THE
RESURRECTION OF
JOSEPH BOURNE

JACK HODGINS

The Resurrection of
Joseph Bourne

OR

A WORD OR TWO ON THOSE
PORT ANNIE MIRACLES

MACMILLAN OF CANADA

TORONTO

Canadian Cataloguing in Publication Data

Hodgins, Jack, 1938-
The resurrection of Joseph Bourne
ISBN 0-7705-1717-X
I. Title.
PS8565.034R48   C813'.5'4   C79-094375-1
PR9199.3.H63R48

*This is a work of fiction. Though Port Annie shares some
of its geography and a little of its history with actual towns in
the northern region of Vancouver Island, it is a product
of the imagination, and its inhabitants are not to be confused
with actual persons, living or dead. Since there is sometimes a tendency to equate fictitious public figures with actual
public figures, it is perhaps necessary to state that Jacob Weins,
who shares some obvious surface characteristics with other
Island mayors, grew naturally from the fictional soil of Port Annie
and is not intended to represent anyone but himself.*

PRINTED IN CANADA FOR
The Macmillan Company of Canada Ltd.
70 Bond Street, Toronto
M5B 1X3

for
DAVE SWANSON

·

for
PETER MCCUE and KEVIN DAVIES
who helped me search for
Joseph Bourne

·

and once again, for
DIANNE

*If we should find out some day that we're wrong,
that he isn't dead at all, will anyone be surprised? Somehow
it seems impossible that such a life could end.*

(from a magazine article at the time of
Joseph Bourne's disappearance)

*What else should our lives be but a continual series of
beginnings, of painful settings out into the unknown, pushing
off from the edges of consciousness into the
mystery of what we have not yet become, except
in dreams. . . .*

(David Malouf: *An Imaginary Life.*
New York, George Braziller Inc., 1978)

*But oh, what fuss these earthbound mortals make
When asked to pull up roots, or new life take;
You'd think the sky had fallen on their heads,
The earth in ruins, or even pets found dead!*

(from Amelia Barnstone's epic poem
"The Last Days of Port Annie", still unpublished)

THE
RESURRECTION OF
JOSEPH BOURNE

OF UNIQUE GIFTS FROM THE SEA AND
THE REMARKABLE CURIOSITY OF PORT ANNIE'S RESIDENTS;
OF JOSEPH BOURNE'S ATTEMPTS TO AVOID THE GIRL
FROM THE PERUVIAN FREIGHTER,

OR,

The Ragged Green Edge
of the World

WHEN THE GIRL FROM THE PERUVIAN FREIGHTER walked for the first time through Port Annie, on the twenty-second day of constant rain, it's true old Magnus Dexter collapsed in front of his daughter's house, but who could blame him? One glimpse of this walking miracle was more than even some younger men could take, and Dexter was a feeble creature after all. As he muttered to his daughter while she held his head up off the spongy grass, life could offer him only disappointments after this: he might as well just cash it in right now. Still, he somehow found the strength to raise himself for a final peek at that girl's incredible walk before she turned the corner to cause a stir on someone else's street.

Everyone noticed her, of course, but no one could provide a name. She was the girl who came in from the sea, or as Eva McCarthy put it, "that cormorant with the cheeky behind".

"A seabird is what she is, but that rear end of hers thinks she's the Queen of Sheba."

Mrs. Landyke had her opinion too: "Something that big wave washed up, and look at the beachcombers come out to gawk."

Even the sun had shown itself—a miracle for sure!

The seabird walked past nearly every doorstep; she seemed determined to visit every street in town. And oh, what a marvellous walk! As George Beeton said, with a walk like that she'd be a fool to stop. He'd already forgotten about the giant wave that had left long strips of kelp hanging from his service-station pumps and patches of salt-water foam on his floor; he was under a car draining the oil when she passed his open door, stepped on the rubber cord to ring his bell, and kept on going. He tripped over the half-filled pan, stumbled through the oil he'd spilled, and rushed out onto the concrete to watch her go. "Holy toledo!" he shouted, to bring the others running. But all life at the service station had already come to a halt. Everyone watched the incredible walk of the girl who'd come

1

in from the sea. Such a spring in her step, George thought, such gorgeous legs, such beautiful hips! He did not even notice, as the woman in the Mercedes waiting for gas was noticing, that her skin was the deep uncertain colour of cinnamon, that her eyes were as dark as those long loose curls that she tossed like a mane as she passed. He noticed only that walk, and wished with all his heart that she would stop and turn around and come back to his service station so that he could watch her walk away from him again.

She walked the waterfront, from one end of the little town to the other. She walked the streets that sloped uphill from the inlet, past the houses with their tiny squares of lawn and gravel driveways and faces watching from the windows. She walked past every shop that faced the square. And everywhere she walked, the dangerous fragrance of some exotic flower seemed to float behind her like a scarf unravelling in the air. "What a show-off!" grumbled Rita Rentalla, herself Port Annie's most accomplished practitioner in the art of turning heads. From the doorway of the hotel beer parlour known as the Kick-and-Kill, she watched with alarm as that fascinating outsider sashayed past—so brazen, and at the same time so apparently unaware of the commotion she was causing on every side!

In the public library she stopped just long enough to glance at the titles down the rows of books, though never pulled one off the shelf. According to Larry Bowman, the librarian, she only touched them here and there with her slender fingers with their long, beautifully tapered nails and seemed to size them up suspiciously out of the corner of her eye, as if she were calculating by some inner mathematics the entire contents of each book, the number of times it had been read, and the kind of secrets it concealed about the people of the town. Then, swinging on her heel, she gave the librarian a wink that caused the whole world to lurch, as he put it, and bounced out the front doorway of the library. Click, click, click, her heels tapped the pavement. Such calves, he exclaimed, and had you ever seen such delicious insteps?

No one had, of course, and no one could talk of anything else. What was she doing here? What kind of woman lived on a freighter with all those men? Had anyone heard her speak, was she South American, what was she looking for? What could she possibly find of interest in a place like this, miles from anything else except mountains and bush, a few houses perched on the steep side of a narrow inlet with nothing to look at but rain and the fuzzy green slope of the facing hill? And why didn't her legs ache from all those miles she'd covered; why wasn't she crying and rubbing her arches and complaining that nobody knew how to make shoes that didn't kill your feet?

No one approached her, of course, no one stopped and asked her, lady, what are you doing here, because everyone knew that Port Annie, like other towns on the northwest coast of Vancouver Island, was full of people whose past was none of your business and whose reasons for being here had to be respected in silence. Still, this universal respect was hardly enough to stamp out natural curiosity. After all, she hadn't exactly picked the most inconspicuous way to make her entrance. That Peruvian freighter had just started up the inlet when an enormous wave heading south from an Alaskan earthquake picked it up, carried it forward like a giant trophy past the town, and set it down in the middle of a log boom floating beside the Mill. Just the tail end of a gigantic wave that had nearly worn itself out, but still it had swept in with enough force to leave salt water and sand, stunned fish and shreds of tortured driftwood on the streets and front yards of houses for two rows up the hill. Long strips of kelp and seedy knots of seaweed lay in doorways, starfish and blue mussels bloomed like brilliant flowers in the spongy grass, and periwinkles spilled themselves like tiny jewels across the roads. When that seabird walked the streets she might just as well have been walking on the bottom of the ocean; it was only natural that every eye should follow her.

According to a song the children had once made up, the dark water of the inlet was where your nightmares came from. Nonsense, of course, according to Eva McCarthy, but still you just couldn't take any chances. Tiny Eva followed that seabird around for most of the day—a half-block behind on her skinny legs, pretending to look for dimes in the weeds— but she found out absolutely nothing at all, except that the girl from the sea must have had a cast-iron bladder at least, while poor Eva had to pay two visits to the washroom at George Beeton's service station.

"No sense of style," was the opinion of Mrs. Barnstone, who was an expert when it came to matters of taste. The line-up behind her in the grocery store could just stand and wait while she tightened one of the rollers in her hair. "Who wears high spiky heels like that nowadays, she'll break her neck. And did you get a look at that too-tight skirt?"

"And can you imagine living on a freighter at all?" Angela Turner said, behind the till. "A person would go crazy with nothing to do through week after week after week."

Mrs. Barnstone lifted her heavy eyelids and pursed her mouth, calling up a fickle British accent to give her words some weight. "Oh, I imagine she was busy enough, dear. She doesn't seem to be travelling with a chaperone. I should imagine she's come ashore for a bit of a rest."

And Papa Magnani was astounded. His fat fingers went wild in his thinning hair. "Such a beautiful woman!" he yelled over the phone to his equally astounded wife. "She come into the rec centre here and walks all around—oh, Rosa, can I tell you how she walked—she stops, looks thisaway looks thataway, she eyes up the rafters with her white hand playing the piano on her hip—I tell you, Rosa, you had to be here—and then she watches those boys dribbling the basketball up and down the floor until they're so rattled they have to stop and pretend their shoelaces are undone. And then, oh Rosa, then she sees me standing here behind my counter like an old fool and starts to walking over this way. 'Yes ma'am,' I say, 'you're the lady off the boat,' and she shows me those perfect teeth in her smile and heaves a look around like she wants to buy the place— oh the hair when she throws it, why am I tell you this Rosa, where are the words? Then the next thing I know she's gone. Oh Rosa, Mamma, if you could be here to see!"

Of course, even while he was reporting to his bedridden wife, Papa Magnani's eyes were still on that girl, who was moving around in the gravel pit next door, looking over the boarded-up trailer that had tried once to become a church. He could remember when the company built a real church there, a tiny place of worship for anyone who wanted it, but the first mudslide had knocked it off its foundations years ago and the second slide had smashed it flat. No one ever bothered attending services in the trailer that had been dragged in for a replacement, so someone nailed sheets of plywood over the broken windows and put a hefty padlock on the door. No use yanking on the lock there, either, Papa Magnani told the seabird in his thoughts, because no one even remembers who's got the key. "Besides, why would a girl like you want to get into a church? God already gave you every thing you need."

High above the trailer, the battered wooden hull of a fishboat floated in the lower branches of a Douglas fir, but the seabird gave it no more than a passing glance—as if such things were everyday fare in her life.

Not even Fat Annie Fartenburg, the founder of this town, could have caused such a stir. Not even if she'd come down from that hotel room where she'd kept herself locked up for the past twenty years and started walking the street. This gal was a mystery, a phenomenon, an insult. And who would ever have thought it would be Jenny Chambers, that ex-stripper with pink hair, who'd come up with the perfect solution, and so simple too? Maybe chewing gum with her mouth open helped her to think. "So what's the matter with old Bourne, that he hasn't invited her onto his radio show? She's managed to strut through the whole blessed town, and still nobody knows a thing." Jenny was on her way home from picket duty, dragging herself up the steep rainy hill, hot and sticky inside her transparent raincoat, and of course she had to stop in at the Corner Store to catch her breath and tell Mrs. Landyke her idea.

And Mrs. Landyke, who never thought anything ever went through Jenny Chambers' head except visions of that crazy Slim Potts she lived with, or the trouble those eight rotten brats were always getting into, threw up her chubby hands in delight. "You're a genius, Jen, because of course he's exactly the one. With his ways, if he can just get her behind a microphone he'll soon have her spilling the beans. No one can resist him." If he stuck a microphone in Mrs. Landyke's ruddy face and asked her the time of day she'd tell him her whole life story, that was the kind of effect he had on her.

"I could resist him easy enough," Jenny said, tossing a package of Spearmint on the counter. "When he looks at me I can feel his eyes just chilling my bones. When he comes up from the inlet in his crazy old rags with his white hair all whipped up by the wind he makes my flesh crawl, like one of those spooky guys in a fairy tale." But still, she had to admit he knew his business, and if anybody could find out about that cheeky so-and-so of a woman he could.

Here was proof, if anyone doubted, that a town like Port Annie needed everyone it could get, even a has-been stripper who'd come in to perform at the Kick-and-Kill and decided to latch onto some local beanpole with eight kids instead of moving on to another town. "Sometimes he has coffee with the mayor, who's a persuasive man," said Mrs. Landyke, stepping back to let the drawer of her till slide out beneath her heavy bosom. "I'll put a bug in his ear."

Mayor Weins was happy to oblige, and no beating around the bush either. But first, just let him holler at these children playing in the puddles. "Hey you kids. See how fast you can get all those dead fish and rotten garbage thrown back in the sea! Because if it's still here when those nosy health people come in to poke around they'll jab you full of needles and maybe throw everybody into jail for letting ourselves be contaminated by that crazy wave."

Stupid kids, they only stared with their mouths open. He'd have to get after them later, the town looked terrible with all this litter scattered everywhere. Even the hotel had ribbons of kelp plastered against the walls and strips flapping like streamers from the windows—a disgrace.

"So what's the matter with you, Bourne, that you still haven't invited her onto your show. And don't play innocent, please, you must have noticed. The young lady from the freighter is the one I'm talking about. No one in town seems to be able to find out a thing, but you could do us all a favour—get her into the studio and start that beautiful mouth talking. People might even listen for a change instead of turning to another station." Though to tell the truth he never listened to any station at all himself, and didn't particularly want to be seen here in public like this, either, squeezed into this booth with a weirdo like Bourne who had the nerve to pretend he didn't know what the mayor was talking about.

And he might as well have been talking to himself, of course, he might as well have saved his breath, because two minutes later old Bourne was outside again, hobbling down the half-mile of pavement between the town of Port Annie and the Squatters' shacks along the shore. Not an ounce of civic responsibility flowed in those ancient veins! The mayor's jowls quivered, his huge ears reddened with indignation. He might have gone after the old fool to talk some sense into his head if it weren't time to have his photo taken for the *Port Annie Crier*, the weekly newspaper. Not a week had gone by without his picture appearing somewhere in it, once at least, shaking someone's hand or receiving someone's cheque or simply smiling at someone's guests—and he wasn't going to let that stubborn old man cause him to miss an issue now. If the women wanted to talk Bourne into something he didn't want to do, let them catch him and do the dirty work themselves, a mayor had more important things on his slate.

"Who needs you, you uncooperative old goat."

Under his breath, of course. A mayor couldn't be overheard yelling out insults, even to a man like that. Still, why should he take time out from a round of important functions, just to humiliate himself by talking to ears that refused to listen?

"Hey you kids, go home and find your rakes and shovels. Get started on that clean-up job, and no stalling either."

But what did Joseph Bourne care about the problems of a big-eared pot-bellied mayor? The tidal wave of sea-gifts had left the lower town decorated with the underwater brilliance of a dream and filled the rainy air with the unfamiliar scent of a stirred-up sea, but the old man hurried away as if he thought there was a spell in it that he needed to escape. His stuck-forward head bobbed like a camel's. The skirts of his tattered rain-soaked kimonos and robes beat in an uproar of colours around the tops of his high rubber boots. His primitive cape, made from a sheet of black plastic snitched off someone's backyard fence, rippled and flapped in the air behind him. Inside all those layers he was an indefinable shape—perhaps as lumpy as a potato, perhaps as thin as a wire, perhaps a shape as changing as his changing moods. With the aid of a long black stick, he hurried past the recreation centre where Papa Magnani was busy shooing some noisy children out the door. Past the library, where Larry Bowman stared into space, still speechless from the shock of his first encounter with the beautiful girl. Past the little boarded-up trailer which had tried once to become a church, and the battered fish-boat riding a Douglas fir much higher than that wave could possibly have reached. On he went, scowling out of his deep-set eyes and running a hand over the puckered skin of his burnt face, until he came to the snaky upstanding mass of roots by the side of the road, where George Beeton, out walking, had stopped for a rest.

"So what do you think, Mr. Bourne? That girl's been driving everyone crazy."

The old man paused to flick up bits of seaweed off the road

with the end of his stick. His rags settled heavily around him, as if he too were draped with sodden strips of kelp like the roadside trees. He didn't speak, but only tugged at one ear with an enormous hand and looked off in the direction of the inlet to watch the bowling-pin shapes of three cormorants riding a log pulled seaward by the receding tide.

"She's been in town for less than a day and already the world is beginning to change," George said. "My clock even stopped. No connection, of course, but what a coincidence when it's kept perfect time for twenty years without even a pause. And my brother-in-law? The minute he sees her, he packs up the car and leaves. If it's all the same he'd just as soon go some other place, he says, because a girl that beautiful will do more damage than a tidal wave or an earthquake, just wait and see."

Bourne sighed, as if with enormous pity or disbelief, and peered at George a moment from under his weedy tufts of eyebrow. Then he started to move away with his robes and rags all whispering around his legs. George looked at his footprints, which seemed to have stained the wet pavement, just as everybody felt that old man stained the air around him wherever he went. "There's more satisfaction in talking to a friggin' tree, you grouch," he said. "I'd rather talk to myself. Go home to your scummy neighbours and see if I give a damn."

Of course George knew that Bourne's neighbours weren't the proper decent people of Port Annie. That was common knowledge. Naturally he'd chosen to live in a two-room shack on the beach at Squatters' Flats, surrounded by people the town considered as undesirable and repulsive as he was—dirty and shifty and unpredictable. Everyone in Port Annie had been down at one time or another to look over the place and pass judgment. Squatters' Flats. It made you ashamed that there were human beings who could sink so low as this. It made you thank your lucky stars you were born with a little pride and some sense of decency. Falling-down shacks and rotten pilings and a bunch of lazy bums. Look at those little kids, poor things, the child-welfare people ought to take them away before they were warped beyond repair. And take a look at that cow of a girl, will you, slopping around in those outlandish rags and you can tell not a thing underneath. And bums, all the men were lazy sloths or they'd have got busy long ago fixing those shacks to look like something a human could live in, they'd be down at the Mill every day trying to get a job, they'd be ashamed to be seen lying around in the daytime like sluggish deadbeats with nothing to do but drink and smoke and fight and make babies. As long as a place like this was allowed to exist it was an insult to everyone else who had to live near it; about time the sawmill company kicked them off the land, evicted them, released it for decent people to build their houses on. A place like that was a graveyard already, the kindest thing you could do was bury the corpses with a bulldozer.

Sometimes on Saturday night, after they'd become bored with watching the bears root around in the dump, young men from the town would drive their motorbikes down the gravel road off the highway and sit for a while with their headlamps lighting up the row of old buildings along the shore and the chain of homemade shacks out on the estuary. Then they shouted and tossed stones and tin cans and pieces of wood. Seldom did anyone ever look out a window to see what was going on, or come out to chase them away—which showed what a bunch of boobs they all were. That crazy old wild man of a Bourne was the only one who ever showed himself; he sometimes opened the door of his cabin and stood there staring into what must have been a blinding light until they left. When you got back up onto the pavement, they said, you felt as if you'd just pulled yourself out of a filthy sewer. Someone ought to set a torch to that stagnant stinkhole of a dump. What kind of a man would live in a mess like that?

"An ugly old grunt," Jenny Chambers called him.

"Senile creep," said Eva McCarthy.

Though Mrs. Landyke was forced to admit she had a weakness for older men with eccentricities.

And he did host that radio show, twice a week, don't ask her how he managed at his age. Apparently when he sat down in front of that microphone most of his crotchety oldness left him, his eyes brightened, his deep voice cleared. He came in to town out of nowhere a few years back, took on the job just because nobody else wanted it, and now people all over town and even in other North Island villages listened to him regularly because he played such a variety of music and could nail his guests to the wall with a fierce perfect aim, though there were some who admitted they listened only because he'd been known to go to sleep in the middle of a program, his snores vibrating in radio sets all over town, while an astonished guest sat across the table wondering what to do next. It was a good laugh. You should

listen, people said, there was always a chance he'd drop dead
in the middle of a sentence, an old man like that, and you
wouldn't want to miss such a treat. If he ever got that seabird
off the Peruvian freighter across the table from him, who knew
what might happen!

A faint hope, though, by the looks of things—at least for the
present time. The old man hurried home just as fast as he could
go to escape that mayor, that town, all that stirred-up gossip.
Down the pavement he went, and then down onto the gravel
road that led to the Flats. Puffing, muttering to himself, swinging his stick to disturb the bushes that had been decorated by
the sea, kicking up stones, thwacking the trunks of trees. Oh,
he was in a rare old mood, anyone could see. He rushed along
the row of sagging houses—a string of old buildings with
shakes missing from the roofs, and flowers spilling out of yellow
plastic pots along the verandah railings, and long grass growing
up through the sea-washed steps; a row of front yards with
mangled car-bodies turning to rust and rose bushes gone wild
from neglect and wringer washing-machines and iceboxes
thrown out by earlier residents who'd never found the time to
haul them away. A barely civil nod to the faces in the windows,
the beards and bushy hair and granny glasses of California
youths whose names he'd never learned. On he went, hurrying
past, with a fierce dangerous scowl on his ancient face.

Yet he paused long enough to offer "Hello" to Dirty Della,
who greeted him with a smile: out walking in the drizzle with
her brood of kids, a United Nations of colours and faces. She
never complained about anything, not even the rain, just so
long as those children of hers were all in top-notch health and
the young men from town continued to come down off the
highway in the middle of the night to have a good time in her
house.

"A lovely day, Mr. Bourne," she said, as if she hadn't noticed
the tangled mess of seaweed she was standing in, or the boards
off someone's wall that lay across the muddy road, or the
purple baby-buggy hanging from the spiky branch of a twisted
snag above her head. She herded her brood ahead of her, like
a flock of noisy geese, but paused to wish him a very good day,
Mr. Bourne, and a pleasant evening.

She might as well have cursed him, though, for all the good
her wishes brought. Because within moments, when he'd got
as far as the two-storey building where some of the Squatters

had a small-time paper-making business, greeting cards and coloured stationery, the gigantic figure of Preserved Crabbe leapt down off the steps waving his big hands like someone trying to flag the police. "Bourne! Bourne!" His voice boomed from his thick heaving chest. Seven feet tall, hairy as a gorilla—a ludicrous figure with his little head all wrapped up in bandages. "Bourne! Just hold it a minute!" The reason for those bandages was no secret, either—far from it. Bourne had heard the four Crabbe brothers come home at five o'clock in the morning, he'd heard all the whooping and hollering about the party they'd been to in a deserted cannery across the Island, and about the fight that Preserved had got himself into, ending up with thirty stitches in his scalp—a great long snaking scar from his forehead to his crown—the art-work of some jealous husband. But none of that was any reason to stop; all he wanted was to get to his own shack, slam the door, and let the silence fall over him again. Get out of the way you hulking bull, or feel the end of this stick in your crotch!

Preserved's huge hand clamped down on his swinging arm just as the club-footed brother came hobbling out onto the step. "We've got to talk, Bourne. Please come inside for a minute."

Talk! His ears still rang with the talk that had rattled his head in the town. Did they think he'd come home for some more of the same? Up in that town they squandered words like rain, never stopping, as if there was no such thing as an end to the supply; but down here his neighbours usually hoarded words like gems. Gentle people, who seldom raised their voices. Even Preserved Crabbe seemed to have a limit of six or seven words a day, mostly curses, but today it looked as if he'd pulled out all the stops. "Look, old man, this is your business too. That tidal wave made a mess of them smaller shacks. Just look. The place is wrecked."

Bourne could hardly see any difference; the shelters out along the boardwalk had always been such patched-up leaning piles of junk. Their loose and mismatched boards seemed to be only rearranged, and decorated a little with colourful debris. His own cabin looked unharmed, and the other sturdier houses along the shore. Why all this fuss? What they ought to be using their energy for was putting things back together or pulling out.

"Hill Gin says it's a sign," Crabbe said.

A sign? He couldn't begin to imagine the philosophies these people lived by.

"All those letters. Threats. Now even the ocean's trying to swipe us off of here."

"And a stranger prowling around," the brother said. "A beautiful woman. Hill Gin says she's here for the sawmill company, to start prying us off their land. She strutted right through here like she owned the place and never talked to nobody. Hill Gin says our days are numbered now. What are we going to do?"

He laughed scornfully. They would go to pieces, that's what they would do. Bourne pulled against the giant's grip. They'd fall apart, behave like babies, come running to him the way they always did, as if he had the answer to everything, including the end of the world, their inevitable eviction off this private land. What else did they expect? How could it turn out any other way? What right did this bunch of Squatters have to think the world should arrange itself in any other pattern for them but the one it had for all—a short uncomfortable visit and then you're gone?

Still, he followed Preserved inside The Paper House—they'd only whine around his cabin if he didn't, they'd whimper like children until he'd heard their complaints.

In the damp pulpy heat of the first room, two of the faceless Californians were hauling old newspapers and advertisements and rags and leaves out of plastic bags and tearing them up into shreds to drop in the tub on the stove. Life went on, even if the brothers Crabbe were falling apart. One of the youths looked at Bourne and tilted his face to sniff at the air. "When my grandpa started to die *he* smelled like rotting turnips."

Red-eyed Louise stirred the boiling pulp on the stove. "Something cock-eyed must've happened in the universe to-day," she told the ceiling. "Everything's started to go nuts. That wave hit us like a sledge-hammer, a good thing it was just the tail end of something or we'd've been drowned for sure. As it was, Tim's shack was washed away in pieces, and Rosemary lost her roof. Broken windows everywhere." She ran a hand over the damp forehead and pushed back her hair. "Then we heard about that stranger prowling around. Something's going on."

"Of course something's going on." Hill Gin stood up to scratch her ankle with the end of her shotgun barrel. A damp cigarette shifted from one end of her lip to the other.

She rolled her own but rarely smoked them. "They should never of let that woman off her boat."

"And that white strip of crap that flows past from the Mill turned black," Louise continued. "I saw it happen—a cloud of seagulls flew up out of it screaming like they'd just been poisoned."

"Ha!" Hill Gin slapped her leg—her point had just been proved. She scratched in frizzy grey hair, then hoisted up her overalls and stomped a foot. "You see! You laugh at me, the whole damn lot of you, but there are people in this world whose thoughts go out in waves to poison everything around them, that's how powerful they are. Don't think I don't know what I'm talking about because I do."

"Hill Gin's a witch," the cripple said, and rolled his eyes. Even amongst this motley crew she was considered odd. And liked to be the centre of attraction as well. "They'll flick us off of here like bits of dust and hardly notice. They can hardly wait to do it, either, I can tell you that. Our days are numbered." She tucked her free hand inside her overalls and turned her smile on everyone with equal smugness. "Don't say I didn't warn you." A witch's job was to make you feel that no matter what happened it was everyone's fault but hers. That was why she spent so much of her time issuing warnings: every possibility had to be covered. Otherwise she could end up looking bad, with egg on her face, and have to resort to gossip and scandal to hold onto people's attention.

Bourne made for the door. He'd heard enough nonsense for one day. If he had to choose between the excited prattle of the town and the frightened hysterics of his neighbours—well, what real choice was there to make? Both made the silence of his two-room cabin all that much more inviting.

Instead of trying to stop him with that tree-trunk arm, Preserved just let his face crumple up like a baby watching someone steal his pacifier, and sat down on a wooden crate to sob into his hands. A perfect move; Bourne couldn't force himself to leave; it wasn't every day you got to see a giant shedding tears.

It wasn't fair, Preserved wailed. Didn't he have enough trouble already, with his scalp hurting like blazes? He didn't want to be kicked out of his home. Why couldn't they stay right where they were, puttering around in The Paper House to make a little money, and selling Louise's homemade belts, and going to parties across the Island? Life wasn't meant to be all worry and work, it was meant to be mostly fun.

The pony-tailed youth whose grandfather smelled like turnips turned his back on this disgusting spectacle. A sharp fart was his only comment on the matter. Let it go at that.

Things got even worse when Red-eyed Louise, too, started weeping. Her soprano wails were a perfect match for the basso-profundo sobs of the bandaged giant, though she had no painful ditch gouged into her skull for her excuse, only her mind's-eye panorama of this whole settlement flattened by bulldozers, and herself out on the road, roofless. A perfect picture if she wanted to be the heroine in a best-selling novel, but nothing she wanted to encounter in her actual life. "Can't anybody do something to stop it from happening?" she said. "Wouldn't it help if we stood up and fought?"

The idea of these gentle childish people fighting anyone was impossible to imagine. Yet Preserved pounded his fists on his knees. "That's what we'll do, we'll fight them! Nobody's going to kick me out of my home!"

Hill Gin, not to be upstaged, spat out her cigarette. "Fight who?"

Heads snapped up to stare at her.

"Fight who?" Now that she had her audience again she was a little inclined to overact—to roll her eyes and slap one hand on her hip and make threatening gestures with her gun. "This isn't a *person* you're talking about, this is the world. Not quite so easy as you think." Instead of all going to pieces like this, she said, why didn't they try to find out the truth for a change? No use getting all upset so soon. Her pale eyes sought out Bourne's. "The person to root it out is that old man over there. He's the one with the job up in town, he's the one that gets to talk to people with power."

His turn now. You can't be an audience for ever. They'd dragged him in here to watch their little performance, now the spotlight was swinging around his way. Everyone looked at Bourne, who looked away. Why hadn't he left when he'd had the chance? What had any of this to do with him? Through the window he could see the sewage from the Mill flowing down the inlet and collecting like a lacy fringe around the edges of the tiny island half a mile away. He could see the steep tree-furry mountain that stood like a vertical wall on the other side of the inlet, pale and indistinct behind the heavy moisture in the air. This was his place to brood, his perch on the edge of this huge green frightening silence, his spot to wait. But it wasn't home, it wasn't home; he couldn't hope that it would never change.

Hill Gin hammered her shotgun on the floor. "You think they won't flick you off here just as fast as the rest of us? You think you got something that'll make them overlook you? You got some other kind of place to run to when they flatten this one?"

Bourne spat on the floor; he stirred up his rags in the doorway like someone preparing to fly. "So let them do it! Let their bulldozers push this whole dump into the sea, it's no more home than anyplace else, it isn't worth the trouble." He rushed across the muddy gravel towards his shack. "If it isn't one kind of eviction that you're faced with, it's going to be another!"

Hill Gin yelped, as if he'd struck her. "That stupid old piece of garbage!" She stepped out onto the porch to watch him go, and raised her voice. "That hunk of crap, he ought to be fed to the seagulls like a stinking fish."

A stinking fish. He laughed. What else had he ever been but carrion? What else—for that matter—were *any* of these people, washed up along this muddy beach? He wasn't even surprised when he heard the pulse of giant wings above him and looked up to see an enormous bird circling out over the inlet, tilting to swoop around in this direction. A turkey buzzard—one of the three he'd seen roosted in the dead limbs of snags along the inlet, their old red vulturous heads pulled into their shoulders while they scanned the beach for food. Dead stinking fish. This is the proper place for you, old bird, come down and start to gorge!

By the time Bourne reached the boardwalk at the side of his cabin and looked up again at the bird, it appeared to have accepted the invitation. It seemed to be flying backwards as it braked, descending, with its claws thrust forward. Maybe Hill Gin was even more of a witch than he'd thought. No, go on, he thought, this piece of meat is far too tough for you anyway.

Just a joke until Preserved yelled, "Look out, Bourne!"

His stomach tightened and he looked in horror up over his shoulder.

"What is this?" Preserved bellowed, and clapped his hands, let out a whoop that sent blackbirds and jays exploding out of every tree up the bank but did nothing to interrupt the buzzard's descent. When Bourne swiped with his stick it lifted on its huge wings, hovered, drifted down, lifted, then dropped to set its claws into that white bush of hair. Bourne roared, and threw himself to the ground, rolling, in an attempt to brush off his attacker. He struck at the bird, grabbed at it, tugged at its claws. But the thing held onto the white thrashing head like a bronco rider, flapping its wings to keep balance, and eventually rode it to rest. Bourne lay on the planks like a heap of flung laundry, his bleeding hands clasped to the splintered rails.

Hill Gin raised her shotgun, got the bird lined up in her sights, and set her feet apart for balance. But Preserved took hold of the barrels and shifted them skyward. "I know you're a dead-eye shot," he said, "but I don't trust the sights on that gun." Hill Gin pulled both triggers anyway, out of disappoint-ment, and brought down the end of a limb from the top of a Douglas fir.

When Bourne stirred at last, and groaned, and pushed him-self up onto his knees, the bird flew up on leisurely wings to settle on the ridge of the old man's roof, where it vomited a string of half-digested meat. Then it watched out of the little eyes in its wrinkled red head while the others helped Bourne to his feet, brushed off his clothes, and led him inside the shack.

"You see!" Hill Gin said, in a stage whisper, with an edge of panic to her voice. "You see, Bourne? You see what is happening now?"

The bird did not leave its roost on the peak of Bourne's sagging roof. Inside his cabin he could hear the scratching of those claws on the cedar shakes, he could sense the restless stretching and flapping of those enormous wings, he could feel the weight of the bird as if it had actually chosen to nest on his aching head.

The old man's skin began to shrivel and tighten over his bones. He stayed all night at his table, his old robes and kimo-nos whispering around his legs, and listened to the sounds of the bird on his roof while he plotted ways to outsmart it. "A bird is only a bird. This isn't a nightmare." Yet more than once he fell asleep sitting up, and dreamed that his hands were around that hideous throat, that he squeezed until the bright eyes went dull and popped out of the head, until the thick worm-like tongue fell out of the beak, until blood bubbled up out of the vicious nostrils.

But he would permit no one else to do it harm. When Hill Gin's double-barrels went off just outside his cabin in the early morning, he flew into a panic, tripped over himself trying to get out his door, rushed out into a shower of floating feathers. The bird flew in high circles, while Hill Gin dropped new shells into her cracked-open gun. "I'll feed that thing to my dogs," she said. But Bourne flew at her like a furious bird himself. She looked at him as if he were mad, glanced up at the soaring buzzard, then hoisted her overalls and headed back to her own house. "Crazy old fool."

Bourne, watching her, could hardly believe his own fury; his heart throbbed with the desire to go after her and beat her into the ground, his hands itched to claw at her back. He hobbled up and down the boardwalk until the buzzard began to circle lower. He tugged at his ear. Then he went inside to listen for the sound of its claws on his roof, and to continue his designs on its life. Sometimes he felt that those claws had pierced all the way through to his heart, or gouged out pieces of his brain. Sometimes he felt there was more of him up on that roof with the bird than there was here below in his cluttered room.

The next day he did not go into Port Annie for his radio show. Let them do without him for a while, he couldn't face that stirred-up noise again. He'd rather stay in the overheated safety of his tiny cabin, trying to keep his mind on a book pulled out of the stack in the corner, or jotting words on scraps of paper that he stuffed into knotholes or threw into the stove, or cleaning up this mess of clothes and magazines and dirty dishes that he lived in.

"Probably remembering his youth," was what people said whenever he dropped out of sight for a while. When you got to such an age all you wanted to do was relive the exciting things that had happened in your life—all the tragedies and love affairs and successes. But the truth was that Bourne remembered none of these, he remembered nothing at all; he didn't know if he had ever had any tragedies or love affairs or successes. His life seemed to have been erasing itself as it unrolled; he recalled nothing at all but an infinite stretch of grey. He knew nothing at all but his life since he came to Port Annie, he knew nothing at all but his life as a foul old dry-boned man. This must be the same as being dead, he thought. That bird was nesting on his coffin. There was more life in those rocks out on the beach; there was more life in those rust-ing car bodies and in those grey telephone poles and in that washed-up kelp. Sometimes it seemed that he'd been here for ever; that he'd never been anywhere else.

When the rain slowed and the cloud lifted high enough he could see most of their precious town against the hill; he could see the mountain that curved like a huge green wall around the back of the town, as if the whole thing were a giant amphitheatre. When he'd first moved in, the loggers had only recently felled the heavy timber off that slope above the buildings, leaving behind the blackened stumps and a charred tangle of fallen smaller trees and bare scorched earth; but rain fell and eventually alder spread across the face of the mountain, and some stands of birch, so that now in summer the back wall of the town was brilliant and alive and brighter than all the surrounding mountains of timber, and in winter when the leaves had fallen and the mist closed in, it was dull and grey and depressing.

In this place it rained every week of the year, it rained for at least part of each day, and sometimes it rained day and night without cease for as long as a month and a half. Enough to make you feel you were drowning, or ought to develop gills. Twice now he had seen it rain so much that one of the mountain streams had got clogged up with logs and mud, starting a small avalanche which gathered other trees and mud with it and pushed right down into the town, shifting houses off their foundations and littering the streets and overturning cars and burying trucks in mud up to the axles and even higher. A terrible mess. Everybody had to move out. He thought the place had died for sure. But those crazy people put everything back exactly the way it was and moved into their houses and forgot all about the hill at their backs. Some even forgot about the rain which fell every day on their heads and on the mountain and into the streams that continued to work their way down the slope. Some day it would happen again.

Brooding under the weight of the bird that wouldn't go away, Bourne felt crabby enough to enjoy the thought of a new slide happening. Let it wipe the town right off the mountain in a single blow this time! One long sweep down into the inlet. Sometimes he was able to keep his mind off that carrion-eater for several minutes by imagining that it was already happening. The mud. The stones. The buildings smashed. The terrified faces. Once he actually felt a rumble deep in the earth beneath his cabin and hurried out onto the boardwalk for a look. But the mountain was still there, solid and green as always, like a dark wall behind the town. What a disappointment! A few patches of old timber stood like feathers in the mist at various places along its ridge.

Now *do* it, he thought, dislodge them properly this time, right into the black and filthy water. Push them right into the stinking sewage from their Mill. But scowls and commands had no effect at all on the mountain, and frustration whirled him this way, whirled him that way, rags in a violent turmoil, looking for someone to blame. He tugged at his ear, he stomped one foot, he twisted his face like a dry pink sponge. He shook his stick at the faces in the windows of the other shacks. He jutted his bristly jaw at those who came out to see what was going on. He hobbled noisily down the full length of the boardwalk, shaking the railings and hammering at the sides of houses with his stick, muttering, growling, and casting hateful looks at the black wings beating the air above him. And at the very end of the boardwalk, above the eelgrass and the stinking low-tide mud, he smiled to imagine that his racket had startled just one tiny pebble into movement high up the mountain, a trickle of stones, the beginning of a landslide, the start of a gigantic avalanche roaring and rumbling and falling over itself down that slope, gathering trees and windfalls and roots, lapping forward on itself in rushes of gravel and stone and timber, pushing the top houses into the next row and rolling over top of both down in a great rush of cracking timbers and human screams and mud and stones down all those rows of buildings into the inlet—a great sheering off into black water, so that there'd be nothing left at all but a brown obscene scar running up that mountain like a fresh sunken grave and silence, silence, the stench of death.

He could smell it, he could nearly taste it. It hung in this place as thick as the mists, it caught in the trees and drifted over the inlet. It was on his face, he could feel it; walking, he pushed himself through it; stopping, he held up his enormous hands to let it curl itself around his fingers. He breathed it deeply, and chuckled.

Cackled, chuckled, slapped his leg. How many fools in that town even suspected what was hidden in the air they breathed? Dregs, dregs, they'd scooped themselves up off the bottom of other places and coming here had thought they'd returned to life. Ex-convicts, failed husbands, misfits, broken-down whores, terrified perverts; he laughed at them all. They all had the habit of checking over their shoulder, they all hid in the cupped safety of that curved mountain, they were all as doomed as he was. Doomed and scared.

"Ah—crazy!" he said, nearly choking on the sudden realization of his own excess. "What am I doing?"

And back in his room, he began to tremble with the horror he felt at his own ravings. Was he a lunatic or a senile fool? Those faces that had watched him from the windows hadn't shown any alarm—they'd only laughed. There's old Bourne blowing off steam again—cracked as a loon—you never know what kind of madness he'll dream up next. Why don't some people just walk into the inlet and float away? Too bad that tidal wave didn't take him out to sea, we'd all be better off—himself included.

He could feel the huge generalized dread that never seemed to go away blooming like a beautiful sea anemone inside him, its long petal-like tentacles brushing against his organs—exploring the intricate network of his lungs, wrapping themselves around his heart, feeding on the maddening progress of this unstoppable time, this ageing old-body decay that scared him. Some of the tentacles, he was sure, had already found their way to his bloodstream and begun their slow imperceptible work of clogging everything up, bringing everything to an eventual stop. Nobody had asked his permission. All he could do was wait. Not even this soundless weeping could stop it. Not even when he leaned his face against the cool glass of this window and tore pieces of clothing to shreds.

If only he *had* got in the way of that wave. To be washed out to sea, powerless, his life out of his own hands for a change. Instead here he sat, on this inlet, only a mile from the open sea that he'd never seen even once since he'd arrived at this place. Just around that corner, and he'd never been able to force himself down to its shore. Instead he stayed here, on the ragged green edge of the world just out of its sight, and could only imagine what terror there would be in looking directly into the infinite expanse of its grey face.

He felt it waiting for him, its long horizon lost in the pale blue haze, the ceaseless roar of its waves drowning all other sound, its long white beaches empty of any life. Even the sight of that Peruvian freighter slipping past his window in the rain raised up no other response but a chilly trembling in his bones, a vision of that deep sunless ocean it was heading for, of the endless desolate Pacific waiting to swallow it.

Of course others, seeing the freighter, had other reactions. A big black piece of junk was what Eva McCarthy thought, standing tiptoe with her tiny hands in a sink full of dishes, and thank goodness that seabird had gone at last. It made you mad to think these two-bit cheapies could sail in out of nowhere, turn the whole place up on its end, and then leave without even telling anybody why they'd come in the first place. But at least now she'd gone and maybe life would regain its sanity. Eva was even thinking of talking Ian into a little down-island trip, about time they got out of this place, and he did have a few days' holiday coming up. Of course he'd rather go fishing in one of the lakes, he never liked to go anywhere else, but if she told him it was his birthday present—a weekend in a Victoria motel—how could he refuse?

"A person has to get some fun out of life."

And the children, who had finally got around to gathering up most of the debris left by the wave, saw it go by while they sang their song about the inlet as the place where your bad dreams come from. They used garden rakes to scrape the strips of shining kelp off the walls; they used shovels to scoop up the heaps of bark at basement windows; they used hoses to wash down the brown clots of stinking Mill-foam and to break up the tangles of tin cans and orange peels that gathered in the doorways of the shops. Only for a moment did they pause to watch that freighter going past before returning to their work.

Linda Weins saw it through the window of the coffee shop and sighed, her big blue eyes threatening to fill with tears. A long boring day ahead of her and that boat going past just made her think of all the places there were in the world that she'd never been to and wanted to see. She wasn't going to be stuck in this dump for ever, either, she intended to get out. That seabird was a smart one, she knew what was what, she'd come ashore with her rump-wiggling walk to sniff out this place, found out there was nothing worth staying for, and gone off to somewhere else more exciting to try again. What a life! Anyone with half a brain in her head would do the same.

Jenny Chambers, walking down from her house to rejoin the marching pickets in front of Severson's Bakery, saw the freighter, good riddance to that cheeky snip of a woman. "Maybe life can get back to normal again," she said to Mrs. Landyke, who'd seen the freighter from the window of her Corner Store and stepped out into the front doorway to watch it pass, snapping off bites of a crisp raw carrot. And Mayor Weins, too, smiling for the newspaper camera under his favourite slogan, "Pulp City of the Western World", saw the freighter pass, and not with regret either, an old tub ready for the junkyard, and the town would be better off without that troublemaker of a woman.

"Better take one more picture, Charlie, in case the others don't turn out."

And Larry Bowman, not yet fully recovered from the seabird's brief but startling visit to his library, noticed the freighter's departure with both relief and disappointment. Watching that beautiful woman walk the streets had all but replaced his usual pastime, which was studying the liquor ads in magazines in order to find the curvaceous breasts and impressive genitals he knew were hidden in the complicated lines of the ice cubes; but he'd lost ten pounds off his already skinny body worrying that she'd step inside the library again and expect him to carry on a conversation with her—a terrifying possibility. After dreaming about her for years, the ideal woman, he was nearly a wreck from having her so close. Life could get back to normal, now that she'd finally gone.

"*Not gone?*" Jenny Chambers couldn't believe her ears. "But everyone in town saw that freighter go by, and good riddance. Now you tell me she wasn't on it?" Chewing gum furiously, she marched back and forth in front of the bakery, ON STRIKE posters hanging against both the front and the back of her plastic raincoat. Eva McCarthy, if she wanted to talk, would have to go along too, try to keep up on her match-stick legs; nothing looked worse than pickets who only lazed around or draped themselves over cars. Just because the strike had gone on for two years now and nobody paid any attention to the pickets any more was no reason to get sloppy about it, some of those blockheads thought it didn't matter what you looked like when you were on duty, but Jen Chambers knew better. She kept them pacing back and forth on the strip of sidewalk from beginning to end of their shift, and didn't hesitate to tell people going in to that place just what they were in her eyes, and once she'd even used her purse to wallop a little fat baldheaded simp that had the nerve to walk up and tell her she was setting the whole union movement back fifty years.

"But, listen, Eva, what do we care? Let her stay, what difference does it make to us?" This fat wad of pink gum was getting the works, double-time chewing and lots of bubbles to snap. "But the little saucebox, though, why would she want to stay here?" Not that Eva would know a thing like that, or even be able to imagine. Eva McCarthy was a scatterbrain; she'd hear a rumour and go all to pieces, but it would never occur to her to investigate. "Look Eva, I'm tied up here for another two hours; you get on over to the hotel and find out is she registered there, find out her name. Somebody will know. Not that it makes any difference to me, the little hussy can settle down here and live to a hundred and eight for all I care." But hadn't her Slim already reported the men were as nosy about her as the women were? She was the talk of the Mill too. "That's the trouble with us, Eva, you and me come into this place by the wrong door, nobody noticed. We came over that rotten gravel road that nearly shakes the fillings out of your teeth. What we should've done is found an old rusty freighter to haul us up the inlet and then they'd be all over us." A good laugh, Eva McCarthy nearly choked on that one it struck her so funny. Of course Jenny Chambers knew very well that when she herself arrived in town as a stripper at the Kick-and-Kill she'd got every bit as much attention as that seabird was getting, the whole town had gone crazy over her: Jenny Flambé. And not only that, she'd stayed around and shocked the living daylights out of them all by moving in with Slim Potts. Flaming Jenny and the beanpole. People called them the Chamber-Potts, but after eight years a few of them were beginning to treat her like she was almost an equal, like someone who'd always been here.

And Jenny hadn't even had time to kick off her shoes to start supper when "Relax, Jenny"—it was Eva on the phone— "because guess what I heard, and this is going to kill you. You're going to get your chance to find out about that cormorant with the cheeky behind after all because Mabel Weins just called to tell me someone from the radio station—it wasn't that old Bourne, don't expect him to get any sense all of a sudden—someone tracked that gal down at the hotel, bought her a coffee in the coffee shop, and got her to agree to an interview. So what do you think of that?"

Well it was about time somebody got the lead out, Jenny said, and good cripes why did some people have to be pushed before they could move? If she were a radio interviewer herself, now, she'd've thought of that the minute the little snip of a slut put her high heels on the pavement, but you couldn't expect anything from that old clot of a Bourne. Maybe it was partly because he was a man, who couldn't be expected to care about such things. Anyway, she'd be sure to listen, and Eva had better listen too, and tell it around so others would too. Who knows, maybe even the management's wives in their houses Down Front along the water's edge would turn off their foreign stations to listen in, stranger things had happened. As long as it wasn't their bridge day.

Bourne cursed when he heard the news. He'd never set foot in that radio station again, he'd never sit down across the table from that woman off the freighter, there wasn't a thing about her that he cared about. Just a tourist, who cared what reasons she had for walking their streets? Leave the poor girl alone, she had a right to wear the heels right off her feet if she wanted to, she could walk her life away and it didn't make the slightest bit of difference to him or to anyone else. He locked himself in his shack; he had things to do. He'd stay at home, thank you, let someone else ask the silly girl some questions if it was so important to them as all that.

But no, no, they wouldn't accept his refusal; Geoffrey the turntable whizz hammered on his door, the date was set, and like it or not, Bourne would have to show up. It was his job. It was his life, all that was left to it, and if he didn't smarten up, old man, he'd find himself without anything at all to do in this world except sit in his own stink and wait for the world to end. Get off your butt, he said, here's your chance to have the whole town listening for a change instead of just a few scattered housewives too lazy to walk over to their sets and change the station. Here's an opportunity to make your useless life useful. Here's a chance to count. And if he wasn't interested, old man, then he'd better pack his bags and buy a ticket out of here because his already miserable life wouldn't even be worth living from now on, the whole town would be so mad, hate his guts, feel like stoning him to death on sight.

They'd chew him up and spit him out. Who did he think he was, some big-shot star who could pick and choose what he wanted to do?

And Bourne tried everything he could think of to avoid that meeting with the girl off the Peruvian freighter. He locked his door and stayed inside, but after three days the owner of the radio station—a Mr. Lewis Park from Vancouver wearing a green wrinkled suit and an orange unnatural tan—crowbarred the door in and propped him up in front of a big salmon casserole which Mrs. Park had baked especially for Bourne and which he would eat, dammit, if Mr. Lewis Park had to shove every spoonful down his throat himself. "Because the radio station is in trouble, can't you see, serious financial trouble. We must've been crazy to set up here in such a remote spot with this handful of villages for listeners but we did it, and if people like you don't jump on this opportunity to get people listening, drag in more advertising, boost the ratings, then we'll be forced to close down the station and fire everyone in sight. Now isn't that a delicious casserole?" His wife had been given the recipe by an Indian lady who'd grown up in the Queen Charlotte Islands before coming down to the city to die of some disease, he said, he couldn't remember the name of the disease, some terrible sickness full of pain and a lot of coughing, choking to death, but not until she'd had time to pass on her recipe to Mrs. Park, who did volunteer work once a week in the hospital.

"I'm not a local gossip," Bourne replied.

Mr. Park said the important thing was that everyone in town was so curious about that girl their teeth itched, and that made Bourne the most valuable person in the place, the one with the power to get the radio station back on its feet again, show that they weren't so crazy after all to set up here.

As soon as Park had returned to Vancouver with his wife's green stoneware pot, Bourne dragged his suitcase out from behind the bed where it had been since the day he'd arrived, and threw a few clothes inside, a few books. Then he waited until midnight, when all the windows in Squatters' Flats had gone dark and nothing showed from Port Annie but a few street lights, and headed up into the mountains. But he hadn't got a mile away before Geoffrey the turntable whizz came after him in his car, jumped out and chased him into the bush, threw his enormous weight on top of the old man when he fell, and dragged him back to the car. "Lord knows what's the matter with you, but I've never seen anyone so determined to escape. It's only a half-hour job, after all, and something you're good at." That girl certainly had Bourne scared, he said, his tiny eyes blinking rapidly behind his thick distorting glasses, and as far as he was concerned he'd be happy to cancel the whole thing because he was fed up with the business anyhow—but the news that Bourne was trying so hard to avoid the encounter had got everyone stirred up worse than ever. That town, he said, was having fits, turning itself inside out with excitement and curiosity. Didn't he think he had a duty to them?

And Bourne, suddenly, knew why he was terrified. He knew why he'd been trying to run away. While he was roller-coasting downhill through the dark in Geoffrey's car an idea touched lightly in his brain, fled, came back like a needle thrust: what that woman had come ashore from her Peruvian freighter to find was Joseph Bourne. She'd travelled all the way up the coast of two continents to find him. She'd paced up and down all the concrete sidewalks of the village of Port Annie, driving everyone crazy with curiosity, for the sole purpose of flushing him out. If he let these people have their way, if he let them drag him in to that hotel to sit across the studio table from their seabird, she'd have got what she was after, she'd have fulfilled her purpose, she'd have found him, and of course he would never come out of that room alive.

He worked himself up into such a panic that he hurried down to the end of the boardwalk in the middle of the following night, untied Preserved Crabbe's little wooden punt, and rowed himself seaward down the inlet. It took little effort, the tide was running and all he had to do was guide the direction of his movement by dragging an oar on this side a while, on that side a while, sliding silently down that darkened channel —no sound at all but the heavy beats of the bird's wings above him—until he ran aground on the shore of the small rocky island that sat ringed with the white foam of effluent out in the middle of the inlet.

But they found him there the next morning. Three men in the town saw his vulture circling the island and came roaring down in a motor boat, laughing and shouting, came skimming down the water and circled the island three times shouting insults at him before running their boat up on the beach and stepping ashore, where they found him at the top of a slope littered with the white bones of long-dead goats, huddled inside a tiny building made of driftwood logs.

"Get on out of here," one of them said, and would have kicked at him like a dog if he hadn't been afraid that what he saw in those eyes was madness. "Come on back where you belong, Bourne, an old man like you isn't safe out here alone, you'll die of exposure or starve to death." They gave each other knowing looks and said that life would be a lot easier for them all if there were an old-folks' home in Port Annie, where there were people whose job it was to chase down foolish old idiots like this, but that unfortunately there was none in the town and there wasn't likely to be one in the future, either, because no one ever stayed around long enough to grow old. Old people with any sense lived elsewhere. Or locked themselves up, like Fat Annie in the hotel. Only a scramble-headed fool like Bourne picked a place like this to live out his dying years.

"Get in that boat," one of them said, and strong-armed him down through the bones to the shore. They dragged Preserved's punt back to the Flats at the end of a rope, swinging from one side to the other of their wide hollowed-out wake. If he tried any more of his silly tricks, they said, they'd be forced to ask a doctor to pump him full of drugs for his own safety, they'd have to keep him locked in the hotel where someone could keep an eye on him night and day, they might even be forced to have him committed to an insane asylum over on the mainland, because it was obvious, for heaven's sake, that he wasn't acting like any sane and rational old man ought to act. He was acting like a screwball, a raving loony, a cracked loopy cuckoo.

But they needn't have worried about any more attempts to escape. Bourne was resigned. His night in the island shack among the goat bones and the kitchen supplies of some long-ago hermit had killed all desire to avoid the confrontation. That woman, whoever she was, had come to give him what he'd travelled several continents in his lifetime to find, what he'd travelled through a life so long to find that all of it but the most recent years had been forgotten long ago, as if it had never happened. She'd come to give him what he'd perched himself here on the edge of the world to wait for. The final eviction.

They didn't need to bother setting up guards by his shack, he told them when he'd climbed out of the boat at the Flats, and they needn't worry about spying on him any more or chasing him up and down the inlet and over the roads. He'd be there on the day of the interview, he would come in to town the same as he always did and face that woman across the studio table like any other guest, and do the best job of it he knew how to do. And he wanted them to know, as well, that whatever happened in that radio studio in the basement of the hotel when he and the seabird finally met they were not to blame themselves, it was only what had been preparing itself to happen for hundreds, or thousands—or, who knows, maybe millions—of years.

They could arrange for him to meet this woman but they couldn't force him to like it. On the day of the interview, in the dim studio light, he indulged in a round of complaints. The place was too dark, full of shadows, couldn't somebody put on a light? Why should Geoffrey get to sit in the lighted control room while he had to work in this grave? Why were they expecting him to do this interview cold—without giving him any of the background information he usually got? All he knew was her name (Raimey), which didn't help him at all. He complained of a rattle in his chest, it was hard for him to breathe; he complained that his head ached, that he could hear a voice calling the roll in the back of his head—a teacher or something, he must be remembering a teacher. His whole life was stored in his head someplace, he imagined, but it wasn't accessible, he had no use for it now. He complained that the girl hadn't been considerate enough to get there a bit early. Geoffrey's voice came on loud: "I've turned off the mikes, old man, I can see you muttering away in there to yourself, but you're wasting your breath. I can't hear you." Behind the glass in that brightly lighted control room he grinned, unimpressed. And still Bourne continued to complain, pacing the floor, while his stirred-up robes whispered around his legs.

And later, when his nostrils had filled with the scent of his own fear and his head reeled with the dizzy ring of that roll-calling voice, Geoffrey burst in to the studio. "They're phoning in to see if it's time yet, people will be listening, man we've never had such interest," and handed him a folded piece of paper which had been delivered, he said, by one of the hotel chambermaids, a hippy blonde just new in town, probably a love letter, you old goat. But Bourne's stomach growled, his bowels rumbled and snarled, he waved the young man away, go back to your hole, and tried with shaking hands to open the paper. His fingers were wooden blocks, he dropped the thing twice, trying to pry it open. He smelled it—the eye-watering stink of smoke and urine; he held it up to the light— just some faint black scrawl; he slapped it down on the table, cursing, and tore it in half so he could pry at it with his thumbs, open it out, and put the two pieces together. His eyes were so hard to control that he had to sit down, lean down close, force himself to focus on that scrawl, those big black sloppy letters, a handwriting he recognized from somewhere, dimly; he'd got notes from this person before, plenty of them, at some time in the forgotten past. His stomach lifted, tightened, in recognition; pain shot across his diaphragm. BOURNE, no dear, no mister, just BOURNE, and then IT HAPPENS, a shaky "s"—this was a child's scrawl or an old person's, SOMETIME, the words slid off to the left, he had to lean right down, aim his eyes at the individual letters, TO, a fancy loop on that "o" and a tiny ALL OF, a big slide back to the left-hand margin of the page, one more word, a huge one, two letters, a U and an S, with one two three four exclamation marks after them, and then a long line of small words he could grasp by sliding the torn paper past his face, BUT DONT SAY I HAVEN'T BEEN WARN-ING YOU ALL THESE YEARS, and now just the one big round signature he'd been half-aware of since starting at the top of the page, the one dark arrogant word he knew now he'd seen on a hundred similar letters in his lifetime before moving to this dump of a place, ANNIE, that fat hag up in her hotel room, the old death-whore herself. This was an old letter, there were dozens just like it in his pockets, it must have fallen out. Back in that grey forgotten life, he sensed, she'd tried her best to frighten him. She didn't scare him now. He scrunched the papers between his hands, rolled them into a ball which he threw on the floor and kicked off to one corner of the room.

But where was that girl? He tore at his hair, he pushed out through the black door and hurried up the steps to the hotel lobby. No girl in sight. He rushed out into the square, into drizzle, and limped down the sidewalk. Faces behind the window of the coffee shop watched him pass. Jeremy Fell in the open doorway of The Threads Shed nodded good morning, his long white fingers interlaced and wriggling, his red eyes narrowed to a squint. Mayor Weins at the back of his shop where he sold magazines and pet food and hardware dropped everything and ran, thumped down to the doorway: "Bourne! Bourne! Have you done it already; have you had the interview?" Bourne whirled, "*What*? *What*?" and whirled again to go on. "Miserable old goat! Would it kill you to smile, or act human?" But on he went, down that concrete, kicking at fragments of left-behind shells, past the coin laundry with its hot blast of air and the row of slouched housewives in kerchiefs and jeans, reading paperbacks or gossiping. Ian McCarthy came out of the post office to watch, scratching at his fuzzy sea-otter face. Customers narrowed their eyes to watch him from behind the liquor-store window. The dark white-eyed faces of the Manku family watched him from inside a car. His weedy eyebrows twitched, his eyes darted, his huge fingers tugged at his ear. He followed the perimeter of the square, his face red with impatience, all the way around to the hotel again, where he stopped, supported himself with a hand against one of the four-by-four posts near the door, and seemed to be sniffing the air, or tasting its wetness.

Even his old ears picked up the sound before he could see her. The click, click, click of her heels on the pavement, somewhere between the buildings and the inlet. His heart seemed to stop; his arms went numb. That heady scent of an unknown equatorial flower seemed to have arrived ahead of her, enough to make him dizzy. Then he saw her, coming up the hill in a black shiny raincoat belted at the waist. A purse slung over her shoulder. Click, click, click, she walked her famous walk right across the square and everyone saw her reach out her hand to take the old man's hand—put the beautiful white tapered hand in his huge old fingers—everyone saw her smile. Everyone saw his confusion, his sudden staggering fall nearly to the pavement, his hand on the post pulling himself upright again.

"That man is on his last legs for sure," Ian McCarthy said. "Let's just hope he lasts long enough to finish the interview."

"Did you see that walk?" George Beeton said, nudging at Larry Bowman beside him. "Did you get a look at that gal? Did you see those legs?"

But the librarian could only swallow, his mouth was too dry to answer. He was certain now that he'd never recover from the sight of this wonderful dream.

Inside the studio, she sat across the table from Bourne with a wide-eyed eager look on her face, wet lips slightly parted showing her perfect teeth, the most beautiful woman he could remember seeing, one lovely hand laid out on the felt between them and the other playing with the front of her blouse, which was unbuttoned down far enough for him to see the delicate skin of one breast, the pale blue veins. Weren't they going to be strapped into their chairs, she wanted to know, because this place reminded her of a gas chamber, it even had that window for reporters to watch their death agonies through. And then she laughed and pressed her elbows into the black felt and leaned towards him as if somehow things had got turned around so that she'd become the host in this confrontation, he the guest. Yes, her name was Raimey just as his piece of paper said and, no, it didn't matter if she had another name and, no, there weren't any questions he couldn't ask her once that red light came on. Anything he had the courage to ask, she had the courage to answer. Behind her, fat Geoffrey in the control room made faces, rolled his weak eyes behind his glasses and let his tongue hang out as if he intended to go mad with passion. He couldn't suck his cigarette fast enough. Bourne's hands shook; there was nothing on his paper but her name. Anything he learned would be as new to him as it was to his listeners, he couldn't possibly know what would be best to ask. He was old, too old for this job. He couldn't remember why he did it; he couldn't even be absolutely sure he really was doing it and not only dreaming it. Why hadn't he dropped dead the moment he saw her? What terrible sort of death did she have in store for him that it was necessary to go through all this first? Maybe it had already happened. Maybe those bells in his head were tolling for his own funeral.

Geoffrey's voice: "Watch me, we'll start when I nod, ten seconds." Geoffrey himself behind that window was only a blur to Bourne, a vague heavy figure hunched over his controls, and even the sound of his own theme music seemed unfamiliar, distant, even threatening, his own voice introducing the show creakier, shakier than ever before. His temples throbbed. Beautiful or not she was here for just one purpose, and already it was becoming harder to breathe in here, there was something wrong with the air. A clammy sweat broke out on his skin.

Certainly she would be happy to tell him why she'd been on that Peruvian freighter, she said, though the route was a

little circuitous—if he had the patience for it. Her dark eyes
smiled; she seemed to have no idea how hard this was for him.
She was in Jamaica, just sitting around in the sunshine eating
oranges right off the tree for her breakfast and swimming in
the warm ocean—the lazy life of the shockingly spoiled, living
with this government bigshot, feeling guilty—when she found
out that she was needed here, that she had to get up here to
Port Annie fast. An old lady told her, a beautiful old brown-
skinned healing lady who lived in this shack outside of town
by herself, a friend of hers, who came to the house high up
the slope from the harbour and told her it was time to go. It
was time for something the old woman had asked her to do
long ago, something she would have done herself if she hadn't
been so old now, unable to travel.

But why? Bourne wanted to know why an old lady would
want to come to Port Annie. What was so important that she
had to send someone else in her place?

Just a minute, she would get to that. First let her get off
that island, which wasn't easy, because the government bigshot
couldn't believe anyone would ever want to leave him. He
even had her followed. Police. But she packed up and got out
of there in the middle of the night, caught the only ship that
happened to be tied up in the harbour at the time, and sailed
south, southeast—not the direction she needed but it was a
start. Living on an island means you can't be fussy about certain things. And then before long she was on her way up the
Amazon River.

On a freighter?

On a freighter. Boats go right up that river every day, right
up the thousands of miles into Peru. She found herself stepping off the freighter in an Indian village somewhere in the
jungle, don't ask her where. Those people nearly adopted her,
one family, she ate their jungle meat with them and Lord
knows what else, they wanted to keep her; but she had to get
moving, and over the Andes she went, with their oldest son as
a guide, slept one night in some ancient ruins—how did he
like that?—and another night in a burial cave on a pile of
skulls, not everybody's idea of fun, but she didn't know that
was where they were until morning. Then down to the coast
she came, down by canoe to the desert coast and right down
to the city of Lima. Okay, she thought, so now I'm on the
right coast at least, and I could walk if I could count on living

forever, just follow the shoreline north past a half-dozen countries in all, but why should I when there was this great big
boat heading north to drop off something in San Francisco
and pick up something else here in Port Annie?

But Bourne's throbbing mind hadn't been able to go on past
that cave full of skulls, he wanted more. Surely she was exaggerating. Why would anyone sleep in a cave full of skulls?

It was the boy's idea, he didn't tell her that was where they
were going, they just stopped there when it was already dark
and she was so dead tired she went to sleep on top of the
bumpy ground, a bed of skeletons—skulls and bones—all
human. Some special burial place, the boy explained in the
morning, but she went screaming out of the cave anyway, there
were bats as well. He tried to tell her a child conceived in a
place like that would grow up to be a leader of men, but she
wasn't interested, the boy had a woman at home but he was
still only a boy, up to here on her and mostly naked, and
thought everything she said was so funny he nearly turned
himself inside out laughing. When she went screaming out of
that cave in the morning he rolled around on those bones
laughing until he was nearly sick. And Bourne's mind, filled
with those skulls still, slid backwards to the Amazon River;
she'd opened a tear in that grey ribbon, there was something
in it he recognized. He peered at her face, at her dark eyes.
He leaned closer to the microphone, could feel her cool breath.
He squinted, tried to squeeze her face into other shapes. Was
he supposed to know who she was? Was she, by some chance,
a granddaughter of his or something?

She laughed. She looked at the microphone, no doubt imagining an audience of home listeners snickering at such a silly
question. No, don't be ridiculous, was he trying to make a
joke? No, don't be silly. But he didn't care if their laughter
brought the mountain down on them all, there was something
here, she'd opened a tear in his mind, he saw miles and miles
of that river. The violent green shore. Riots of colour and
noise. No, no, this was crazy, her father was a fisherman, she
assured him, in Barbados. She ran away from home when she
was fourteen years old, full-grown and with a mind of her
own. She lived everywhere, visited people in all parts of the
world. She'd sat on Skellig Michael. She'd seen the Norwegian
fiords. She'd climbed old Fujiyama. She'd visited the Isle of
Patmos.

It was nearly impossible for him to breathe. He could drown
in this dark thick air. Or melt from the heat. His hands on the
felt tablecloth appeared to move on their own, to float as if
they were unattached to him.

All that travelling, all that continent-crossing, what had she
done it for? Why was she here? He'd been up the Amazon
once himself, long ago, he was sure of it now—he'd been God-
knows-where all his life, searching for something, in Jamaica
probably, and Europe, all the countries of the world maybe
back in that grey fog that had been his life, and up the Amazon
too like her—but why had she gone to all that effort, all that
travel, just to end up in a place like this, a place like Port
Annie, a few buildings perched on the edge of nothing? Why
had that old woman sent her?

She smiled. Oh those beautiful teeth. Her famous walk had
nothing on those teeth, that incredible smile. Because she
knew, she said, she knew it would be in a place like this that
she'd find him, she knew that by now he'd have worked his
way to the very brink of something, that he would have moved
until he'd come to a place where there was nowhere else to
go. That he would have come here to meet her.

No, no, his head was about to split, he felt the screaming
sound of his whole body being torn open, pieces of him pushing to be born. A face, an earlier face, a soft brown earlier
face.

Of the healing lady, yes, she told him, a Mrs. Bourne, the
lady in Jamaica, a beautiful old abandoned lady she'd loved
very much, a healing lady, who'd made her promise this, living in that shack where he'd left her sometime in his life when
he'd passed through there as he'd passed through nearly everywhere, had made her promise that she'd seek him out like this,
just like this, where she knew even then he would be, an old
sour cramp of a man terrified on the brink of eternity stewing
in his own foul juices, told her to seek him out at the last
possible moment and—

And what? He saw skulls, the table was littered with her
bed of skulls, his hands played with them, his fingers hooked
in their eye-holes. The air was full of booming, full of that
voice still calling the roll, full of darkness. And what? And
what?

And simply bring him to this moment when there was
nothing left for him to do, nothing left in the world for him

to do but the most terrifying thing of all, the one thing he would resist with all his strength until there was no choice left in the matter—to turn his vision back until he was forced to see his own life, his own soul, his—

Then she *had* come for him. Oh God, he cried, and his fingers in those skulls were no longer fingers, they were alive, white and squirming. Bourne reared up from the table, screaming, shaking his hands. Trying to detach himself from his own fingers. There was no air in here, she'd used it all up. There was no light. He was drowning. He tried to crawl up the space towards the ceiling, straining for air, and felt himself collapse across the black felt on the table.

Blood bubbled at his lips. His eyes bulged. He slid off the table and fell to the floor. His fingers clawed at his throat, as if the thick grey mist which had separated him from his own life all this time had opened up or burned away at last and the sudden overwhelming vision of it were choking him. A terrible whispering filled the room, like moving curtains, tiny whirlwinds—a disordered conspiracy of noises that licked at walls, that spun in corners, that whirred in his ears and increased its volume to fill up the world, explode beyond sound in his skull.

Geoffrey said it first, *the death of Bourne*, like someone testing to see if an idea worked, then carried the news out into the lobby and the hallways of the hotel and into the dining room and the coffee shop where people one after the other, hearing it, began to whisper too, *the death of Bourne, the death of Bourne*, as if they'd been entrusted with a secret. And the doctor who rushed to the studio with his wrinkled bag rose up from his knees to confirm it, *the death of Bourne*, no question here, the man was as dead as a stone, a chilling announcement which spread across the sea-washed town by telephone and backyard gossip and the radio itself to every home, and even down the road past the boarded-up church with the boat in a tree to Squatters' Flats, where his neighbours, awaiting word of their own expropriation, heard of it, *the death of Bourne*, and even the raindrops falling on that whole green place of mountain and town and inlet seemed to be swollen with the sound of it, while the great dark bird set out on his enormous wings as if to follow some dim persistent memory down the inlet and past the coastal beaches and out into the pale blue haze that hangs above the sea.

2

Of Extraordinary News from Squatters' Flats,
Some Digging Around in the Past, and
Considerable Feverish Planning for the Future
(Much of It Considered by Mabel Weins
To Be in Questionable Taste);
of a Lover's Noble Suffering and His
Decision To Act,
or,

The Old Man and
His Deeds

Just when Angela Turner had decided to give up and leave Port Annie, where nothing ever happened to a girl except this never-ending rain that would drive her crazy, the giant wave had washed up into town and left a Peruvian sailor on the flowered sheets of her unmade bed. Fortunately her rooms were on the ground floor of an apartment building set right at the water's edge, squeezed between two of the Down Front homes, so she got more than her share of benefits from that tidal surprise. When the water had sucked back out of her bedroom, leaving crabs and broken window glass and a pair of someone else's panties stranded on her spongy carpet, she got up from the corner where she'd been thrown and found the man—no apparition—lying on the soaked yellow daisies of her sheets. Limpets glued themselves to his shoulders; periwinkles nested in the curly hairs of his belly. "Oh, Lord," she said, "I hope this isn't a mirage."

At first, she had trouble believing her eyes, even after all those months of standing behind her cash register and dreaming about the man who would someday rescue her from this place. A refined man was what she'd ordered, not one of these coarse and vulgar types who worked at the Mill. And maybe here he was. A handsome jaw, arrogant eyes—so far, exactly what she'd hoped for! And a magnificent body stretched out naked and soaking wet, like a youthful god. Perhaps it was just too perfect, she was a little afraid to believe it, but when he winked one eye and wiggled the toes of his long pale feet, she quickly closed the door which had let the ocean in and pulled the blind down over the broken window. It would be sheer stupidity, she thought, to question such marvellous luck.

Of course, her visitor hadn't been able to speak a word of English, but that did not prove to be a serious impediment. His genteel behaviour, his aristocratic manner, his way of treating a girl like a lady while driving her crazy with the passion he aroused (and then so ably satisfied), all spoke clearly

39

in his every movement, the look in his eyes, the touch of his slender fingers—there was no need for speech. Port Annie had never seen such a man. Even Angela's dreams hadn't managed to cook up such absolute perfection. And he refused to step outside her apartment either—a great relief, no need to share him with anyone else that way, though it made going to work in the morning a horrible chore. For three days and nights her life alternated between the slow, boring frustration of standing behind that till and the perfect ecstasy of being at home with her gift from the sea. There seemed to be no end to what he would teach her—all with the refinement of a real gentleman, of course—and no limits to his imagination, his generosity, his fantastic physical abilities. An encyclopedia of techniques, a paragon of finesse—real class—a wild man with the manners of a count when it came to his treatment of a young woman.

Unfortunately, when his freighter was ready to take off for the open sea again, loaded down with pulp, the sailor was not able to think of a single reason to stay behind in this town. His perfect aristocratic manners just suddenly evaporated; he couldn't understand a thing when she tried to suggest that he take her along on that floating bucket of rust. He wrapped himself up in a flowered housecoat from her closet and hurried down to the Mill, where his fellow crew members, who'd written him off as drowned, welcomed him back with a great deal of excited talk and backslapping and laughing at his silly get-up. When the freighter sailed past town, Angela Turner refused to raise the blind on her window or go to the door to watch. Her face burned as she imagined him telling his friends what a stroke of luck he'd fallen upon—a lot better than drowning, boys—and what a fool she'd been to think he'd intended to stay. A real pushover! Her red face was burning with both shame and rage—to be dumped like that, when she'd made such a fool of herself over him; to be left with nothing but this empty sinking embarrassment, this nagging feeling that, like it or not, he'd left something of himself behind in her, perhaps even more than she'd have wanted if he'd warned her. After all, she wasn't equipped like the waxy leaves of the Mist Maiden flower for shedding seawater before it could do her damage.

The most humiliating part of it all was that, despite her dreams, despite the eagerness with which she welcomed that unexpected gift from the sea, Angela Turner wanted to be a modern woman with nothing but contempt for females who let their happiness depend on a man. Not for her the life of that male-hungry Linda Weins in the coffee shop, a teen-aged nympho who went all to pieces every time a man passed within fifty yards. Not for her, either, a future like those house-wives whose talk never got very far away from the size of their husbands' cheques, the state of their husbands' health, the im-pressiveness of their husbands' demands. No, they didn't need to let this pretty figure fool them, or these large brown eyes that seemed to be always ready to fill up with tears; she in-tended to be an independent young woman who put sex in its place—just one small part of a woman's life—and filled her days with thoughts of a better future. Career, money, power.

What shame then, to have lost her sense over a horny Peru-vian male! A different matter if she'd only had a rip-roaring time, then thrown him out on his ear when she'd had enough —like a modern woman. But to have gone crazy, lost all inter-est in anything else, filled up her whole life with sex! A good thing she hadn't blabbed to anyone. A good thing no one had come banging on her door to discover what she'd been up to. A good thing that freighter was on its way out to sea; by the time it came back she'd be long gone from this town, only a faint memory in people's heads, not even missed. If that sailor returned to look for her here, eager to make a fool of her once again, she'd be miles away, starting a new life, safe from the likes of him.

But running away from this place wasn't so easy to do. After all, she'd come here to get as far as she could from home, to find independence. Who wanted to give up so soon, call yourself a flop? Or start hopping from one town to the next? She'd made a bad choice, she had to admit; no girl with her eye on the future ought to pick a town like this one, a dead-end place so far from the rest of the world. Yet there were a few things she would miss, strange as it seemed. The chilled silence, for example. And it was a breathtakingly beautiful spot—the dark water, that steep green mountain across the inlet when the shreds of mist were caught in its feathery trees. And much as she hated to admit it, she'd prob-ably miss living in a town that was made up mostly of men— even if they were crude, not her type at all, and looked at her in a way that made her go cold.

She would even—hard to imagine this—miss that clutch of women who gathered for coffee in the hotel every day at three —exactly her own afternoon break—to sit in the booths and gossip. Eva McCarthy, Mabel Weins (the mayor's wife), Mrs. Barnstone, and others, all miles older than she was, another generation, yet she liked spending some time with them there. They made sure they all arrived for their mail every day at precisely the same time, so that they could convene for coffee in the hotel and catch up on the latest news, compare opinions, and pass comments on everyone who walked by the windows —especially that shameless clothes-horse of a Rita Rentalla, who hurried past every day at this time, set free from her part-time job as the doctor's receptionist and in a big hurry to spend the rest of her day hanging around in the Kick-and-Kill right up until closing time. Every day there was something different about her to criticize—her tight dress, her long scarlet fingernails, her nose in the air, her notorious red hair—and of course there were the women of the Manku family, once in a while, whose colourful costumes came in for a great deal of good-natured disapproval. Angela herself never joined in when it got vicious—live and let live was her motto—but she couldn't help feeling good in the company of those women whose lives she officially despised. What a conundrum! She wanted to stand up and shout at them, "Haven't you anything better to do with yourselves than pull people apart?" but she also wanted to hug them all close to her, like her own mother, and burst into tears. Sometimes she just couldn't help loving people, even when she felt that she ought to be loathing them. It didn't even bother her very much that their opinion of her was so far from what she wanted the world to think. Such a lovely girl, according to them, the picture of innocence with those large eyes of a startled deer. Everyone's dream of a daughter. Not someone you'd worry about, no, a girl with old-fashioned manners and a smile that would melt icy hearts. They behaved as if they'd adopted her as a group, or saw their own pasts in her eyes.

"Tell us, Angela, do you have the linen for your hope chest yet? I noticed some lovely sheets in the latest catalogue."

She'd never even got around to telling them that a hope chest in this day and age was beneath contempt.

But she still hadn't managed to pack up and leave the day that Mayor Weins came into the coffee shop and told them the news from Squatters' Flats. He was all worn out, a wreck, slumped into a corner to puff for a while. "They had to pick the day I'm all dressed up in my Thunderbird costume, of course. It's heavy as the dickens, and I'm sweating to death— can't somebody turn down the heat?" It was his favourite outfit, which he wore periodically to honour the band of Indians that had fled the inlet when Fat Annie Fartenburg and her husband started this town. Too bad the wire-and-paper wings were a little battered from going in and out of doors that weren't wide enough, and the enormous beak that protruded from his forehead was bent in the middle, but other than that it was good as new, and colourful, a perfect costume for getting his picture taken for the *Port Annie Crier*.

It made him a little bit ill in the stomach to admit it, and no kidding either, he announced, but the rumours had turned out to be true. He'd gone down to check them, just part of his civic duty, one of the little things a mayor was happy to do for his town. Not a word of a lie, Joseph Bourne was alive. The old man hadn't been snuffed out, he'd come around: the girl from the Peruvian freighter hadn't arrived to kill him, she'd brought him back to life. What did they think of that?

"Honestly, I could spit," Mrs. Barnstone said. "Those Squatters are quite impossible. Surely it's all a joke."

It was no joke, however; it was true. No one had ever heard anything like it. Who could have guessed that the crazy old man would survive his very own death? As Eva McCarthy put it, staring into her cup, it was enough to shake your trust in the natural order of things. The entire universe, now, was suspect.

"You saw him?" Mabel Weins said, dismissing the universe with her hand and narrowing her eyes to see right into her husband's skull, through Thunderbird head and all.

He nodded. "*And* talked to the girl."

A lesson, he added, for those who read signs in nature.

Though Mrs. Barnstone, having digested the news, wondered if an ageing woman like herself couldn't take some hope from such a reversal of things.

Hope? Hope? What was this talk of hope? Mayor Weins fanned his face with a menu. "Not that I wish a death on anyone, ever, but what's the matter with that man that he can't act normal and kick off when his number comes up?"

"Thank goodness he wasn't a churchy man," Mabel Weins

said, "or the first thing we know they'd be calling it a miracle
and, Lord help us, people would be making that shack into
a shrine." She'd been to university once, for a year, and
learned a few lessons from history. "Better if no one else even
hears of it, something to keep to ourselves."

"For the time being, at least," was all that Charlie Reynolds
would agree to in the adjoining booth. As editor of the *Port
Annie Crier*, he was never far from the mayor, and knew he'd
get a story out of this thing sooner or later. But he'd decided
to wait for more details to show themselves rather than make
a fool of himself by jumping in with a hasty headline. It was
safer to stick to the kind of thing that he'd always done, like
taking the mayor's picture every Friday when he presented an
Award of Merit to whichever merchant had made the healthiest
profit during the week. "And besides, no one in his right mind
really believes the man was ever dead," he added with a sneer.
"Not even in this gullible dump of a town."

"But the doctor checked him over, right in the hotel, pro-
nounced him dead as a mackerel. I was there. I saw him."

"And what about Angela? What do you think? Did this kind
of thing happen in Fredericton, dear? Do old men in Fredericton make a habit of dropping off when their time comes up,
and then popping back for some more?"

Angela didn't know what to say because she felt like laughing and crying at the same time, and shouting something. Her
eyes were filled with tears, damn them, but her stomach
trembled with the laughter that was trying to burst free. She
heard a voice in her head, *Come forth! Come forth!*, which
she didn't recognize but which she sensed to be terribly funny
and horribly sad at the same time, awe-inspiring. She clamped
a hand over her mouth, "Excuse me," and hurried out through
the coffee-shop door.

Across the square in the rain, down the slope to the dock,
over the slippery planks that floated on logs. From the very
end of the dock she could see the shacks of Squatters' Flats,
she could see the roof of Joseph Bourne's cabin, she could see
the shreds of smoke that escaped his metal chimney. So Joseph
Bourne was alive, he wasn't dead—not everything after all had
to come to an ugly end. The seabird had arrived in town to
save him; not everything off a Peruvian freighter came here
to hurt and betray. Angela Turner, laughing, crying, tore off
her coat, her dress, and leapt into the cold salty water that

had delivered the gift of a perfect man to her sheets and a garden of shells to her floor. And laughing, crying, she set out into the inlet with the long sure strokes of a champion swimmer.

By the time the mayor had fought his way out through the coffee-shop door in order to call her back, or save her—battering his wings even worse than before and snapping his beak right in two—it was clear to everyone in the window booth that Angela Turner needed no help, she was a magnificent swimmer, a champ. Look at those strokes. No one had seen such speed. She could swim to the other side of the inlet with no trouble at all, she could swim to the open sea if she wished. She could swim (she knew this herself) in the rolling Pacific until she caught up to that freighter if she wanted, and could probably pass it, thumbing her nose at those sailors before she set off with her expert strokes of a champion into the mysterious sea. Or into the world.

And yet she returned. One trip across the inlet and back was enough. By the time she dropped in at the library later the same day to see if Larry Bowman had heard the news from the Flats, she'd become the subject of excited chatter herself. Port Annie's hope for the Olympics, some called her. Cracking up, said others. But she behaved as if her spectacular feat had not even happened, or had erased itself from her memory as it was taking place.

"Some people don't want to believe it," she said, referring to Bourne's revival.

But Larry Bowman had no trouble believing it at all. That seabird's beauty by itself was enough to raise the dead. When she told him the news he only smiled and nodded and looked away, as if this was just exactly what he'd been expecting to hear all along.

And who was in a better position to know what that girl off the freighter was capable of doing? Hadn't his own first glimpse of her been enough to raise up something that he'd thought was dead in him, his manhood? His library had never been the same since that day she'd come inside, given him a wink, and tilted his whole world up on end. Such a quiet man, so insignificant that hardly anyone even remembered he existed, and yet the sight of that incredible walk, her brilliant smile, had started a sweaty trembling fever burning in him that matched the suffering of the lustiest hearts in any book up there on his library shelves. The girl was herself a miracle—of course she'd brought a dead man back to life, no question about it, not a serious problem for someone as talented as that.

Naturally he didn't mention a word of this to Angela Turner. He didn't even *think* it until she'd gone. As long as she was in the library, finding herself a book, his brain was just as scrambled and confused as it always was when an attractive single woman was breathing the same air he was. He kept his back turned—his neck hot and red, his upper lip beaded with sweat—hating himself for having so little control, for reacting like this when it was only Angela Turner—pretty and confident but nobody to be afraid of, more like the best friend of your younger sister. Not until he'd stamped her book and heard her leave was he able to look up, breathe again, and curse himself properly. What an idiot! When that seabird had restored his masculine hopes, why hadn't she gone the whole way, completed the job!

Better to be a brute, an animal. He'd rather be a gorilla like Preserved Crabbe down in the Flats. Imagine having that scar on his scalp as a badge! Imagine being so confident over a woman that he'd risk his life, steal someone else's wife, get into a fight.

And then to go *back*, yesterday, and *steal* that woman—snatch her away from her husband and bring her home. So what if she was a thick-legged penguin, sullen-faced and dull? So what if an overly generous backside wasn't everyone's taste, or big yellow thick-nailed toes, or spaces between her teeth? Preserved Crabbe had been confident enough, he'd cared enough, to go back and steal her away from her dangerous husband.

The fact that she'd run away from him almost immediately didn't matter. One look at the floating bunkhouse she was expected to live in, one look at her motley brothers-in-law, her neighbours, one look at that whole shacky mess of a Squatters' Flats and she'd bolted, fled. But that didn't matter—even if it made Crabbe look like a bit of a fool—because he was man enough to go into a towering rage, to break down and howl like a baby, smash things, and go chasing off after her like a raving maniac. Maybe he'd never catch up, maybe he'd never be seen again, but any man with that kind of unthinking confidence had Larry Bowman's respect, not to mention his admiration and envy. He was romantic, heroic, a real man.

Now that would be a true resurrection, Mr. Bourne! To wake up some morning and find that he'd been turned into a brute, a lady-killer, a man of terrific confidence. Not so ugly and stupid as Crabbe, perhaps, not a chauvinist pig either, but someone with enough courage to approach that seabird— not just dream about her like an adolescent but make himself known, approach her, make her knees go weak with the cool look from his eyes, cause her to fall head over heels in love with him.

Poor Larry, always dreaming. He shook his head, why did he torture himself with such idle hopes? His future behind this barricade of books was about as bright as that dull green rain that never stopped falling, drowning the grass and washing out plants that lay with their little white roots exposed on the ground and making the town appear like something under the sea. If that girl was so handy with miracles, now, why didn't she shut off this rain? Otherwise it was going to be a long uncomfortable summer.

Jenny Chambers up in her house at the top of the town saw right away what kind of summer it was going to be. Stupid rain falling on them without ever stopping, turning the whole town into a waterfall. If this kept up they could be looking at another one of those rotten slides. It had taken her a year to recover from the last one, mud two-foot deep on all her floors, and Slim still hadn't shovelled the leftover gravel and muck back over the fence. A losing battle, the poor man. The run-off ditches were so full of rain water now it wasn't safe to let your kids outside, not to mention the way a car passing by on the street sent a spray up so high it got your living-room windows every time. "Maybe that dumb-looking woman of Preserved Crabbe's is the only one with brains after all," she told Eva McCarthy on the phone. "At least she's escaped from this endless rain."

As for herself, she hoped Slim's union got busy and called another strike at the Mill pretty soon, so they could all get out of this town for a while, holiday in the sun.

But Eva McCarthy at the other end of the line wanted to talk about Bourne—even her brand-new refrigerator had to take a back seat for a change. It was driving her crazy that she hadn't got into that cabin yet, to find out what that sea-bird was doing to the old man. She was tempted to march down there and hammer on the door, demand to be let in, but she'd heard the old woman with the gun wouldn't let you go near.

But Jenny couldn't talk about it now, Eva, because there were eight rotten brats fighting at her supper table and Slim didn't even seem to be noticing. Over a sausage that Edna kept pushing off onto other people's plates. It was impossible to hear anyway, they were all yelling, except Regina who was sixteen and of course superior to everyone else in the house with her pinch-nosed face. And when Edna stood up and tossed the sausage to Liz, who threw it back splashing into the creamed corn, Jenny yelled, "Get out of my kitchen!" before realizing she still held the phone in her hand. "Excuse me, Eva, I've got to hang up." And grabbed for the broom.

Albert started to cry, and then fat Min: chair legs scraped and they all stood up. Regina stomped out, tossing her head, and slammed a door, but the others thought Jenny was fooling and moved off only far enough to be out of broom-reach. "Git!" She ran three short steps towards them, and they retreated, screaming. Fire-eyed Jenny, she looked as if she could scorch their hides. But they stopped again, half giggling at her anger, until she took more running steps, slapping her feet on the floor so hard that they hurt. "Out! Git out! No one fights at the table, you bunch of barbarians. Go on to your bedroom. No dessert! Go read a book or something."

They would do no such thing and she knew it. They would sneak out the back, all eight of them—Regina to meet that sneery-faced creep of a Conrad boy somewhere, the older boys to hang around the rec centre with no money to spend until they were kicked out, the younger kids to play in the water running down the streets, swearing like mill-workers until people started yelling out of car windows for them to go home where they belonged if they didn't want to get killed. Housewives would come out into their porches to say What was the matter with Jenny Chambers that she hadn't taught them anything about safety or manners? A string of curses was all they'd get for an answer, language to curl their toes, and then they'd go inside clucking their tongues and say what a shame those kids hadn't been given to their own real mother instead of being dragged up by an ex-stripper who didn't even own a wedding ring or want one.

Oh, she knew what they thought, but let them blab. What did she care? At least now it was quiet in here for a change.

"That Eva just can't get her mind off Bourne, he's driving her crazy," she told Slim, who read yesterday's paper at his end of the table, his feet crossed on the seat of Liz's chair. At least he had his cowboy boots off, but his Stetson still sat on the back of his head. "But how could I tell her I don't want to talk to her *at all?*" Maybe never again. Not about Bourne or anything else.

Slim showed no sign of paying attention but she told him anyway, she'd always found it easier to do her thinking right out loud: she'd stayed home from picket-duty today, Slim, just to show off her new catalogue wardrobe. A new fur coat, and wouldn't you think one person in this wet dump of a place would notice and tell her how nice she looked? A day-long visit to every corner of this town in the pouring rain in her new clothes, and how was a person to tell who her friends were if not one of them in all that time could be bothered to compliment her on those new catalogue clothes or even let their eyes turn a little green from envy and travel down the length of her stylish get-up? Not even Eva McCarthy, that house-proud scatterbrain, had asked to try on her fur. Not that she'd have let her, the little minnow, but you'd think that at least one person in this place would have asked to run their hands down its softness.

"Do you want to know—are you listening?—do you want to know what that Eva McCarthy said when I stopped at her house? She didn't offer me even a cup of her stupid imitation coffee that tastes like melted-down trucks, not a cookie or a cup of tea, though she could see I was pooped and puffing from the climb. All she could talk about was her new yellow fridge and the stupid birdbath she bought for that front lawn of hers, already littered with enough plastic ducks and geese and pink flamingos to fill a barnyard. Of course what does she know about style? She never steps outside her house in anything else but that satin baseball jacket with her name on the sleeve and that old-fashioned beehive mess of artificial hair. And at the other houses—not even when I told about your promotion did one of those babes say So that's why you're wearing those new clothes and can I try on that fur? Practically a foreman at the Mill, I said, but of course they only looked sour at that. I should've known. It's easy to find people who want to hear every word of your troubles, but just try to tell them about a little bit of good luck for a change and suddenly they're deaf as posts. Sometimes I think I'm as much a stranger here in this town as I was the first day I set foot in it. Sometimes I think it should've been me and not old Bourne that dropped dead. I would've had the good sense not to come back."

"A complete mystery, that Mr. Bourne," Papa Magnani said, to Mr. Kamaljit Manku in the men's change room of the recreation centre. Eyes ready to pop, hands wringing one another under his dimpled chin. "A complete mystery, Mr. Manku! The strangest thing!"

"An amazing thing," said Mr. Manku, paying no real attention at all to Papa Magnani. He stood barefoot on the concrete floor in a brand new pair of swimming trunks—the first time in his long life he had been exposed like this in public—and looked down over his huge brown belly. His heart pounded, but not with excitement over that old man's amazing recovery—he'd heard of such things before now. The truly exciting thing was that he was about to embark on an adventure himself. He'd walked out of his house that was overflowing with the noise of his sons and his daughters-in-law and his grandchildren and a basement full of his wife's nephew's family just arrived from India—had walked out with a purpose in mind so important and so exciting that he could hardly breathe. He intended—oh, his heart flopped around like a fish in his fat chest—he intended to be the first person in all that noisy crowd to do something courageous in this country—something that meant something. "There is more to becoming a citizen than signing those government papers," he'd tried to explain to the others. But, "Try not to be too much the fool," Harbans had said to him (in Punjabi of course—he had never encouraged his wife to learn English, no need for it when she rarely stepped outside the house), and even Joginder his son had interrupted his reading of Guru Granth Sahib to come out of his room of worship and ask what kind of madness was going on. Still waving his angel-hair wand, too, so dumbfounded by Mr. Manku's announcement that he was breaking a hundred traditions all at once.

"Get back to your book," Mr. Manku said (in English, in order to protect his wife from the shock of hearing such disrespect from his mouth) before he stepped outside and shut the door on them all.

Of course he had not told even his wife of the particular

way he intended to go about completing his citizenship. Something not only courageous but embarrassing as well—he would do the one thing he had never succeeded in doing in his childhood village or in all the long years since. A small thing but so important: he would overcome his fear of water, he would learn to swallow his terror and put his face down in the pool and to swim like all those other laughing people he'd watched through the wire fence around the swimming pool for several nights before he'd made up his mind.

He wished now that he had not been so rude to Joginder. As the only practising Sikh in the family, his son should not be mocked at a time like this. Rather, his holy devotions could have been a source of some strength now that he faced this moment of no return.

And there it waited for him, outside the open door: the dancing blue water of the pool, spotted all over with the falling raindrops. Little splashes. The great floodlights that shone down on it from above made it seem to him like a stage in a theatre, a magic place; the trees all around were dark and shadowy, hardly visible; even the bleachers just outside the fence (where those noisy Chamber-Potts children were playing like a lot of wild animals) seemed like the rows of seats in a theatre. An audience. Mr. Manku took a deep breath, he felt like a great actor about to go out on that stage and take part in an important play, perhaps the biggest drama of his life when he considered how frightened he'd always been of water, how shocked his family would be if they knew he was here, how unusual it was to be exposing his fat brown body in front of these pale North Americans.

"Yes, yes, a marvellous thing," he said to Papa Magnani. And pulled a white rubber swim hat over his head, to protect his ears, and snapped it under his chin. A place didn't become your home, he believed, until you'd claimed it—by committing at least one act of tremendous courage.

"And how much information has anyone got out of that beautiful girl when she walks in to town for her groceries?" Papa Magnani said, to Mr. Manku's back. "Hardly anything. Too much mystery, there's too much mystery here I think. Ah, the way the world, Mr. Manku, can serve you up such mysteries!"

Mysteries made some people uneasy. This whole business of the old man who came back to life upset Jeremy Fell badly;

he hadn't slept a wink since he'd heard about the amazing recovery, just lay on his back the whole night beside his wife's hot heaving body and watched the shadows on the ceiling while his red eyes burned and his body seemed to be stretched out from his neck like a pulled rubber band down the length of the bed. Not a very nice way to spend the night, especially since his body suffered enough already in the daytime just from standing so long on that cement floor of The Threads Shed and from tensing himself to hear every word that was said by every person in this town. And then he realized that what he had begun to do with his long sleepless nights was talk in his mind to an image he had of old Bourne dressed up like a judge—enough to make his blood run cold— that old scarred face looking down at him nodding, nodding, like all the real judges he'd ever had to address in his life, just nodding and listening and looking at him as if to say *Yes, hmm, and then what?*

This town never changed, Your Honour, it was exactly the same as the day he arrived, only soggier, but forgive him if he took no small pleasure in knowing that his work here would eventually change it to something completely different, a future so rosy he had to force himself not to think of it very often in case he forgot and told someone, which was forbidden. Not even good old Cynthia, here at his side, Your Honour, and snoring like a hibernating bear, not even she knew a thing about the details, only that there was *something* up, because as Mr. Frederick Herbert told him in that panelled office with the view of the Golden Gate Bridge, if Cyn knew what was up she'd never be able to keep it to herself, and then what use would Jeremy Fell be to anyone, up here in Port Annie, they'd be better off to send a bachelor who didn't have to worry about a yappy wife. There was too much money tied up in the affair to risk losing everything. This place was just going to waste now, Your Honour, and Jeremy Fell was the man who would make it possible for these other people to put it to good use, make a fortune out of this countryside, put this town on the map and money in the pockets of all his neighbours, not to mention himself.

For all people knew he was just the simple balding manager of a clothing store, Your Honour, nothing more. He'd come into this town with orders to get to know everyone, top to bottom, and that was exactly what he did and did fast; but getting to know everyone hadn't meant what he'd expected it to mean, it only meant that he knew everyone's business and everyone's weaknesses and everyone's goals and was still as much an outsider as ever. He knew, for instance, that George Beeton, the mechanic who ran the service station, had run a larger station on the mainland once, until a tire he'd put on a car fell off, causing a fatal accident, and he was sued by the survivors for thousands. He knew, too, that George had a dream to break out of here, to disappear even farther north, without his wife—a dream he'd shared with no one at all in Port Annie except Jeremy Fell, once, when the two of them were drunk together last Christmas Eve at the Kick-and-Kill. One intimacy, one shared secret, but did it lead to anything else, Your Honour? No, not at all, because George Beeton still only nodded coldly when he saw Jeremy Fell, still only said the surface things that people say who wish they didn't have to say anything at all, a dry expressionless face, eyes turned away to study fingernails being cleaned.

There was Cyn, of course, but poor Cyn hardly counted for anything—a dry hot discontented woman, who offered him only one part of herself, grudgingly, once a week like Sunday chicken (only quicker, and with less attention), but clung to him anyway like a barnacle as if she wanted to be always there in case someone else offered him more. Fat but dry, no juices flowed in her at all, she might have been made from cut cedar —strong grain and pleasant smell, but sapless. A smile would crack her open like kindling. A youngish woman still, her soul was already withered, an old hag, a big mistake, an error of the first order, a nothing. Her breathing smelled dusty, Your Honour; even in this rainforest dampness he sometimes could swear he saw clouds of fine powdery granules float out into the air from her nose, her open mouth. He should have left her where he found her, no question, in that ridiculous museum of her grandmother's down in Victoria—a tourist trap full of old dirty relics and gritty air, the cast-off junk of forgotten thieves and forgers and two-bit murderers, faded photographs of plagues and wars, rusty instruments of destruction. The Museum of Evil. But she'd grafted herself onto him, sucked what little life she enjoyed from his veins, saw nothing he didn't point her towards, registered no response that didn't pass through his head first. A wife, Your Honour, but he'd seen how other people's wives treated them—he'd seen married people, even friends in crowds of strangers, let just their glance brush across the glance of one another and say a million things that no one in his forty-five years had ever said to Jeremy Fell: You're still here then, that's good; I know what you're thinking; this reminds me of the time you and I did such and such; yes, I still feel what you're feeling; yes, I still love you; yes.

That would be a nice thing to have, Your Honour, in a place like this. After a whole day's drive up the Island—on dusty logging road as rough as a dry creek bed (two tire blowouts and a broken windshield) through mountains and valleys, and then on new grey pavement roller-coasting fifty more miles through mountains logged bald and ugly, a desolate ruined place—after that whole day's terrible drive, with car loaded down with all the belongings they could tie onto it, he stopped at the bottom of it all, on the road that ran along the inlet past the hotel and the shopping square, and looked up at the tiers of wet houses. Here is where he would do something important, here is where he would have some purpose for the first time, and be an important part in changing all that he could see, bringing a new life to these people, prosperity and progress, a great future. What irony, Your Honour, that he should come here to bring a new life, and look what he'd found for himself.

All night long he talked to the nodding face of that old man Bourne, someone he'd never said more than hello to in real life, though he'd seen him often enough come puffing up into the square on his way to the radio station in the basement of the hotel. Now he'd become an obsession, a face hanging over his bed the whole night long; and to top it off, what was it that he had to listen to all the day, in his shop and out in the square and especially in the coffee shop? Talk of the same man, people saying they could hardly hold themselves back from going down to that cabin at Squatters' Flats and knocking on the door and demanding to see the miracle man, the Lazarus man. It wasn't good enough for them that a policeman had gone down, and a doctor, to prove he was really there and being cared for; they wanted to see for themselves.

And not only that, some people were beginning to get a little bit curious about the old man's past. Who was he, anyway? Where did he come from? What kind of secrets had he been keeping from them down in his shack? Seventy years or more

were a mystery; someone ought to get busy and find out what
Bourne had been up to before he came here to Port Annie.

But the only thing that anyone in the Kick-and-Kill could
remember the old man saying about himself was that he had
no past at all, no past or future, no age, no mother, no father
—nameless and homeless and ageless as that shaggy old man
on Tolstoy's ferry. He was Melchizedek if you please. Which
helped a lot, thank you, George Beeton said, because he didn't
understand a single word of the explanation. Maybe the old
man had been even crazier than they used to think. Because
who the blazes cared about Tolstoy? And as for that other
name, that mouthful of unpronounceable nonsense, it was
probably just something he'd dreamed up in that filthy shack
he lived in, in the days before that Peruvian seabird had moved
in to do her thing. No father, no mother, what was he then,
a stone or a cabbage?

A stone or a cabbage maybe, but something about the whole
affair was beginning to sound familiar to Larry Bowman, maybe something he'd read in a magazine somewhere, and come
to think of it so did the name of Joseph Bourne, though he'd
never thought of it before. So he rolled up his sleeves—"This
will be no easy job, gentlemen, but curiosity's a powerful
thing"—and dragged out the dozens and dozens of old magazines and newspapers his predecessor had stored in the back
room of his library with the broken-back books he intended
to fix some day, and the stacks of medieval histories and
romances Larry couldn't get enough of. Something to take his
mind off his hopeless mooning over that girl. "I'll need time,"
he said, and locked up the library for three days while he
worked his way down through one pile after another, sitting
on the floor, flipping page after page with a freshly licked
finger, reading titles and subtitles and captions under pictures
and sometimes getting waylaid by old cartoons that seemed as
funny now as they had the first time he read them, until he
found something that made the flesh on the back of his neck
crawl—a large black-and-white photo of that old face puckered and shiny from burns—and ran to his phone to dial the
mayor's office. "He's a poet!" he said. "A famous poet, of all
things."

He slammed down the phone to go back to the piles of magazines, where he thumbed pages hungrily now, greedily, finding

an article here, an article there, which he tossed aside into a
separate pile, until he'd gone through the whole stack and the
pile of set-aside magazines had grown as high as the stool he
stood on for the highest shelves. He kept the door locked for
one more day while he read, then he walked in the rain to the
coffee shop of the hotel where he drank a cup of burnt coffee
poured for him by Linda Weins and waited until word got
around that he was there and people started coming in out of
the rain to see what he had dug up for them to know about.
Even the mayor showed up, in his Spanish-explorer costume—
gold earrings and a black eye-patch included. Esteban José
Martinez was the first white man to see this inlet, but no one
had ever seen a photograph of him to know whether the
mayor's costume was authentic.

Such a shy man—many people thought that Larry Bowman
probably wouldn't be able to spit it out when he got everyone
together and saw them looking at him, expecting something.
But Bowman, who was nearly tongue-tied when it came to
making conversation with individuals in the library, where he
spent most of his time behind a wall of books, was also the
local tutor for students of the invisible and amorphous North
Island College and had no trouble at all in talking to groups,
large or small, where he could pretend he was a televised pro-
fessor or a faceless tape-recorder. Give him an audience and
he was a different person.

This Joseph Bourne was no ordinary man, he told them,
this wasn't just another of your ageing cranks. There wasn't
a person in this room who hadn't heard of him before, it had
just never occurred to anyone to link that famous name up
with the—you know—miserable cuss who lived in Squatters'
Flats. "A famous poet," he said, "mostly in other countries
where they don't seem to mind making a fuss over people like
that. He's even been introduced to royalty in some little place
in Europe, and read his stuff to crowds across the United
States. A somebody in New York, even. You might have even
heard about the time that someone years ago showed up nude
to get a prize?—well that was him." Larry Bowman watched
the faces of his listeners; it was clear that no one believed a
word he'd said. "He wasn't always so old, you know, there was
a time the women used to come in truckloads just to meet him,
like some kind of rock star nowadays. He always had an eye
for a beautiful woman and you never knew who it was going

to be until after he'd done his show, they were crazy about him—especially all those university girls, they turned up their noses at movie stars but thought it was all right to swoon over an eccentric poet. The papers sent their photographers when he arrived in town because he could always be counted on to say something that would offend the city fathers and never balked at having his picture taken with his arms around half a dozen girls. More photographed even than Jacob Weins, if that was possible. Everyone laughed and looked at the mayor, who shrugged, pulled out his black eye-patch, and let it snap back into place.

This Bourne, Larry Bowman continued, was one of those sort of—you know—legends, one of those writers that people who'd never be caught dead reading his books know all about. Travels in exotic places, public fights, gorgeous women, conspicuous prizes, once even a speech that offended the President of the United States—he was public property before he disappeared.

"Disappeared?"

"He was an amazing success, flying all over the world to countries where people treated him like I told you. It looked as if he had nothing ahead of him but an old age full of money and attention and international respect. In other words, he had it made. But then one morning after an appearance in . . . in Montana it must've been, he flew up into the Rocky Mountains in his lemon-yellow twin-engine plane and disappeared off the face of the earth. Three weeks of searching by a rescue squad in helicopters turned up nothing. Not a trace. As far as the magazines are concerned after that, he was dead. They even had memorial services for him in the East. Records of his voice sold like crazy. New York made a fuss. People even bought posters to hang on their walls."

Ian McCarthy whistled. "I wonder where he ditched that plane."

Larry spread his armload of magazines out on the table. A good teacher used visual aids when he could. "Now listen to this. The story of his life. These magazine writers have to doctor things up a bit to make them interesting, but still this is going to be pretty impressive stuff. It makes me think of that Joseph Somebody-else in the Bible—remember that fellow?— who never gave up no matter what happened."

He opened a magazine. Pictures would help tell the story.

But don't expect baby photos, ladies, gentlemen—there just
weren't any. Not a single bearskin rug or first-day-of-school
picture, or snapshot of Momma and Papa under the apple
tree. This man just may not have had any childhood at all
as far as these magazines were concerned. Maybe he'd been
alive for ever. Maybe he was immortal. Here was the earliest
picture, a young man standing on a dock, in front of a windjammer. Look at the teeth in that smile. Skin sunburned. He
was almost what you might call handsome, it was easy to see
how those women used to go for him back then in the old
days. Look at those huge hands. That wasn't a sailor suit of
any kind in the photo, so if he was going to get on that ship,
it wasn't as a member of the crew.

He did get on it, though, and look at this. A whole page of
coloured photos. Palm trees. Sandy beaches. Brown bodies.
A hillside of white houses curved around a bay. This was
Jamaica. That windjammer caught fire three times with him
on it, all the magazines agreed on this, and finally burned to
the water line right out in the middle of the Gulf of Mexico
while he and some of the crew floated around in lifeboats with
their eyes peeled for sharks. One of the others died and he
ended up in Jamaica, nearly dead himself. But immediately
fell in love with a beautiful dark-skinned woman whose mysterious religion enabled her to exorcise his nightmares in no
time flat, cure his swollen pus-filled eyes in a matter of days,
mend his broken leg in a week, and waltz him down the aisle
to marry her in a little church that overlooked the sunken
Port Royal whose history became the subject of an epic poem
he was to write off and on all the rest of his life. He hadn't
finished it all that lifetime later when he disappeared. Maybe
he'd been even working on it here.

There were no photos, anywhere, of the wife. If the magazines were to be believed, she was even more stunning and
enchanting than a certain recent arrival in Port Annie, if such
a thing was possible.

Venezuela this time. A blurry black-and-white snapshot of
the youthful Bourne standing in ankle-deep water with his
pants rolled up to his knees. Not even that Jamaican beauty
could hold him for long. He was restless, and very young. He
headed south to Venezuela, then farther south along the coast
to Brazil, where a band of thieves fished him up off the beach,
roughed him up a bit, and marched him in their Carnival

Parade through the streets of a hot and noisy city. Then they beat him, tortured him, raped him, spat in his face, broke half his bones, and left him to die in an alley beside the heaps of garbage. There were no photographs of Bourne in this state, of course, but Larry Bowman was able to produce large dazzling photos of the town itself, with crowds of costumed people in the streets, and a close-up shaded picture of a rat-infested alley that could very easily have been the one where he was thrown. He didn't stay there long, though, because within the day his wife arrived on the scene and brought him back to life with her mumbo-jumbo or her prayers or whatever. Already she could see some purpose in his life, she told him. Because every disaster and setback was only another opportunity to prove the guidance of good, not to mention the ultimate triumph of perfection. "And a whole lot of stuff like that, which was no doubt a bunch of nonsense," Larry Bowman said, "but anyway got him back on his feet."

Then he disappeared. No photos for this. Several years unrecorded. He and that wife sailed to Europe and seemed to be swallowed up—none of the magazines had much to offer on this, only that it was during these years he began writing that long sequence of books he would start to publish much later. Travel and research maybe, or simple seclusion—he would never talk about this period to those reporters who hounded him later on in his life. "The next time he surfaced it was back here, believe it or not, on this same island he was born on. And started working for a while somewhere down-island in the camps where no one paid him any attention at all until one day a house exploded with Bourne in it." Two photos of the house. Before and after. A big farmhouse needing paint. A black-singed windowless shell. That explosion sprayed window glass all over three fields of grazing cattle and threw a door right across the road and left his face a shiny puckered mess of scars. But even at that he wasn't halted. First there was his wife again, of course, appearing out of nowhere, to whisper her advice in his ear about the ultimate triumph of good and all that kind of thing, and to heal his wounds before he was off again, this time to the East, where he surfaced again in government circles. Naturally, from now on there would be more photos than enough.

Bourne working miracles among the poor. Bourne making a speech to a roomful of cabinet members. Bourne at a huge

mahogany desk. Bourne addressing a whole village of Indians
who had marched hundreds of miles through the snows of
winter to see this man who was supposed to save people from
starvation and poverty by whatever magic he had. A man who
could be everywhere at once and heal the world. Bourne holding his first book. Bourne signing copies. Bourne reading from
behind a lectern. Bourne beside his own plane. Pages and
pages of photos. Bourne in Japan, in Australia, in Chile, in
Alaska. Here was Bourne in the garden of his wife's house in
Jamaica, overlooking Port Royal where it is said you can hear
the bells of the sunken city when a wind stirs the water of the
bay. His last visit to her. Again, she was not pictured.

Author. Healer. Statesman. A man whose name became
synonymous with *care* to a large part of the population, synonymous with *stardom* to another even larger part. Another
photo here, full-page black-and-white of his head and shoulders, on the occasion of receiving an international prize. The
last one taken, apparently, just before he disappeared.

When he disappeared into the Rocky Mountains so suddenly, like that, the newspapers made a fuss for weeks—everybody was out looking, everybody was guessing what might
have happened, even the psychiatrists were writing articles on
how success can lead some people to suicide. It took a long
time for people to forget him, apparently, and even Bowman's
most recent magazines mentioned him once in a while, wondering where he'd ended up. "But no one ever seemed to guess
he'd found himself in Port Annie, living like a pig in that
shack, hanging around with Squatters and getting older and
crankier every minute."

A strange story, the librarian apologized for telling them so
much of it, though he'd left out acres of details that no one
would be interested in. But it did explain why the man might
be easier to bring back to life than another person might be;
he was used to it, it was always happening to him.

The others fingered the librarian's notes, peered at his scribble, stared out at the rain bouncing off the pavement in the
square, wondered if the poor timid man was so starved for
attention that he'd made it all up. Pictures or no pictures. "It's
what happens when a wallflower like Bowman stays too long
in the library, reading books," said Rita Rentalla.

The librarian began to protest, his feelings were hurt. All
that research and so little gratitude. But the words stuck in

his throat—his mouth went dry—the girl from the Peruvian freighter was standing just inside the doorway, watching him, with her head tilted back just a little as if she were measuring him for something. His throat closed, he nearly choked, cold sweat sprang out across his upper lip. How long had she been there watching? How much had she heard? Why was she smiling like that just at him?

When the others turned to look at her, she moved forward, walked forward as if each step were a carefully planned move, without taking the cool challenging gaze of her eyes off him, then stopped and put one hand on Larry Bowman's shoulder. All that research and so little gratitude, she said—gently, to everyone, yet looking only at him. He felt his face redden, his shoulder burn under her touch; he didn't know where to look. If they didn't believe the librarian's story, she said, they could probably stop in at the library to go through the magazines for themselves.

Larry did not hear what else the seabird had to say, he was too busy trying to keep his breathing calm and regular, he was too aware of that beautiful hand so close to his face, he was too conscious of those incredible legs, those fantastic ankles, that mysterious scent of some invisible exotic flower that made him light-headed, dizzy. What if he fainted right here in front of everyone! He'd be a town joke for ever, like a pubescent boy being touched by his very first girl.

He was no more confused by this episode, however, than Angela Turner was. That ambiguous young woman had listened to the whole story like a small child listening to a fairy tale, ready to believe every word, enchanted by the sound of Larry Bowman's voice, thanking her lucky stars that she lived in this town where such a thing could take place. And the sudden arrival of that seabird—just a beautiful sexpot up until now— had knocked her breath out. The woman was no sexpot at all, more like a visitor from some better place. When Angela left the coffee shop to go back to her grocery till, she was ready to burst into tears, her head was spinning with Larry's story, completely scrambled when it came to deciding what to do next.

Whatever had happened to her decision to get up the gumption and get out of this town? On the one hand she wanted to say good riddance as fast as she could, give everyone here a big raspberry, and head out of this rain for a city with some excitement, night life and plenty of opportunities for a career; yet how many places could you live where a Peruvian sailor could land in your bed out of the sea, where dead men could come back to life and grouchy old cranks turn into famous celebrities, where the grass and sidewalks were studded with beautiful shells and glittering stones from the ocean even after a hundred people had spent hours trying to get rid of them— as if they multiplied by themselves, or as if someone was scattering them around in the night while no one was looking? Now she was curious to see what could possibly happen next.

When the news was passed along to Mrs. Barnstone that Bourne was a famous poet, she refused to believe it. "Impossible," she said. "The man's so ugly!" And besides, how could he be famous when she—who was a member of the Port Annie Creative Writing Club—had never heard of him? This place was isolated, heaven knew, but it wasn't completely out of touch with the rest of the world. "Honestly," she said, "I could spit."

And she wasn't at all surprised to hear that no one else in the club had heard of him either. Because of course she called all four ladies to her home immediately to find out, and Corina Matthews collapsed in a fit of laughter. "Incredible," she exclaimed, "and I wouldn't even have guessed the man could put a decent sentence down on paper." Though it was poetry, after all, that he wrote, reminded Opal Dexter, and as they already knew, modern poetry needn't be anything more than a collection of obscenities to win you fame. And Honorelle Skinner insisted the whole thing was only a joke. "My cousin in Vancouver reads *everything* that's worth while," she said, "and he's never even mentioned this creature's name!"

By the time a delicious pineapple square had been devoured and several cups of coffee drunk the initial disbelief had mellowed into sober depression. As Opal Dexter put it, "It doesn't matter whether you've got a speck of talent when it comes to getting published, he's proof of that; the only thing that matters is that you be outlandish enough." And Mrs. Barnstone, sensing that her world was sinking rapidly, suggested someone call the librarian, find out if a copy of anything by this man could be found in town. "I suppose if he really has had poems published we owe it to ourselves to read them. If we can get borrowed copies, of course. No need to buy our own."

When he answered her phone call, Larry Bowman, who had

not yet recovered from yesterday's episode at the coffee shop, had given up his attempts to fight down the images of the Peruvian seabird which plagued him, and was back to studying the liquor ads in magazines in order to find the hidden figures in the ice cubes. Sometimes it took hours to find them, but once they'd revealed themselves he was amazed at how obvious they'd suddenly become, and a little shocked at the lengths the manufacturers would go in order to sell their booze. In the end it didn't help at all because those figures in the ice, when they appeared, only called up new images of that beautiful girl, rubbing in the hopelessness of his situation.

The sound of Mrs. Barnstone's fake-English voice, however —a regular library user, but someone who had a way of making him feel guilty—jolted him out of his concentration. No, he said, he had no books on the shelves by Joseph Bourne, he would have noticed the coincidence long ago if he had, and yes he would phone down-island to the headquarters of the library to see if anything was available there. No there wasn't, he told her when he called her back. The woman in the office said she'd bought one once, a single copy of his very first book, but some dishonest sneak had immediately stolen it off the shelf, probably a relative, and she'd decided then and there that Bourne was a waste of the taxpayers' money. Mrs. Barnstone could buy herself a copy if she wanted, he would give her an address. But no, she said, that would be going a little too far, and anyway she thought he ought to do what he was paid to do and find a copy they all could use. That's what libraries were invented for.

"He'll try," she told the club. "But listen, ladies, I had a marvellous thought while I was talking on the phone. What a story it would make, to write about, that old goat come back to life like that and turning out to be a famous man. I can feel my fingers itching to do something with it." Well it would be all right to write up as an *incident*, Honorelle Skinner said, but you'd never want to tackle it as a *story*, because of course the narrative was dead, a useless dated form of literature as everyone knew. And besides, said Opal Dexter, no one would ever believe it, you couldn't expect a reader in this day and age to believe an old man like Bourne could actually revive, be better than new, as if nature had reversed itself. Even if it *had* happened in real life.

The hardest part, Gloria Anderson said, would be knowing

how to end it. She was the member of the club who'd had a story published once and, "Goodness knows the problems you run up against! If you leave things hanging in the air the real story-lovers will think you've cheated them, but if you tie things up and finish it off the intellectuals will think you've gone and monkeyed with reality." No sense starting something you couldn't finish was her motto now, and that was why she devoted her creative talents to criticizing the other ladies' efforts, rather than writing things of her own.

Corina Matthews snorted, she'd thought of something: "There'd be no problem ending *this* one if you want to try it, because of course the man will have to die *some* day."

"We can only hope so," said Mrs. Barnstone. "Because goodness knows he's certainly old enough. Honestly, I could spit."

II

IN THE CONVERSATION that took place that night at the Kick-and-Kill, Bourne and his amazing past had to take a back seat for a while. Famous or not, he wasn't the centre of the world as far as the regular customers were concerned—not at the corner table reserved every night of the week for George Beeton and Christie and Bald-headed Pete. Usually they hashed over the day's work at the Mill, and reported the seabird's latest movements about town, and argued about the terrible performance of Port Annie's baseball team in the North Island League, but tonight the topic was Fat Annie Fartenburg. Bald-headed Pete was fairly new in town and could hardly believe there was a woman upstairs who'd been there for twenty years. Who was the old bag anyway, he wanted to know, and why did he have to look at that giant statue carved with a chain saw out of a cedar stump every time he came into this place?

George Beeton, examining his black-rimmed fingernails, suggested that Christie fill the poor bugger in. How could you live in this place and not know?

Christie figured you had to start somewhere, eh, so he swallowed a long drink and told Pete what he'd heard himself, from his grandparents, members of the band of natives whose longhouses and sweat baths had once stood by the edge of the inlet, less than a mile away from here. This was not so far back as that Esteban José Martinez, who sailed past the mouth of the inlet and named it El Golfo de Nuestra Señora del Fin del Mundo. And not even so far back as old Vancouver, eh, who renamed the inlet Esteban's Gut in honour of the Spaniard. But it was far enough back that these people of the inlet, who'd seen these foreign sailors snooping around in their big ships and knew the sea never got tired of dishing up surprises, were still simple enough to be scared shitless when the ocean swelled up during a huge earthquake and suddenly belched up a gigantic blue whale, which shot up the inlet and found itself beached a hundred yards up the shore. Tons of blubber, eh, bigger by far than any of those nosy ships had been; obviously some god had decided to give them ten years' worth of food and candle-oil and bones for their tools all at once, a windfall they could hardly believe. But—and this was the hard part to swallow, boys—the whale cried like a human, threw its weight around, breaking off trees, slapped its enormous tail on the ground to cause tremors that rivalled the original quake. Everyone ran away. Or that's what they said.

And said, too, that when they came back the next day there was no whale in sight, just this female human sitting on the beach, a great fat lady with pale blue skin, miraculously tiny ears, and a mouth that could swallow you whole. She scratched in her armpits and yawned, she looked over her audience as if trying to decide which she would gobble up first, then let out a laugh which sent everyone running for the trees. Only one man was brave enough to come back and watch from behind a log while the fat woman gathered herself a lot of dry twigs from under the trees, tied them together with vines and seaweed, and played with the little doll man until it responded to her caresses and started to breathe.

"That's what those old guys were like, eh?" Christie said. "Expect you to believe anything. Dieter Fartenburg and Fat Annie, a whale and a pile of sticks, that's nothing compared to some of the stories they told me. But not even that bravest of braves stayed around to see what the whale-lady would do. The whole tribe took off. The rest of the story is history, everyone knows it."

Christie saw someone come down the steps into the foyer and walk in through the door to the Kick-and-Kill, but it wasn't Fat Annie. It was redheaded Rita Rentalla, rummaging through her purse, churning things up with her hand. "How's things, Christie?" she paused to ask by their table, cocking her hip in that skin-tight dress and laying her perfect vermilion fingernails against her throat. Then she moved on past and Christie watched her legs as she sashayed her way amongst the tables, looking for someone. A beautiful woman, eh, but she tended to move right in on you and stay put if you gave her too much encouragement.

"Maybe the rest is history to you guys," Pete said, "but I never heard it."

Still watching Rita Rentalla's legs, Christie lifted his glass and drank all that was left of the beer, then pulled across a full one from the supply in the centre of the table. A story of two lovebirds, eh, a couple of ridiculous sweethearts. Fat Annie and her little Fartenburg looked at all those mountains covered with trees, as far as their eyes could see, and decided to stay right where they were, start up a logging camp, and make a killing. It seemed that the fat lady, once she'd achieved her incredible translation from whale, had also discovered a memory of her own which included a history of careers, a business education, and a terrific understanding of human weaknesses. She was able to teach her little man everything he needed to know. She had an uncle, she said—for her grafted-on memory also included a whole lot of relatives, as well as numerous friends all over the world, including some in positions of unimaginable power—she had an uncle who'd started out with a single stick of firewood, which he stole from his parents' woodbox as a boy, and through a long series of business transactions conducted with only a hint of the required blackmail and an absolute minimum of the necessary acceptable fraud had built himself up a multinational network of woodfibre companies by the time he was seventeen. A clever kid, but not the cleverest. There was also a cousin, on her mother's side, who'd sold a tiny eastern-seaboard woodlot in such a complicated dazzling jigsaw of brilliant deals that he'd ended up as the sheik of some Arab kingdom without a single penny changing hands. The woodlot, in fact, was still in the family. It was all in the genes, she said, and chopped her first tree to the ground with the edge of her hand.

The most amazing thing about the Fartenburg Logging Company was not the way it prospered—it didn't, despite her array of successful relatives—it was the exuberance of the love affair those two carried on, right under the noses of their startled crew. They were so crazy about each other that they got that whole float-camp rocking every night of their lives together and sent waves sloshing up and down the inlet that would've capsized any boat that got itself caught in it. Fat Annie's great jubilant whoops clapped thunder-like across the bay, kept everyone awake, the only thing the loggers found to complain about in the early years. They called Fat Annie their tub of love and secretly envied the little bundle of dried sticks who had the power to provoke such shouts of joy, such hoots of satisfaction, to kindle such an abundance of overflowing love. There wasn't a man in the camp who didn't dream every night of wallowing in that enormous tub of love, tickling those generous folds of fat, causing those sighs and moans and ecstatic whoops to escape from that gargantuan mouth. In fact, when those noises of love-making penetrated their sleep, they would sigh and turn over in the hot lather of their own bodies and fall into a deeper sleep, convinced that they themselves had been the cause of such miraculous joy.

If such uncomplicated happiness had only lasted! Then there would never have been the grisly murder. The logging camp would never have fallen into ruin. The big American company might never have got all the timber rights to this part of the Island, and built the Mill. And, who knows, the town of Port Annie might never have come into being, the Kick-and-Kill never have been built, and Christie never have had the pleasure of drinking with George and Bald-headed Pete. All on account of someone named Billy Goat Jake.

For years after they set up camp, Fat Annie didn't even know about Billy Goat Jake, she was too busy keeping everyone happy ever to notice. Then one day she looked up and saw the thin line of smoke drifting up from the little island down the inlet, and rowed out to take a look. Ho, phew pew, there he was, this old smelly whiskery man with his six nannies and one billy goat, living in a shack thrown together out of driftwood on the backside of the island; he'd been there a whole year and nobody'd noticed, come from San Francisco where he chopped a man open with an axe. Of course he didn't tell her about the murder right away. Annie got into the habit of rowing out to his little island nearly every day, she stole food out of her own cookhouse for him, to fatten him up a bit—he looked half-starved—she snuck away while everyone including her husband was hard at work and thinking she was the same in the cookhouse. Old Billy Goat Jake just opened up in the face of all that attention, out of gratitude, and told her his whole life story, murder and all. And then, suddenly, he had more to be grateful for than he'd ever hoped. A woman as big and generous as Fat Annie couldn't be expected to give it all to one man her whole life, she was too big for that, she could have accommodated a thousand men and still had enough left over for the bundle of twigs.

For three years she rowed herself out down that inlet every day, right down past the townsite, on down past the floating log booms to his little island, bringing him food and news-papers and the great warmth of her own body, while old Fartenburg was up over the mountain cutting timber. In all that time the little German never once let on if he knew some-thing fishy was going on—perhaps too stupid to guess, maybe frightened to bring it out in the open. How could he help but notice the smell she must've brought home with her every day, in her clothes and her hair and on her skin, the smell of those goats and old Billy Goat Jake?

Both of the men disappeared the same day. When Annie rowed out to the island, no Jake, just a lot of goats running around wild-eyed and confused. When the men came in for their supper, no Fartenburg: where'd he get to, they asked her, how come he disappeared halfway through the afternoon, we thought he'd come back in to camp. How do I know anything, Fat Annie said, something rotten's happened to somebody. A month later neither man had shown up, so she rowed out to the island and spent a full day slaughtering those goats. Cry-ing, wailing so loud the little trees shivered right down to their roots, she chased one after the other of those animals, cornered some, followed some right into the sea, and calling out for her man, her men, drew their heads back in the crook of her arm so that she could look into the eye-rolling terror of their faces and slice her knife across the straining throats. Up to her ankles in blood, she stalked the island until she'd killed them all—even the billy, who fought back, knocking her down into the gore with his head, kicking her hard enough to break three of her fingers, tearing her flesh open with one of his horns. Eventually she got him too—somehow climbed onto his back and rode him to death, and even then slit open his throat so his blood flowed with the others', including her own. Then she set out again, dipped her oars into the crimson water and rowed back to the camp, where she collapsed in a swoon into the arms of a dozen horrified men.

She would frighten them even more. With her fingers in bandages, her gashed-open thigh bound up in sheets, she rowed up and down the inlet every day, hallooing in every direction. Calling their names. Once she rowed all the way out to the open sea and back. Tramping up over the hills, through logged-off slopes and deep timber, hollering for her man, her men. No one could get any work done, she never fed them, no one could get to sleep at night. Finally they started to drift away, to find other places to work. When there was nobody left but herself, Fat Annie walked over land to the east coast, caught a boat south, and sold everything to the first company that showed the slightest interest in her business. Then she came back to live on the inlet the same as before, to wait for one or the other of those two men to return. In the original company town the children threw rocks when they saw her on the boardwalks; lovers surprised by her in the bush accused her of terrible things. Loggers complained she was mad—they would cut a tree down and then find her standing only inches from the swaying branches, nearly scaring them to death. It was not unusual to wake up in the morning and find her already out in the inlet, walking the booms, the logs sinking beneath her weight, and the water all stirred up sloshing back and forth from her movement as she hallooed out over the water, her echo coming back from the mountains. Once some boys caught her, worn out from her walking, weak from the tremendous weight of her grief, and tied an alder tree to her back—made her drag it uphill past the picket fences of the houses right to the top of the town, until someone's father saw what was happening and stormed out to chase them away.

It wasn't until the Mill had been built and the company had started construction of the new town of Port Annie that Dieter Fartenburg's body was found. The construction crew clearing the spot for the hotel uncovered his remains, beneath the complicated mass of roots of a giant stump so old that even when it was cut down it had nine hundred and thirty-four rings. They had no idea how he'd got there, twelve feet down under that weight, but when Fat Annie was summoned to view the body—a smashed-in skull, a skeleton, and an old tin lunch bucket—she had no trouble explaining it. The earthquake started it, she said, or an unimaginable wind. When one of those giant trees fell all by itself in the forest, sometimes its shallowest roots tipped up out of the ground with it, leaving a hole. She kicked at the stump, disturbing some wet earth that trickled down onto the black-rimmed teeth in the skull. You see them, she said, sometimes a hole as wide as a house, filled up with water, and the roots standing up above them like a colony of snakes trying to get to the sky. But what some people don't know, she added, slamming her fist into the shiny blade of the yellow cat, was that if you cut through the trunk of the fallen tree near the base the whole mass of roots would flop back into place, into its hole, as if it had never come out. Weeping great tears, Fat Annie gathered the little collection of bones—less even than the bundle of twigs she'd created him from—and squeezed them to powder in her hand. Then, while the workmen and the children and the company officials from the Mill watched in amazement, she pushed the handful of powder into her mouth and swallowed it down.

Someone handed her the flattened lunch bucket, no doubt hoping to see her do the same with it, but she only held it in her hand a moment, looking contemptuously at the person who had given it to her, and tossed it spinning off the side of the mountain, well up into the air, and down into the centre of the inlet, where it sank immediately, without sending back to the surface so much as a single bubble to show where it had come to rest.

And soon after that, Fat Annie decided to ascend.

"She waited until this hotel was built on top of her husband's grave," Christie said, and swallowed another long drink of beer. "Then she hauled all her things in here and went up those steps, eh, and nobody's seen her since except Vincent, who keeps an eye on her. That's twenty years now. She said she'd come down again some day, but not until she damn well felt like it."

Pete clamped both hands on the top of his own shiny head and took a good look at the chain-saw statue while he sucked at his lips. "Okay," he said, and lifted his eyes to the ceiling. "Okay, so I'm sitting right on top of that hole, where they found him."

"Where she swallowed him up. Right on the spot."

"And I'm sitting, okay I'm sitting right under the room where she's been sitting for twenty years. Right now, this minute, she's up there, waiting. Sitting on my head."

"Once a year we have a celebration in here, eh, on her birthday, every November. And one of the things is a contest to see who can raise enough racket to bring her down. Just a game, a bit of fun, an excuse for a blowout, but so far nobody has managed to shake her loose."

"Maybe she's dead."

Even the neighbouring tables went silent at this. Christie was so disgusted he had to turn away. "She's alive. Vincent would tell us if she wasn't. She's alive. He takes up her food every day."

Rita Rentalla arrived from across the room, "Hi boys," one hand holding her glass of beer and the other resting on her thrust-out hip. "Is it okay for me to perch here a while?"

"When she comes down those steps I sure hope I'm here to see it," George said, ignoring Rita. "I hope she picks a time when I'm here in this place."

"There's a good chance of that," Christie said. "You're in here more time than you're not, but don't worry, wherever you are you'll feel the earth trembling when it starts to happen." He for one could just see her coming down, huger than ever, with her little pig eyes buried in lard.

"Bald as a baby's arse," George said. "Bald and naked old swollen flesh flopping down them steps."

"*Not bald!*" Christie's fist rattled the glasses on the table. "Fat Annie will never go bald, not if she lives to a hundred and fifty; she had a fine head of hair. It'll be white, eh, floating out around her head like a halo; she'll come down these steps all surrounded in light, slow and smooth as if she's floating."

"Lord!" Rita Rentalla decided to sit. Some people had no manners at all.

Pete laughed. "She'll get halfway down, with the lights swaying and the walls buckling. Then she'll trip. She'll roll forward somersaulting down those steps and land flat on her back, shuddering, jellying, splaylegged, huge mountain of flesh, sending out shock waves through floor and earth to tremor the whole Island. Then she'll pee her pants all over the carpet and lie there laughing."

"Shut up, you don't know anything." Christie's face began to turn a brilliant pink. "Shut up, you don't know a goddam thing."

"A hundred years old, I know," George said.

"Maybe there never was a Fat Annie," Pete said.

"What you think don't make any difference to what *is*," Christie said. "You can't touch Fat Annie with what you think. Do you think she cares what goes on in your stupid brain?"

"They probably hauled her away in the back of a moving

van and locked her up in a loony bin," Pete said. "Don't push
me, take your paws off of me."

"Son of a bitch." On the floor Pete rolled away easily, then
sprang to his feet, wiping the blood from his lips. "Bigshot,
what the hell do you know about anything?" He tried a tough-
guy smile but it didn't work. His lip quivered.

Rita Rentalla thrust her ring-cluttered hands up into air.
"Has anyone ever seen such a bunch of stupes? Children, children, they ought to be locked up to teach them a lesson."

George yelled to a waiter, who looked as if he planned to
interfere, "Back off! This is our fight." The dirt-bikers at the
neighbouring table shrugged. "Maybe they think if they cause
enough ruckus she'll come down to see what's been going on,
some people are crazy."

Christie and Pete, locked in a grunting embrace, went slamming against the wall, bounced off the table, and fell to the
floor. Christie's fist forced itself into Pete's mouth. "I'll rip
out your tongue you—"

But Pete's fingers clawed into Christie's eyes, and Pete spat,
choked, kicked his boots up Christie's back, and rolled himself
free, then leapt kicking at Christie, brought him down again
crashing against a chair, splintering it. "You bastard," rolling
across the room, "kiss my"—and Christie, leaping up, jumped
with both feet on Pete's stomach, fell, and they rolled again,
crashing this time into a table, bringing it down, glasses and all.
"Lying son of a bitch," and Vincent the hotel manager stood
up on a table yelling, "Stop, stop everybody, stand back, don't
touch them, they'll pay for this," and the thrashing bodies hit
his table, too, pushed it up against the wall, and they rolled
across the top of it grunting and blam, Pete's head slammed
against the wall again and again until he dived for Christie's
legs, dragging him down to the floor again. "You two'll pay
for this damage."

As they lurched towards her Rita leapt back, spilling beer
down the front of her dress and shrieking, "You dummies!"
Rubbing at the stain, she screamed, "Gouge out his eyes,
choke the crazy fishface!" and took a kick at somebody's ankles
as they rolled by.

"Police!" Vincent yelled from behind the bar. "I'm calling
the police!" He waved the telephone receiver in a threatening
way, to show that he meant business.

A visit from the police meant the Kick-and-Kill would be declared off-limits for some—no small punishment, a disaster in fact, because where else was there to go in this town? "Watch out, watch out, watch out." George moved in to kick them apart with his boots. "Get up out of there, you two idiots, that's enough. Take it outside before he brings the cops down on us. Come on, move your asses out of here."

Christie and Pete let others help them to their feet, then leaned into one another for support as far as the door, where they broke apart, spilled out into the square, then flew at each other again. Christie pushed Pete up against a parked car and drove a fist into his stomach, once, twice, before Pete, grunting brought his knee up towards Christie's crotch, missed, and brought it up again with more success.

"And she didn't even stir!" someone screamed at them from the doorway. "You didn't bring her down. You crazy buggers, all your carrying on didn't touch her at all."

"What stupes," Rita Rentalla said. Her beautiful red fingernails pressed against her white throat. "What ignorant stupes, has anyone ever seen such ignorant stupes?"

No one answered her, because the entire population of the Kick-and-Kill—except for Vincent himself and old Belchy McFadden asleep in the corner—was pouring out through the door into the rainy night after the fighters. Outside, uninhibited by indoor manners and breakable furniture, they felt free at last to join in. Greg Wong took offence at the sight of George Beeton trying to pry Christie and Pete apart, leapt up onto George's back, and rode him forward until he collapsed to his knees on the pavement. This was not to be tolerated, as far as Linda Weins in the coffee shop was concerned. She left her Pyrex coffee pot and her single late-night customer to march outside and give Wong a piece of her mind.

By the time she put foot on pavement, however, the whole square had exploded into chaos—fist fights, wrestling matches, dog-piles, Indian wrestling (all in the spirit of good fun, of course, with more shouts than blows, more laughs than curses, more good-natured bruising than actual bloodshed). Poor Linda decided the only safe place for a girl like her was inside, behind glass. When several of the combatants ransacked their cars for sports equipment and quickly converted the square into a softball field (with the post-office door for backstop and

the roofs of the cars for bleachers to hold the screaming spec-
tators), no one paid any attention to the fight between Christie and Pete. The dirt-bikers, led by Greg Wong and assisted
by the entire graveyard shift of the Mill's digester building,
were the first up to bat, and greeted each of Eddy Deck the
bank manager's sloppy pitches with such noisy hoots of deri-
sion and howls of contempt that windows opened in the apartment building down by the dock, sliding-glass doors opened
in the Down Front houses, and people came out onto the sun-
decks of their homes up the hill. Within minutes, people all
over town were putting on their coats and hurrying through
the rain towards the source of the commotion. No hope of
getting to sleep in this racket, you might as well join them.
And there was nothing like a noisy game of softball under
the streetlights to make you forget your troubles, that lousy
Mill, anything that was nagging at you. Besides, this could go
on until morning, with unexpected twists of plot, spontaneous
singalongs, impromptu parties, plenty of booze, exciting readjustments to marriages and other living arrangements—and
who wanted to miss out on a thing like that just for the sake
of a little sleep?

"Honestly, this whole town is populated by overgrown children," Mrs. Barnstone said, hearing the ruckus from her bed
far up the hill. "Somebody down there must've started talking
about Fat Annie."

"What stupes," Rita said from the doorway of the Kick-
and-Kill, watching Pete and Christie roll weakly from second
base towards the sidewalk, still pummelling away. "What a
bunch of ignorant stupes." She turned to Vincent, who was
beginning to put things back into place. "Just listen to that
racket. Every time somebody brings up that woman's name
you can count on the whole place getting into an uproar."

"Shut the door," Vincent said. "Shut the goddam door. Let
them do what they want to each other out there but just shut
my goddam door."

III

THE WHOLE WORLD should hear about this, as far as Mayor
Weins was concerned. Good grief, it would make Port Annie
just as famous as the old man was, and no kidding either—
this town would be known on every continent as the home of
Joseph Bourne, the place of his miraculous recovery. Photos

in every important magazine—some photographers would no doubt insist on including the mayor in the pictures, after all he did represent the town, their elected leader and figurehead. Television and radio interviews in every language if the old man was all that Bowman had made him out to be. What a magnificent plum for the town, an unexpected windfall, maybe the event he'd been looking for to change the direction of all their lives!

Because it drove the mayor crazy that no one out there had ever heard of Port Annie. And it made him furious that year after year no real tourists ever came in to visit. When he opened his Hydro bill and found the little pamphlet from the Minister of Tourism listing ten suggestions that he (and everyone else in the province) ought to be putting into practice in order to be nice to out-of-province visitors, complete with a photograph of the Minister demonstrating the most effective way to smile when one of these visitors approached, he felt so left out that he trembled with rage and disappointment. Would he ever get a chance to try out that smile? Would he ever get the opportunity to put those ten directives into practice? Tourists were pouring in to other North Island towns, he knew— people who praised their beauty and charm and left plenty of money filling their tills. Tourists were pouring into every other town in the province, he was sure, but there was no reason for them to come here—in the first place because they didn't know it existed, and in the second place because the town still hadn't come up with a spectacular tourist attraction to make that long uncomfortable trip worth their while.

The first thing he saw in his mind when the librarian had strung out that tale of the old man's fame was a picture of a huge banner, spanning the road just where it started down into town from the mountain, with the enormous letters PORT ANNIE, THE HOME OF MIRACLES across it. And another, smaller sign at the top of the road to the Flats: *This way to the Bourne literary shrine, re-birth place of the famous poet.* He saw people arriving in droves—the road would be plugged with American visitors slung with cameras, Europeans talking strange languages, students in crowded Volkswagens wanting to work on their theses, university professors on bicycles making a pilgrimage, miles and miles of the naturally curious, the tourists who would follow other tourists practically anywhere and pay whatever you charge just to be made to feel that

something important was happening in their lives. Bourne
would be only a beginning. The whole town would benefit.
Stores would do a wonderful business, expand, even multiply.
The hotel wouldn't be big enough, motels would go up along
the highway, restaurants, other tourist attractions would
spring up. This place would get onto the map at last, thanks
to that old man, and of course thanks to the fertile imagination of Jacob Weins.

And about time it happened, too. He'd nearly given up.
How could a modern town hold up its head if it didn't have
at least one tourist trap to its name? Doomed to obscurity.
Everybody with any sense accepted that, there was no question about it; but had he succeeded in getting anyone in this
place to make the first move?

Lord knows, he'd tried hard enough to get people off their
backsides for a change. His imagination had come up with a
wealth of schemes, but just try to get anyone to put out any
energy in this town. How about the World's Biggest Beer-
Drinking Contest he'd suggested to Vincent in the Kick-and-
Kill. That ought to bring them in. But Vincent only shrugged,
he was too busy serving the customers he had, to contend with
an influx of thirsty contestants. Then what about Christie
Jimmy— couldn't he throw up a couple of longhouses or something in the bush and charge people to go through an authentic
Indian village? It would be doing his own people a favour at
the same time; he could wrap himself up in a blanket and tell
stories—the more far-fetched the better, tourists would love
it. Lord knows, Christie could tell some whoppers when he
wanted to. But Christie hadn't been interested, his job at the
Mill kept him busy enough, why would he want to start fooling
around with tourists? Typical Indian, the mayor decided, no
get-up-and-go, no imagination, no modern drives. He offered
to finance Ian McCarthy if only he'd throw up a fence around
ten acres of bush on the outskirts of town, slash out some
trails through it, and put up a sign calling it the Magical Forest.
He wouldn't even have to quit his job at the post office, Eva
could sell the tickets. But, "Are you kidding?" was Ian's response. "By the time he's got here the poor bugger's already
driven through one hundred and fifty miles of the real boring
thing."

The only scheme that had ever had any hope of getting off
the ground was The World's Biggest Slug Race, an interna-

tional-championship event. There was no trouble finding plenty of slugs in these rainy woods and the Mill management had been almost persuaded to sponsor it by giving enormous prizes that would bring people here from all over the globe. The mainland newspapers would have co-operated, they loved this type of thing. But someone higher up in the Mill, someone in an office in Vancouver or Seattle, had turned thumbs down on the deal. Too undignified for a company with an international reputation to protect. How would it look if their customers in Japan got wind of the thing?

So Bourne was his salvation. The salvation of the whole town. The mayor hadn't breathed a word to the outside yet, he'd kept mum just as Charlie Reynolds had suggested, because he needed a little more time to let the project develop fully in his head. If people outside got ahold of the news the whole thing would be ripped out of his hands, someone else would reap all the benefits, and before anyone knew it the old man would be frightened away to somewhere else that didn't need him. Or worse still, die again, just out of spite. It wouldn't hurt to find out what others right here in the town thought of his scheme, either. Subtly of course, and without giving too much of it away.

A wonderful plan, according to Charlie Reynolds. The mayor could count, as usual, on the full support of his paper. Juicy as this whole business was, front-page stuff, he would hold off from printing any of it until the program was fully developed. No sense spilling the beans too fast and giving the usual nay-sayers a chance to be heard. Announce the whole thing when it was practically an accomplished fact. He himself had connections and would send photos to every newspaper in the country, invite journalists in to town when the time came, whip up a rare old fuss.

"And something else you might think about," he suggested, "is having someone important come in for an official opening. The lieutenant-governor, for instance, or even an Olympic athlete."

Of course Weins's own wife was against the whole thing. The very thought of it brought on a migraine. Mabel Weins saw religious fanatics pouring in by the millions, cripples and imbeciles and who knows what-all on their knees, preachers and evangelists and—God help us—priests. Someone would open up that trailer for a church again, and their Sunday morn-

ings would be ruined by the caterwauling of hymns. She had
to swallow four pills before she could even discuss the matter.
"Leave well enough alone," she said. "It's a time bomb. Start
monkeying with metaphysics and something will blow up in
your face."

"Thank you very much," the mayor said, as coldly as possible. "That's one more opinion to add to my list."

"And what's more," she continued, "your scheme is in questionable taste."

Questionable taste? How could anyone suggest such a thing?
How could making a fuss over a wonderful act of Providence
be in questionable taste? Far from it, couldn't those softheaded
religious people see that if God hadn't wanted them to make a
million dollars out of this and put themselves on the map at
the same time, He would never have directed Joseph Bourne
to Port Annie in the first place? All the same, he decided to
check it out with Papa Magnani, who was a religious man himself. Well, not exactly religious, but he *was* Italian.

"Jesus Christ!" Papa Magnani nearly exploded when he
heard the scheme. Then, shocked at his own vehemence, he
stuttered, apologized in every direction. "I'm sorry, good gracious, I'm sorry." He dug his fingers into his hair. "I tell you
this, Mr. Mayor: if that man in his shack is all that Larry has
told us, I tell you this, that he doesn't belong to us, he belongs
to the world. If you go through with such a ridiculous scheme,
you will make all of us look like fools. And you will drive
him away. And, Mr. Mayor sir, you will force me to punch
you right in the nose—me, a coward from way back, a pacifist,
and a gentleman. Right in the nose."

Even after the mayor had left, obviously offended, Papa
Magnani's head was in danger of falling off. "Banners! Signs!
Tourists!" He stomped back through the men's changing room.
"The man is crazy!" he shouted to Mr. Manku who was just
stepping into the shallow end of the pool. "He wants to turn
Mr. Bourne into a sideshow! He wants to make our town a
laughingstock!"

But Mr. Manku, who could see that Papa Magnani was saying something to him but could not hear through the rubber
swim cap, just gave a little wave and lowered his body, with
the slow dignity of an elephant seal, to sit on the cement bottom of the pool. The water—warm in comparison with this

cold rain that fell on his shoulders—came up to the top of the round belly that stuck out just below his slack womanly breasts. Ah, it felt good. He imagined the look on Harbans' face if she should come around that corner by mistake and see him there—no chance of that, she never left the house—she'd have a heart attack and die on the spot.

But he was not going to be allowed to sit like a child in his bathtub. Just as she had done every evening now since he'd started coming here, the instructor came around the edge of the pool and crouched down in her orange slicker above him. "Now come on," she said—she talked to him as if he were a stupid child, but he didn't mind, she was very young, with pimples on her face, and her voice was barely strong enough to penetrate his rubber cap even when she shouted. "So hold my hand, okay? and walk with me, okay? it's getting deeper but don't worry, just hold my hand, okay?" Yes, yes, okay, Mr. Manku thought, but the water was up to his chin now, he would drown! He started moving back towards the shallowest end where he sat again, and put his face right down within inches of the water's surface. Oh so close!

So *don't* get excited about it, Papa Magnani said, to himself. So maybe with your great Eastern wisdom you don't care that we have an idiot for a mayor. Maybe it doesn't matter to you that I have just lost my temper for the first time in years. Ah Rosa, Rosa, the man is as deaf as a post once he gets in that pool! Splashing around like a little baby, look at him sitting there trying to get his face wet.

And a good thing, too, that he was deaf as a post, because just as Papa Magnani was turning to go back to his kitchen, his face still red from his explosion, he heard one of those Chamber-Potts kids, still horsing around on the bleachers, shout out, "Look at the water rise when that elephant sits!" They all screamed with laughter, and slapped at each other, and threw themselves around on the seats. "Everybody out of the pool, the rug-rider's fleas'll get you."

The swimming instructor, who was sitting on the edge of the pool, holding Mr. Manku's hand while he bent his face down towards the surface of the water, looked up alarmed, and shouted. "Will you kids keep it down out there!"

"Keep it down! Keep it down!" The Chamber-Pottses went into fits trying to keep it down. They threw themselves down on the wet ground, fought against their own arms, "It's coming up, it's coming up, oh now it's down, now I'm keeping it down!", making more noise than before.

"Shut up!" Papa Magnani yelled, and stomped his feet on the concrete. "You kids there you just shut up, y⁓u hear me! Just shut up."

They stared for a moment, mouths open, then started to giggle.

"Come on," the instructor said to Mr. Manku. "I know another way to try this." She led him over to the edge of the pool, with his back to those kids, and got him to stand in the water holding on to the edge. "Now see if we can get your feet to float out behind you, then you'll learn to trust the water, and getting your face wet won't seem like anything at all."

The Chamber-Potts children soon got bored with themselves and went next door to throw rocks at the boat that floated in the tree, but Papa Magnani by this time was disgusted with the entire world. Weins . . . Chamber-Potts kids . . . they were equally obscene.

Italians were too emotional to think straight, the mayor had decided. No use listening to Papa Magnani. Jeremy Fell, on the other hand, could be trusted. A sensible man. He thought the mayor was onto a wonderful thing. A refreshing change to see someone in this place with business sense and a concern for the future. "You can count on my help," he promised. He would even consider changing the name of his store. Instead of The Threads Shed, how about Miracle Wear? Or The Poet's Wardrobe? He would devote one corner of the shop to whatever clothes bookish people liked to wear, to attract those students when they came in. And T-shirt souvenirs, with a picture of Bourne on the front. Or a photo of that shack—patched up a little to make it look properly romantic. The name of Port Annie, of course, would be clearly printed across the stomach in brilliant green, the perfect colour to remind visitors of their stay in these mountains.

"Congratulations!" He even shook the mayor's hand, making the fat man beam from ear to ear. "It's good to know a fellow businessman, someone who can smell an opportunity without having to have it rubbed in his face. There's hope for this town after all, Mr. Mayor, with a man like you at the helm!"

"I'm grateful to hear it, and no beating around the bush either," the mayor said. "Because to tell you the truth I was beginning to feel a little let down by the place. Nobody cares about progress."

Fell was elated. Maybe there was hope for himself yet. That pompous fool could turn into a valuable acquaintance. It was about time that something around here began to change, maybe he could even begin to shake off those long monologues addressed to Bourne that left him shaken and white, sleepless and full of dread.

Because now it wasn't only at night while he lay sleepless in bed that he found himself talking to old man Bourne dressed up like a judge, but in the daytime as well, whenever The Threads Shed was deserted.

Draped over the rack of dress slacks, staring off into space and hearing nothing at all but the sound of the steady maddening rain on the roof and on the pavement outside his door, he had to tell these things to *somebody*, because his whole reason for being here had depended on complete secrecy from the very beginning. As far as anyone else was concerned he was here to open a small clothing store, nothing else—work clothes and boots, gloves, jeans and underwear and handkerchiefs, rubber rainclothes, a few dozen pairs of socks, a rack of ties, three felt hats and six peaked caps, gum boots. The Threads Shed he called it, to bring in the younger people, but they were after styles he couldn't keep up with even as well as the Sears catalogue. It was the Mill workers who kept him going, people who had always bought all their work clothes and outdoor clothes once a year on a trip "out" and found it easier (and cheaper) just to send their wives into his store with an order and a list of measurements. No one ever came in to see how things looked, they came in to see if his prices compared with catalogue prices, if he carried the brands their husbands were used to, if he had the right size in stock. The young single men who made up half the work force of the Mill stayed in town only long enough to wear out the one pair of work clothes they'd brought with them. They hardly crossed his threshold, and those wives when they did come in were not there for making friendships—they hardly saw him, a balding middle-aged man with burning eyes.

This distance they kept didn't make his job easy—he was supposed to produce a file on every one of them that mattered, and most of the files were empty for the first two years. He hadn't been blessed with the gift of long-distance hearing,

Your Honour, or X-ray vision either, for that matter. These people in the south just had to sit tight and wait for his reports; he ignored their impatient notes and phone calls and did all he could to get close to people, find out what made them tick, discover where the money was, where the ambition was, where the greed was, where the weaknesses were. Five years he'd been at it now: he had a whole room full of files, each filled with carbon copies of the reports he'd taken down-island four times a year (did he think he'd use Her Majesty's Mail, Your Honour, in a place like this where the post office was nearly the emotional centre of town, after the Kick-and-Kill?) when he'd gone out to replenish his stock from the warehouses in Victoria and Vancouver. He knew everyone's business—it was all there in that room, typed up—but it wasn't as if he was going to use it against anyone, or to harm them; no, it was so that he could play his part in bringing them progress and development.

He knew secrets that people told only their closest friends, he knew secrets people told no one at all, he even knew things about people in this town that they hadn't got around to telling themselves yet, and there wasn't a one of them who knew a thing about him—not one person whose glance, brushing past his in a crowd, would say, Yes, I know what it's like to be you. When the bulldozers moved in (sweet music to wake up this dreary silence) it would be nice, Your Honour, if there were someone to dance with him leaping and laughing around the town square and shouting *Jeremy you did it, you'll make us all rich, you've brought a future to a place that had none at all!*

Maybe it would take a poet to understand, Your Honour. Maybe the one person who would know what it felt like to be Jeremy Fell had been there all the time, an old crank of a man named Bourne, who maybe could have been that person, if only he'd had the sense to approach him, to see past that ugly exterior. And maybe, Your Honour, that fat fool of a mayor would become just what he'd been looking for, just what he needed, because of this tourist-attraction affair. But only if he hurried up, otherwise it would be a lost cause; if that damned doctor was right, with his cardiac-this and his cardiac-that, there'd be no Jeremy Fell left here at all. Time was important; time wasn't something that went on forever.

Naturally the mayor didn't even think of asking Jenny

Chambers' opinion of his scheme, but she had one all the same. It had never entered his head to call her on the phone or knock on her door. He'd forgotten she'd once been a woman of the world, the toast of dozens of towns, a smart talented gal with a head on her shoulders, who might have been counted on to voice an intelligent thought. He didn't think to ask her, but when rumours of his scheme reached her ears she had no trouble sorting out how she felt about it. She was all for the plan. In fact, she decided, it was about time someone did something to right what she'd just decided was a terrible wrong.

Look at the way this town had treated the man who'd turned out to be a world-famous poet. Something ought to be done. Nobody knew better than she did what it was like to come into this town from the outside, have people make a fuss over you for a while, and then turn around and treat you like dirt when they got used to you. She could speak from personal experience.

She didn't have any trouble remembering what it was like the day she came here, a shapely sexy broad, believe it or not, and how they made her welcome for a while and then reversed themselves and made her feel a stranger again, the very people she'd thought were friends, by showing their true colours when they refused even to notice that she'd got herself new clothes out of the catalogue, and of course couldn't be expected to break their necks offering congratulations when her Slim was given a promotion at the Mill. She hadn't been just anybody, either, she'd been the first stripper ever to perform at the Kick-and-Kill. Jenny Flambé, there was a leftover poster somewhere in the house. A real knockout, too, she'd been a sensation. That beer parlour was packed, standing room only—every house in town had drained downhill through its doors to watch her perform, do her tricks. Of course it was illegal to have entertainment in a beer parlour then, but Vincent the hotel owner had arranged for a drunken brawl to break out on the other side of the Island so that the local cops had to be called away. By the time they got back Jenny Chambers had gone through her act five times, gathered up five pots of thrown money, been the fought-over guest at nearly every table in that huge room, and signed a contract to perform nightly for the next month (let the police just try to stop her now). She phoned her manager and told him she'd fallen into a gold mine, made him promise not to send anyone else into the place until she tired of it or got herself kicked out. It felt like the end of the world, she said, so far from anywhere, and it took a lifetime to find it, but once she'd arrived it was worth the trip, a gold mine and a dream come true. Flaming Jenny they called her. She knew how to light fires in every heart.

It was the next morning before she saw the gold mine in daylight, if the haze could be called daylight—this small town clinging to the side of a mountain, this quiet inlet, this square of tiny shops outside the hotel, this rain rain rain. She'd never heard anything so quiet, she'd never breathed air so wet. Standing in the front doorway of the hotel, watching that rain fall, she started to cry. She chewed her gum furiously until it was full of air bubbles that snapped with every bite, she fished a white handkerchief out of her purse to blow her nose.

The long skinny man who came in through the door in a Stetson and cowboy boots barely glanced at her as he went by; he got all the way to the coffee-shop entrance and came back. "Miss?" he said. He was chewing too, and for a moment they stood looking at each other. A rat's face, narrow and pointed. "Just got off graveyard shift and I'm starving. I'll buy you a cup of coffee and a fried egg if you want."

What a long stringy boob, did he think she was so easy? Still, it was better than standing there blubbering like a baby, so in she went, sat across the table from him, slap up against a window where she could see the rain. He was getting trans- ferred to the maintenance crew at the Mill, he said, no more graveyard shifts for him, and what line of work was she in?

"If you don't know, you must've been the only man in this town who didn't show up in the Kick-and-Kill last night."

He looked uneasy, glanced down at her bust, then up at her eyes. "Beer gives me gas," he said. "Bloats me up like a balloon."

"You live in this hotel?"

"Naw, I only eat here. I've got a house up at the top and eight kids. I eat breakfast out so's I'll get one decent meal in a day."

Eight kids? She couldn't imagine. "Your wife too busy chas- ing those kids to cook you a meal?"

He sipped at coffee, glanced out the window. "She's too busy chasing men is more like it. Last I heard she'd chased one as far as Toronto, changed her mind and chased another all the way to New Mexico. The baby's not even a year old yet. Regina's the oldest, going crazy trying to keep order."

He took her home. What else was there to do in this place? One look at the town and she'd known that any direction she could take for a walk led only to mountain, thick forest, or black water. And hotel rooms depressed her—eight kids ripping a house apart promised more entertainment.

And delivered. When they walked in that front door those crazy animals of kids were going wild, acting like a zoo. The oldest, red-faced and furious, stood in the middle of the living room screaming orders that no one noticed; she looked as if her eyes would pop right out of her head and zing like bullets into the wall, while two boys raced with toy aeroplanes, around and around the room, up over stools, across the chesterfield, under tables. A small baby sat in a play pen, naked, his hands and face smeared with his own crap, the wall behind him scrawled with patterns he'd traced with his greasy hands. Two girls crawled out from under the chesterfield, crying, and threw themselves at one another—biting, scratching, punching, throwing themselves this way and that until they knocked over a stepladder, and with it the boy who'd been head-standing on its top rung. When he landed—thud—on the floor, there was silence for a moment, then everything resumed. The fallen boy leapt up and threw himself on the two girls who'd brought him down.

Slim Potts cleared his throat, but only Jenny Chambers heard. Then he went back and shut the front door again. No one paid any attention. He shut the door a third time, loudly, and everything stopped. Everyone stared at Jen Chambers, glittering like a Christmas tree in her jewellery.

"This is Miss Chambers," he said, his softest voice. "She takes off her clothes for a living down at the hotel, where we've just had breakfast together. A little quiet please, and some respect."

They gave her more quiet than she could stand—two seconds of staring—and all the respect they thought she deserved —the sight of their backsides high-tailing it out of the room. Only the baby remained, slapping its greasy hands together and grinning at them. She cleaned him up quick, she'd wiped up worse messes on adults forty times his age, and laid him down on the first bed she found—that kid needed a sleep, his eyes closed the minute his back touched sheet.

When she came back into that living room, Slim had stepped

over the mess to get to some photo albums piled under a table. "Are they always like this?" she asked.

He looked at her, blankly. "Like what?" Two beats more of blank look, then they both burst out roaring with laughter. Jenny Chambers had to press her thighs together to keep from wetting her pants, something that happened every time she sneezed or lost control of herself in a good laugh.

When she straightened up at last, wiping tears, she found a photo album stuck in her face. "This here's my wife here, Gloria." A finger pointed at a snapshot but Jenny pushed it away, she hadn't come up here to look at pictures of runaway Glorias. She walked to the window and got a full view of this whole town from the top—rows and rows of roofs going downhill to water, then across the inlet that green misty wall of mountain.

"Mr. Potts," she said. "What do people *do* in this place?"

"Do?" He sounded as if the thought had never occurred to him before. "Do? They live their lives I guess, same as anywhere else. They work and eat and worry about their kids and make love with somebody if they're lucky, and sleep. Some fish. Some hunt. Others hike. Most drink."

He took her through the house to a back window so she could see his machines—lawn mowers and garden tractors and a small bulldozer and even an old schoolbus—lined up neatly against the back fence in the mud which had pushed downhill into the yard from a mountain slide. "My hobby," he said.

"I'd go crazy. I'll never last the week."

Still, she did last that week. And she didn't go crazy, unless you called it crazy of her to quit her job with one quick phone call, pack her few belongings in a suitcase, and move up that hill and into Slim Potts's house and bed. So long to Jenny Flambé. Just because he'd been so attentive all week (never stepping foot in the Kick-and-Kill), kissed her once down at the water's edge after dark, made her a gift of three ugly figures he'd carved out of wood, and asked her politely if she'd consider sharing her life with his.

"Sure," she said the third time he asked, and "Why not?", and tried not to think of those kids, who needed her more than he did (and would appreciate her less). "But if I hear you just once mention wedding or marriage you won't see my ass for the dust." A quick glance at the rain told her that what she'd just said was impossible—this place had likely never seen dust, except under beds. But he knew what she meant, promised never to mention it, and went home to warn his brood she was coming. No weddings, she promised herself. This would be a free, modern couple. She treasured her independence too much to walk into anyone's harness.

It was the town, not her, that went crazy at the end of the week when they heard the news. That pink-haired hussy of a stripper with the big headlights had moved in with quiet Slim Potts. Shacking up, too, no marriage ceremony for them, a couple of degenerates wallowing around up there at the back of town with all those kids. No wonder she was so tight-assed and proper to everyone else, she was saving it all for Slim Potts, that sly rat-faced son of a gun. Flaming Jenny and the beanpole. But it wasn't the lack of marriage certificate that excited them (Jenny found out soon enough that three-quarters of the people in town were not married to the people they happened to be living with), it was the fact that someone as exotic as a stripper had settled in their town. They broke their necks to be friendly, especially the women. She was coffeed every morning until she thought she'd float away—cripes, her stomach soured just to remember it—she was pumped for the story of her life so often she got bored with it and started making up new, more exciting material; she and Slim were invited out to so many parties and dinners that she began putting on weight and Slim called a halt (he hated going out at all, he finally admitted). One of the management wives in a Down Front house even invited her in for a bridge game one afternoon—out of curiosity, no doubt—but even with a scatter-brained partner she'd beat the pants off the whole lot of those snooty babes and they never invited her back.

The fuss died down when people began to realize she was not very different from anyone else—no exotic flower at all—and lessened when Slim made it clear he was getting tired of so much socializing and only wanted her to be part of his home with him and not stir up a fuss, and then it died to nothing at all when eventually it became clear to everyone that Jenny Chambers' presence in that house up the hill had not done one thing to civilize those eight monsters who terrorized other kids, wrecked property, and treated adults with less respect than they had for the slugs they stomped into slime on the road. Jenny became so normal that eventually she even took a part-time job in Severson's Bakery until the union went

on strike, then marched in the picket line every day for two
years without anyone paying any attention.

She'd had three good friends, all she really needed—Eva
McCarthy and Mrs. Landyke and sometimes that hypochon-
driac Mabel Weins—until she found out they weren't the
friends she'd thought they were. So that old man down in his
shack didn't need to think he was the first person ever to come
into this town looking for a new home to belong to and discover it was just the same as other places, only worse. A
famous poet, and a well-known humanitarian too, who'd been
celebrated in all the important cities of the world, proclaimed
a hero with prizes and honours—it made a girl like Jenny
Chambers feel absolutely sick to think how these people (herself included, goodness knows) had never given him any respect at all, or even paid him half the attention he must have
got from all those other towns. But he didn't need to think
for a minute that he was the only one they treated that way,
she'd had her share and she wasn't even a poet. The very least
she could do was support a scheme that would set things right
again, give him the kind of honour he deserved. It might even
make up for all the years of treating him so badly.

The mayor, of course, did not know he had Jenny Chambers' approval. No doubt he would have been delighted if he'd
been told—a travelled entertainer, no less. But at the moment
he was on his way back to his magazine shop from the post
office—wearing his Captain Vancouver costume today, complete with long black telescope—and stopped in for a short
visit with Jeremy Fell in The Threads Shed. "A whole pile of
postcards from that Crabbe fellow. Addressed to his brothers,
of course, but Ian could hardly help reading them, the script
is so large. And not only that, it's one long letter so that you
have to line one postcard up under another to get it all. The
silly fool didn't think he could save himself stamps by putting
them all in an envelope."

The chase was still on, the mayor reported to Jeremy Fell
in The Threads Shed and later to his own daughter in the
hotel coffee shop and to Angela Turner in the grocery store.
The runaway was still running and Preserved Crabbe was still
hot on the trail. He'd chased her across the Island to that village where he'd found her in the first place and made his way
to the door of the one house he recognized, where an enormous

man reached out and dragged him inside. Someone even bigger than Preserved, if you could believe it.

"Who you want?"

"Marguerite."

"Marguerite?"

"Marguerite."

"You hor hosband?"

And found himself in the middle of a gigantic party of
neighbours and friends, drinking like fish, while his Marguerite's mother—a little woman in braids—kicked his shins
every time she passed by, until it seemed that somehow the
whole village had crammed itself inside the house, scores of
hot steaming bodies, all weeping with pity for a man so weak
that he could not keep his stolen woman at home for more
than a few minutes. Eventually he passed out—though not
before he'd deposited the contents of his stomach on the floor
between his feet—and was carried through the crowd to a
back bedroom, where he was laid out on a bed and watched
by the little woman in braids for fourteen hours until he came
to. The first thing he saw when he opened his eyes was her
face, grinning.

"Lie still," the woman said. "Hor hosband, he's coming."

"What?"

"Hor hosband, he's coming to kill you. That Marguerite,
she was opstairs the whole time, all through the party. She was
listening. This morning, early, she come down the steps, to see
what was hoppen, and one look she took off again. Heading
south."

He found all the clothes he really needed, his pants, his
coat, someone's rubber boots, and rushed out through the
houseful of sleeping stinking bodies to the front door, then ran
for one of the many taxis that cruised the wet streets. "To the
ferry!' he shouted at the driver, and already felt himself plunging south beneath the surface of his world, a diver, straining
towards Marguerite and all that she meant.

"He put all that in a postcard?" people asked the mayor.

"You know the kind of maniac that Preserved is. All that
and more, believe me. Beautiful script that goes on from postcard to postcard, you ought to see them."

And all afternoon one person after another, dropping in to
the post office for his own mail, sidled up to Ian McCarthy's

wicket, where he just happened to have all the postcards laid out in order, waiting for the crippled brother to come up from Squatters' Flats to collect them. There was even more than the mayor had reported. Plunging south after his woman, Preserved had already gone through flood and fire for her (fallen off the ferry and had to be fished out of the chuck; then barely escaped with his life when the cheap hotel where he'd stayed the night burned to the ground), and despite the fact that he'd already forgotten what she looked like, was discovering just how desperately he needed to find her, the only person in the world who mattered to him any more.

"A real love story," Angela Turner sighed. "The man is obviously out of his tree over the woman." She put her hand over her own stirring belly to remind herself of what could happen when men fell out of their trees. Maybe Crabbe in his travels could find out where *this* one had gone.

"Touching," Mrs. Barnstone said, when the story was reported to her. "I hadn't realized those Squatters were capable of such devotion. Ordinarily they appear so . . . primitive?"

"Romantic savages," Opal Dexter suggested.

Though Mabel Weins, when she stopped by the post office for her turn at the cards, found the whole thing a little disgusting. "He's making a fool of himself, and for what? The worst kind of woman there is. A coy temptress, and ugly to boot, which makes it all slightly distasteful. He'd be better off staying at home and drinking himself to death. Anguish is better than what lies ahead if he catches her."

"Which he won't," Mrs. Barnstone said. "That last postcard says he heard she'd headed for Victoria. Try and find anyone in *that* maze!"

But Mabel Weins didn't like the way that Squatters' Flats seemed to be forcing itself on their attention all the time when it deserved to be totally ignored. Up to now all they'd had to put up with was wild-eyed Hill Gin with her shotgun periodically stomping through town to announce the end of the world, crazy woman. And Dirty Della with her silly smile dragging her skirts and her train of variegated children into town once a week to give away—force on you free of charge, whether you wanted them or not—all the products of her week's labour —jars of wild-berry jam, lopsided pottery, immature watercolours, braided belts, and seashell jewellery. You couldn't say no to her, but at least you could throw her stuff in the garbage and have a good wash, she was easily forgotten. But now, every time she turned around someone was reminding her of that filthy place which made her flesh crawl. She didn't even want to listen when Mrs. Barnstone told her about the debauchery that went on in Dirty Della's shack last night. Fourteen men in her house at the same time, Greg Wong and all his dirt-bikers plus friends from across the Island, kicking up such a racket that even the other Squatters threatened to call the police, something unheard of in that place.

The one person who wasn't particularly interested in the odyssey of Preserved Crabbe or the latest sins of Dirty Della or the mayor's scheme for capturing tourist dollars was Larry Bowman, the librarian, who had his nose buried in something more important—a book of Bourne's poems which had arrived in the morning's delivery. A thin book, which was a relief, he'd had visions of ploughing through a great fat intimidating Collected Works. It was called *Possessing Me*, and had a large black-and-white photograph on the back cover of a scarred face that couldn't be anyone else's but Bourne's. And not a poem in it that wasn't easy to read, a lot of simple enough words and quite ordinary punctuation, except that the notions put forth were so outlandish he had to go back and read them again and again to find out what he suspected was hidden in the words—like those figures concealed in the ice cubes of liquor ads. He suspected, too, that the disguised meanings, once he'd unmasked them, would turn out to be every bit as perverse and filthy-minded as those ads. He cancelled his tutorial appointments and locked the door of the library in order to pursue the task of unmasking without disturbances.

> We possess nothing,
> the world refuses us;
> we possess no one,
> not even ourselves.

Simple words a kid could understand, but where did he get his ideas? They all started out talking about something a person could relax about, like a walk through an alder grove, then just when you were nodding yes you knew what he was talking about, he snuck up and hit you with something bizarre that went hand in hand with what you'd just agreed to. One of the poems told the librarian, just when he was nodding in recognition over a described boat journey up a coastal inlet, that a

search for a home in this earth was pointless, life couldn't be
nailed to a spot. Another suggested that the librarian himself
(the poem spoke to him as "you") was really a windowpane!
His sole purpose on earth, according to the poem, was to let
through a light that shone from somewhere else. It was full of
words like "penetration" and "thrust", which made him suspicious. He slammed the book shut and resolved that he would
not pass it along to Mrs. Barnstone and the Creative Writing
Club of Port Annie until he'd had time to study every page, in
order to be certain it contained nothing to offend them. He
would not see another one of his college students until he
solved the puzzle of this enigmatic book.

Peering at those words and trying to detect the offences they
concealed soon gave him bloodshot eyes and headaches, however, and any references to sex or body organs he uncovered
seemed to slide away out of sight almost immediately, like a
mirage, so he decided it would be necessary to involve one
more pair of eyes in the search. "This is something for Jenny
Chambers to decide," he said aloud, because everyone knew
that Jenny Chambers had been a stripper once, when she was
younger, and being a stripper she'd know more than anyone
else in town what was sex and what wasn't sex. By nine o'clock
the next morning he'd persuaded her to come into the library
(her first visit, the only time they'd talked before had been in
Mrs. Landyke's Corner Store) and had talked her into reading
the questionable book with the blinds down while he stood by,
tapping his fingernails on his desk. "What's this?" she said,
making a face, as if she'd never seen a book before; and
"Cripes almighty, what's *this*?" when she saw the words laid
out on the pages in twisted uneven columns.

"Poetry," Larry Bowman said. "The man's a poet, remember? No Chaucer by a long shot, but famous just the same."

She screwed up her eyes and read. After a few pages she
looked up, shook her head, "Why doesn't he say what he means
straight out like you and me?", and unbuttoned her fur. She
started again at the beginning. "One thing this dry stick of a
book isn't about is sex, and that's for sure," she said, somewhere in the middle. "Sex has more fun in it than this." But
soon she was lost in the words, as if something had reached
out and grabbed her and pulled her right in, these dry pages
weren't so bad after all, and an hour later when she ought to
be up the hill making lunch for those rotten kids she came out

the other end, blinking, and closed the book carefully, as if with regret. "So what's the matter with you that you can't see what it's about? I thought librarians were educated people." She had hardly any education at all, she told him, in fact that was the first book of poems she'd ever read in her life—cripes, it wasn't bad, either, considering—but she had no trouble at all in seeing what the thing was about. Obvious, too. What every poem in that book was about was the terrible feeling of looking for a place where you belonged. "If I wasn't such a hard-bitten old crust of a broad I'd be hauling out a handkerchief right now for a good cry. That stuff hurts."

The librarian stood in the doorway and watched her walk away from him through the rain—her fur coat protected by a transparent raincoat, her pink hair protected by a plastic bread-bag—and wondered if he had the courage to read the book again. He'd tried, once, to show someone else what he'd found in those liquor ads—an old friend who'd worked at the Mill but had since moved away—and the friend hadn't been able to see a thing, even when the librarian traced the shapes of vaginas and penises out for him. "What you need is to get married," the friend had said. "A big healthy Swede, like my wife. Then you wouldn't be seeing things in those magazines." Larry Bowman, knowing that what he saw in the ads really was there, and not a figment of his imagination, wanted to scream. And the sight of Jenny Chambers' retreating figure made him feel much the same way. He went back to the book to read it again. He would become the world expert on this one book of poems by Bourne. He would be able to write a PH D thesis on it. And this time there was no doubt about it, the whole book—every word—was about copulation. Pure and simple pornography.

He would never have had the nerve to ask Angela Turner such a favour if she hadn't come into the library anyway at the time and asked him what he was reading. If the book was as dirty as he suspected, how could he put it into the hands of a single young woman like her, pretty and confident, with the look of innocence always on her face? Pure cheekiness shone in those dark eyes of hers when she looked for the title. He was sure she was doing it just to make fun of him, to watch his neck going red. Still, she was a serious reader—the only person in town besides himself who'd ever taken a book of poetry off those shelves, or Mallory—so he couldn't afford to

let his timidity force him to pass up this chance. Even so, the
best he could do was toss the book down as if it was hardly
of any consequence. "Some poems of Bourne's," and then, as
if an afterthought, "I don't suppose you'd be interested in looking them over." She was interested, of course, she'd be happy
not only to look them over but to read the book from cover
to cover. A great big sigh when she finished, those eyes full of
tears as she stared into space, fingering the pages. "And to
think I was tempted to get out of this place," she said. "Now
I know why I stayed." He hadn't the nerve to prod her, only
to wait. "The most beautiful love poems I've ever read," she
explained, as she gave him the book. "I didn't know it was possible to put those things into words, the longing, the purest
emotion of all. He raises human love to the divine, where it
belongs. That man knows more about us than we do ourselves."

More frustrated than ever, he called Charlie Reynolds of
the *Port Annie Crier*. "I've got something you'd like to see.
Maybe you'll want to write a book review for your paper."

Reynolds wanted to take the book back to his office to read,
but Bowman would not let it out of his library. "Read it here,"
he said. And the newspaperman sat where Jenny Chambers
had sat and where Angela Turner had sat. He skimmed through
the book, licking his thumb, reading a phrase here a phrase
there. "Hmmm," he said. "Hmmm." But no, the librarian said,
if you were going to find out what it was about you had to read
it from beginning to end, every word. "Just sampling," the
newspaperman said, waving Larry away. "Just sizing her up
before I tackle her." When he did tackle the book he opened
it up on the desk and pushed his chair back so that he was
lying on his laid-out arms, only inches from the page. He stuck
his tongue out between his teeth. "Holy old shit!" he said,
when he'd got about halfway through. "You know what this
son of a bitch is about!"

"Sex?" the librarian said.

"No. This little baby is about communication!"

The librarian sat down, exhausted.

"That old man down there in his shack is an expert on the
whole field of human communication." And sure enough, the
newspaperman was able to read out whole long passages which
were full of references to ideas and the methods of their dis-
semination. Even the poem that had triggered the librarian's

suspicion in the first place, with its windowpane image and its use of words like "thrust" and "penetrate". Larry had never seen such excitement in anyone's face. "What I'm going to do is take this thing down and confront him with it. He's hidden out in that shack of his for long enough, it's time we did a front-page story on the resurrection of Joseph Bourne!"

His heart sinking, Larry Bowman watched his book disappear out the door—not even signed out either—and resolved that as soon as he got it back, if he ever got it back, he'd hand it over to Mrs. Barnstone immediately. Let her and the other biddies in her Creative Writing Club make what they could of it. It would only drive him crazy sooner or later if he kept it any longer. But one thing he knew for sure: that book was about sex. And just to prove it, he'd have the main office down-island buy copies of the old goat's other books and send them up.

Once again he'd been abandoned, his hands empty, left with nothing to occupy his mind but his adventure novels and medieval poems and those cursed liquor ads, nothing at all between him and the tantalizing images of Raimey, the insolent seabird—images which would begin to overwhelm him again now any moment. But anger came first: to think that that old sex maniac of a crazy poet was monopolizing her down there, selfishly taking up all her time so that a man like Larry Bowman had to be satisfied with just a glimpse of her twice a day, as she walked past the library on her way in to town for groceries and then went past again on her way back to the Flats and his shack. He had brief visions of her incredible walk, enough to throw him into frantic rage if someone were in the library signing out a book at the time, but not once had he got up the nerve to do what he'd dreamed of doing—step out onto the road and introduce himself. All the rest of her time was wasted on that old man who'd defied nature and refused to die; she didn't even know Larry Bowman existed, let alone the fact that he was burning up with desire just to be close to her for a few moments, never mind touching her or anything else. All he could do was feel this powerful rage building up inside him—rage both at that old man's selfishness and at his own cowardly weakness.

Charlie Reynolds in the meantime stopped in at the coffee shop for a cup of Linda Weins's burned coffee (made drinkable by the addition of some rum from his pocket flask). He

read the book through from cover to cover, then announced
to everyone in the room—all of whom had looked up when he
slapped the book closed and let out a great long "Aaaaah!"—
that this was the real thing, dammit, that old goat really knew
his stuff, and he was going down into that stinkhole of a
Squatters' Flats to get himself a story. And if that delicious
woman off the freighter tried to stop him he'd just eat her up,
nibble on those juicy bones, and step inside to corner the
famous poet in his own smelly nest of a cluttered shack.

"Bravo!" someone shouted. "It's time someone went down
and found out what really goes on in that place. Probably
something kinky."

"Go get yourself a story."

He did, too, and the next night's paper offered the proof.
Beside the photo of Mayor Weins at his desk proclaiming this
to be Think-Tourism-Week, giant headlines announced.

POET J.B. A NEW MAN

Says He Has Lots of Life Left To Live Yet

Reynolds had chosen to refer to the old man as J.B. throughout his story because he knew some copies of the paper were
bound to find their way outside Port Annie and he didn't want
to trigger off an avalanche of reporters rushing in to town
just yet. Time enough for that when he'd got the whole story
himself. He'd considered the clever substitution of a synonym
for Bourne and had looked the name up in a dictionary, but
there were so many words meaning the same thing that he decided to keep matters simple and just use the initials, which
everyone in town would recognize. J.B., he reported, was indeed a well man, indeed better than all those years he'd lived
in Squatters' Flats, rejuvenated and reborn. The famous five
W's went out the window when he wrote this story, to hell
with them, this was no big-city paper where you had to figure
no one knew what the story was going to be about. And out
the window went all he'd learned in journalism classes about
the inverted pyramid, too, which was okay when you figured
no one was going to read past the first paragraph but made
no sense at all in Port Annie where everyone would read every
word, and more than once, too. Reynolds just wrote the story
the way it happened, his visit in the shack from beginning to
end, and left it to the reader to draw his own conclusions.

And Mayor Weins's conclusion was that Reynolds was into

the sauce again. "Well, look at this mess. No two sentences that connect up. And who's going to believe all that nonsense? A lot of hogwash."

This earth could buck you off its back just any time it wanted to, Bourne was reported as saying. And as easy as turning over. But it took a little talent to hold onto something sturdier when it tried. The something sturdier wasn't exactly heaven, he said, but it came to much the same thing—he called it life. Others might call it something else.

"He's only reporting what the old man told him, dear," his wife said. "And don't forget Mr. Bourne is a poet, and that poets tend to . . . romanticize?" It was something she'd learned in her year at the university.

"If that's the same as being crazy then I'll agree."

And, "Honestly, I could spit," said Mrs. Barnstone. "When I think of how long the Creative Writing Club has been meeting in this town and not once got a bit of publicity in the paper." Proof once again of what she'd said a hundred times: that you had to be warped to be noticed in the literary world.

What bothered Mrs. Landyke most was the fact that there was no photograph. She opened the paper out on the counter of her little Corner Store and read every word of Reynolds' visit to the shack, but still she wasn't satisfied. So the old man was alive and healthier than ever. So the Peruvian seabird had brought back his memory and all the strength he'd built up during those years. So he'd rediscovered his faith in the absolute power of good. So he intended to stay in Port Annie for a while yet and do what he could to help make it a better place to live. What Mrs. Landyke wanted to see—as she wrote in her letter to her married daughter Irma—was a photograph of Joseph Bourne sitting on the side of his bed or on a chair down in his shack, grinning at the camera—proof that he really was a flesh-and-blood human man down there, and not a figment of everyone's imagination, not a fairy tale dreamed up by Reynolds or by someone else, not a supernatural saint or something spooky. Why should she believe the words in this newspaper any more than she believed gossip? She'd believe in Joseph Bourne the day he walked into this store, slapped down his money on the counter, and asked for a quart of milk.

Larry Bowman skimmed through the whole story (three full-length columns) looking for the only thing that interested him, some reference to the books, the poems, those respectable-

looking packages of hidden sex. And found what he was looking for in the final column, halfway down—the report of a
conversation about writing. Poems aren't about things, the old
man said, with a typical vagueness that made the librarian
clamp his teeth together in irritation. Poems weren't *about*
things, poems *did* things. They threw light on things so that
you saw not only what they appeared to be but also what they
were.

The librarian scrunched up the paper, threw it on the floor,
kicked it across the room. Just see if he ever read any of the
pompous old lecher's other books! He'd burn them first. He'd
pass them on to that old Barnstone crow and let her and her
cohorts get their claws into them, rip them to shreds, destroy
all his nonsense about *light*, for crying out loud. What did the
old man think he was talking to, a bunch of English professors? How could a beautiful woman like that Raimey waste
her time on a man like him, an ancient fanatic? What she
needed was a sensitive man, someone younger, who could show
her what it was like to have a man loving you more than his
own life, never letting you out of his thoughts, worshipping
the ground you walked on with that incredible walk which
drove people mad. What she needed was no old has-been of a
famous person, just a normal man that no one had ever heard
of, someone who'd never written a poem in his life, or ever
wanted to, but who burned with a passion equal to all the pas-
sions in all the phony poems ever written and wasn't afraid
to promise to love her every minute of her life without fail,
no matter what else happened, and to devote his whole life to
nothing else but serving her. He was a new man, just watch
him. This was the bravest he'd felt since before he'd fallen
for Patsy McKay back in high school, a gorgeous long-legged
redhead who laughed in his face when he asked her to a movie,
told him to get lost—the first time he discovered how frightening women could be. He'd felt like Marhalt when those ladies
threw their filth on his pure white shield and circulated ugly
stories about his manhood, but the seabird Raimey had made
none of this important any more, he'd survived.

Mayor Weins didn't even read the article right through. He
didn't have to. Charlie Reynolds had come into the magazine
shop and told him everything before he'd written it up. And
then that sloppy irresponsible drunk had gone and opened his
mouth just once too often, and spoiled everything.

"While I was down there, Weins, I took the opportunity to feel them out."

"Feel them out? What are you talking about?"

"About your plans. The tourist idea. Only hints, of course, I didn't give any specifics, just to find out if they had any feelings on the matter."

The mayor nearly turned himself inside out holding his breath. That bloody fool! That royal arse! Weins had wanted to spring the news himself, when it was all sewed up, a complete package so attractive the old man was sure to go for it. He'd even dreamed of the occasion more than once—himself in a brand-new costume, something appropriate, copied from a picture of William Shakespeare, maybe—himself and the council and a handful of businessmen who'd been in on the ground floor going down to that shack and delivering the honour with appropriate speeches, leather-bound copies of the old guy's books, perhaps a gold medallion to fasten to his door. Those artsy types were a pushover for attention and prizes— maybe he'd even offer to turn Squatters' Flats into a writers' colony once those other bums were kicked off, give a big Joseph Bourne Bursary to some kid every year. And now this boozy bastard had gone and got the jump on him, stolen the fun of delivering the news for himself—and prematurely at that.

"And what did they have to say?" the mayor asked, trying to keep the disappointment out of his voice.

"The girl forbade it."

"That doesn't matter." Weins's hand waved the girl's opinion aside. "And the old man?"

"He said that the day you put your obscene plot into motion he would burn down his shack and leave this town for good."

So the mayor didn't need to read Reynolds' article when the paper came out. He looked at the headlines and the first paragraph and threw the thing in the garbage. He cursed the newspaperman. He cursed the girl from the Peruvian freighter. He cursed the famous poet. This had been the opportunity of a lifetime, and he hated the thought of making even a minor adjustment to his perfect plans. Without the old man's shack they'd have to fix up one of those other junk heaps in the Flats, pretend it was his. It might turn out to be a good thing to have the old man out of the picture—not around to throw any monkey wrenches into the works with his famous grouchiness—but still it was a disappointment, bound to lose them a few hundred of the tourists he'd counted on, especially the ones who wanted to talk to the Lazarus man himself. Damn that Charlie Reynolds and his *Port Annie Crier*!

"And what an insult," Eva McCarthy told Jenny on the phone. She folded the newspaper back and prepared to read. "Listen to this, his reasons for moving here to Port Annie." She read out the long paragraph in which the told man told Charlie Reynolds about the pressures of fame, about the loneliness of success, about the sudden feeling that had come over him that his life was over, that it added up to nothing at all, that he belonged nowhere in the world, belonged to no one, no place, that he was a homeless friendless purposeless man. "So what he did, Jen, was decide to get as far as he could from everything that represented life and wait for the end here on the edge of nothingness. He actually said that, Jen, the creep, the edge of nothingness. Too bad we didn't push him *over* the edge while we had the chance."

Jenny Chambers hung up as soon as she could, with as little comment as she could get away with, because that skinny minnow of an Eva McCarthy was still off her list, a traitor, and why should she waste her afternoon listening to that voice droning on and on not knowing when to stop?

Besides, Jenny still hadn't recovered from her first brush with Bourne's poetry. Those silly things had really knocked her out, left her breathless; a lot of little blobs of print on a piece of paper, really, but they'd given her the impression somehow that that ugly old man she'd crabbed about so often had been able to see right into her, that he knew what Jenny Chambers felt like. It gave her the willies, made her heart race, and yet it was thrilling, too. Of course he'd put those words down on paper long before he'd ever clapped eyes on her, long before he'd ever set foot in this mess of a town, but still it was as if he knew. And it inspired her to fight back. If an old goat like him could fight his way back from the edge of death, who was she to give up her fight so easily? Cripes, wasn't it obvious in these poems that what he'd spent his lifetime doing was just exactly the same thing as she was after?

"Listen!" she said right out loud, astonished by a wonderful thought that had suddenly occurred. Fight back was exactly what she would do. If those catalogue clothes hadn't been enough to turn a few heads, she'd go out, get some in person, spend a fortune if necessary. She'd been what they'd all called a "looker" once, she'd be one again, and so what if it cost her a fortune. Think of the money Slim spent on his silly machines —tractors and snowploughs and old pickups and dune buggies lined up across the backyard, with no purpose in life except to collect his admiration and take up his time with waxing and fixing when he ought to be doing little things around the house. He'd thrown away a king's ransom on those rigs, so why should she feel guilty about a few dresses?

She picked up the phone to tell Eva McCarthy—no, Mrs. Landyke—no, Mabel Weins was the one she could trust to spread it around—that, guess what, she was heading south, and tomorrow! That dumb duty on the picket line could just drop dead, she'd quit that job the minute she got back and besides it didn't look good for a woman of her social position to be traipsing up and down with a placard like an ordinary worker, she'd have to watch her step from now on. And listen, Mabel, don't spread the word too far, because everyone knew the minute a person let on she was heading *out* the whole town descended with orders for things they wanted brought back. She knew for example right now that Gerda Beeton was just waiting for someone to go out because her dad down in Campbell River had butchered a beef for her and was keeping it in his freezer; well Jen didn't mind doing favours for people, as Mabel well knew—soft-heartedness was one of her faults— but hauling a frozen beef back was too much; and if she wasn't mistaken that old Bill Nichols was just waiting to pounce on someone to bring him back a big order of cheap down-island groceries (he'd threatened to starve before he'd pay *these* prices) and his wife had three wedding presents she wanted delivered in Courtenay, all breakable, the silly nit didn't have enough sense to buy things you could mail. Just tell Eva Jen went out on a buying spree—selfish as all get-out for a change —and would be back to show off before she got packed for *her* holiday.

Three days later she was on the phone again, to Mabel (let Eva wait, the skinny traitor) : two days in Nanaimo, it was like a dream, Mabel. She stayed in the Tally-ho, no less, with a view over the swimming pool and under a bridge and out to the harbour where there were sailboats; she hated to leave the room. But she did, because cripes, guess what—it didn't rain a drop the whole time she was there, she could hardly believe air could be so dry, she didn't even wear her fur, just carried

it over her arm, and stores stores stores—she'd forgotten it
was possible to come out of one store and go into the next and
in and out all down the street, no two the same and all with
people who sometimes smiled at you and didn't know all your
business and private thoughts already. "You must be going on
a long trip, buying so many clothes," one saleslady told her,
but no, Jen said, only stocking up on a few decent things to
wear because her Slim was being made foreman at the Mill.
"My husband works at the Mill too," the lady said. "Do they
know each other?" Not likely, Jen told her, because the Mill
she was talking about was at Port Annie, she was down on a
shopping spree, treating herself a little, and seeing some sights.
"Port Annie?" That lady's face shrivelled up with distaste.
"Isn't that where they keep sliding into the sea? How can anyone live in a place that's so dangerous?" But no, there was no
danger that you ever thought of, Jenny said, and besides there
was more than one place up there that went sliding downhill
every once in a while. "Then how can you stand being so far
away?" the lady said, and cripes, Jen told her, "Far away from
what?" Every place you could name was far away from some
other place you could name, but the lady said, "Far away
from the whole world," meaning right here where she happened to be standing at that minute. She looked at Jenny as
if what she said she'd come from was Mars, or Siberia, or a
prison camp in the Yukon.

Oh, she had a wonderful time, Mabel, and couldn't she just
imagine this gal strutting those streets after clothes, as if every
one of those sales clerks was put there in their stations just for
her. Just wait till she saw the load she'd come back with, she
wasn't even sure she'd be able to get it all in the little plane,
but thank goodness one other person had no luggage at all.
But don't think buying was all this woman did, she treated
herself like royalty the whole time; ate every meal in a different restaurant (clam chowder on the waterfront, and pizza
in the shopping mall, and Chinese food in this place where
every single one of the waitresses had long dresses to the floor,
and boys poured out ice water and wine); and visited all the
tourist spots, including a little island out in the harbour where
she got invited to join in on a big picnic this club was having
for blind people. And don't think she sat in her hotel room
every evening either; she dressed up in her new clothes and
went into cocktail lounges where she nursed tomato juice and

watched the people until one couple moved in and made a friend of her and eventually took her home with them, where they called up others to come on over and meet this new lady from "Port Annie of all places".

Like a real person is how they treated her, with respect, and she almost hated to leave, but that didn't mean she wasn't happy and relieved to be back here where she belonged with her two feet flat on the ground and the sound of Slim's brats screeching around her. Home was home and it was a treat to see how glad Slim was to have her back, you'd think she'd been gone a whole month. Every woman that could afford it should go off on a spree like that for a while just for the pleasures of coming home afterward, though of course she understood that Mabel had good reasons for never going anywhere, don't think she didn't know that, it was a different story when you were the constant victim of migraines and arthritis and stomach upset and jittery nerves, not to mention sickness from even a few miles in a car or a boat or a plane. What Jenny meant was that every woman who *wanted* to should get out on a shopping trip whenever she could. It did you good, and now watch out for her because rain or no rain she was going out for a walk this afternoon and would no doubt find herself on Mabel's street sooner or later panting for a cup of tea.

And every day that following week she went out for a walk, a whole different outfit of clothes each time. By the end of the week it was clear—in this town she'd been welcomed to with such a fuss all those years ago, where she'd felt more at home than any other place she'd been in her life including a childhood spent in a Saskatchewan river-town, in this place that she'd learned to like despite the rain that could drive you crazy and the isolation that sometimes scared you and the small-minded way that so many people got into the habit of thinking—she was finally friendless. Except for Slim and those monsters of his (who hated her, she was sure of it) she was every bit as alone as that old Bourne had been, down in his shack in the Flats like a miserable hermit.

Eva McCarthy, when Jenny stopped in at her house, had just waited for Jen to get through talking so she could tell about her own holiday and how it was put off for the time being because civil servants couldn't do just whatever they wanted like other people, and then went on and on about the new wallpaper she'd ordered for her kitchen and that new vacuum cleaner she loved to play with like a kid with a toy, and didn't Jenny think the chesterfield looked better with its back to the window? Mrs. Landyke was just on her way out the door, her daily visit to her husband's grave—and would Jen like to come along? But all that woman did was talk about what a wonderful man her Herbert had been, and then made a complete fool of herself by kneeling on the damp ground to pray. Right in front of Jen, a real embarrassment. Mabel Weins, wife of the mayor and a great reader and club person besides, was someone she should be able to count on, but surprise: that short shrimp of a whiner was as bad as the rest. She told Jenny that one just doesn't wear red with pink and that a fur coat in summer seemed a bit extreme even in this climate and then catalogued a list of her own health problems, head to feet, with detailed descriptions of every medicine and herb and Indian potion and health food she'd tried without success, and every word the doctor had said to her on every one of her visits to his poky little office. Arthritis and lumbago and pinched nerves and varicose veins and nervous tension and migraine. She wasn't the slightest bit interested in Jenny's clothes or Jenny's holiday or Slim's promotion. A wet blanket, a bucket of cold water, enough to put out all the fire that was left in Flaming Jenny, nothing but a steaming heap of ashes.

And during the evenings Mr. Manku continued to walk down the hill from his house full of noisy relatives, his big stomach hard from the delicious cooking done by his wife and by his four daughters-in-law, and put on his bathing suit to have his swimming lesson in the community pool. Citizen Manku, he thought to himself, the only one in that household to break out of the little safe cluster and do something that these westerners liked to do, do something individual and brave and shocking. Sometimes he thought of the rest of his family with contempt—he was the oldest of them all, he and Harbans had been the first to leave the Punjab and put foot in the new country, so he had the right to scorn their timidity, their refusal to change any of their ways. They'd guessed he'd taken up bowling, and laughed at him—such a silly pastime, they said. Harbans jeered at him. "Rolling black balls down a gutter!" But he could hardly wait for the day he could reveal the truth, the day he could invite them down here to see what he'd been doing, the day when he'd be able to put his face down in the water at last and swim like a fish. Swim up and down the length of this pool just like those other students.

"A brave man," Papa Magnani said. He'd got into the habit of watching every evening, of standing in the change-room door for the forty minutes that Mr. Manku and his instructor worked together on this terrible problem of his fear of getting water on his face. A brave man. And that instructor—so patient—tried everything she could think of to help, everything she'd ever learned herself or read in books or got one of the other instructors to tell her. And every time it was failure, every evening the brave Mr. Manku had to step out of the pool at the end of his forty minutes no closer to success than he'd been on the first day, and strip off that bathing suit in the change room, where everyone including Papa Magnani could see the water-shrivelled nakedness of his old flesh and the desperate look of determination on his face. Sometimes Papa Magnani thought he was a fool to watch—his heart would break if this went on much longer, oh Rosa how this hurt him! —but he stayed to watch every night so that he could be the one to yell "Shut up!" at those terrible unfeeling Chamber-Potts brats when they started up their laughing and their shouted insults about Mr. Manku's size and colour and race, and their imitations of his activities in the water. They came every evening, and made faces at Papa Magnani when he told them to shut up, but so far Mr. Manku seemed not to have heard their insults, he seemed to be completely unaware that they even existed. Like the dignity of a great actor on stage. If he was aware of anything outside that fence at all, it would be only of a huge silent audience he imagined watching him with awe.

But oh how glad Papa Magnani was that he continued to watch, because the day finally came when it happened. A rainy evening, like all the others, and Papa Magnani was startled to see that beautiful seabird creature standing just outside the fence, in the shadow of her own gigantic umbrella, watching Mr. Manku too with a half-smile on her face, as if he were an amusement that had distracted her from something else. Papa Magnani's heart raced—as it did whenever he caught even so much as a glimpse of that girl, or the scent of that invisible flower—but there was no time for admiring her mysterious beauty because suddenly what a fuss broke out! When no one was looking Mr. Manku held onto the edge of the pool, let his feet float out behind him, and simply put his face down into the water. He came up sputtering. "I did it!" In a high voice. "I did it!" The instructor came running and he did it

again. When she screamed, laughed, clapped her hands, practically cried, everyone else in the pool stopped what he was
doing, climbed out, and ran down to the shallow end to see
Mr. Manku do it again. Everyone clapped, congratulated one
another. And Mr. Manku did it over and over again until he
was tired of it, until he was absolutely certain that he would
always be able to do it, then came up out of the pool laughing
and crying and forgetting all about the dignity of a great actor.

Papa Magnani, who'd never cared a fig for dignity in his
life, ran out onto the deck, weeping openly, and threw his
arms around that huge wet body. The two men danced in turning circles, laughing and crying, until the instructor clapped
her hands together and shouted, "Okay! Everyone back in the
pool!" And even then they were reluctant to break apart—
Papa Magnani held onto Mr. Manku's hand and pumped it
up and down, "Congratulations, congratulations!", and narrowed his eyes to see if that seabird was still watching from
the shadows. But she was gone, nowhere in sight, and Mr.
Manku stepped back to face the bleachers and made a deep
bow in the direction of the Chamber-Potts children. Papa Magnani, to cover up their hysterical screeches, started to applaud
again, as loudly as he could, and soon everyone else in the pool
was applauding with him. They clapped until the Chamber-
Potts children had jumped down off the bleacher seats and gone
off into the gravel pit next door, where they tried to climb up
the fir tree to get at the derelict boat. Even the lowest branches
were too high for them, though, and all they could do was
throw themselves up the trunk and hold on while they slid
back down.

And during the time that Jenny Chambers was walking the
streets in the daytime and Mr. Manku was persevering with
his swimming lessons in the rain, Jeremy Fell—still unable to
get to sleep in his bed—had begun to walk out into the rain
every night after the streets had been deserted, down the paved
road out of town until he was above Squatters' Flats, where he
climbed uphill into bush to sit on a high black stump and look
down over the shacks, the beach, the inlet. He knew which was
Bourne's roof, that little boarded-up boathouse right on the
high-water line. And it just wasn't possible to sleep, Your
Honour, whenever he began to hear those bulldozers' motors
in his head, the sounds of power saws roaring and trees cracking and shacks collapsing into rubble, the smell of diesel oil

and burning slash piles, the imagined sight of hard-hatted sur-
veyors looking through instruments and driving stakes into the
ground and huddling together for conferences. As beautiful
as the poems he'd heard of, Your Honour, and no one he
could share it with yet, that vision of a future which was coming nearer and nearer. In fact, if he could believe the letters
he got back in answer to his fat packages of reports, a future
only months away now perhaps, because one thing was sure:
once they made the decision, once the way was made clear by
government and companies and everyone else who had their
fingers on the strings of power, they would do it all fast, get
it done so quickly, that people who were told about it at the
last minute would wake up practically the next day and discover the gift was already delivered, a new future, and those
grumbling drag-backs who never saw any good in change
wouldn't have the time to raise any of their usual hue and cry
of ludicrous charges or to drag up their red herrings and com-
plications in an attempt to halt progress. That hundred miles
of gravel logging-road was going to be replaced any day now
by pavement, Your Honour, a modern highway joining all this
to the rest of the Island, and once that happened just watch
those hang-backs fight a losing battle trying to stay in the Dark
Ages, they just couldn't seem to get it into their heads that this
was the frontier they lived in, and what they were trying to
beat down was the frontier spirit of progress that moved this
country from just a lot of useless wasted land into a buzzing
hive of industry and progress and fantastic growth. Jeremy
Fell was only doing his small part.

A small part, but an important one. And it was absolutely
essential that no one suspect why he was here, they'd think
something crooked was up, so a low profile was what was
needed, and someone who could size people up fast, find out
what kind of town this was up here in the bush, and let the
company know.

When these people saw later on what had happened to them,
what he'd done, they would recognize that Jeremy Fell had
turned out to be their saviour. They would make a hero out
of him, put Jeremy Fell in their history books. Too late,
though, if something didn't hurry up, they wouldn't know until
it was too late what he had done. And what hideous irony!
Only a matter of time, according to the doctor, who wanted to
haul him off to a hospital somewhere, Your Honour, cut him

open and hook him up to a little machine he could keep in his
pocket. Forget it. Where he would be when they wanted to
thank him for what he'd done was under the ground, buried,
almost forgotten.

Going home in the middle of the night always made him
feel a little ashamed. What if people had noticed? Was he
beginning to go a little insane? Nobody liked to think he was
doing something that nobody else in the world would want to
do—nobody wanted to feel like a freak. And all this dark
drizzly quiet was enough to give you the creeps about yourself.

So it was with some relief that he discovered a light on in
Weins's magazine shop one night, the mayor himself sitting
behind his counter. The fat man was dressed in his Captain
Vancouver costume again, drinking from a tall glass of some
amber liquid, and—if Jeremy Fell's eyes didn't deceive him—
talking to himself. Those little eyes were red and puffy, that
mouth was chewing over unintelligible sounds. He was tempted
to go on past, pretend he'd never seen, but the mayor was the
one man in town he felt was a kindred spirit, and he would
have felt even more ashamed if he'd ignored him there.

"The scheme's fallen through altogether," Weins announced,
putting one hand over his eyes. "The Bourne affair's off.
There's not going to be any literary shrine. There's not going
to be any sign over the road, no Joseph Bourne T-shirts, no
souvenirs. There aren't going to be any tourists."

"What happened? What went wrong?"

"My wife. The only person in the world who could stop a
first-class idea like that. She said she would leave me."

Jeremy Fell looked down at his hands. "She won't change
her mind? You can't talk her into it?"

"Mabel has never changed her mind about anything in her
life. She's hard. No one has ever budged her on anything."

The mayor hiccoughed, and swiped a handkerchief across
his eyes. His Captain Vancouver hat fell on the floor. "God
damn it, Fell, I feel terrible about this thing. I wanted to see
that sign go up over the road in the damnedest way. I needed
to see those tourists pouring in to gawk at the shack. I could
practically taste their excitement. That whole scheme was a
stroke of genius, Fell, it ought to have happened. It just isn't
fair."

Fell sensed a rage building inside himself—that stupid
woman, to wreck such a beautiful plan!—but he swallowed

it down. No sense letting Weins see how he felt. "It was a terrific idea, Weins, but you'll come up with others."

"It was a fantastic idea, a stroke of genius, and no kidding either. It could've put this place on the map."

"So don't give up just because one little scheme fell apart, the world is full of ideas and all you have to do is pick the right one out of the air. People will pay to see anything at all, so long as you make them think they can't find it in their own living room. You've got to have a little faith."

The mayor hiccoughed so loud that both men jumped. It was, after all, very late. Even the rain outside on the pavement seemed to have taken on a hushed, menacing tone.

Jeremy Fell was tempted to let Weins in on a few secrets, to help him to get over this blow by telling him about the exciting days that were ahead. The eyes would bug out of his head. That little scheme of his would seem like pretty small potatoes compared to the changes that were coming. Too bad, though, it wasn't allowed, this was still too early to be spilling the beans. Besides, when the news got told, it wouldn't be Fell who would tell it. "Listen," he said. "Let me tell you something. A Bourne shrine isn't the only way to collar the tourist trade. Listen. The first building I put foot in when I arrived in this country from the States was a ridiculous museum run by a white-haired woman named Mrs. Wagonwheel." After a lifetime of drifting, he said, he was stopped in his tracks when she looked up at him with her blue eyes blinking in a hideously overpainted face and said, "Aren't you someone I know?" No, he wasn't, just Jeremy Fell from here there and everywhere, ma'am, and what was this place supposed to be, with its huge hand-lettered sign:

MUSEUM OF EVIL

and how much did it cost to go through? It was an old house down a side street, porches and balconies and cherry trees, looked more like a boarding house than a place you paid to walk through. There were plenty of tourist traps on the Island, she told him; everyone wanted to get in on the act. But there wasn't another place like this one. You had to have a gimmick to get people in off the road and she was sure she'd come up with the one that people couldn't resist. "Everyone wants to believe it's a thing of the past," she told him, and Jeremy Fell said, "What is?"

"Evil," she said, and led him around the first room, past shelf after shelf of displays, mementos of killers and thieves and every sort of outlaw imaginable, photographs of world-famous villains, records and details of sicknesses that had wiped out whole families right there in that city, paintings of wartime hillsides littered with broken and bleeding bodies, photographs of starving children, records and newspaper articles about injustices done to innocent people, guns and animal traps and bottles labelled poison and models of guillotines and electric chairs. She made him try on a black hangman's hood she claimed she'd had smuggled out of the mainland penitentiary. When people had been through her place, she told him, they felt that mankind had long ago conquered and destroyed all evil, all illness and cruelty and death. Put something in a museum and you imply that it's defeated at last.

So he'd stayed there for a while, Mr. Weins, to help her out in that museum, taking money from the eager tourists and showing them through, and going out on trips to scrounge up new displays whenever they got wind of a bargain—a nice life, not too much work and there was the fun of seeing those tourists swallow that whole parcel of hoaxes, and not a thing illegal about it, every single thing in the place was legitimate, no phonies.

Weins made an attempt to get up, then fell back with a grunt into his chair and shook his head. "Oh, don't worry about me," he said. "I'll get over it, and no broken bones either; it isn't the end of the world. There must've been something wrong with the plan, maybe this way we've been saved from some bigger letdown in the future, maybe the decks just had to be cleared for a project of even greater dimensions."

In fact, the mayor added, putting his Captain Vancouver hat back on, even while he saw this whole scheme going down the drain an idea was beginning to form in his head. "As you suggested yourself, there's no limit to the imagination." Just the beginning of an idea, but no doubt it would blossom. A sudden flash of a face started it growing, his cousin who lived down in Arizona, a little dry snake of a man who'd visited here once, years ago, and complained the whole time about rain.

Weins picked up Captain Vancouver's long black spyglass, raised it to one eye, and aimed it at Jeremy Fell's face. He held it there, like a sailor studying land, while he talked. "To tell you the truth, Jeremy, I've been getting just a bit sick and tired lately of the way even the people who live here are always complaining about the rain. How are we supposed to get tourists to flock into our town if we keep knocking it ourselves? You know what happens when it *doesn't* rain? That pulp-mill smoke comes down and wraps the whole town up in its stink, so thick you have to turn your car lights on to see ten feet in front of you. I say we're lucky it rains; complaining is crazy. So I've come up with this idea, much better than the last one and no kidding either. No doubt it will make both of us as famous as Bourne."

The telescope made a quick probe into the corners of the room and then came back to settle on Jeremy's face again. What they were going to do was this, the mayor explained. Down in Arizona where his cousin lived they had giant cactuses growing in the desert, some of them as high as fifty feet. "Who dares to say it rains too much in Port Annie? We'll prove this place is more than a watery jungle and no question about it either. We'll import a few of those prickly giants and start a desert garden down along the water's edge to prove our point."

He could see it now. What a beautiful sight, enough to bring tears to your eyes! The tallest one—fifty feet high, Jeremy!— would be higher than the hotel, higher than anything around, seen from everywhere in the town, one of the wonders of the world. They'd plant it in a barge full of sand down at the dock, and it would flower, Jeremy, in the spring, a magnificent sight, a living statue, it would bear fruit every fall. An inspiring tower, a work of nature's art, a beautiful column of their faith in the future, disappearing with its upraised branches into the clouds. And tourists, Jeremy, tourists would flock here by the hundreds to see it, the country's Biggest Natural-Growing Cactus! What was the opposite of an oasis in the desert, Jeremy? This was going to be a desert blooming in the middle of a rainforest. Who could resist the temptation to travel for miles just to see such a wonder? No question about it, this was a certainty, gasps of astonishment would be everyday fare in this town.

IV

BUSY TONIGHT at the Kick-and-Kill, a thirsty crowd. Vincent was going crazy just keeping everyone happy. If Port Annie ever had a heat wave, with honest-to-goodness sunshine for a change, it was staggering to imagine just how much beer would be consumed. Even during rain some kind of record was broken every night of the week. Not a closing-time passed without an announcement from Belchy McFadden that he'd once again passed some astonishing milestone, some incredible volume of suds taken in, more than you'd think a human was able to hold. Of course Belchy had more storage room in his body than most—a truly gigantic stomach, with no valuable space ever wasted on food. And his Plimsoll line had obviously moved up to the top of his head—there was room for brains and beer both in that skull, and any time he felt the need Belchy could pee in his pants to clear a little more space. He was a model customer for sure, someone the others could copy. Already there were several not far behind, neck-and-neck in a race to be the second-biggest drinker in town. It was not clear yet whether the winner would be Jim Smithers or Lanky Torrero, or maybe even Charlie Reynolds—the newspaper editor—who seemed to be coming up fast from the rear, determined to catch up to the others and pass them.

Rita Rentalla looked at the newspaperman from across the room—a hazy figure through all that smoke—and rested a hand on her thrust-out hip. "Why don't the police go down for another look? Maybe he died after all—I wouldn't believe something just because that souse-head writes it up in his paper. Maybe that gal is watching the old guy rot down there in his shack."

"Rita, be sensible." Christie hooked his boot into a chair and dragged it over for her to sit on.

"Who knows?" Rita said, not sitting yet. "Maybe we ought to be throwing a funeral for the poor old man."

"Don't be stupid," Christie said. "When was the last time you ever saw a funeral in Port Annie, eh? People usually go home to die, they have themselves buried where they came from. No one ever wants to be buried here."

"Well pardon me for living," Rita said. "I guess I only imagined I saw Fat Annie's funeral right here on these streets."

"That's different, eh. And twenty years ago."

Bald-headed Pete placed a hand on his scalp and fingered the scar that Christie had left on his crown. "That woman again? I thought she was supposed to be still alive."

"That didn't stop her from having a funeral," Rita said, perching daintily on the chair. "When they found her old man's remains she decided to make it a double affair. If you wait till you're dead for a funeral then you'll miss out on most of the fun."

Christie sighed and took a long drink from his beer. It was time to tell Pete some more about Fat Annie, but he didn't know if Rita could be counted on not to butt in. "She rode in a coffin all of her own, eh, right behind his—both of them rented, naturally, there were no remains to bury, don't forget, once she'd gulped him down. Polished walnut, they tell me, with shiny handles and all white satin inside. Too small for a woman her size, each of her thighs needed a coffin of its own, but she squeezed her arse end into it anyway."

Rita Rentalla pressed hands to either side of her face, buried her nails in her hair. "The first problem they ran into was the fact that Port Annie's only got one garbage truck to its name."

"I'll tell this," Christie cut his hand down through air, as if separating Rita from the rest of them. "Port Annie don't have a hearse, Pete, because there's hardly ever any need for one. But when somebody forgets to go home, or nobody sends for them, eh, or they want to be buried up over the hill, we scrub out the dump truck that's used for garbage and throw a lot of flowers and stuff onto it for a disguise and use that, no kidding. So when Fat Annie told it around that she was having a double funeral everyone figures they'd put both coffins on the same truck, eh, but no sir, she made them borrow a second one from across the Island and scrub it up too and decorate it and have a parade."

"Half a mile long," Rita said. She had one of her long vermilion nails caught between her teeth and they waited, un-moving, until she got it free. "It started with a huge party out in the inlet on barges, then came past on trucks through the town."

Christie looked at Rita until she got his message: keep out of this damn story. But she sniffed, offended, and grabbed her purse up off the table, to stand up. "Excuse me, please. I guess I won't be tempted to put my two bits' worth in if I'm sitting at somebody else's table. Maybe Belchy could stand my company for a while."

"Just don't bring him back with you when you come. You know what he's like about Annie."

Christie watched her sashay across the room, swinging her rear end just for his benefit, until she stopped to talk with someone he didn't recognize. Then he sat back and bellowed, *"Rita,"* so that everyone else in the room except Rita Rentalla looked at him alarmed and he bellowed, *"Rita get back over here,"* so loud the veins in his throat filled up like hoses and his fingers went white on the table.

Everyone turned to look at Rita now but she behaved as if there was nothing at all behind her. She stirred around in her purse after a cigarette, lighted it off a candle on someone's table, and then turned slowly and looked at Christie across the room, long enough to let a lungful of smoke drift out of her mouth.

"Lord, Lord." Her hands went up into the air again. "I don't know why I stay in a place where the best you can find for a friend is someone like Christie." Then she moved on, dismissing him, and worked her way to a back table, where a hand reached out and grabbed her arm. Laughing, she allowed herself to be pulled down onto a chair at the dirt-bikers' table, where Gregory Wong and his friends had moved in on Belchy McFadden. For a moment Christie saw her look back at him. A woman in a softball jacket looked from one to the other and leaned closer to her companion: "Them two are crazy."

So Christie, keeping an eye on that red hair of Rita Rentalla's, told Bald-headed Pete about Fat Annie's funeral. He remembered seeing it himself, eh, when it came down through the old original townsite that they kicked everyone out of when they built this new town. What a sight! Dieter Fartenburg's box went by, and then Fat Annie in the second truck, propped up in that gleaming brown coffin of hers, surrounded by flowers and waving to everybody like Queen Victoria, and the driver too, waving too, like he was hauling the May Queen to her coronation.

Christie hawked up some phlegm in his throat and then swallowed it down. Nobody had ever seen anything like this funeral, eh, first the mayor in an open-top car and his wife, who wore gloves, and then the MLA in a black convertible with his mistress from Victoria and then poor old Dieter Fartenburg's coffin on the back of the flower-covered garbage truck and then Fat Annie grinning like mad and waving from the back of that garbage truck borrowed from across the Island and then forty-seven baton-twirling majorettes and the North Island Dance Band marching and playing "Who's Sorry Now?" and the whole management of the Mill itself and a sign saying

WHERE WOULD ANY OF US BE WITHOUT YOU ANNIE? flying out from the smokestack, eh, and all their kids sitting around the edge singing "The Sweetheart of Sigma Chi" with their feet swinging back and forth, flowers spelling out WHERE IS THY STING? along either side. A mile long at least, by the time you include the Vancouver delegation and that long flowered float sent up by the big American company she'd sold the place to when her husband died and that gold and purple marching band from Seattle you see in every parade you go to no matter where it is in this part of the world. It wound its way down from the Mill through all the streets of the Old Town and then along the inlet to the New Town and along the bottom street and up into the square, and then out the other end, heading inland, to cross the Island and give a treat to the other towns.

"But didn't make it," Christie said, holding up a hand for Vincent to get some more beer over here in a hurry.

Because the garbage-truck drivers started getting frisky, once they got out of town, and managed to turn the funeral parade into a race over the mountains. Faster and faster, up and down the slopes and around the lake, first one of them ahead and then the other one ahead, drivers yelling curses at each other and shaking fists out the windows and blowing their horns. The people behind tried to keep up, scared stiff but not wanting to miss anything, placing bets on who would get there first and what the people of that other town would think lined up along their main street when they saw those two trucks racing for them like a couple of dragsters with all those other cars behind. Then, heading downhill neck-and-neck on one of those switchbacks that could make a person's eyes pop even at low speed, both trucks turned the same sharp blind corner too fast and shot both coffins off the back end out over the cliff to go sliding downhill side by side, riding a small avalanche of rocks, to land right in the river and go floating off downstream. One of the coffins didn't have much to say about it, but Fat Annie sat up and howled like a banshee. She sailed away as helpless as a floating log on that Greenwater River and went out of sight down a canyon.

And so the chase was on. The whole parade had to get turned around and come racing back, trying to keep Fat Annie in sight, and they nearly broke their necks in an attempt to get to the plank bridge over the river before she got there. And did, too, but couldn't think of anything else to do but line up across the bridge and watch her come around the corner out of the deep shadows and sail right under them, cursing and yowling and waving her arms, and then run to the other side of the bridge to see her pass on out of sight again behind more trees and go rocketing off towards the ocean. Some of them heard language that day they'd never heard before.

"The inlet," Rita said. "Off towards the inlet." She'd come back, with her purse hanging at her elbow, and Belchy McFadden seemed to have followed her. He held onto the back of the chair for support and drained one of the glasses from the middle of Christie's table.

"The inlet, okay, with her husband's coffin right behind her, riding higher in the water than she was." Christie looked at the cigarette that waited between the long pale fingers for someone to produce a match. "Belchy, buy your own damn beer."

"Okay," Pete said, "and I guess I'm forty kinds of fool to bring this up, but isn't there part of the story missing?"

"You mean you wanted to hear about every bloody thing that was in the parade and the name of every sonofabitch that saw it, and the names of the truck-drivers as well?"

That wasn't what Pete meant, what he meant was that the last he saw of Fat Annie Fartenburg she was floating off into the inlet and presumably right down the inlet to the open sea and then into the Japanese current for all he knew and ended up in Asia, turned back into a whale, so why was it he was expected to believe she was alive still and sitting in this same building with him, only somewhere above his head and waiting for a chance to come down again and stir up all kinds of crap?

"That's another story," Rita said, lowering herself elegantly into the chair and stretching every bone in her body. "She waded ashore just down there at the foot of this hill. And walked right up to here, and Christie you've got to tell what happened next." She fished a matchbook out of her purse and lit the cigarette herself.

Christie shrugged. "Tell it yourself."

"I won't. You started this, now finish it."

"Well there isn't all that much to say," Christie said, trying to ignore Belchy McFadden, who'd pulled up a chair beside Rita and put a hand on her leg. "You can imagine her right over there in the foyer, in her black silk funeral dress, eh, soaking wet and sticking to her body. Plastered all over like this town with bits of kelp and weeds and seedy yellow pods and chips of bark, with broken shells in her hair."

"Belchy here was in love with Fat Annie Fartenburg," Rita said, removing the hand from her thigh and placing it carefully on the table. "He told me he was crazy about her then."

The old man winked at Christie and wiped at the drool that escaped from one corner of his mouth. "Of course I was. I stood over there and cried like a baby."

"So did others," Christie said. "When she said she was going upstairs to stay, they didn't want her to go."

"You silly old fart," was what Fat Annie said. "What are you blubbering about?"

"Cried like a baby," said Belchy proudly. No matter how much he'd had to drink, his voice and his eyes remained as clear as they'd been years ago, last time he was sober. "My heart was busted, I tell you. How could she do it? I'd followed that woman around like a dog, she knew I'd do anything at all that she wanted. An arm and a leg if she'd asked. I was twenty years younger than her but I'd've married her in a minute."

"Back off, Belchy," someone had told him. "Leave her alone, let her do what she has to do."

"If I was tempted to change my mind," Fat Annie said, "your slobbering sure as hell wouldn't be why." She pulled her wet dress away from her breasts and released tiny black silver-eyed fish that fell to the floor and thrashed themselves to death on the carpet. "I'm tired, McFadden, I'm sick of this world. I just want to go upstairs for a rest."

"Is that what she told you?" Rita said.

One after another men came in off the square with her belongings, which they carried past her and on up the stairs: trunks and boxes heaped with cooking pots from her cookhouse days and racks of clothes and pieces of old broken furniture and a gigantic four-poster bed that had to be taken up piece by piece in six or seven trips by those grunting sweaty men.

"She took everything she owned up there?" Pete wanted to know.

Christie nodded. "Anything she cared about."

"Half a dozen fish tanks," Belchy said. "I saw this slimy damn octopus looking out at me through the glass, with his yellow knobby eyes."

"Be careful with those little buggers," Fat Annie said. "Don't scare them half to death, go easy."

"Change your mind," Belchy said. "This is crazy, Annie,

change your mind. You can move that junk up into my house as easy as here. If you want to get away from the rest of them, that's okay, but don't go away from me."

"A regular Romeo," Rita said.

"Shut up," Christie said. "The man was nuts about a woman, anything wrong with that? Some things should never be made fun of, never."

"Pardon me for living," Rita said.

Finally, all of the furniture and fish and bedclothes had disappeared up the staircase and down a hall. "Stand back, McFadden," Annie said, "I'm on my way." She moved to the foot of the stairs, where she could be seen through the door by all the people crowded outside, undid the zipper down the front of her dress, shrugged out of it, and let it drop like a shed skin on the floor around her feet. People gasped. She stood in a satin slip with a long embroidered vine snaking its way up the front, all the way from the lacy hem, up over those stump-thighs and curving over the bulging stomach, where it sprouted leaves and brilliant flowers and golden fruit and separated into two narrowing branches that burst suddenly into leafy crowns over her enormous breasts. For a moment she stood motionless in a sudden beam of sunlight, a shivering shimmering tree. Strips of seaweed glittered in her hair. Her tiny feet were strapped into rhinestone-studded dancing shoes. Then she dipped, to grab the hem and pull the slip inside out, up over her body, and off.

"My God," Pete said.

"But don't worry, nobody saw her," Rita said. "They turned away, there wasn't a person in Port Annie who would dare to look at such a sight. By the time they looked again, through fingers or over shoulders or through squinted eyelids, she'd gone. There was nothing of her left but the pools of water and the heap of dress and slip, and halfway up the staircase a pair of pants, and farther still a brassiere."

"I saw her," Belchy said. "I didn't turn away for nobody, I saw her as clear as I'm seeing you. I fell apart. I went crazy. I started acting like a madman."

"What is the idiot doing? He's got a gun."

"Come down from there! Somebody grab him, quick!"

Someone caught his foot from behind, and brought him crashing to his face on the stairs. He kicked himself free and crawled, scrambling, up the steps, yelling for Annie, but someone else grabbed a leg and dragged him backwards. He kicked, twisted, turned himself over and shot the gun off in the direction of the upstairs hallway, then pointed it with both hands at those who would hold him down. "Let me go, you sonsabitches, let me go."

They released him quickly and moved back, alarmed. "What are you going to do? You're crazy, McFadden, get ahold of yourself."

"She shouldn't have done that to you," Rita said. "After all she'd been through herself she ought to've known how it felt."

"She did it anyway. So I shot myself."

"But missed," Christie said. "I was there, don't forget. All you did was shoot off half your ear. My God, blood was flying everywhere. You had to be carried out kicking and screaming, eh, hollering for Annie to come on down and help you, but she never budged."

"She was an old bitch," Belchy said. "She knew how crazy I was about her. I asked her twice to marry me, before she found the body. I would've done anything for her and she knew it, but the old bitch didn't give a shit for me or anyone else. All she wanted was to get upstairs where she could be free of everything and never have to care about anybody again. She didn't care what happened to me or anyone else, she was up in her room like somebody safely dead."

"Sometimes I hate this place," Rita said. "It makes me feel like having a damn good cry."

"I hate this place too," Belchy said, "but somehow I never get away. As long as that woman is up there I'll never be able to move."

"That's stupid," Christie said. "All it takes is a little backbone."

"Of course it's stupid," Belchy said. "But that doesn't change the facts. I'm stuck here, like it or not, until she decides to come down."

V

NOTHING COULD DISTRACT LARRY BOWMAN from mooning over that seabird—not his job in the library, not the coloured liquor ads or Sir Walter Scott, not his tutorial sessions with the local students of the North Island College struggling with their texts and cassette tapes and examinations. Not even the news that a fresh batch of postcards from Preserved Crabbe had arrived at the post office could raise a flicker of interest—his admiration for that foolish giant from the Flats had disappeared. So what if the big ape of a Squatter had been sidetracked onto a commune in the mountains where he'd been lulled into a euphoric stupor by the cigarettes they offered him and almost tricked into forgetting his mission by the habit people had of walking around naked and of sharing everything including their women with visitors? What did Bowman care if he'd been shanghaied in Nanaimo onto a plastic bathtub across the strait to Vancouver, where he'd had to smuggle himself onto a ferry, all his money stolen, in order to get back to the Island? And what difference did it make if a fat woman on a pig farm pulled him in off the road to fix her water tap and refused to let him go until he'd worked the squeaks out of her bedsprings while she sang him obscene lullabies she'd written for her pigs? All of that was exactly what you had to expect when you went off on a chase after a woman you hardly knew and didn't own, so why should anyone care?

Larry Bowman was unable to keep his mind on anything at all except his daydreams about the girl named Raimey. It was obvious that the time had come for him to make his move, show himself, stand up like a man and declare his feelings for that woman. No more fantasies. Though it made his arms go cold with fear and his stomach tighten into a painful knot, it was evident that the time had come for the man of love to become a man of action. All his oldest instincts were to lock up the library and hide, but this newer instinct—this passion that was threatening to make him ill—told him there was no escape. What he would do was still a mystery, but it was clear that it had to be imaginative, aggressive, courageous, and flamboyant—in other words an act worthy of all those lusty heroes who had the advantage of living only between the pages of books, without the less romantic minute-by-minute hazards that lay in wait for the heroes of real-life dramas.

Such as cramps. No hero in any of those books ever got so nervous that he found it necessary to make several painful trips to the bathroom when the clock told him his ladylove was due to pass by the library door any moment on her way to town—his opportunity to approach her for the first time and make his presence and his feelings known. Nor did any of those heroes have to put up with the arrival at the last minute of three of his college students wanting him and his shelf of encyclopedias

THE RESURRECTION OF JOSEPH BOURNE

to solve the confusing puzzle of the jargon of their corres-
pondence lesson. And it was very unlikely, too, that any of
those paper heroes had ever got himself so worked up into a
frantic confusion at the sound of his loved one's approaching
footsteps that he fell on his face going down the steps and bit
his lip, causing great squirts of blood to spray out between the
fingers he held over his mouth.

Fortunately, the seabird did not notice his noisy fall and kept
on going down the road without a break in the rhythm of her
step. Click, click, click. Those high narrow heels. Those shapely
legs. That maddening rocking of the hips. It took several
moments of watching that magnificent walk before Larry
Bowman, lying in the wet, even began to feel the pain in his
mouth.

"Damn it to hell," he said to himself, just loud enough to
alarm the students who'd come out of the library to help him
to his feet.

So Larry Bowman set about the tough job of turning himself
into a lover who would be as irresistible to that seabird as she
was to him. He saw that a transformation from an insignificant
timid librarian into a vibrant and dashing masculine hero was
going to be no small feat, requiring every spark of imagination
and courage he could dredge up from the corners of his
timorous soul.

It would be necessary, for instance, to forget all about Patsy
McKay, the high-school beauty queen with the long legs and
the sensational mouth, laughing in his face. "Are you kidding,
Larry Bowman? With *you*?" It would be a good idea, too, to
push far back to the farthest corners of his head the memory
of Marilyn Mossfield, who'd almost become his wife before he
moved up here to Port Annie. For two years they'd seen each
other almost every night. Movies. Picnics. Shopping. Day-trips
to the mainland. For two years she successfully protected her
precious chastity—"Not before marriage, Larry, you know
better than that"—just as he'd wanted her to, though of course
he did everything in his power to change her mind, just in case.
For two years he turned himself inside out with desire, secretly
buying property, planning the house he would build, hinting
to everybody that there was bound to be a wedding in the
family soon, don't ask him whose.

Then she'd looked out the window of Larry's car on the way
to a movie, and had seen a sailor rolling a cigarette under the

overhang of the General Store, a tall handsome uniform with dark eyes and a mysterious smile. "Stop," she said. "He looks like he needs a ride." In the twenty minutes of highway driving between the General Store and the movie theatre in town, she found out all she needed to know about the stranger, and in the week that followed she wrote Larry the seven-page letter which tried to explain, in her perfumed scribble, just why it was that she couldn't help herself from running away to marry this man of her dreams. After all they'd been through together, she wrote, she hoped that they'd always be friends. In fact, she'd be stricken if he didn't drop in to visit her just whenever he happened to be passing through Halifax and found himself with time on his hands.

If that was the kind of person she was he didn't want her was his way of reacting. But he'd had to move up to Port Annie in order to be able to stand it. And he still spent too much time going over and over that evening in his head, trying to keep himself from putting his foot on the brake pedal and letting the uniform into his car.

As a reader of thousands of books full of heroics, Larry knew that it was possible to achieve love only through acts of incredible valour and terrifying self-sacrifice. That was the one constant you could find between almost all sets of covers. And who was he to hope for anything easier? In order to scrape up the courage that was needed, he would first have to push all that humiliating past right out of sight and forget it. Become a new man: someone who felt differently, dreamed differently, thought of himself in a different way. Not an easy task, but he was sure that it wasn't exactly impossible.

A quick down-island trip was a help. From somewhere in his back rooms a clothing-store clerk brought out an amazing wardrobe that a less-desperate Larry Bowman would never even have tried on—even in the privacy of his own home—let alone bought. But this was no time for conservatism; he took a deep breath and did the unimaginable—came out of that shop wearing clothes he hadn't known existed, except in travel posters: high-heeled boots that added inches to his height and reflected the sky in their shiny black toes; a lacy white full-sleeved shirt with no buttons to do up over his chest, just laces, and a leather jerkin to hang open; pants so tight in the hips he could feel every muscle in his buttocks move while he walked, and bottoms so wide and loose they whipped around his ankles

like a skirt. All he needed now was a whip, the clerk suggested
with a wink. And perhaps a leather patch over one eye. Larry
drew the line at that, but agreed it wouldn't hurt to start a
moustache if he could, and he even let the clerk push his hair
around this way and that until he found a way it looked more
modern and manly. He really wasn't such a bad-looking fellow
after all, the clerk said, and Larry Bowman, looking at himself
in the mirror, was inclined to agree.

Thank goodness, though, that to get back to Port Annie he
had to put on the same old raincoat as before. People wouldn't
see the peacock he'd become, at least for a while. He dreamed,
that night, that the shack in Squatters' Flats went up in flames
and he, of course, was the first one there to rescue the beautiful
seabird, who was trapped inside behind a wall of fire. Just as he
suspected, she was not the least bit miserly about showing him
her gratitude.

People could hardly help noticing the transformation. Who
would ever have guessed that an insignificant man like Larry
Bowman could turn out to be so good-looking after all? Just a
change of clothes and a little determination in his face and
Angela Turner, for one, was ready to call him handsome.
Maybe it was even a good thing he was so shy, she said, it was
a good thing he just didn't know the effect he could have on a
girl. Those eyes he always turned away from you were actually
too beautiful for a man when he raised them up, large and a
little slanted, and with long lashes too. Strange she'd never
noticed it before.

A transformation of an astonishing sort, and yet Larry
Bowman had no real confidence that it would make any difference to the way the seabird felt. After that day in the coffee
shop she'd never again paid him any attention. When she
passed his library she never looked to one side or the other,
never acknowledged his presence, even when he stood out at
the edge of his walk and waited for her. Never gave him any
more attention than the trees she passed, or the telephone poles
and the garbage cans at the side of the road. Clearly, he was
going to have to do more than simply put on his clothes and
stand around in obvious places.

As soon as he had gathered up enough courage, he pressed
his new clothes, rubbed his boots until they shone like marble,
read quickly through two or three of the fiercest, most heroic
love poems from his shelves (and a few pornographic ones as

well), and set out in the drizzle down the road towards Squatters' Flats reciting lines, over and over, to keep from going to pieces and running home. But all of this steeling himself was for nothing, anyway, since Hill Gin and her pack of dogs met him at the foot of the hill and stopped him dead—shoved two shells into her shotgun's barrels and snapped it closed, while her dogs twisted themselves so close around his ankles that he would have fallen off those awkward heels if he'd taken another step. "No one bothers the old man," Hill Gin said, "not while he's healing in there." And only cocked a cheeky eyebrow at him when he said it was the girl he'd come to see. A cheeky eyebrow and a knowing sneer. The crazy brothers Crabbe came out of their floating bunkhouse and ambled down to stare at him, scratching in their whiskers—seven feet tall, the three of them—and guessed aloud that he must have been on his way to a costume party in such a get-up, he had obviously got himself turned down a wrong road. Two women came out of The Paper House (he could smell the steam from the boiling newsprint) and, once they'd discovered who he was, went back inside to come out with a load of overdue books. "We never seem to remember when we're going up that way," one of them said, "so maybe you'll be a hero and take them back for us, before we owe a fortune." And he couldn't help himself, librarian to the core, from taking just a peek inside to see that, yes, they owed a fortune in fines already, which they had no intention of paying, and no money to pay it with if they'd wanted to. It was Dirty Della who rescued him, came down the road past all those other houses with her head cocked to one side, wiping her hands on her blouse, like a farm wife come out to see what was coming up her drive. She led him out of that mess, as if she'd been expecting him for days and could hardly wait to make him feel at home. Led him all the way down the road, yelling at her kids to get lost (which they did—scurrying off into bush or down over logs without a whimper of protest, admirably trained) and right inside her house before he realized that what she had in mind once she'd lifted those library books out of his arms was peeling the skintight pants right off his body and pushing him over towards her bed. A temptation, of course, since he'd already gone to so much trouble to work his courage up, but a fleeting thought of that girl who came in from the sea was all that was needed to bring him to his senses, hoist up his pants, and get out of there. He was horny, yes, but he wasn't blind.

The next day he sat up in the woods, with a clear view of the cabin, waiting for a glimpse of the Peruvian seabird. He said her name to himself, Raimey, Raimey—it was like the name of some exotic jungle bird, or a gorgeous flower—and tried to send down through the air from his head to hers a hundred reasons for leaving that shack, tried to will her out of it. And nearly jumped out of his skin when a sudden crashing in the bush moved towards him (a bear! a cougar!), which turned out to be a sweating red-faced youth in a yellow slicker and hard hat, dripping wet, who burst into the little clearing and looked, for a moment, as startled as Larry was. No one Larry had ever seen before. He was a surveyor goddammit, he said, one of a crew working this piece of land, and some sonofabitch kept pulling up the stakes they put in, was it *him*? Then, satisfied that it wasn't frightened Larry who'd been stalking through the forest undoing every night the work which had been done the day before, he moved crashing off into the trees again, swearing to castrate the bastard if he ever caught him, swearing to grind his skull into a meaty pulp. The noise of the heavy boots and the swishing tree limbs had hardly faded when the seabird did come out of the cabin (though not without pausing to make certain it was locked behind her) and started walking down the shore of the inlet, in the opposite direction from town. With a fishing rod, for Pete's sake, over her shoulder. A sleek black raincoat and a fishing rod. Larry moved downhill to the water's edge, his heart slamming like a fist inside his chest, and followed her a good hundred feet behind. He stopped when she stopped, pulling back into the underbrush while she set herself up beneath an overhanging fir. She was barefoot—no narrow heels on this rocky beach—and those tiny feet, those delicious insteps, were even more indescribably beautiful than he'd hoped. Yet he didn't make his presence known, he watched her all afternoon, he sat back against a damp tangle of root, with wet salal in his face, watching her fish. She arched back— that white curve of throat!—and cast her line in a long clean arc out over the surface of the inlet, far out, a little plop, and started—slowly—to drag that colourful fly back in towards her, the soft squeal of her reel the only sound aside from the rain on the leaves, on the water. She might as well have gone fishing in a sewer, Larry thought, because any fish that wanted her fly would have to swim up through a black surface scum that was a foot thick, before bursting into light. She didn't know a thing about fishing. Yet astonishingly she brought them up, raised them one after the other up through that muck to take her lure, brought fish after fish up from the dark bottom of that inlet to snap at her bait and go flying up into air with it, a thrilling silver curve in the daylight. She cast that line like a spell out over the sea, and stood motionless as a dark goddess on the edge to wait for the spell to take. She raised them up and reeled them in, one after the other, raised them up to reel them in, and stopped only long enough for her quick white hands to do with them whatever it was she did before she stood again to cast her spell another time. Pure goddess, and Larry, hidden in the cold wet brush, was himself spellbound. He felt himself rise every time to her lure and leap with it, he felt all his body pulled towards her again and again, sliding through water, towards her and back and towards her again, completely in her power, just as he suspected the whole world was that came into contact with her.

The next day when she set out it was without a rod and he followed her all the way down the inlet this time, to the open sea. There, in a small bay where the breakers spread out like foamy lace on the level sand, she stood barefoot amongst the sea-carved driftwood and stranded intertidal life to look out across the waves into the haze that obscured the horizon. What will you raise up here? And Larry half expected sunken ships and old whales to burst free into light. But nothing surfaced, and she stepped back as far as the nearest log, unbuttoned her raincoat, and let it drop.

She was naked. Totally. Her skin, though cinnamon-dark, appeared to have the nearly transparent delicacy of petals. His face, surprised, flushed. All of his insides dropped and immediately rose. He sat. Larry had never seen a woman completely naked before, except in pictures. And nothing in those magazines had prepared him for this exquisite beauty, or for this breathlessness. Not even the magnificent breasts in the ice cubes of the liquor ads had prepared him for this moment. He felt dizzy and had to close his eyes.

Yet he revived in time to see her walk across the sand and into the sea; that waist; those side-kicking hips; those full legs and slender ankles. Right into foam, into low-breaking waves, into the full sweep of the sea, where she turned, briefly, and faced him just long enough to back into an enormous wave that broke over her and swept her forward with it onto the sand and left her there with the moonsnail shells and the sand dollars and the broken shreds of feather boa kelp. She went back again, tossing that jet-black hair—wet now, and heavy. He followed her, out onto the sand at first so she could see him, hardly able to breathe, amazed at his own courage, and waited until she'd seen him standing above her coat and lifted her hand to him as if she'd been waiting for this to happen, and then he took off the leather jerkin and kicked off the boots and shrugged the shirt up over his head and peeled down the skin-tight pants, until all of his things were lying with her raincoat in the sand around his feet and he was as naked as she was in this chill air that was somehow warm, and started walking out towards her hardly able to believe that this was him, this was Larry Bowman, this was himself burst free at last of those clothes and that timidity and all the years of hiding, and striding now across the sand and into the foam that bubbled around his feet and out into the ice-cold waves where she stood waiting for him just as she'd stood yesterday waiting for those fish she'd raised, while the sea rose and fell around her legs.

They swam together, that's all. Side by side. In that incredible cold. Out into free-flowing sea, then riding the waves and running hands-clasped together until swept off their feet and thrown against one another, away from each other, rolled over and under one another, turned and turned and spun into laughing turmoil. They swam together, that's all, and even Larry couldn't believe that was all that happened until they'd already walked out onto the sand again. She looked down to where it was obvious that even the ice-cold sea hadn't put out all of his fire, then smiled as if what she saw was an enormous compliment. A single lifted eyebrow, though, a certain twinkle in her eye, reminded him that a knight was more than his sword. Once he was into his clothes again they walked hand-in-hand back up the inlet nearly as far as the Flats. Then near a fallen tree she stopped, put one hand up against the side of his face for a chill moment, smiled, and left him there alone.

He got all the way back to his library, nearly sightless from the blood that pounded behind his eyes, before he realized that they had not done any of the things together that he'd dreamed of doing, none of the touching and caressing and thrusting and groaning that he'd hoped for. His groin ached, his insides hurt, his head throbbed. This was worse than before, when everything had been only fantasy, this was worse than he had even been able to imagine anything could be. The wet greenish buildings of Port Annie looked foreign; he'd stepped out of their world into something else and knew that he couldn't return, like someone heavily drugged who feels a thick invisible extra skin between himself and the rest of the world, setting himself apart, giving everything the frightening unpredictable air of the unreal.

Yet he went with her again, still ripe and swollen with hope, this time up into the mountains behind town. Not his idea, he would have stayed behind closed doors all day trying to adjust to this new thing, or gone down to the Flats to follow her seaward again, hoping; but she came to him this time, knocked on his door, and asked if he felt like a walk. Flustered, confused, he said "Yes" and "Just a minute" and found his old plaid mackinaw to put on over the same plain loose insignificant clothes he'd worn for years—the *macho* outfit in a heap on the floor beside his bed, maybe he'd never wear those things again. They walked uphill, slowly—even that wonderful walk of hers was reduced to strained climbing on these steep hills—and this time she talked. A strange town, she said, that would rather have an old man safely dead than face the implications that his return would suggest, where everyone treated her like some kind of foreign creature, not even human, when as far as she could see there was not a person in the place who wasn't as foreign as she was, every one of them came from somewhere else. And yes, he said, it was a crazy town, completely nuts, but she mustn't forget that living up here made people twice as suspicious as they might have been if they'd stayed somewhere else. And she shouldn't forget, either, that nearly everyone in this place had come here to forget some other place, and the sight of a mysterious beautiful woman like herself walking amongst them made them uneasy. Naturally they were going to treat her with suspicion, it couldn't be avoided.

She stopped and watched an eagle soar, then cocked her head to listen to something—grouse perhaps—thumping or fluttering in the bush. Then she moved on, and he did too, beside her, until they reached the top of the first long, slow rise and could stand on roadside gravel to look out over miles of mountains and valleys, all logged, all whiskered with black charred stumps and tangled slash, and flushed over with pink fireweed patches. Black stumps and fireweed, miles and miles of logged-off desolate landscape, and every scalped knoll made even more ridiculous by a thin fringe of trees left standing at the top, a few feathers. "An Indian headdress," she said. But he explained that those trees were left there on purpose by the logging companies, in order to drop their seeds and start another forest growing up along the slopes of all those hills. Believe it or not, he said, the whole ruined world had been reforested, he'd even helped once when he first moved here; he and the rest of the crew had set out with millions of tiny seedling firs and hemlock to plant every so far apart in that tangled mess. If she looked she could see them pushing up through the burnt limbs and charred windfalls, nearly as high now as the fireweed, just look at all those drooped-over lacy tops. But she only nodded, as if what he'd said was exactly what she'd have expected, here or anywhere, and looked off somewhere across those hills into the grey cloud that had descended to drop this rain on them and to obscure the farther mountains and the snowy peaks of the mainland mountains which he knew could be seen if ever the sun shone again and the cloud lifted. Did he think, she said, that the town was ready yet for the return of Joseph Bourne?

He looked at her face, the petal-soft skin wet with rain, the lips parted just enough to reveal a glimpse of those beautiful teeth. He saw her naked, again, like yesterday, and felt some of that temporary courage return. The town would probably breathe a sigh of relief, he said, turning to walk back down the hill. People were beginning to think he was really dead after all. But as far as he was concerned it didn't matter, Bourne meant nothing at all to him, but it would be a relief to see her shake herself free from the old man's attentions and have a little more time for somebody else.

At the bottom of the steep hill, when she stopped, he put his hand on the side of her face, lightly, as she'd done to him, and expected her to step closer, perhaps even to press her face against his chest. But she pushed his hand away. He could tell them, she said, that by tomorrow they'd be seeing Joseph Bourne again. As for herself, she would be long gone by the time the old man got as far as the town. She'd done everything she'd come here to do. She was off to other places, other people.

She smiled the smile that made the world lurch for him every time. A smile which he saw now was not only woman-beautiful to an unspeakable degree, as he'd always known it was, but another kind of beautiful, too, that had nothing at all to do with being a desirable woman. This was some other quality that had been there all along, of course, though less immediate, some other quality that had made her capable of raising up Bourne just as she'd raised up those fish from the dark bottom of the sea. And he knew, suddenly, that it would be the loss of that other thing he saw in her, more than the loss of Raimey-the-woman, which he was likely to mourn from this moment of their parting for the rest of his life.

The rest of his *terrible* life, he thought, alone at the library door. He'd come close to something and lost it and was more alone now than ever before. The pale green silent rainy buildings of Port Annie sat crowded together up the slope of the mountain, under the low grey ceiling of cloud that had sat on them for all of this summer, and he couldn't imagine that in any of those buildings there was someone who felt as desolate as he did, as abandoned and tossed-up, as useless and foolish.

Of course he did not know that at that moment Jenny Chambers, up in that top row closest to the cloud, was flat on her back with problems of her own, a nervous wreck. She had no idea of Larry Bowman's transformation, or of his adventures with the seabird, or of his new and painful abandonment. She lay on her bed with the blind pulled down, with damp cloths on her forehead, with none of her new clothes on at all—only an old slip she'd had for years, and not a thing under it. What was the use? Why bother getting dressed in the first place when all it did was encourage people to show their true colours and snub you?

Now that those three ex-friends had betrayed her she'd decided she was aiming too low, they were just too common for her. A well-travelled woman like herself, with an exotic background in show business, living with a Mill foreman—she had just been too humble to recognize her proper place, that was the problem, she needed to look for her friends among her own kind—those world-travelled educated wives in the Down Front houses along the inlet, the management people. Well cripes, hadn't she been invited to that Erma Cripps's house the once, for bridge? The only reason they'd never asked her back was because she hadn't had enough sense to lose the game. That, and the fact her Slim at the time was still a labourer at the Mill, no foreman yet. What she needed to do now was invite Erma and her bigshot husband up to dinner and pretty soon she'd be as thick as thieves with that whole Down Front row, these other excuses for friends could stew in their low-class juices. She was climbing the ladder a little.

Yet she still hadn't quite mustered the nerve. What if Erma Cripps—her last hope—turned down the invitation? There was no use asking any of the others after that, those babes were as thick as thieves down there, they did all their thinking in unison, whatever one did they all did the same. If Erma Cripps, that snooty bitch, gave Jenny Chambers the brushoff, the others would follow suit. And then, what if she *did* accept? Cripes, how could she get all the repairs done that would have to be done around here? The house was falling apart. And what kind of menu could she possibly dream up for people who'd lived all over the world, eaten in French restaurants in Paris, dined out in Spain? How would her new wardrobe stack up against those gowns that Erma Cripps went down to San Francisco every year to pay out-of-this-world prices for? And worst of all—she broke out in a sweat at the thought—what would she do with the eight rotten brats? Chloroform them? Pay them to stay out in the streets? They were bound to show up in the middle of the meal and get into a fight, ruin everything. Make her look like a slob. No, she just couldn't face it, not yet. She hadn't the courage yet to take on that Down Front group.

Oh, the delicious self-pity! She might as well stay here in bed, just fade away and die, she was a person who was dead anyway—written off by everyone in town—no one would miss her. Everyone, she thought, would be better off if she left—not that they'd really notice. If they did notice they'd have a big party and celebrate: that has-been old stripper with not a friend in the world was gone at last. Jenny Chambers, who didn't belong anywhere. She might as well lock herself up right now, like that Fat Annie Fartenburg down in the hotel.

When Slim came in to sit by her bed she knew she should try to cheer up. But not even the fact that he'd torn himself away from his beloved machines for her sake was enough to lift her spirits. All it did was make her feel even more like an invalid, a complete failure, a has-been. She pouted. "What do you want?"

"I was thinking," he said. "Sometimes I wish I was still back on shift work. Up in the digesters."

Her heart nearly stopped. "Give up being foreman?" She saw him sliding back down the ladder even faster than he'd gone rocketing up. What would her chances be then?

He put a hand on hers. Rough and hard as lumber. "I'm not talking about what I will do. I'm just remembering the shift work, back when you first moved in. You used to come out in the night, when I was on graveyard shift, and bring me a snack."

Yes, and she could smell the rotten stink of that place right now if she wanted to. And feel that damp heat.

"You had to sneak past the watchman to do it," he said, "but nobody seemed to mind. All the men used to look forward to it and ask what I had that made me such a lucky bastard. The only woman that ever did it, Jen, snuck into the Mill with a small feast every night and looked like a million dollars to boot."

Poor Slim. She took off his cowboy hat, tossed it into a corner, and put one hand on either side of his narrow head. "Those guys were just hoping I'd go into one of my acts for them. Thought they'd get a free peek at the goods."

He grinned, and leaned down to kiss her on the mouth. "Maybe so. But mostly they were jealous. Who ever went to that trouble to bring them a lunch at three in the morning? How many of them had a beautiful woman who dressed up like that just for a ten-minute snack?"

"Are you trying to tell me I've turned into a frump? Or just that I don't care enough to go traipsing out to that Mill any more with a bucket of fancy sandwiches?"

He sat up, offended. "Forget it. I wasn't trying to tell you nothing." He got up to leave.

She turned away, faced the drawn blind, and waited for the sound of the door slamming. Back to his precious machines, he was probably relieved to get out of the way. He hated scenes, he hated self-pity, he hated getting tangled in feelings. A crescent wrench and a differential he could deal with, don't confuse him with human emotions.

Who knew what might have become of her if she'd had the sense not to stay here? A big success maybe, a star of her own show by now, in Las Vegas. She could've become the greatest stripper on the continent, she had the potential. Cripes, by now she'd be named to Jenny Lee's Stripper Hall of Fame, along with Sally Rand and those other babes, no question she would've become as good as they were. And she'd seen the quality of stripper they were putting out these days, no class at all, the Kick-and-Kill had tried a couple since Jenny'd retired. One girl came out on the stage, bored before she'd even started, bumped her knee a few times to the beat of the music,

then quick as you please tore all of her clothes off, like someone in a hurry. No art to that, and not even much of a body
once those clothes were off. Jenny could have shown her a
thing or two, about movement and the art of teasing. She
could've become one of the world's greatest, instead of rotting
here in this rainy town. Waiting for something to lift her up, if
it dared. All she had the energy for was thumbing through the
scrapbook from under her bed, pages and pages of articles
about strippers, some even with photographs. Dancers who
hadn't quit. And one page with a picture of herself in action,
a long-legged beauty in sequins and fur—a scared beginner, it
was her first night in public. Flaming Jenny, before the fire had
been stomped out and buried.

Brooding around in her house, when she should have been
looking after those yard-apes of hers, thought Rosa Magnani,
who could see the Chamber-Potts house through her bedroom
window. "Something is wrong up there, I know it," she told
her husband on the telephone. "That Slim, he comes in and out
from work, he shovels a little the mud in the yard, he starts up
the motors one after another of all his machines and then shuts
them off, and those kids they run wild. But no Jenny, no Jenny
in sight for days. Something is wrong, I tell you."

But Papa Magnani had to hang up, because here was Mr.
Manku coming into the rec centre again, just in time for his
swimming lesson, accompanied by a whole crowd of East
Indians Papa Magnani couldn't remember ever seeing before.

"My family," Mr. Manku said, and introduced them.
Harbans, his wife—a tall old frowning woman with breasts in
her silky costume as large and thrusting as Mr. Manku's belly,
the brown pigment apparently wearing off her wrinkly face,
leaving patches of pink. His eldest son, Raminder, who worked
at the Mill. And his wife. His son Gininder, a tall handsome
man with round black eyes, "who also works at the Mill, and
his wife". His son Ravinder, an uncomfortable-looking middle-
aged man, already greying, "who like his brothers works at the
Mill". And his son Joginder, a grinning friendly youth, who
unlike his brothers did not work at the Mill at all, because he
was a practising Sikh and refused to wear a hard hat over his
turban. And all these, Mr. Manku said with a sweep of his
hand, were his grandchildren. Including, he said, his beautiful
grandson Kamaljit. He scooped up the small boy whose face,
Papa Magnani had to admit, was indeed the most beautiful he

had ever seen—more beautiful even than the photograph he had seen of his own grandson, Marcos, who lived in Italy. "Named of course for me," Mr. Manku said.

The small child smiled angelically at Papa Magnani—Santa Maria, a heartbreaker already!—then squirmed around to look at the women, one of whom broke away from the others and rushed forward to rescue him from his grandfather, while throwing accusing looks at Papa Magnani.

"Now, go, go!" Mr. Manku said, and herded them all back to the door. "Go, go!" And pointed out to them where they were expected to sit, under the plastic rain-cover, in the bleachers. Most of the family started to move, but his wife clung to his arm, clearly afraid that he'd taken leave of his senses; she had to be shaken loose.

Papa Magnani saw the Chamber-Potts kids—kicked out of the rec centre only half an hour ago and drenched from the rain—take one look at Mr. Manku's family and start to follow in a pack, towards the bleachers. The insults were already bubbling at their lips, dancing in their eyes. Oh mamma mia, what Papa Magnani would like to do to those miserable excuses for humanity. Teach them a lesson on their backsides with a stick, get the police after them, drag them all together up the hill to their door and insist that either Slim Potts or that Jenny strip-teaser punish them right then and there.

He followed Mr. Manku into the change room. "One day, Mr. Manku, you must come with me after your lesson to my house for some coffee or a glass of wine, to meet my Rosa, now that I've met your family. My Rosa, of course, she cannot leave her bed."

"Yes, yes." Mr. Manku was paying no attention. He took off his shirt and handed it to Papa Magnani, like a great actor getting ready for a performance—a great actor used to servants. Soon he was stark naked—all his clothes folded over Papa Magnani's arm—and rubbed his huge belly proudly. There was a strange mysterious smile on his face the whole time he was stepping into his trunks and pulling them up— Papa Magnani had never seen such dignity in all his life—and an even deeper, more mysterious smile when he pulled that rubber swim-cap over his head and snapped it under his chin.

Soon he was ready. Papa Magnani himself had become so excited his stomach was all fluttery. He followed Mr. Manku to the door, where Mr. Manku took a deep breath before striding out onto the deck and shaking the instructor's hand, as he had done every evening this summer. He stepped down into the water at the shallow end of the pool.

Papa Magnani heard someone in the bleachers shriek— probably the old woman—then a confusion of gobbling voices. Telling her to shut up, no doubt. The Manku family was strung out across the top two rows of the bleachers, in the shadows, and the Chamber-Potts kids were sitting on the bottom seats, some facing the pool, some turned to stare open-mouthed at the people above them.

Mr. Manku faced the deep end of the pool, straightened his shoulders, stuck out his great belly, and started to walk. He heard his wife squeal, even under his cap—she probably thought he'd arranged for her to witness an elaborate suicide— and only smiled more mysteriously than before. Do not worry, he thought, for you're about to see how your husband has made a great and symbolic gesture. When the water reached his knees he paused, and realized that he was the only actor in this drama. The other students had all got out of the pool and crouched down against the fence, with the instructors, to watch. He was aware of the bright light, streaming down on him through the slanted rain from high on the posts at the pool corners. He was aware of the dark silent world outside the fence as an enormous audience, holding its breath. He was the centre of everything. Kamaljit Manku, who had always been afraid of water, who had huddled in that small community of Indians for safety all these years, who had done nothing at all before this—except sign those citizenship papers—as a gesture towards belonging in this new world. It had taken him so many years to put his foot in this pool. As the water climbed his thighs, he thought of Harbans—how very beautiful and how frightened she'd been when they'd arrived, how terrified she'd been for him when they'd moved to this town, how nervous she had remained for herself living among these strange people with their strange ways. "Let me calm your fears." When the water reached his waist he thought of his four grown sons, four handsome men who (except for Joginder) wanted more than anything else to spend their money on fancy cars and trips to the city and American hamburgers and all the other things that would make them just the same as everyone else, but who saved their money instead for a house of their own and hadn't in all these years brought a single non-Indian friend inside the house to meet their father. Proud, proud of him when they were together with other Punjabis; ashamed of him when it came to the people they worked with, the people they knew were the real people of the town. And when the water reached the top of his belly he thought of little Kamaljit, his grandson, who would never in all his life forget this wonderful moment when he saw his grandfather float face-down in water.

Mr. Manku leaned forward into the water, stretched out his arms, felt his body rise to the surface. For several moments he floated out over the deep end of the pool with his face down in the water, only the back of his head and his shoulders and his big buttocks above the surface. He thought of his family in the bleachers, astounded by his performance, no doubt bursting with pride.

But when he came up for air, something was wrong. His son Gininder was inside the fence, crouched down at the edge of the pool, shouting something at Mr. Manku. Raminder too, looking fiercely angry, was beside him, also shouting. Mr. Manku was so alarmed that he forgot how to conduct himself, felt himself go under, gulped water, and had to be rescued by the instructor with her aluminum pole. "Get out of there, old man!" Gininder, furious, roughly helped Mr. Manku up onto the deck, yanked off his cap. "Get out of there. Can't you see what you've caused?" And Raminder too: "Trouble, trouble. What have you done to us?"

Mr. Manku saw his wife, wailing and tearing her hair, in the centre of a jabbering cluster of daughters-in-law and children outside the fence. He saw Joginder holding on to one of those small children that played around the pool, beating him on the head and body with his free hand. He saw Ravinder engaged in a shouting match with one of the instructors, waving his arms and making wild threats. He saw Papa Magnani running this way, shaking his head, wringing his hands.

"What is it?" Mr. Manku said. "What has happened? Has something happened to my little Kamaljit?"

His two oldest sons started yelling again, their voices too loud for the words to be heard, so Mr. Manku just bowed his head until they'd run down, then looked up to Papa Magnani for an explanation.

"It was those children," Papa Magnani said, still shaking his head, wringing his hands worse than ever. "Your family, Mr. Manku, your family took offence."

"The butt of children's jokes," Gininder said.

"Making fools of us all!' Raminder said.

"It's a great wonder that our mother did not have a heart attack and die on the spot."

"Come home with us, please. Before the whole town is laughing. You have been the cause of violence—Joginder has gone wild and beaten all those kids he could catch, and Ravinder has kicked one of them in the face, blood everywhere. You get yourself dressed and come home immediately."

Mr. Manku told his sons to let the children go, to take the women home. He would be along soon after them, he said, but he would go home alone.

"Stupid ignorant kids," Papa Magnani said. "Not a brain in their heads, no manners at all, nobody should pay attention to a word they say, they don't know any better, just dragged up by parents who don't care. Not a word they said was worth listening to, Mr. Manku, just the kind of brainless insults that kids can make up—nothing personal at all—just the kind of thing they might pick up from listening to stupid parents or equally stupid friends at school. Stupid thoughtless words, nothing important enough to spoil a wonderful day, certainly nothing to make a man wonder if he'd made a mistake."

Mr. Manku stood where he was—on the concrete deck at the deep end of the pool—and waited until his family had all been herded into cars which roared out of the parking lot and up the hill, until Papa Magnani had finished with his long apologies and silly explanations and gone back inside the rec centre, and the instructors had gone back inside their little room where he could see through the glass that they had three of those Chamber-Potts children prisoner. Then he breathed in as deeply as he could, pulled his shoulders back, and walked down the length of the pool, on the side farthest from the bleachers, without looking to the left or to the right. When his own instructor—that young girl who'd done everything she'd known how to do and finally got him floating with his face in the water—when she stepped outside the little hut and started to say something ("Please, Mr. Manku, you mustn't . . ."), he shook his head without looking at her, waved her away with the slightest movement of his hand. Inside the change room he stripped off his bathing suit, towelled himself, put on the clothes which Papa Magnani had folded so carefully into the square box of a locker. Then he went outside again and began the uphill walk in the rain towards his home.

Papa Magnani watched the figure walking in the rain, and shook his head. A terrible day. But his telephone rang and, "Guess what?" It was his wife again, his Rosa. "I can see it from here. The surprise."

Papa Magnani held out the phone to scowl at it. "What? What are you talking about? We've just had a tragedy here and what is this that you're babbling about?"

"The mayor's surprise, it's arrived, I can see it right now from my bed with no trouble at all, as big as a house!"

Rosa Magnani was not the only one to notice the new addition to the Port Annie skyline. When Mrs. Landyke phoned to tell Jenny to look out her window, Jenny was still lying on that bed feeling sorry for herself. The phone rang eleven times —impossible to ignore—and Mrs. Landyke's voice shouted at her, "Just turn around, Jen, look out the window. What do you see?"

What she saw, at the foot of the town, was a giant cactus— thirty or forty feet tall—sitting in the rain in a barge full of sand tied up to the little wharf. The thing was as high as the hotel, higher—one thick trunk growing up out of the sand, with a ring of shorter branches stretched up around it from a point somewhere about the level of the lower hotel windows.

"I'm going down for a closer look," Mrs. Landyke shouted into the phone. "Grab your umbrella and join me, Jen, this ought to be something to see!"

But Jenny had barely put the telephone down when it rang again—the swimming instructor calling from the pool. Those rotten brats had really done it this time, not only made a nuisance of themselves the way they always did but insulted people as well, and caused a lot of trouble. "Next time we see those kids around the pool at all we call the police," the instructor said. "Don't bother telling me about it," Jenny said, "just tie them up and dump them in the chuck." She slammed the telephone down again, peeled the silver paper off a new stick of gum, then started putting on some clothes—nothing special, just the first thing she could grab out of the closet. Going out for another walk was the last thing in the world she wanted, but if she didn't go down to find out what was up, she could be sure that none of those others would bother to tell her about it.

A small crowd had already gathered when she got there, people in the square and down onto the dock. Jeremy Fell, slouched in his doorway. And Ian McCarthy—that whiskery sea otter—Jenny couldn't look at him without imagining him on his back, eating his supper off his chest, floating around in the ocean. Where was his traitorous wife? Mrs. Landyke was over by the delicatessen, gesturing for Jen to join her there under the overhang, as if the old bag only had to crook her finger for Jen to come crawling. Why should she stand there? Jenny wanted to go right down on the dock for a decent look. The men standing in the open door of the Kick-and-Kill stretched their necks to look up at that freakish sight—forty feet of desert cactus soaring up above the buildings of the town. Someone in nearly every hotel window, too, laughing at the sight. And Larry What's-his-name, the librarian, was down on the dock looking as if his world had fallen apart. Biting his nails off and spitting them out into the rain.

"That big thing," someone yelled out to Jenny as she passed, "it looks like it's giving us all the finger!"

Of course he was right. The biggest obscene gesture in the world. All the fingers pointed up, but the middle one, the trunk, soared above everything else. Grotesque was what it was. Even in this mood, she could see that the inlet was beautiful in comparison. Everything was green, even the dark water which mirrored the green mountain. The tide was in, full and calm, and didn't smell of the Mill, or the rotting muck that stank up the beaches when the tide was out. That cactus couldn't have looked more out of place, or ridiculous.

Mayor Weins was right out at the end of the wharf supervising a pair of carpenters down on their knees hammering a few boards together. He was dressed in his Dieter Fartenburg costume today—a fat logger in plaid shirt and torn jeans, laced boots and a bushy false beard, his face red with excitement. He seemed to have worked himself up into a frenzy, giving orders to those carpenters and entertaining his audience at the same time.

"Take a look at that beauty, all the way from Arizona— make sure those nails are strong enough now, better put an extra one or two up in this corner—this thing will grow up to fifty feet, a living statue, right in front of your eyes, everyone in town gets the benefit of it, and just you wait until word of it spreads, there'll be tourists pouring in to this place from all over the country—take it easy with that board, you don't want to scrape the letters off the sign."

Did they think it rained too much in this town? he shouted. Did they think they lived in the arctic, a bunch of Eskimos? Did they think this place would grow nothing but rainforest jungle? Well, history was about to be made. This beauty they saw towering above them was going to be the salvation of them all, no kidding either. Just wait and see what a difference it made.

Larry Bowman moved up to stand under Jenny's umbrella. "It looks like an overgrown hatrack to me."

Jenny snorted. He was right. A hatrack for giants.

"In the spring there'll be great big flowers growing on it, wait and see," the mayor said. "And fruit that looks like melons by next summer. Back where this thing comes from, the Indians use the ribs for building their houses—but don't let that give you any ideas," he said to the carpenters at his feet. "No eyeing this up as a source of free lumber, you'll be the first we suspect if it disappears!"

Weins laughed, "Just joking, just joking!", then swung right around and leaned as far back as he dared in order to see all the way to the top. By the time he turned to his audience again, shaking his head and ready to deliver still more in the way of a speech, someone had already spotted Bourne.

Necks stretched. Heads turned. Was it really him? Larry Bowman's heart started to pound. There was the old man all right, coming this way through the wet, but he was definitely alone. No sign of the girl, she'd meant what she said. Just that old man all alone on the road, his makeshift plastic cape flapping and popping behind him, his long black stick cutting arcs and loops in the air like a conductor's baton.

Jenny's elbow nudged at Larry. "I've got this urge to go up and touch him, to see if he's flesh and blood."

But no one touched. If it wasn't flesh that hung on his ancient bones they'd never know; if it wasn't blood that pumped through those veins it was something else that did the job as well. Or better, they didn't want to know for sure. An old man come back to life was mystery enough without raising any other kinds of doubt. What seemed body could be the substance of soul, what seemed blood-life could be the anima-tion of pure spirit, it wouldn't matter. And if Ian McCarthy or someone had gone up to the old man now and passed his hand through that body without encountering a material thing to stop it, no one would have been more than a little surprised.

George Beeton headed into a coughing fit that started out as only a tickle but got louder and louder in that strange silence which had descended on the crowd until poor George was doubled up, with his red face between his knees, choking and drooling and struggling to catch his breath. He got out of there, scrambled wheezing up to the hotel, where there would be a washroom he could hide in until he'd got himself under control.

So here was Bourne the restored, Bourne the newly raised as wet as anyone else in this rain, alive and moving in just as much of a hurry as he'd always done whenever he'd come up from the inlet to do his show at the radio station in the hotel. In a hurry, but something was different: he was using that stick to stir up the air, to test the walls of the buildings, to poke at the drowning grass and prod the drooping shrubs that grew beside the gravel ramp to the dock. No ragged kimonos flapped around his knees; wool tweed pants were stuffed inside his rubber boots, and sweater on top of sweater bulged beneath that plastic cape.

For a moment, everyone was quiet. Then someone shouted, "Well, you fooled them!" An edge of hysteria in his voice, whoever it was. "We thought you'd kicked the bucket but you showed us."

The old man paused when he saw so many people watching him. For a moment it appeared as if he might be frightened off, he prepared to turn and run. But suddenly he raised a clenched fist above his head and laughed—the first time anyone had ever seen such a thing. For a second they held their breaths— who did he think he was, a victorious gladiator, or what? But he doubled over in a deep bow, sweeping his arm across like an actor acknowledging applause, and everyone knew he was making fun of himself. He didn't want to be welcomed back from the grave with too much solemnity. After all, hadn't he played a joke on death? The crowd burst into laughter, and gladly gave him his applause—if he didn't want them to take him seriously, they'd be more than relieved to comply. Larry thought he saw a mischievous glint in the old man's eyes—even at this distance—as if he were thinking of shaking up those ancient bones in a comic dance. But instead he chose to move in closer and gaze on every face with deliberate care, one after the other, as if they all held some importance for him now and needed to be singly thanked. Silence replaced the outburst, or something like silence: the steady hiss of the rain that fell on

the pavement and on the plastic coats and on the plank deck of
the wharf. No one moved. Larry felt his heart speed up as he
watched that old man's face turn slowly past them all to take
in every person with a steady look. And then to let his curious
gaze go up the trunk of that immigrant cactus.

"Welcome home," someone blurted nervously. Then giggled,
afraid of sounding silly.

Welcome home? The old man raised a bushy eyebrow as if
he believed that cactus to be some kind of gift they'd imported
just for him. If this were a joke, he was more than ready to
share in a laugh.

"Saguarus!" the mayor shouted. "You're looking at the
future of this town."

Bourne tugged at his ear and grinned. He peered at the wet
sand that filled the barge, and rested two fingers against his
bottom lip. His gaze came up again, and locked on Larry
Bowman's for a moment, two eyes frozen on two, a silence.
Was he daring the librarian to join him in a rich full-bodied
laugh at all this nonsense? Larry couldn't be sure but he felt
himself move forward past the others until he was in the space
where Joseph Bourne, grinning, stood alone. This man was
more than just alive, he was nearly bursting. What had that
seabird done?

"Yes," Bourne said, in his deep radio-announcer's voice,
"let's go inside and shake off some of this rain." One hand
grasped Larry's arm and urged him uphill towards the hotel.
"Home!" The old man chuckled, and shook his head. " 'Welcome home,' that woman said, as if I'd actually belonged here
once." The black stick described a circle in the air, then jabbed
at a clod of grass the rain had washed up out of the ground.
"Our roots grow somewhere else, Larry Bowman, and that's a
fact. Our real roots grow upward, no one could ever find a
home on *this* mountainside, or under those flimsy roofs. We
aren't trees, that anchor themselves in earth."

"Wait! Wait!"

Mayor Weins hurried up the slope from the wharf, puffing
noisily. "Let me welcome you too, Mr. Bourne." With his hand
outstretched he shouldered Larry aside, still grinning as if he
hadn't noticed the way the librarian lost his balance and nearly
fell. "Where's Charlie Reynolds? Tell him to get out here
quick, I want a picture of the two of us together for the paper.
Wonderful to see you, Bourne, you're looking fit as a fiddle.

Just step over this way a little bit." He dragged the old man over into a better light, best friends reunited at last, one arm across the back of the old man's shoulders holding him rigid and close. "We'll get the cactus in the background." Reynolds looked up from his camera. "Impossible, Weins. Just take a look at the size of that blasted thing."

"Then get as much as you can."

At that moment the carpenters raised their sign and began to nail it to the side of the barge.

CANADA'S LARGEST NATURAL-GROWING CACTUS
Port Annie Saguarus

"There," Weins said. "Isn't that something? Take your picture now."

As soon as the camera had clicked, the mayor's smile died, the old man was pushed away. "Now let me get back to that barge, this is a big day for this town, come on, Reynolds, I want plenty of photos taken of that thing from every angle, from all over the town. Don't be cheap with the film, take it in colour, every way you can think of, you take it."

Bourne looked at Larry Bowman and laughed. "What luck," he said, "to be welcomed back from the grave by one of the natural wonders of the world!"

Someone, overhearing, wanted to know if he was talking about the cactus or the mayor.

With the old man's hand on his arm, Larry pushed in through the glass doors of the hotel. Where were they going? He didn't know. Maybe Bourne felt like a cup of coffee, that's all, maybe he just wanted to go down into the radio station and visit the studio where he'd come face to face with the girl, maybe he intended to register in one of the rooms, move out of his shack. It didn't matter. What Larry Bowman was waiting for—never giving up, not now—was some message that the seabird may have left him, some goodbye word that she'd asked the old man to deliver. Why would Joseph Bourne have picked him out of all that crowd to hang onto if not to get him alone for a while and pass on some farewell words, maybe even mention some plans for meeting again in the future? Once raised, Larry Bowman would not be easily put down again. After all, it was only in modern novels that believers were always made to look like fools, with empty hands. In the poems and heroic romances that Bowman read, hoping was not considered to be a crime.

OF THE BATTLE OF LIFE AND DEATH IN ITS NEW DISGUISE;
OF MRS. BARNSTONE'S AMBITIOUS EPIC POEM AND
THE PROMISED DESCENT OF FAT ANNIE
(GOD OF THIS WORLD)
AT LAST,
WITH CALAMITIES FOLLOWING,
OR,

The New Man

SEVERAL MORE WEEKS had to pass before some people could accept the fact that the seabird had gone. "Honest to Pete, I just can't stand it," George Beeton announced. "What'll I do without that walk of hers to keep me alive?" He used to wake up with a smile on his face every morning, knowing he'd see her go past his garage at least once in the day, but now she had gone he didn't even want to get out of his bed. He pulled down his blinds and stayed put.

And Larry Bowman, as everyone knew, had been driven back to his books, a shaken and heartbroken man. A timid recluse, by the looks of him now, he seldom poked his nose out the library door. Lord, the men of this place had just fallen apart, according to Rita Rentalla. A lot of weak-kneed romantics, with one-track minds, their brains were all down in their groins. Let them suffer!

Of course she changed her tune just a little the day the good-looking stranger came into town. Her pulse raced, her throat flushed, her heart seemed to be thumping too fast. And naturally none of this had anything to do with the white Porsche he drove, low and sleek as a skateboard, nor did it have anything to do with the thousand-dollar suit that he wore or the coloured fire that flashed off the rings on his hand. A tall handsome man with a mouth full of teeth, a jacket full of muscles, and eyes that made you feel naked, he was a lecher for sure and no doubt an arrogant rooster, but—oh well—she freshened her lipstick and set herself up where she could follow his every move. It wasn't too often you got to observe such a savoury hunk in action.

The savoury hunk walked every street in the town, he didn't miss a thing. He parked his Porsche at one side of the square, put on a belted raincoat, then walked the length of the waterfront end to end, hardly noticing the rain that streamed down his face. He paused long enough on the dock to give the cactus an admiring smile, and stopped in the gravel pit to scratch

147

his head over the tree-stranded boat. He climbed every street like an athlete, all the way to the top of the town, where he could see everything below him, including the inlet and Squatters' Flats and the facing green mountain, and could see everything above him as well, including the second-growth brush and the gravel scars left by the slides. He strolled along all of the cross streets, inspecting the lawns with their drowned grass and their adornments of starfish and shells, examining the cars left with flat tires and slide-damaged bodies in yards, marvelling at the noisy incessant squawking of the thousands of Steller's jays which had descended on the town this fall from all up and down the coast, jays in everyone's yard, like a plague of too much life, too much colour and excitement and noise. He flashed those teeth at the children who played in the fast-running ditches, as if he were bursting with some gift he intended to offer but couldn't announce just yet for a while.

Eva McCarthy choked when he came into sight: a movie actor at least! Look at that cleft in his chin, those dimples, look at those long hard legs, and where else could you get hair the colour of wheat except in the Hollywood sun? Naturally she ducked so he wouldn't see her gawking out the window, and only stood up when she was sure he'd gone past. But she came up too soon, he hadn't gone past; he gave her a quick salute, the impertinent devil!

Mrs. Landyke did not escape so easily. He came into her store—such a shock that she had to sit down on a chair. "And hinted at good times ahead, said a business like mine would be booming one day, I could look forward to holidays spent on the golden sands of Hawaii." Enough teeth for a barracuda but such powerful masculine hands, such hairy wrists, she'd nearly fainted when he reached out to shake goodbye.

And stopped for a cup of Linda Weins's coffee, a natural thing to do, but Linda was almost too terrified to serve him, the cup would rattle in the saucer, she'd trip and fall on her face, she'd spill it down his suit. But she'd kill anyone else who tried to do it for her, she'd seen him first. And not only did she not make a total fool of herself, as she'd feared, she fell so completely under the spell of those eyes that she sat down across the table from him, to heck with her other customers, let them wait on themselves, and asked him what kind of business brought him here to Port Annie. Tantalizing hints that something exciting was up, promises of new days ahead, prosperity and progress. But she hardly listened, she was too much in love with his arrogant eyes full of erotic promises. And his face. So mature—this was no androgynous boy, no baby-fat here—this was a strong adult face, with character lines and skin that had been exposed to the weather. Exactly the kind of man you'd expect to come into a town on a rainy day like this one and ride off with the sweet young waitress who'd got so sick of this boring job in this boring place that she could just curl up and die from yawning!

History repeating itself was what Angela Turner thought of it all, with one hand on her thickening belly. Had that Peruvian sailor spread word of the easy pickings to be found in this town? Since this was one of the days in which she felt like a modern woman, she could see very clearly that this stranger was a foolish caricature, a ridiculous strutting male, cocky and absurd. There was nothing so silly as a man who considered himself pretty hot, unless it was the woman who fell for his act.

But Rita Rentalla, who had no interest in the modern approach to things, looked at Christie and Bald-headed Pete in the Kick-and-Kill and wondered if her own orgy of watching that savoury hunk had completely destroyed her taste for the men of Port Annie, commonplace males that they were.

It was George Beeton, out of bed to see what the fuss was about, who noticed that the world had changed colour. The rain seemed to be falling heavier than ever out of a high cloudless sky, a pure white ceiling of light so harsh that it made you squint. The bush, the houses, the inlet, everything looked as if it had been washed over with brilliant unnatural colours, like a garish jungle painting. "It's not safe to go to bed in this place," he said when he arrived at the Kick-and-Kill. "The minute you pull down the blinds someone changes the world."

Even the air had altered its smell. Instead of the usual sharp odour of salty inlet and the rained-on hemlock smell of the mountains, he detected a scent that he couldn't quite name. The odour of wealth, they told him. While the dazzling smile of that stranger was breaking hearts, his tongue was scattering intimations of money all over town. You'd think the fellow was planning to buy up the whole blasted place. It was obvious he knew plenty he wasn't telling, something that was

going to change all their lives, something that could fill all
their pockets with dough. He had the look on his face of someone who had plans for major adjustments to the world.

"But not too much," Charlie Reynolds promised the Kick-
and-Kill crowd. "If it was something drastic I'd have heard
of it down at the paper."

"You'll read it in the outside papers the same time the rest
of us do," Christie said. "After it's happened, eh. Are you so
stupid that you still think people tell the public their plans
before it's too late to stop them?"

And Ian McCarthy felt there was good reason to be alarmed. That swaggering peacock had come into the post office,
too, and asked who was who in this town, and nodded to everything Ian said as if he'd already known it. "Asked this and that
about people you'd never think that he'd heard of."

Rita Rentalla stood up, too excited to sit, and started to
circle the table. Did he speak with an American accent or just
like us? Did he mention San Francisco or Hollywood or Hous-
ton, Texas? Maybe he was a filthy-rich philanthropist looking
for some place to throw all his money.

"I never noticed before," Christie said, "but Rita walks just
like your seabird! That girl must've given her lessons."

Jeremy Fell, of course, knew what the stranger was up to,
but he had no one's permission to let the news out just yet.
In The Threads Shed he was putting price stickers on socks
and listening to his doomed beating heart when that stranger
stepped inside out of the glare and looked around with his
hands at his waist as if he owned the whole store. But Jeremy
Fell acted as if he'd never seen him before, had no idea why he
was here. He asked could he be of some help, pressed his narrow hands together, and scrunched his red-rimmed eyes into
an appearance of storekeeper solicitude. Looking, the man said,
just looking, and prowled the aisles and fingered the unisex
jeans and held up the see-through shirts; just looking and
thinking, he said, and winked at Jeremy Fell, "How's Cyn?"
A nice place if you liked this type of a set-up, he said, the
scenery was just as beautiful as he'd been told, and from what
he'd been able to gather the people of this town were exactly
the way someone had described them, no disappointment at
all. Yes sir, yes sir, said Jeremy Fell, and he had rubber boots
at a low price too if the gentleman intended to do much more
walking in this rain. As he himself had said many times both

in conversation and on paper, no one would ever be a success in this town who kept waiting for the rain to dry up. You had to exploit what there was.

Yes, yes, the man said, he was sure he'd read something exactly like that some time in a letter perhaps, and was the mayor of this town that big-eared old coot in the magazine shop? It was time, he supposed, to go make the fellow's acquaintance.

Jenny Chambers caught a glimpse of the Hollywood hunk going into the magazine shop but, cripes, who had the time any more to be bothering your head about strangers? The mail order box in her arms was so big she could hardly see over it—yards and yards of pure white material for her wedding dress, not to mention acres of pink for the six bridesmaids and the two little brats of flower girls. She still hadn't quite got used to the complete reversal in her position, but it was amazing what a woman could do when she was desperate enough.

She'd run out of ideas. This was the only thing left. She'd taken a deep breath and announced to everybody that she and Slim were going to get married at last, make it legal, a big white wedding with all the trimmings. And it had turned out to be a stroke of pure genius. Just as she'd hoped, it had brought her more friends than enough. Overnight. A bride was always the most popular girl in the town. Everyone had come flocking around her, turning themselves inside out with excitement over the wedding of an ex-stripper right in their town. Everyone wanted to be her friend now. She had hardly a minute to herself. Even the annual neighbourhood crab-canning party up Rupert's Arm had to be cancelled this year. Too much work was still waiting to be done right here at home. She nearly tripped over her own feet in her hurry to get back to the house and open the carton and run her hands through all this material. Of course the bridesmaids' dresses would have to be sewed up first, she wouldn't dare touch her own for a long time yet, she was on a starvation diet to get her old figure back as fast as she could—almost nothing to eat, and a ten-mile walk every day. With so much on her mind and so little on her stomach she could hardly be expected to notice even if that handsome stud had come in to town with a bomb and threatened to blow up the Mill.

Larry Bowman saw that peacock go right past his library

door in this unearthly new light, but paid no more attention than Jenny Chambers had done—what was one more stranger to him when his life was still lying in pieces? There was a time when he would have perked up at the sight of that Porsche, cars were his hobby, but who cared about things like that now? His days were spent with his nose buried in books of medieval fiction, about knights who saved kingdoms and won admiration from hundreds of feminine hearts, a magical world where everyone was courageous and women belonged to a separate race that had vanished ages ago. And when he wasn't reading, or helping the young single men who came down from the hotel with their college assignments under their arm, he spent his time in the doorway of his library, staring off across the inlet and trying to force himself to believe that his seabird really had disappeared.

He'd been ill for several days after she'd gone. He hadn't even opened up the library, nor did he open the door of his rooms to Angela Turner, who'd come knocking, who'd hollered through his window at him that she was worried, that she'd tried to phone him but no answer, that she'd like to come in and make him something to eat, talk a while. He told her to go away and leave him alone. He tossed all his magazines with their suggestive liquor ads into the garbage, he hauled all his ridiculous new clothes after dark out to the dump, where those Squatters' Flats people would find them and tear them up for their paper machines, good luck to them.

Not even his old books allowed him the comfort he'd always found there. Passages leapt out to mock him:

> My lady yaf me al hooly
> The noble yiftë of his mercy . . .
> As helpë me God, I was as blyvë
> Reysed, as fro deth to lyvë.

He thought of picking up and moving out of here for good, but he knew that wherever he went it would only drive him crazy to think that in his absence the lovely seabird could return to Port Annie, perhaps even to look for him, and he wouldn't be there to greet her and tell her face to face the things he'd only whispered in his head at night. Like it or not he was stuck in this town, he just couldn't leave.

Nor could Angela Turner, who'd been trying. This stranger

was one more reason for putting it off. "It wouldn't kill him to let us know what he's got up his sleeve," she said. And abandoned her till to stand outside the door for a few minutes, under the overhang, to get a full view of the square.

No stranger in sight, he'd gone into the magazine shop and never come out; he must have had some kind of long-winded business to talk with the mayor. Instead, all she saw was the figure of Joseph Bourne—gumboots and sweaters and fluttering plastic cape—hurrying in through the big glass doors of the hotel, where he was late for his radio show. Living so many lives at once—now that he'd bounced back from the grave, defying all the natural laws of the world—he was always late, always hurrying, always eating on the run, as if he intended to learn how to be everywhere at once, how to touch everyone's life at once like the rain, like those noisy jays that invaded the town.

Of course he still spent a good deal of his time down in Squatters' Flats, helping in The Paper House, turning garbage into some kind of notepaper that no one in Port Annie had ever seen but which was rumoured to bring in good money when they delivered it down-island twice a year. He'd also been helping renovate one of those houses along the shore-line for Preserved Crabbe to live in with his thick-legged penguin, now that he'd run her to earth and dragged her back home and refused to take his hands off her in case she escaped again. A hopeless job, trying to turn that old falling-down shack into a decent house, but still the three of them went at it as if they believed in miracles; one room after another got cleared out, scrubbed, repainted, and furnished with patched junk dragged out of dumps all over the North Island bush, some even bought at an auction sale. They hung curtains in the windows, they dug wild plants up out of forest soil and rooted them in tin cans along the verandah ledge, they painted the front a blue so bright that the young men from town who went down to visit Dirty Della in the middle of Saturday nights said it glowed in the dark, right in the middle of Squatters' Flats, like a beacon. A beautiful job, every bride's dream, and now it was said the rest of those people down there were starting to talk about fixing their own shacks up, to follow the old man's example.

And some of the merchants in town were singing his praises as well. On the day they gathered out in the square to discuss the possibility of a facelift for those drab storefronts, Bourne had arrived on the scene and immediately thrown himself into the job. Even Mayor Weins had to give him a little credit this time, no holding back, here was a new man for sure. No climbing ladders, of course; despite his amazing display of energy, they wouldn't allow him to go up those rickety things to replace light bulbs and slap new coats of paint over the faded words and touch up the rain-worn letters on the signs, but he did carry pots of paint to where they were needed, he rushed cups of coffee and sandwiches out for their breaks, he gave advice like No that sign's not quite level, a little too high on the left. Eddy Deck could not say enough good things about the old man who'd helped him pick out the new bright colour for the front of the bank and then helped him plan that new sign for the window. And Ian McCarthy said, what the hell, if the government didn't like lemon-lime walls on the post office they could repaint them themselves, he was tired of battleship grey.

The ex-convicts in town had their reasons for praising him, too. He'd called together all the young Mill workers who lived in the hotel, a meeting downstairs in the empty dining room, where he'd had beer brought in for everyone, and confessed —while he tugged at one ear and wolfed down a sandwich— that he knew a good half of them had come here straight out of the pen, still on parole. Nobody knew who they were, he said, and it wasn't really any of his business, but he wanted them to know that he and his radio program were at their disposal if anyone wanted to work with him there, to come up with a series of conversations about the prison system, maybe, and the problems of trying to adjust to life in a town like Port Annie. They drank their beer and left, scowling at the nerve of the old crackpot, but within a week ten of the men were meeting in the hotel in the evenings, to help him plan a series of half-hour programs. "Crazy!" Greg Wong reported. "And he promised he wouldn't bleep out all our goddam cursin' either."

Miss Cleary the schoolteacher wouldn't trade him for any-thing, not even a school board made up of people with some intelligence for the first time in Port Annie's history—because Joseph Bourne had saved her life. She had thirty-one grade threes and fours already bursting her classroom walls, more than any one person could handle without breaking her neck and wearing herself to a frazzle, and what did they go and throw in with the rest for good measure but three East Indians without a word of English, right off the boat, some distant relatives living up in Mr. Manku's house. Fat chance she had of ever doing them any good, with all those other kids to teach. The very thought of what she didn't have time to do was giving her headaches so bad she had to lie down and fan herself on the bench at the front of the classroom two or three times a day in order to keep herself from screaming and running off into the bush. Then along came that old man, flapping and thumping his way down the hall in the middle of her writing lesson on capital "E" to hammer at her door, poke his head in to see what was going on. He tossed candies to every one of those open-faced little kids, then offered two hours of his day, every day, to sit with those three puzzled foreigners, pumping English words into them until they had enough to ask where the bathroom was and tell the other kids to go fly a kite when they teased them.

Now every day he came wind-fluttering up the road from his shack to the school and sat out in the hall at a table with those three children, teaching them as if the whole world depended on it and delivering them back to her classroom afterwards with all four faces shining, theirs and his. Oh, he was disastrous at first. Out in that hall the four of them just sat looking at one another across the table, blankly, unable to believe that the silence could be broken in any way that all four of them could understand. Eventually he picked up one of the books she'd given him and said, "This is a book," so loud the students inside the room had to smother giggles behind their hands. The three brown faces only looked, no expression. "This is a book," again, even louder, as if he would force it through their foreheads. Again "This is a book, say it, say, 'This is a book.'" Over and over, "Say, 'This is a book,'" until the three little children looked at one another, unable to believe that they weren't being insulted, and got up to walk back into her room and sit in their desks with tears resting on the bottom lids of their eyes. "Oh no you don't," she said, and marched them out again. "Mr. Bourne, this is a desperate matter, keep trying, please."

So he did, with Larry Bowman's help. He read every book ever written on the subject, had those children starting to talk, even told her how to help out by changing her lessons just the slightest bit when those three little kids were in the room. Never mind the vocabulary, he told her, they'll gather words as they need them, no problem. The important thing is to help them get the sentence patterns, make the patterns second nature. He gave them order, he gave them patterns, and they loved the old man, did everything they could think of to please him—which was not only to learn English at an amazing rate but also to bring him gifts, exotic-looking foods, and even to invite him home to their rooms in the basement of the Manku house, where the parents treated him like something between royalty and God, ready to force all their most treasured possessions on him to show how much they appreciated what he was doing.

What a worker! He was so glad to be alive that he was in danger of killing himself with all this effort. Restored, he'd become a restorer. Repaired and resurrected, it looked as if he'd set about repairing and resurrecting everything in sight. Eating, eating, always eating—apples and bananas and folded-over slices of bread and whole raw carrots. His pockets were full, his mouth was full, his huge hands never stopped searching for something to eat in the dozens of pockets he had in all those layers of sweaters. Eating and laughing at the same time, while his eyes were forever on the lookout for whatever job it was that he ought to leap into next with his great whoop of surprise and wonder. Who could imagine where all this would end? Would they wake up some day and discover the cemetery turned into a mess of sprung-open graves, a noisy party of dancing revitalized corpses?

Naturally, there was a touching side to all of this, too. For all his apparently endless supply of energy and his eagerness to be always busy, you never knew when you might discover him, quite unexpectedly, and in the most unlikely places, worn out and fast asleep. In a dim back corner of the Kick-and-Kill, for instance, or curled up on a gym mat at the rec centre, or in a booth of the coffee shop with the side of his face pressed up against the glass of the window. Softly snoring, and with one hand hanging onto some piece of half-eaten food.

Recharging his batteries. Because the old man could not walk anywhere in town without being followed by a dozen kids all hollering for his attention, he could not walk a block without people coming out of their houses to stand in the rain blocking his way in order to talk to an old man come back to life, and he could go nowhere at all, it seemed, without raising a thousand brilliant jays from out of the bushes and around the doorsteps and along the fences, a noisy confusion of birds darting and hopping and swooping around him like too much life, too much joy.

Tell us about that seabird, some people demanded, and dragged him in to their houses to sit by the silent snowstorm of their television set, where he fished raw carrots out of his pocket and told them in his rich radio-announcer voice how he missed that girl, she'd been nearly as beautiful as his wife in Jamaica, a lovely dark-skinned woman he'd met and married in Kingston so long ago and never stopped loving for a minute of his life—not even when he travelled all over the world without her, not even while he made her life a trial by forever getting himself into messes that only she could get him out of. Not even, he believed, when he'd come here to Port Annie and forgotten that she even existed. Until that girl had arrived and brought everything back. She had the same touch, the same deep understanding of things, the same healing strength that his wife had had; and indeed it was from that remarkable woman that she had learned what she needed to know, and it was even from that woman that she had received her orders to come here and snap Bourne out of the dark despair which was leading him straight to death. Never, he said— except in the case of his wife, of course—never had he met anyone so full of the strength of spirit, the vitality of life, the gentleness of love, the beauty of soul . . . and so on and so on, you could add all the other synonyms you could think of for God, never anyone in this world so pure. "Maybe so, Mr. Bourne," they told him. "But when you think of God walking the earth you don't usually imagine such a cheeky rear end, or ankles that could make a man foam at the mouth." True, he had to laugh at the notion, but then neither could they deny that she'd caused them to *notice*. Hadn't they sat up and paid attention? And then he rose up out of his seat by the silent television set to head for the door, still a hero, who'd be welcome, Mr. Bourne, just whenever he felt like dropping in for another visit.

Or tell us about your travels, they insisted, now that he had his past again. Was it true he'd seen nearly every country in the world? They hauled him in off the street—the renovating and the facelifting and the rehabilitating and the schoolteach-

ing could wait—while he told them, no, not every country in
the world exactly, but enough for any one person to digest in
a lifetime. But he could tell them, while he munched down a
whole bag of oatmeal cookies, about waiting for a plane in
Calcutta, where the air was thick with the smoke of burning
cow dung and this Brahmin businessman, who was also a
famous poet and the author of fourteen novels—no older than
thirty—engaged him in conversation there in the airport and
then proceeded to read his own novels aloud to Bourne all
that night in the waiting room in some mellifluous language
that Bourne couldn't understand, and then again all the next
day and night in the hotel where they were put to wait for
the plane that seemed to have got lost on its way across the
country, confused perhaps by the static of insults radioed back
and forth between the officials of Calcutta and the officials of
Bombay. And similar incidents in Stockholm, in Belgrade, in
London, always someone to touch you and corner you to read
endlessly from the precious work of his lifetime, bad poetry
and good, epic novels of grand events and sordid novels of
gutters and back alleys, panting as they read, so that you sometimes thought you were witnessing something you shouldn't
see. Only up the Amazon did he escape them, and in the Alps,
and in the desert of central Australia—no poets there, and
instead there were beautiful women who'd never read a word
that you'd written, never heard your name, nor ever thought
of writing something themselves, just wanting to enjoy the fact
that you were two people together in a part of this beautiful
world. Oh, he could go on and on, with stories about Luisa
the mad madam from Brasilia, who had feathers growing
where other women had hair, and of Mary Maguire from the
city of Cork, who sang songs that made the birds turn green,
and of Two-Ton Trixie from Perth, who fed him lizard eggs
raw. "Yes, yes," they said. "And since you're so good at repairing things, maybe you'll take a look at this broken chair that
Pete's been promising to fix for over a year."
    And what was it like to be a world-famous poet? they wanted
to know. Not that they read poetry themselves, sir, at least
not since school, but couldn't he come in out of this miserable
rain for a few minutes—have a hot toddy, the kettle was already boiling—and explain how a person went about writing
a poem and then, once it was written, what he should do with
it? No, he didn't particularly want to talk about it very much,

not even to the Creative Writing Club of Port Annie, all dressed up eating little cakes at Mrs. Barnstone's house on a Wednesday evening, because to tell the truth it only got harder, not easier, look at how long it was taking him to finish his Port Royal poem, down in his shack. The more attention you got the harder it was, and even if you'd published a hundred best-selling masterpieces there was always the fear that this next time your editor would send it back and say, "Why are you showing me this piece of junk?" A terrifying way to spend your life, and the more people noticed you, the more terror there was in it, but don't misunderstand, please, he wouldn't have traded a minute of it. Okay, okay, but perhaps since he was already in the house, sir, he wouldn't mind stepping into the bedroom, where little Margie had been sick for several days, no improvement at all, and had begged them please to get Mr. Bourne in here to sit with her, she just knew it would get her back on her feet again in no time, the man was so obviously a miracle-worker.

A few of the braver ones tried to get him onto the topic of dying. Carefully, of course, as if it didn't really matter in order not to seem prying. But they couldn't help wondering, they said, if any of the things that they'd read were true, that people who died were supposed to feel themselves float free of their bodies and hover above, watching others mourn—people had come back from a few minutes dead to report things like that, it was even in magazines—or if you really heard choirs singing and saw loved ones who'd died long ago coming to gather you in. It was a hard subject, they admitted, and one people didn't want to talk about much, but it was something they worried about, Mr. Bourne, especially as they felt themselves getting older, something they'd appreciate having more information about. But this was the one topic Bourne would not talk about. Death? he said, searching in this pocket and that pocket for something to eat. Was there even such a thing as death? As far as he was concerned there was only life. If he believed that death was anything more than a temptation and a mistaken belief he wouldn't be here this minute, walking these streets.

He'd become a special person, no doubt about it. Not the same thing to everyone, of course, but still he was welcomed nearly everywhere he went—not even just welcomed, he was hoarded, people wanted him to themselves, like a good-luck charm, and if they could manage it without making it look too obvious they would touch him, just briefly, as if to take some magic from him. Doors that had been closed to him were suddenly opened, and he was dragged inside. How else could he have found himself making polite noises over the long and detailed plans for Jenny Chambers' wedding, or listening for what seemed like hours to the blow-by-blow description of her starvation diet? She'd had a knockout figure once, she told him, and she'd have it again in time for the wedding if it killed her. Cripes, she had less than two months to go before the big day and she still had to finalize her list of bridesmaids and flower girls and caterers and bartender and orchestra, as well as her Slim's best man and ushers. And on top of it all she was expected to be a decent mother to those eight spoiled-rotten kids, she said, who nearly drove her crazy with their fighting and cheekiness and playing hookey from school and starting to smoke and drink and God knows what all behind her back.

And Slim, too, before he could get away, dragged him outside to admire his backyard full of parked and perfectly clean machines that he had been buying for years; and made him stand in the rain to watch him take a lawn mower apart, wash all the pieces in a bucket of gasoline, and put them together again. "I'm never so happy as when I'm up to my elbows in grease."

And had to follow Mrs. Landyke out to the little grown-over cemetery on the edge of town while she paid a visit to the graves of her husband and son. They'd been fishermen, she said, they'd lost their lives like so many others in a heavy herring season. A little greedy perhaps, they left their net down a little too long, and seven tons of trapped herring for some reason or other all dived for the bottom at once, sounded, and pulled the boat over, sank it. A freak accident, a terrible thing. She couldn't leave these graves, she told him with one hand gripped to his elbow, she couldn't stand to live where she wasn't able to visit these graves every day, they were the reason this place was home to her. No use trying to tell her how wrong she was, of course, how earthbound she was letting herself become, no more use than trying to convince Mr. Manku, when he opened the door of his home to Bourne, that he was making a mistake to hide in his house just because his family,

since the day of the swimming-pool fiasco, was convinced that
he was senile, a public embarrassment. Whenever the distin-
guished Mr. Manku invited him inside there was only a moment
or two of stiff meaningless conversation before Bourne went
down into the basement suites where the children and the
children's parents and Mr. Manku's beautiful grandson Kamaljit were waiting to make a fuss over him, fill him full with
a delicious meal, talk his ear off, treat him like a wise man and
a funny pet and a member of the family all at once.

It was just as hopeless trying to resist Eva McCarthy's techniques for seducing him into her house and setting him to
work: standing on her step when he went by, "Oh not doing
so well, Mr. Bourne, this skin rash is driving me nuts," and
telling him trouble after trouble of an oh-so-hard-done-by
woman, who was never satisfied, until it was clear that refus-
ing to go inside for a cup of her imitation coffee would be the
same as a slap in the face, one more hardship in her catalogue.
Before he knew it, he was helping her repaint or repaper or
revarnish or refurnish some part of her perfect sterilized house
which was never the same two weeks in a row. She was all tied
up in knots buying new furniture, new furnishings, new wallpaper; she couldn't catch up because every time she'd finally
got her house redecorated, Mr. Bourne, she'd go into someone
else's house and see something she didn't have, or open a magazine and see something she'd die without. There was no end
to it. And she couldn't throw anything out, old furniture didn't
go down to the basement or off to the auction, it just moved
back to make room for the new things. In the living room, he
helped her lay out a brown circular braided rug on top of a
red carpet, which was itself already sitting on top of a sisal
rug that could be seen around the edges but, "Oh, I love my
house, even it it will drive me crazy, there isn't anything I like
better than getting that furniture to shine and pinging my
finger on the spotless glass of my crystal."

Poor woman. And he knew what she said the minute he left
—to her friends on the phone or to Ian home for his supper—
that Bourne had become a perfect model of an old man, a
paragon of virtue, a living demonstration of goodness, a saint!
In short he made you sick, because how could you stand to
have a man like that around without starting to feel guilty
yourself? It depressed her to see the energy that old man was

willing to burn up for the sake of other people. Sometimes she hoped he'd do something downright selfish and cruel for a change, to show he was the same as everyone else.

And of course Eva McCarthy was not the only individual in town who saw him as less than heroic. On the same day that the Hollywood hunk walked the streets of Port Annie, Bourne stood for a few minutes in the doorway of Jeremy Fell's store eating a chocolate bar he'd found in his pocket and making small talk about this and that and trying to find out if Fell knew what that stranger was up to in the magazine shop. But the storekeeper stood rigid, no expression at all on his face, not a sound out of that throat where a blue vein throbbed visibly. Then, after several minutes of listening to Bourne's talk, he hawked up a wad of phlegm to spit perfectly, quickly, onto the wet pavement by the old man's feet. "Don't look at *me* with your disgusting compassion, it only makes me want to be sick."

Bourne stepped back, surprised. What had he done to bring this on? He hadn't been unaware of the turmoil this man had been going through all summer. Why this sudden hostility? Why the pure hatred in those eyes? What had he wanted Bourne to do that he hadn't done? Jeremy Fell looked as if he could happily have slit the old man's throat. "Keep away from me, you. Just keep away."

Almost immediately the stranger came out of the magazine shop, followed by Weins dressed up in his Depression costume —torn pants, a too-tight jacket, shoes without laces, like someone about to ask for a dime. As soon as the Hollywood hunk had gone inside the hotel, Weins rushed over to Jeremy Fell. "He told me about it. I'm calling a meeting. Tonight we'll tell the whole town."

Joseph Bourne was ignored. The mayor had pushed right past to get at Fell's hand and start pumping it. "Wonderful news! And to think you knew all along. I guessed from the start there was something about you I'd like."

"Come in, come in." Fell tried to drag the mayor inside. "Let's talk where half the world isn't listening in."

"Yes, yes," the mayor said. "But I've got to get to a phone. One call to the Mill, one to the radio station, and one to my wife. That way everyone'll know within minutes. We'll have the meeting right after supper, and no putting it off, either."

Naturally, everyone came. Who could stay away? Who

could be found in that whole town who was so indifferent to everything—the man's charm, the smell of money, the hints of changes ahead? Even having to find your own chair under the stage at the rec centre, unfolding it, and setting it up in the hall, was not enough of a detraction. Nor was having to listen to a P.A. system that worked only half the time, and the rest of the time blasted out shrill noises to break your eardrums. Besides finding out why this handsome devil was prowling the town, you would also get to smell—even taste—Papa Magnani's coffee and doughnuts, you would get to see all the people you didn't bump into once a day at the post office or out at the Mill, you would even get to find out for yourself if that was really an engagement ring on Opal Dexter's finger or only a disappointing birthstone. Nobody wanted to be left out. Only the afternoon shift at the Mill, a skeleton crew, had to wait until later to be told what was up.

Only Larry Bowman was reluctant. Angela Turner had to drag him out his door. "Put down that book and let's go. Afterwards, you can mope again all you want, today let's go see what's up. A little distraction won't hurt."

A distraction was not what this was intended to be, however, as far as the mayor was concerned. This was the most important event in the history of the town—even more important than the death of Dieter Fartenburg, far more important than the arrival of Fat Annie as a whale or whatever those crazy Indians claimed. And in keeping with the importance and dignity and absolute urgency of the occasion he showed up in the purple robes of a mayor, chains and medals clanging and shooting off sparks of light—the first time he had worn the full costume in public. Captain Vancouver and Thunderbird and all the other costumes stayed in the closet tonight, this was an occasion of far too much weight for frivolities. And as if to prove it, he began shouting orders the minute he stepped onto the basketball floor of the rec centre: "Get your own chairs, get your own chairs, line them up across here, there's room for a few more in this row. Haven't you got that microphone hooked up yet? Bring those tables down here, Magnani, so people can help themselves. Are you sure there's enough coffee in that urn, it doesn't look like enough to me. Get your own chair, come on, help yourself to a chair. Let's get this show on the road and no fooling either. Charlie, don't sit so far back, I want you up in the very front row so you can get every word. You can check that paper bag with me if you want, I'll take care of the bottle until after. Ian, there'll be no standing along the walls as long as there are chairs to sit on. Come on, come on, let's get this show on the road."

That purple robe with its white fur trim and the gold chains was unquestionably a knockout, a dramatic touch that was guaranteed to draw everyone's attention to him just as soon as they entered the room, even without all the shouting. No one had ever seen the mayor look so regal. Yet all that finery paled the minute the Hollywood hunk entered the room, carrying a leather case. The mayor did the introductions—as full and flowery as he could whip up in the little time he'd been given—but nobody heard, he might as well have been reciting a recipe for borscht; all eyes were devouring the stranger, trying to guess his intentions, wondering where he'd come from and what he would look like without that rakish moustache, and what kind of a man wore a gold stud in his left ear lobe. The councilmen in the front row compared their own wrinkled suits to his immaculate wardrobe. Papa Magnani admired that trim waist, the man obviously kept in shape, probably worked out every day in a gym. Mrs. Barnstone frowned when he lit up one of those narrow cigars—couldn't he see the signs plastered all over the walls, thanking him for *not* indulging in such a filthy habit? Would everyone, now, think it was all right to light up, fill the whole room up with their fumes?

George Beeton estimated that those hands had not done an honest day's work in their life. Too white. And look at those perfect clean nails.

As soon as the mayor's speech had ended, to a round of applause, the centre of all this attention stood up to unzip his leather case and pull out some papers, smiling at the front row. Mrs. Landyke couldn't keep her eyes off those hairy wrists. Such a strong masculine man! Jenny Chambers, like the councilmen, was more impressed with the suit; she was scared to imagine how much it would cost, twenty times the price she'd finally persuaded her Slim to spend on an outfit for their wedding, she bet, and cripes, this one even had a vest to match.

"I'll make it short," he said. "I can tell you everything I've come here to say in five minutes. It's good to see so many people out on such short notice, a healthy sign of community interest, and if you've got questions I'll be happy to answer them when I'm finished." Such a sexy voice, nearly a whisper, and yet he could be heard in every corner of the hall. The teeth were nearly blinding in this artificial light. His name was Damon West, he said, and he represented the Evergreen Realty Company—in fact he was its chairman and largest shareholder. As everyone here undoubtedly knew already, that parcel of land just north of town, between the road and the inlet and stretching along the shore for more than a mile, had been owned for years by a down-island sawmill company, a piece of Crown land given to the company by the government years ago to encourage new industry in the area, but deserted and going to waste since the sawmill was abandoned. "A piece of prime land, very desirable, contributing absolutely nothing to the economic progress of this part of the Island," he said, and turned his smile on Mayor Weins, who beamed right back. A movie actor, Jenny thought, with a perfect face for a hero, don't waste your smile on that big-eared blob. He went on to say, with his voice dropped low so that they all had to strain to hear, that his company had been acting as agent for the sawmill people for the past few years now, and had sold the land to some wonderful folks from below the border, who would develop it in a way that would benefit everyone here. He counted the ways on his fingers: by improving the appearance of that neglected and rundown piece of realty, by putting Port Annie on the map at last and making her famous throughout the United States of America, by making the place an attractive location for other industries searching for new development areas, and by bringing to this part of the Island an unpredictable number of tourists, who would be happy to spend their money in the shops and service centres of the town. "A dream come true is what I'm here to announce, ladies and gentlemen," and his white smile embraced them all. "Everyone's dream, not just the dream of the merchants, or the Mill management, who will be finding Port Annie an easier place to attract workers to and hold them, or the young people growing up, who will no longer have to leave this inlet to find jobs in strange cities. Everyone. And what I want to show you now is the specific plan these people have for the development of that property, a development my own company will be carrying out on their behalf, but according to their exact and detailed specifications." He unfolded a large piece of heavy paper and held it up—some sort of map. "This company, ladies and gentlemen, has its headquarters in San Francisco but has created similar developments in various parts of the United States, as well as Latin America and Eastern Canada." What they were now looking at was a rough sketch, he told them, though to everyone but the front row of aldermen it was nothing but a blur of dark lines. Similar in most respects to their other developments, of course, but adjusted architecturally and in general conception to conform to the local climate and terrain, what they were looking at on this piece of paper, ladies and gentlemen, were the plans for an enormous and rather exclusive holiday resort, to be called the Cathay Towers Resort. A name to conjure with, he added, legendary hope of all the explorers.

Someone down in San Francisco must be psychic, people thought, because Cathay Towers was already the name of the hotel in town, always had been, though nobody ever called it that. "Hotel" was what you called it when it was hotel you meant, and "Kick-and-Kill" was what everyone called the beer parlour.

Dead silence for a moment after the announcement. Linda Weins shivered. The way that fellow could talk! It was enough just to sit here and look at him, but the music that came out of his mouth was an added attraction. Who cared if it made any sense? Then a large guffaw from somewhere in the middle section. Heads turned—how rude could you get?—it was George Beeton. Mrs. Landyke looked down and shook her head—some people just didn't have any manners at all. "In this rain? Who'd be crazy enough to spend money for a holiday in this place?"

Mr. West held out his hands to calm the chaos of voices and smiled as if this was exactly the question he'd expected. "Not you or I, perhaps, sir, but you'd be surprised how someone's point of view is different if he's been brought up in a dry hot desert. The clientele will be exclusively Americans, of course, who presumably see more romance in that liquid sunshine than we do." A flash of teeth, some laughter. "And as I mentioned earlier, the whole thing will be adjusted to suit the climate. The guests will be fishing, hunting, horseback riding, and indulging in all the other activities this area offers, but they'll also be spending a good deal of time indoors, or at least under roofs, where they can enjoy the scenery without getting wet."

That was telling the grease monkey a thing or two; Eva

McCarthy turned right around in her seat to give George a scowl. What was this Mr. West going to think of the town if everyone asked stupid questions like that? (And would he be staying for dinner, she wondered; probably already tied up with an invitation from Mabel Weins, a social climber if there ever was one.)

George Beeton returned her scowl for scowl: shut up, you bag, just put that fancy dandy in a grease pit for a while and see if he's much of a man. How much good would his flashy smile do him there?

Another voice, from somewhere near the front. "Will they be paying for the privilege of swimming in the sewage from the Mill, I wonder?"

"Oh for Pete's sake," Mrs. Landyke said aloud, before she could slap her hand over her mouth.

This time the Hollywood hunk did not look amused. No, he said, there was an agreement being worked out at the present time with the Mill. In future, the flow would be considerably less poisonous and much less visible. "Besides," he added, finding his smile again, "Texans and Californians will not be coming here to swim. You and I, sir, find it cold enough. To them it would seem like the frozen arctic."

A smattering of applause, led most vigorously by Linda Weins—right up front beside her dad. Mr. West tilted his head towards her, as if in gratitude. Then winked, to show her not to take this thing too seriously, it was just his job.

One more hand up, and this time it was Hill Gin, from the Flats. What was that old witch doing here? This was no business of hers. Who was the fool who let her know about it? A disgrace, in those old overalls, and she probably hadn't even washed her face.

Hill Gin had been standing along the back row, but stepped forward to speak. She pushed the grey hair off her forehead, then folded her arms and addressed the ceiling. "Does this San Francisco crew know there's already people living on that piece of property? Don't your company care about the ruckus there's gonna be when the public hears you're kicking more than a dozen people out of the homes they've been living in for years?"

Mr. West shook his head. "It's always bad business removing people from public land, even when you have the right to do it. If that land was under a tree-farm licence the government would probably not have released it in the first place; it costs them more money to relocate people and absorb them into the welfare system than to leave them alone. But this is different, madam." He smiled as broadly as if what he was saying ought to be marvellous news. "I know there's been some squatters living there, but removing them won't be any problem. That's been private property all along. They're trespassers and the RCMP can be asked to remove them, no public embarrassment at all."

Hill Gin grunted and stepped back to lean on her piece of the wall, dwarfed by the hulking bodies of the brothers Crabbe. But this seemed to trigger off a whole flurry of voices, all speaking at once. People stood up all over the room. Eva McCarthy's face was a brilliant red, she just couldn't imagine what this handsome rich man from the south must be thinking of them. A bunch of hicks from the sticks, at least.

"Lord knows . . ." someone shouted—it was Dr. Harmon and he had to shout even louder to get others to shut up their talking—"Lord knows most of us would be happy to see the end of those shacks in the Flats, but what we better think about is—" but Christie seemed to have taken over the floor, drowned him right out, "need to realize, eh, that this thing you just told us about will make a big difference to this town. It won't only add something to it, it will *change* everything, and I . . ." But Weins leapt to his feet, waved everyone quiet, his face the colour of his robe: "What's the matter with you? What's the matter with you? Can't you see what this man is bringing us? Can't you see he's giving us a chance to join the rest of the world? Catch up to the twentieth century? Doesn't anyone here have the good sense to see that a new business in town will put money in all of our pockets?"

Slim Potts stood up, the first time anyone had heard him try to make a speech in public. He didn't shout anyone down, he just waited until the sight of him standing up at the front of the room looking back at them out of his ridiculous narrow face caused the racket to die out of plain curiosity. He had to clear his throat once more, he shuffled his feet. Some people needed more stability in their lives than others did, he said. At least for a while. Some people need to know that every morning when they wake up their neighbours will be the same people they were yesterday, not strangers, the trees will all be in the same place, not bulldozed out of the way for a building, the sea the same as it always was, not filled in for a parking lot.

"There have to be places for people like that, sir, and Port Annie is one of them. Don't expect us to jump up and down with delight over your big fancy plans for a resort."

The Hollywood hunk waited with a patient smile on his face while Slim talked—how childish! how charmingly rural!—then returned to the microphone. A very good point. Exactly why he was here. Because the project would not go ahead without approval of City Council. A full public debate was what he wanted to encourage.

"And listen," the mayor said, before anyone else could respond. "Make no mistake about *this*. Turn down this offer and you're saying goodbye to the future. You're saying no thank you to tourist dollars, to bigger stores, to more hotels. You're saying so long to movie stars and millionaires on our streets. Doesn't it drive you crazy that we haven't a single fast-food outlet—nowhere to get a quick hamburger like everybody else? Doesn't it make you mad that to buy a new car you have to drive the old one a hundred and fifty miles to find it? Well, here's your chance if you'il take it. A dozen used-car lots right on your doorstep before you know it. A dozen hamburger drive-ins along the highway, with golden arches and rotating buckets and neon lights as far as the eye can see. Just let them build their resort and all of civilization will follow. You'll wonder how you ever stood it before."

The meeting disintegrated into chaos. Everyone had to have his say, all at the same time, and no one bothered to listen. Arguments for, arguments against, expressions of hope, expressions of horror—voices went right out of control. Mayor Weins tried to bring the meeting back to order, but for what? The Hollywood hunk was already zipping up his leather case, letting his eyes flicker out over the women in the crowd, as if trying to make up his mind, and settling finally on Linda Weins, to whom he offered the gift of his knee-melting smile. Not the slightest bit interested in the outcome of this fray, he had other things on his mind. A few faces went hot just imagining what it was. Linda Weins rose up out of her seat as if she were hypnotized and gave him her arm while they hurried together out the nearest exit as if there were a train to catch somewhere. Hardly more than a girl! This was scandalous. Really going too far.

Several eyes narrowed as they watched those two leave. No question about it, the man was a cradle-robber. There was nothing so disgusting as the sight of a middle-aged man with an eye for little girls. A foolish conceited peacock, and not nearly as good-looking as he thought he was. Probably had a fat middle-aged wife at home, and seven kids; he got his thrills out of snatching babies from their mothers' arms. When it came right down to delivering the goods he promised in every look from those arrogant eyes he was probably a dud and knew it, he probably wouldn't dare take on an experienced woman who'd know right away how unimpressive he was when it came to performance, only a greenhorn like Linda would be sure to be thrilled with his half-a-job efforts.

"Don't be alarmed," the mayor shouted. "Don't get excited. No one is going to force this thing on us. Open debate, all aboveboard, everyone will be heard. That company will wait for our answer, up to a month, while we decide if we want to see progress enter our lives, or if we want to remain a back-water forever—written off by the rest of the world. Too stupid and lazy to care if we move forward or not."

"Have you made up your own mind which side you are on?" George Beeton shouted. "Or are you going to stay as unbiased as you've been tonight?"

Everyone laughed. Chair legs scraped. People stood up. There was plenty of time for more meetings, these chairs were hard on the rump. Next time bring cushions and settle in for a long juicy fight, but right now it was more important to laugh at that mayor, click your tongue over his shameless daughter, and admire the smooth practised delivery of that Hollywood hunk—it showed what an education could do, the man could make speeches as easy as the rest of us make mistakes, no problem at all.

It was also important to seek out the people you were used to, your friends and usual confidants, to reassure yourself that you thought the same on this issue too. "Put your chairs away!" someone yelled, and people who'd nearly escaped came back, laughing, clamping cigarettes in their teeth and squinting against the smoke while they joined the clatter and clash of chairs being folded, stacked, pushed back under the stage. "What a bombshell! Just what old Weins has been looking for. Much better than that silly cactus he's nursing down at the dock."

"That thing takes up more of his time than a baby," said Ian McCarthy. He'd even had to get the doctor down to it last week! To drain it again before something terrible could happen. Those accordion pleats in the cactus had swollen up ready to explode from all the moisture the poor thing had taken in, confused by the change in climate. Another day and there'd have been pieces of Arizona hanging from every tree on the inlet, a terrible mess.

But what was the matter with Joseph Bourne that he hadn't spoken up at the meeting, Jenny Chambers wanted to know. He'd been there in the crowd, but no one had heard a peep. With his talents he should have been able to stand up at the front and put everything right into its place, so they'd know what to think. A man like him could save this town from an ugly end if he wanted to. Considering what had happened in the past, wasn't it safe to suggest he get that cradle-snatcher onto his radio show, pump him full of questions, have a debate?

Right now wasn't the time to suggest it, not to the old man at least. Bourne was out on the steps, standing to one side of the crowd going out, while Jeremy Fell was screaming at him like a maniac. Obviously he was in a panic about something. Bourne must have upset him. Fell was so angry that many of his words weren't even clear. Trying to stop things, trying to ruin things, trying to hold back the future, seemed to be his theme. Old Bourne answered too softly for anyone else to hear (though dozens stood to watch, and to listen) and Jeremy Fell, leaping back, went all to pieces, his face like a terrified child, screaming and crying, "And what about me, damn you, what do I do? You can't stop what's happening to me, you're a fake!" Naturally, everyone fell silent at that, even those who'd gone on talking in clusters at the door. What could it possibly mean? A person couldn't let it be seen that he was listening, and yet someone had to stop this thing. And why was Fell blue in the face, and wheezing—hardly able to breathe?

George Beeton grabbed Fell's arm and swung him around. "Get ahold of yourself. Who the hell do you think you are?"

White and shaky, Fell looked at George, a tic beating in his eyelid. Then he broke away, and pushed through the crowd a few feet before turning back.

"I'll leave you my corpse, Bourne. In my will. Someone can hang it around your neck so the whole world will see there are some things you can't stop, not even you."

"What was that all about?" someone said, as Fell hurried

away. "What did he say? What's going on? What does any of that have to do with this meeting? Is he against the development or what?"

Since no one wanted to spend long outside in this rain, most people had soon hurried away—down to the coffee shop or the Kick-and-Kill—to try and make sense of it all. Even the Squatters had gone back to their doomed shacks, taking the old man along with them. Within a few minutes there was no one left on the steps of the recreation centre but Larry Bowman and Angela Turner and Papa Magnani, who had to lock up. Angela struggled with a stubborn umbrella.

"She'sa bad news," Papa Magnani said, exaggerating his slight accent on purpose. "That mayor, you watch, he'sa gonna go crazy." He threw out his arms in the expected manner, then bit his thumb at the departing crowd.

Angela laughed, a crystal fountain of sound so familiar to Larry that he felt cold shocks go down his arm. Where had he heard it before? "He's crazy already, Magnani, he's crazy already." The umbrella gave up its battle, sprang open in Bowman's face, and swung up to hold off the rain. "And I wonder what his daughter's up to right now."

In his mind's eye Larry glimpsed a wedge of Linda Weins's flesh—thigh perhaps—moving against the dark upholstery of that pure-white Porsche. He snapped off the picture before it expanded into detail. "Fraternizing," he said. "The first person in town to embrace the future."

Angela laughed again as she started down the steps. "Come on," she said, "I'll let you share my umbrella as far as your door."

"I never noticed before, but you laugh just like that seabird," Papa Magnani said. "That girl, she must have given you lessons."

II

TRUST HILL GIN to leap on a figure of speech and turn it into a sign. That Hollywood hunk hadn't been gone from town an hour when she came up from the Flats to claim that she'd just seen the corpse of Jeremy Fell draped over Joseph Bourne's back. In keeping with her desire to look like the kind of witch that people took seriously—no teacup-reader you could easily dismiss—she patrolled the streets with her hair messed up like the nest of a giant bird and her wild eyes rolling as if she'd just caught a glimpse of hell. No halfway measures for her, she spread the news like someone down from the mountain carrying tablets: pale as wax, she told Eva McCarthy in front of the coffee shop, no weight at all, that corpse was riding the old man's shoulder like a shadow or a trick of light. And don't try to tell her it was an optical illusion, either, she'd seen it with these eyes as clearly as she'd ever seen anything in her life. People could make what they wanted of it, but she knew exactly what it meant: the end of the world was coming even faster than anyone might have thought.

Always eager to take the wind out of people's sails (in case they were tempted to take themselves too seriously, a crime), Eva McCarthy was quick to dismiss the idea. "The power of suggestion. Your eyes are getting old, you're only making a stupid fool of yourself." Yet she nearly broke her own neck in her hurry to get to the phone and be the first to spread the word around town, even before Hill Gin herself. "What do you think of this, that mad woman is roaming the streets with a story about Bourne with a corpse on his back. Those Squatters get more disgusting every day."

"Bad sports," said Mabel Weins. "Terrible losers. They just want to raise a stink because their days are numbered."

There was no question that Hill Gin was making it up. Everyone knew that Jeremy Fell was still alive, you only had to walk past the front of his shop to see him. Getting paler every day, grey-blue in the face and looking more like a cadaver than some already buried in coffins, at least he was breathing and moving around, talking if he was forced to and serving customers who came in for a pair of jeans or some underwear. Yet once the old woman from the Flats had spread her news, planting the idea in dozens of heads, people watched Joseph Bourne wherever he went in case there was something in what she'd said. Obviously Hill Gin was nuts, a fruitcake that no one would ever take seriously, but it wasn't hard to imagine that you'd caught something suspicious out of the corner of an eye just as you turned away, something that disappeared the second you turned back for a better look at the old man going past. It was enough to give you the creeps. This harsh unnatural light, the pouring rain, the unceasing movement of jays, it was easy to imagine that figure draped over one shoulder and down his back.

Larry Bowman couldn't afford to see anything. How would

it look for a college tutor, an educated man, to start seeing corpses where there was nothing at all? Could a man paid by two different employers to broaden the educational horizons of this town afford to treat a self-proclaimed witch with anything but contempt, or allow his eyes to see what he knew wasn't there? Of course not. What he should be doing was making fun of that ridiculous woman every chance that came along, turning her into a joke, and correcting those people who were tempted to take her seriously. What he should be doing was helping everyone to see that Joseph Bourne was a man like any other, nothing unnatural about him just because he'd been through an unusual experience. The trouble was that people around here watched him as if they expected him to do something spectacular any minute, like a conjuror or a superman or a risen Christ.

Yet even Larry was guilty of expecting something special out of Bourne. Even educated people could sometimes wish they had the simple wonder of children. Once in a while they might even hope that the laws they'd been living by would turn out to be the wrong laws all along, and that another more marvellous set they'd overlooked would be discovered at work. Why not? What was the matter, for instance, with a man like Larry Bowman becoming so fascinated with Joseph Bourne that he hated to let him out of his sight? "Blast you, Bourne, I want to figure you out."

But what was there to figure out? The ability to be everywhere at once, touching everyone's life? That walk—as if his feet never quite touched earth? That willingness to burn up enough energy for a hundred men in order to do something for someone else? That power he had, at least according to rumour, to raise sick children from their beds? Angela Turner told him he would crack his skull if he tried to understand such a thing, better forget it. Keep your mind on your job was what she meant, because now his job included her. She'd become a college student, enrolled in a business-administration course; she'd be coming to him for help every chance she could get and she wanted his full attention on her assignments, not floating out the window after Bourne or trying to solve the mystery of the old man's power.

But there wasn't much chance for him to do any kind of thinking at all as long as Angela Turner was in the library. She made sure that this course, which was intended to catapult her into the position of store manager just as soon as her boss left the scene, filled up as much of his time as possible. What kind of notebooks should she buy? How many pens? Would she be able to rely on this library alone or would she have to send out? How much of his time would he permit her to take up before he booted her out to make room for the others? Did he think she'd be able to whip through the course in half the time that other people took? After all, she was in a hurry.

She was also in the way; he never had a minute to himself any more. She hung around so much that he was even getting used to her—no more butterflies—he was even beginning to realize that he admired her ambitious spirit, enjoyed her lively company, and couldn't get enough of that beautiful laugh. But a part of him was also getting a little fed up with the loss of privacy. He wouldn't mind enjoying her in smaller doses. He was so busy reacting to her while she bustled around in his library that he never found the time any more just to scrutinize his emotions, weigh his thoughts, find out how he felt. Attracted as he was to her, he still hoped she wouldn't turn out to be one of those students who think they own the teacher, eager to keep him busy every minute, afraid to let him out of sight in case he dare to pay attention to somebody else.

He needn't have worried, of course. This was the same Angela Turner who'd run away from home to escape parents who didn't know the meaning of privacy, who'd deliberately gone about setting up the kind of life that suited a bachelor career-girl with her own ambitions. She knew what it was like to go overboard with that Peruvian sailor she'd found in her bed, and then to feel the shame that came afterwards. Not much chance that she was going to throw herself at Larry Bowman. She knew how easy it would be to scare him off.

But still the guy was pretty slow. If she waited for him to make a move it could take forever. No doubt he had the seabird on his mind still. (She knew all about his obsession with that woman, it was common knowledge, but naturally she wasn't foolish enough to let him guess she knew.) Obviously he needed a gentle push. No one could blame a girl for deciding that this was one of those situations where she'd have to act or find herself waiting around until the cows came home.

"Why don't you tell me her name?"

Already he looked ready to jump; maybe this was pushing just a bit too far.

"I know there's got to be a woman out there somewhere in the world." She felt clumsy at this kind of thing, hardly recognized her own teasing voice. "I've seen you looking at the girls around here, but you never do anything else but look, there's got to be someone you're crazy about out there." One minute a teasing flirt, the next minute a stern, serious woman. She didn't know what approach to take with this man.

"Name someone I've ignored." He was responding to the serious part of her only. He thought she was accusing him of offending someone.

"One bit of encouragement from you and I know that Linda Weins, for instance, would be putty in your hands."

Now he couldn't help but know she was only teasing. Linda Weins was everybody's joke. Even the men at the Mill knew better than to give her a second glance; at the slightest encouragement she'd have them down the aisle with their pants still down around their ankles.

He laughed. Thank goodness. If he'd taken even the mention of Linda Weins seriously then she would have known that she ought to give up. "Poor Linda! Did you see how long it took her to say goodbye at the door of that Porsche? Soaking wet, with tears streaming down her face, her night with the bigshot must've been really something. From now on it won't be safe to drink a cup of her coffee."

Cleverly veered off the subject, but she'd bring him back. "So who is this woman you've got hidden away somewhere? Who is the lucky girl? I've never seen anyone so faithful."

Now she'd gone too far. He looked hurt and confused at the same time. Maybe she'd put her big foot into something she didn't know about. Maybe he'd been married once, lost his woman, a widower. All she was doing with her clumsy probing was making him feel uncomfortable. She took his hand in hers. Cold as ice, he had a long way yet to go. "Well never mind, you don't need to think you're the only person who's felt that ache."

Then she did a foolish thing. On impulse, not even thinking. A complete lapse for a girl with so much control. She drew the palm of his hand over against her swelling waist so that he could feel the movement that was going on inside. The little Peruvian bugger was already trying to get out, with several months to go, just as impatient as his father when it came to planning an escape. But what a stupid thing to do! She saw immediately that it was a mistake, scaring him to death. He snatched back his hand as if her skirt were the top of a blazing stove. His face reddened, he didn't know where to look. When Mrs. Barnstone opened the library door, he nearly tore himself in two trying to hide his embarrassment and at the same time falling all over her in his eagerness to escape Angela's clumsy efforts to apologize.

"Mrs. Barnstone! Good to see you. A big pile of books to return, I see. And I've put something away that I thought might appeal to you. Just a minute, where did I hide that thing?"

He was so flustered that even Mrs. Barnstone started to blush, guessing she'd stumbled in on something unimaginably shocking. She looked at Angela as if surprised to see that she was fully dressed, not even the buttons ripped off her blouse or her hair mussed up. She tried her best to avoid glancing down at the front of Larry's pants, but lost the battle. At least he was zipped. She'd long ago given up any hope she'd had for the moral fibre of the young, but she still couldn't get over the way they insisted on inventing ever-new ways to wallow in their disgusting lust. "Never mind whatever you're looking for," she said, gathering all the force of her disapproval into her voice. "I'll come back some other time and find something new to read." By the time she came to the end of the sentence she was already pulling the door closed behind her.

Mrs. Barnstone wasn't one to spread malicious gossip, heaven knows. After all, she was a creative writer, and kept her most delicious suspicions and discoveries to herself for later use in poems and stories. Why waste good material on idle gossip? Yet she was so unsettled by the uncharacteristic signs of guilt and confusion on Larry Bowman's face that she just couldn't keep herself from saying something to the first person she met—who happened to be Jacob Weins. "Honestly I could spit," she said, in order to divert his attention from his cactus. "When a person steps inside a public library she has the right to expect she isn't stumbling into a private bedroom." That meek and mild librarian may be a little more complicated than anybody thought, she said, and proceeded to fill the mayor in on all her suspicions, sticking mostly to what she'd seen, but elaborating just a little with what she'd guessed, to add a little spice and keep the mayor's attention. After all, she added, hadn't they been shocked once already to discover their dear Miss Angela Turner wasn't the innocent everyone had believed her to be?

Luckily, the story didn't go any further. Having once expressed her concern, Mrs. Barnstone was again content to store it away for later use. And Jacob Weins certainly wasn't about to repeat such a flimsy tale. He was a public figure, an elected official, above such things. And besides, he was far too busy with his cactus, which he was beginning to suspect would eventually drive him insane. The country's Largest Natural-Growing Cactus was causing him so much trouble that he didn't have time for anything else, he didn't even have time to enjoy his anticipation of the promised changes ahead for this town. No time to dream of the money that would be tinkling in his pockets, filling up his till, pouring into this town —there was always something going wrong with his forty-foot sure-fire tourist trap. And naturally he was the only one around who could take care of the problems when they came up.

First, the thing had been on the verge of exploding. It was the nature of a cactus to store up as much moisture as it could for the hot rainless days on the desert, it was the nature of this type of cactus to expand as it took in water, but it was not the nature of any cactus to cope with the amount of rain that fell on Port Annie in the months that followed the Saguarus's arrival. The mysterious inner workings of this handsome giant must have gone completely out of control, nothing to do but turn it over to Dr. Harmon, who had no previous experience in draining cactuses but was certainly the most qualified man in the town. If the mayor could trust him with the delicate health of his wife, trust him to give her the correct sample pills every time, then surely he could trust the doctor with his beloved tourist attraction as well. And now all his attention was on that enormous structure being built up around his cactus—a tower of powerful steel legs and cross-braces to hold up a roof. Something to keep off the rain. Not only did the giant insist on bloating itself over and over, but it had taken on an unmistakable hint of the smell of mould. If it didn't explode from inside, it would rot away from the outside. Ridiculous as it would look, like a wheat elevator without walls, a roof was a definite must. So what if municipal funds were dangerously low, it would pay for its keep a thousand times over before long. The important thing now was to keep it in excellent health. He had discovered in an ancient encyclopedia that it wasn't enough to keep a cactus dry, it had to have some sun. Sunlight. Sunheat. No wonder the thing looked pale. No wonder its hard crusty surface was beginning to feel like over-ripe squash. The cactus was suffering from cold.

But when the four high-powered sunlamps arrived from Vancouver, he was so fed up that he wanted nothing to do with the installation. "Go wire them up," he told the young men he hired in the Kick-and-Kill. "Hang them from the corners of the roof. Turn them on. Just come back for your money when you've finished, I don't want to go anywhere near it." Nor did he want to think of the fight he would have on his hands the next time the town council met. Those lamps had cost a good deal more than he'd thought.

The maddening part of it all, as Mabel Weins explained to the other bridesmaids when they met at Jenny's house to plan the wedding, was that not a single tourist had come in to see it in all this time. Not one Californian or Albertan or cowboy from Denver had driven up through the mountains for a look at the thing. All those brochures he'd had made with photos of himself standing in front of the cactus were a waste of good money. Not a single one of those ads in the down-island papers had resulted in even a nibble. The poor man's heart was be-ginning to break. And now, ladies, he was out there every day, working like a slave. Because sunlamps weren't good enough by themselves, you see. The damp air was still harming the thing. What he was having to do now was fit the sides of that monstrous tower with walls of glass. The cactus was going to be kept in a lighted display cage, like the valuable jewels of the Queen.

Gossip about the Giant Cactus was not permitted for long in Jenny Chambers' house, not when the bridesmaids were working. Jenny herself saw to that. They could talk about cactuses any time they wanted, but as long as they were in her house she would see they kept to topics that she herself found interesting. Eva McCarthy wanted to talk about those three yellow bulldozers which had mysteriously appeared out of nowhere the day after Damon West left town, parked on a heap of dirt down by the road to the Flats. Didn't anyone else think they were rushing things? Where was the mayor's promise of open debate? Opal Dexter said she'd heard that the Flats people were preparing for war, carrying out drills and making weapons, she hoped that there wasn't going to be bloodshed over this business. Gloria Anderson tried to keep the talk centred on her children, those precious darlings she thought she knew how to raise. She couldn't stop harping about her Randy, who was impossible to train out of peeing on the toilet seat. Not even the signs she taped on the seat were helping—CAREFUL, THE SEAT IS WIRED. YOU COULD BE ELEC- TROCUTED! Spankings, screaming matches, threats, nothing worked, she just didn't know what to do, teach him to sit like a *girl*?

It may have been a mistake to invite Gloria Anderson at all. Like everyone else, she'd wanted to be a bridesmaid, but she hadn't a good word to say about anything to do with weddings or brides, or even with marriage itself. Being married was dull. The only excitement she could find in her own marriage, she said, was the static electricity she got when she pulled her washing out of the drier. Everything else was boring. "At any rate, it's not going to make the slightest bit of difference in Jenny's life. I can't even imagine why she's doing it." She al- most added "at this late date" but remembered that she was nearly the same age as Jen herself, and it wasn't quite as old as she'd expected it to be. "One way or the other, marriage is bound to be boring, I'm sure, compared to the glamorous life of a stripper."

"The stripping world has gone downhill without me, I can tell you," Jenny said, pouring tea (for everyone but Mrs. Lan- dyke, who carried her own teabags everywhere with her in her pocket, and used the hot-water tap). "It isn't what it used to be." Cripes, she said, she'd heard about this pub down-island where their regular stripper didn't show up one night—sick or something—so the waiter went on and did it for her. A twenty-seven-year-old man!

And threw herself back into her seat to show her complete disgust, while everyone screamed.

"What I'd give to see the looks on those people's faces," Eva said.

Jenny threw up her hands. "They loved it. He's still doing it. A logging town, too. It makes you wonder." And grunted, pulling herself ahead to get back to work. Gossip time was over. Down to business. "It's no world for a stripper any more. I'm just as glad to be out of it."

But once the ladies had gone she couldn't help brooding

just a little. There were days, naturally, when she wondered why she'd ever quit. Days when she remembered the music. She looked out over the damp dull roofs below her and saw faces bloated with excitement, eyes bulging, she heard the shouts and whistles, the calls. She remembered the way the music seemed to enter her body—still did, if she turned the radio on—and become a warm exciting force that started to fill her bones with life, her flesh with movement. She was a dancer; the stripping was incidental, just part of the dance itself; and every movement she ever made was controlled by the music. She was the best in the business, no kidding, because she responded to the music and not simply to the drooling demands of her audience—those other babes were clumsy cows compared to her, just twisting flopping flesh, they might as well have come on already naked and stood there for people to stare at. Jenny Flambé when she danced could make things happen in people's souls, not just in their glands.

Sometimes she danced for Slim, right here in the living room, just to keep in practice and to show herself that she hadn't lost the touch. She could make him sigh when she wanted to, or laugh, she could make him feel sad or happy just by the way she moved, and she could have those little eyes popping right out of his head when she started to take things off. Dancing was like the music itself, it could be used to make people feel any way that you liked. A big loss to the business, she knew that, they hadn't been able to find many like her out there, but she'd made her choice and stuck to it.

Sometimes, when she started brooding about her dancing days, only a long walk would help. Once, after the bridesmaids had gone, she packed a small feast of cakes and cream puffs and warmed-up breakfast coffee in an old bucket of Slim's and walked all the way out to the Mill, a mile or more, just in time for the afternoon break. There was a new spring in her step these days—a result of this relentless diet perhaps, and the memories of her dancing days that kept flooding in. A couple of months ago she might have dragged herself up to the entrance gate, ready to argue her way past the timekeeper-watchman, but today she sashayed up to the window as if she were Rita Rentalla, "Hello there, Morgan," and opened the bucket. "I'm taking the old man a treat. He tells me he can't stand to wait through a whole day of work without seeing me, by the time he gets home he's dangerous."

The racket in this place was just what she remembered. The whining of machines from inside the walls of the main building, the whirring of conveyor belts, the irritating roar of the little 'dozer boat pushing logs around in the pond. Nobody had done much about improving the smell, either. Like rotten eggs.

She found Slim and his crew inside the little shack the yard crew used for its headquarters—a storehouse for shovels and rakes as well as his office with a desk piled high with pieces of paper marked up with dirty fingerprints and pencil scribble. They were just sitting down on a bench along one wall to have a cup of coffee or light up a cigarette.

"What's this?" Slim was so surprised to see her at the door that he stood up. "What are you doing here?" Pleasure and anxiety in his face at the same time.

She stepped inside. These male hide-outs had never been able to frighten her off, not even the coloured photos of big-breasted women on the wall. "Time for the feminine touch, gentlemen, I've brought you some calories. Anyone for a bath in whipped cream?" She looked at Slim while she ran her tongue across her upper lip. "I knew a dancer once who went out on stage dressed in nothing but a few dabs of custard. When she came backstage later there was never enough left to feed a canary."

They dug in, the way she liked to see men behave; if Slim had had a finicky appetite she'd have left him long ago. In a few minutes there was nothing on the bottom of the bucket but a few scattered crumbs.

"You'll spoil us, Jen," Slim said. "These buggers'll be too full to work for the rest of the day; they'll lie around like stuffed pigs and I'll have to crack the whip just to get their backsides into gear."

"Crack it now," Jen said. "You fellows had your treat, now take your shovels and get back to your ditches, I want to have your boss's ear alone for a minute."

"What's up?" Slim said.

"Those women will smother me if I don't watch out. I just wanted to breathe some masculine air."

He laughed. "Pulp-mill stink is masculine?"

"It's kind of free of tension. If there's any competition in this air it's only over your job, not your soul. Those bridesmaids drain me dry."

She flipped through some of the paperwork on his desk. If the dates at the tops of the pages meant anything, he was letting this part of his job fall behind. He'd rather be out with the crew, doing what he called "real work"—hauling gravel, burying pipes, fixing the roads.

"And you're wondering if you made a mistake," he said. "Don't mess those up, I got everything in order."

"Order?" It looked as if everything had been dumped on the top of the desk out of an overturned box. "Of course I made a mistake. Everything's worked out just the way I wanted it to—more friends than I'll ever need—but it was still a mistake. Dishonest, for one thing. What the hell am I doing having a big white wedding with eight bridesmaids and two flower girls and all the rest of that fuss? They break their necks to be friends while they're in my house, but if they've got any brains in their heads they're making fun of me behind my back. Jenny Chambers throwing herself a royal wedding, what a joke!"

Beanpole Slim looked as if he didn't know what to do with his hands. "It's not a joke," he said, "not if it's what you want."

She grabbed the empty bucket up off the bench. "Oh how the hell should I know what I want? You better get out to your crew, they've probably dug halfway to China without you there to tell them to stop. Let me out of this place. How the hell should I know what I want?"

What Jacob Weins wanted most was much more easily identified: he hungered night and day for Port Annie's very first tourist. By the time the expensive glass walls were installed in the cactus tower, the complicated dehumidifiers added, the electric heater with thermostat control wired up, and two suspended Mill workers hired to act as caretakers for Canada's Largest Natural-Growing Cactus, he was more than ready, he was desperate. He was so obsessed with this need for a tourist, in fact, that when one of George Beeton's children came into the magazine shop to tell him the miracle had actually happened, he nearly swooned. Only his natural disbelief saved him from blacking out altogether. Surely it was only a very bad joke. But no, the child insisted, and led the mayor to the front of the shop, from where he could see a cluster of people hastily putting up umbrellas. "You see!" Weins shouted. "You see! There's a lesson in this for you all!"

"They're lost," the boy said. "They were looking for San

Josef and the Cape Scott Trail. They've got this great big
mobile home and wanted to know where our campsite was so
I said we don't got one. Then they noticed the cactus."

"And that's them out there now?"

Weins knew that it would be unseemly for the mayor of the
town to rush out of his shop to greet a family of tourists, you
didn't want to appear too eager or grateful, so he pulled a
chair over to his window and watched the umbrellas walk
across the square and down the slope to the wharf. What he
would give to be able to listen in! He was almost sorry that he
already knew about the presence of the cactus, he would never
experience the wonder and delight of driving into this rainy
town on the edge of a rainforest and noticing that mammoth
of the desert standing forty feet in the air at the foot of the
town in its own glass case. Those people were probably stricken
with awe.

After a few minutes (oh, his heart would go right out of
control!) the umbrellas all swung around and started back up
the slope. What did they think, what did they think? Weins
was on the verge of abandoning his self-control (unthinkable
that they should leave without registering their astonishment)
when he saw the man of the family stoop to talk again with the
Beeton boy, who'd gone outside to play with the dead fish he
dragged everywhere on a string.

"They've got Arizona licence plates," the boy reported, as
soon as the big mobile had driven away.

"Never mind that, boy. What did he say?"

The child pulled in his string and held the fish in one hand—
eyeless and rotting, a relic from the great wave of several
months ago—while he picked some pieces of dirt off its scales.
"He said the cactus is dead."

Now Weins was certain his heart would give out. This was
the kind of joke that could kill him. "Don't be a smart-ass,
little boy. What did the man really say?"

"He said he grew up with them things all around him and he
knows for a fact that your cactus is dead as a doornail."

"But it doesn't *look* dead!" the mayor shouted. "It doesn't
look dead!" It wasn't fair! It just wasn't fair! But even before
his brain had totally absorbed the news, even before that child
had scurried outside for his safety, Weins was already deciding
that he would leave the thing right where it was, dammit, until
it rotted and fell to the sand. There were millions of tourists
out there in the world, and not more than a handful could tell

a dead cactus from a living one; so until the thing toppled over and fell it would stay where it was. Any day now his publicity campaign would begin to pay off, word would begin to spread, and hundreds of cars would start hurrying through those mountains for a look at Port Annie's great wonder. When they got here, the largest natural-growing cactus in the country would be standing, just like the pictures, to give them a welcome. Not everyone lived in Arizona. And for all he knew, cactuses may not even rot when they died—they could just stay the same as before, like petrified wood.

It did not occur to Weins until several days later that he had not made provisions for selling tickets for a close look at the tourist attraction. That family had got its look free. And not only that, they'd been allowed to leave town without spending a single penny in any of the stores; they hadn't even bought gas for that monster they drove or stopped for lunch in the hotel. What a failure! He would have to make sure that kind of thing didn't happen again.

Those tourists weighed so heavily on Weins's mind that night —driving into his dreams in their luxurious mobile home that took up the whole width of the road and yelling into his face over and over again that his cactus was dead, was dead, was dead you old fool, and looking around at his town with contemptuous smiles on their distorted foreign faces—that when he woke up in the early morning and smelled smoke, his first thought was that they'd come back and were burning his house. When he staggered to the window and looked out at the faint light of dawn, he thought they were burning the whole town, like that place in *Gone with the Wind*. And even when he'd gone out onto his sundeck to see where the thick funnel of smoke was coming from, he was still confused enough to wonder why those people would want to pick old Joseph Bourne to be the one they fried to a crisp.

The tourists from Arizona by this time were probably up to their knees in mud, starting the Cape Scott Trail, and would know nothing at all about the fire that was destroying Bourne's cabin. Whoever had set that fire, if anyone, would have to be someone with licence plates from closer to home. By the time the mayor was awake enough to realize this, others in town had noticed the smoke as well.

Of course this included Eva McCarthy, who noticed everything. She saw what was happening from her kitchen window when she put on the kettle for a pre-breakfast cup of her imitation coffee. Giant clouds of black smoke rolled up from the beach and spread out over the town. Just some shack down at the Flats, she thought, and nearly forgot about it. But what if no one was putting it out, the danger could spread to the town and do damage to something of value. Even as far as your own house. One of her worst nightmares featured flames that devoured this house which meant everything to her, her beautiful furniture included. She awoke every time from it sobbing, wanting to die. Nothing could have been worse. She dragged Ian out of bed—"Let's go see, just in case"—but by the time they got down to the Flats several of the Squatters and a few men from town, volunteer firemen, were already standing around watching the shack blaze and crackle, sparks flying up in the rain. "Isn't anyone going to do something?" she said.

When Larry Bowman smelled the smoke, wakening from his own kind of dream, he knew immediately what was going on. With a coat thrown on over his pyjamas, and his feet stuck into gumboots, he ran as fast as he could down the road. The old man was trapped, he knew it, burning to death in that coffin of a shack. Probably unconscious in his bed, knocked out by the smoke, he wouldn't even know what was happening. Larry would have to break a window or knock down the door and go in and carry him out. Just in the nick of time, too, the roof would fall in just as he stepped outside with the old man in his arms. Everything behind him would collapse in a shower of sparks. It even passed through his head that if the daring rescue got into a few newspapers there was a slight chance that Raimey would read of it somewhere and know what he'd done.

When he got down to the Flats, however, the shack was such a mass of flames that even the bravest of heroes in his books would not have been stupid enough to go in. Certain suicide. The old man was obviously long past saving. The only thing they could do, one of the men told him, was make sure that it didn't spread to the others. A few sparks in the wrong place and this dump would be a carbon copy of hell, don't count on the rain to put it out.

Larry did not want to stay and watch that funeral pyre, nor did he like the idea of breathing the heavy death-filled smoke that thickened the air, but he couldn't tear himself away. And anyway, what would it look like if he just gave a shrug and left—for all anyone knew to go back to bed and get some more sleep? The least he could do was stay and look as if he were keeping his eye open for sparks, show some concern (while his stomach heaved at the thought of that old man being licked by the flames). His face burned from the heat—he had to back up a few steps, the smell of singed hair could easily have been his own. Like everyone else, he had to move back even farther when the roof fell in, sending birds of fire flying up into the sky. Red-hot floating ashes burned holes in the sleeve of his coat. What a useless man, standing like a stupid helpless donkey while someone burned to death a few yards away.

Suddenly a voice, somewhere in the dark: "Those bastards intend to burn us out one after the other. Tomorrow night it'll be someone else's house."

It was Hill Gin. Larry could see her moving his way, past the other dark figures standing in the flickering light from the fire. "They think we'll stand by and wring our hands. They think we haven't the guts to fight back." When she got as far as Larry, she stopped and jabbed a finger into his chest. "We're not leaving, we're not budging. If you burn us out we'll build again. And if you burn us out again we'll live under the logs, under the rocks, in the trees, you won't scare us off. We're going to stay!" The finger gave a final thrust. Waving her shotgun she moved on to someone else. "When you go to bed tonight, up there in your town, ask yourself whose house will burn to pay for this one."

Jenny Chambers dug Slim in the ribs with her elbow, "Wake up, it's a fire!" and threw on her raincoat. But by the time they got down to the Flats—Slim was a slowpoke, just try lighting a fire under *him*—there was hardly anything left to see. A circle of black human figures standing in the glow from that collapsed pile of embers and charred wood. A twinge of disappointment, especially when she saw Eva McCarthy amongst them—no doubt here from the beginning, eager to tell the whole world what she'd seen. Had there been screams? A face at the window? How long would they have to wait for the thing to cool down enough to go poking around for bones?

But the bones, she saw, were still upright. Still covered with flesh. The old man was standing like the others, staring at the remains, just a few feet behind the librarian. Eating, of course—munching on what looked like a raw potato. Did anyone else even know he was there?

"Watch out, you better hold onto him," she told Larry

Bowman. She'd seen men go to pieces over shocks like this
before now.

Larry jumped. Hold onto who? That figure he'd sensed
behind him had been only a faceless shadow, another one of
the crowd. But he saw now that it was Bourne. Acknowledging
Larry's alarm with a nod, a bit of a smile, the old man moved
forward a step, two steps, and grasped his arm. It was Larry,
not Bourne, who staggered a little. Where had Bourne come
from? How long had he been there? And could he see now, in
Larry's eyes, the tattered fragments of those heroic intentions,
those silly visions of rescue, headlines, and praise?

Despite what the bridesmaids said later, Jenny did not jump
in with her suggestion right at that moment. She had no designs
on the old man, no plans. In the excitement of all that smoke,
how could she have been so fast? It didn't occur to her until
later that now the old man would be looking for a new place
to live.

Try telling that to the bridesmaids. They behaved as if
they'd lost a race. In there like Flint, they said, the fire hadn't
even cooled yet, as if she were the only person in town who
knew the meaning of charity. "Trying to show the rest of us
up." As if she didn't have enough, with eight kids and a wedding coming up. That stripper must've been losing more than
fat with her starvation diet, she must've been losing her sense
as well. The worst housekeeper in town, the most disorganized
woman anybody had ever seen, a complete flop when it came
to running a house, how could she take in a boarder? And
where would she put him—her house wasn't any bigger than
anyone else's—unless she stacked those brats like firewood in
a single bedroom? Or moved them out to the garage to sleep
with Slim's tools. And wouldn't he be underfoot, a nuisance,
while everyone traipsed in and out of the house every day on
business to do with the wedding?

Maybe Jenny had a martyr complex, someone suggested.
Maybe she was one of those people who took on more than
they should, just so they could complain about it. "Any day
now she'll be starting to badmouth the rest of us because we
didn't throw our doors wide open to him, not that she gave us
a chance."

They flocked to her house as often as they could in order
to help her get ready for the wedding (to be held in the Kick-
and-Kill during the Fat Annie Festival), hoping to hear some

sensible reason for her taking on this extra burden. Hoping, too, quite naturally, to find out what it was like to live in the same house as a resurrected man. And even hoping that once in a while they would bump into him, exchange a few words in the hallway perhaps. But Jenny Chambers offered no explanations, just the same thing she'd said before, that generosity was one of her biggest faults. She was a pushover, she said, whenever someone needed her. And to prove it she threw out her hands, to take in the house, Slim, all those kids. Would anyone who wasn't a pushover have ended up with any of this?

And what difference did one more mouth at the table make? She just threw one extra potato in the pot and let him fight like the rest for what he got. Around here, she said, the biggest pig always got the most trough.

He was subject-matter for long afternoons over the wedding preparations. Was he saint or nuisance to have around the house? Lips clamped tight on straight pins muttered guesses: probably both . . . what man wasn't? . . . hold still a minute until this hem is up. And more than one curious lady, coming back from the bathroom, accidentally pressed a wrist against his slightly open door, to see if the room he shared with the oldest boy looked just like anyone else's. It did, a disappointment; even the beds were made—quite likely the only ones in the house that were (they'd never know for sure, the other doors were always tightly closed) and someone had even put an enormous bowl of salal leaves on his dresser, to add some colour to the room.

He was too old to be much help to Slim, of course, Jenny told her friends, but still he did whatever he could. Even learning how to run a machine, if you could just imagine such a thing. Slim had so many engines of one kind or another lined up across the yard that he'd decided to put a roof over the whole bunch of them to keep the weather off his precious babies—just one long slanted roof of corrugated iron up on posts, the full width of the lot—but then he'd discovered he needed to buy a posthole digger to do it. He went across to the other side of the Island to buy one and bought himself a near-new back-hoe while he was at it. He raised the shovel up into the air to stand on while he hammered the iron around the edges of the roof. Bourne sat at the controls and moved the whole thing along whenever Slim gave him the sign. Quite a pair, the two of them, you should come and have a gander over the fence some time, it was quite a sight. If those two ever settled on something to do together that made a little sense they'd be a highball outfit for sure.

And he was out of the house every morning, to teach those little Punjabis down at the school, then off to the Flats at noon, to hang around with his old neighbours there. And eating lunch with them—Lord knew what kind of food those people ate, probably mushrooms and ferns and grubs, certainly nothing normal—while they talked and talked and talked. And he helped them out, too, with little jobs that needed doing around their shacks.

"Making a show of himself," said Mrs. Barnstone, who was not a bridesmaid yet, but sometimes came along to help, and listen.

"But I won't let anyone say a word against him in this house," Jenny said, taking everyone in with a sweep of her eyes around the room. Daring them. "That old stick of a man is just doing what comes natural to him, being decent to other people." If there was anything dishonest about him, she added, if it was just popularity that he wanted, all he had to do was leave this place and go out to the world where people were panting to make a great big fuss over him. But she couldn't even imagine someone like that old man desperate after popularity, she couldn't imagine him doing a thing he didn't want to do just to make a lot of people like him—it wasn't necessary. He wasn't scared enough, there was no trace of loneliness in him now—he looked as if he'd be just as happy if he was the only man alive. Only frightened people had to crawl on their bellies after friendship.

In the afternoons, before he went down to the radio station, he locked himself in his room to work on that epic poem that had been burned in the fire. Starting all over again, right from the first word, something about a place in Jamaica, Jenny said, something in history. Port Royal. And cripes, spent the whole afternoon in there by himself. Eating steadily. You'd think it would be quiet, a poet at work over a piece of paper, but no, he snorted and snuffled, he stomped around the room, he came out to the bathroom a dozen times, he sharpened pencils and rustled around in his boxes of junk for new pens, he'd start reading books and forget all about time. Like a lunatic in there, or a caged animal. Practised the lines out loud, as if he had an audience, the old fool, over and over again, changing the odd little word here and there, and sometimes growling and snarling as if he were eating the thing up or grinding it into the floor under his foot. And sometimes so pleased with himself that he yelped right out loud, laughed, clapped his hands, she was sure she could hear him dancing around the room. Who could ever have imagined that so much of a commotion went into the writing of one silly poem?

"And you know, it's funny," Jenny told her bridesmaids, "but for all his flying here, flying there, living the life of ten different men all at once, there's a calmness to him that you'd never expect. Cripes, it must be nice to be like that. Just having him around makes me feel calmer sometimes, and happy."

So everyone knew what Jenny Chambers thought about having the old man in her house—but what about Slim? What were his feelings? In the lunchroom out at the Mill, Christie wanted to know if Slim wasn't scared he'd be crowded out of his own house one of these days by that famous ex-corpse. There was a limit to the number of bodies you could get into a space, and Bourne looked like the type who'd want plenty of room. Did some of them kids have to sleep between Jenny and Slim?

Slim opened his bucket, unfolded the waxed paper, took a sniff at one of his sandwiches. Just making sure, as he did every day, that she hadn't sprung any surprises. "Naw, there's lots of space left," he said, ready to bite. "And he's never home anyway, he's always out visiting, teaching them kids, all the things that he does, you know. He hasn't got time for hanging around home."

Christie winked at the man who sat across the table. Watch this. Wasn't Slim a little afraid the old man would come home with a chocolate-coloured face one of these days, eh, from hanging around so much with those Punjabi kids? Did he make Jenny throw curry into everything she cooked for him? Next thing they knew the old geezer would be wearing a turban and trying to put one on Slim's head too.

Slim leaned forward and raised his voice, so Christie could hear him above the noise of other voices. "One man's the same as the next to me. I don't have no feelings about colour. I'm sitting with you, ain't I, and my face is as white as it ever was."

Christie didn't mean nothing like that, eh, what the hell. "Look at the colours *I* got to work with. It don't bother me none."

"Now don't get me wrong about this," Slim said. "But I wouldn't let any of them into a house that I owned. They tell me when them people live in a house, the smell gets into the woodwork so bad you can't get it out no matter what you do. The only thing is to set a match to the place, nobody else will ever buy it or rent it." He chomped down on Jenny's sandwich —cheese and jam, his favourite, the only kind he'd had in the eight years since she'd arrived. "It's that terrible food they eat," he said, through the mouthful, "made out of stuff so strong it'll curl your toes."

Bald-headed Pete leaned in to say that he couldn't see why anybody should have to spend his days teaching their goddam kids how to speak the language of the goddam country. Why couldn't their goddam parents do it?

"Because their parents can't speak it either," Slim explained.

Christie dug his fingers into his scalp for a good scratch. "I guess it don't take any special talent to do it, eh, they say it's just like training a dog, going over and over something till you get it. You can train anything you want if you work at it long enough."

"I heard of pigs that was toilet trained," Pete said. "They rang a goddam bell when they wanted the goddam trap door to open."

"Well I had turkeys once," Slim said, "and I'm going to tell you you can't train them to do *nothing*, no matter what you say. Some things can't be trained and turkeys is one of them. Turkeys are stupid. Stomp your foot and they stampede. I've seen them suffocate from being too close together and not even complain about it. Turkeys are so damn stupid that if you move their feed dish they'll just go right on pecking in the same spot. Don't tell me you can train anything you want. Try training a turkey."

"Of course, old Bourne, he figures he can do anything he goddam sets his mind to," Pete said, slamming his bucket shut. "Once you've goddam conquered death, everything else must seem goddam easy. If you gave him a goddam pen of turkeys he'd be goddam teaching them how to sing in goddam harmony."

When Mr. Manku learned that Bourne was still teaching those children after surviving a fire and uprooting his life, his restlessness increased. While that old man behaved as if there were no limits at all in this world, Mr. Manku had allowed his own house to become a prison. He'd pretended, of course, that his family's displeasure had been the force which had kept him inside, and to a certain extent he was right. They could not afford, in this town, to let the head of their household make a public spectacle of himself again. Too many out there would be only too happy to laugh, to say, "See what happens when you let those rag-heads into the country?" Yet he knew that he *hadn't* made a spectacle of himself, he knew that the others had over-reacted. And he knew, also, that the real reason for huddling here in his house like an imbecilic relative or a hopeless cripple was simply his own silly fear.

And look what he'd been doing with himself all these lonely weeks. Eating. All day long he sat over plate after plate of steaming food, stuffing himself. It was disgusting. He was getting even fatter, his clothes were too tight. All he ever seemed to do any more was sit with a piece of roti folded between his fingers to scoop up mouthful after mouthful of rice and curried chicken and vegetable dishes seasoned with plenty of hot garam-masala. Harbans never complained, of course; she was in her glory watching him make a pig of himself with her food.

Yet she did not raise any objections when he began to get ready to go out. She just went on with her long precise preparations for the next meal while he put on his best white dress shirt, his tie, his dark suit, hardly worn. "Just stepping out," he told her, and she only shrugged. Perhaps she felt it was impossible to make a spectacle of yourself while dressed in your best suit.

But it was much more than "just stepping out". Much more. When he had oiled his hair, checked himself in the full-length mirror, brushed lint off his shoulders, and put on his overcoat sprayed with rainproofing liquid, Mr. Manku walked with quick deliberate steps down the hill to the school.

He'd never been inside a school in this country, for any reason; he had very little idea what happened to the children once they'd passed through those doors, only vague tales overheard at home, of embarrassments and punishments and humiliating competition, but neither the cold sweat which had broken out on his face nor the trembling of his hands stopped him from going inside and walking down the hall and finding the spot where Bourne and the three children were sitting in tiny desks arranged in a circle.

The old man made no fuss, simply got up and found a chair for Mr. Manku and continued with the lesson. All eyes were on a giant colour-photo of Port Annie, taken from the air. What is that? the old man wanted to know, pointing with his large hand at one corner of the photo. "That is the Mill," the children chanted. And what is that? "That is the library." And what is that? "That is the post office." And what is that? "That is the rec, the recre, the centre." The what? "The recreation centre." And what is that? Silence. He pointed again, told them to look closer, told them to stand up and push their faces right against the picture if they needed to. What is that? Oh, oh, their faces burst wide with laughter, then tightened into frowns for a better look. Oh, oh, they all burst out at once, that was their house, that was home, that was—as one of them said while pointing at Mr. Manku—that was Mr. Manku's castle!

Castle? Castle? The old man pulled down his weedy eyebrows with mock disbelief. Were there castles in Port Annie? he wanted to know. Were there real castles here in this town, like those pictures of castles they'd looked at the other day? Was it really possible that right here in Port Annie three children were fortunate enough to live in an honest-to-goodness castle?

The children smiled, uncertain. They looked at Bourne and then they looked at Mr. Manku. They looked at one another and frowned down at their hands.

"It is a small joke," Mr. Manku explained. His voice in this building seemed thin and weak. "Because my house is so far up the hill and because enough people live in it to fill a king's enormous palace, the children and I refer to it as the castle. A silly thing, embarrassing, and now it has caused them to learn something wrong which will hinder their progress in school."

Bourne clapped his hands together and laughed. Ah, now he understood, now it was clear. Mr. Manku lived in a castle, he said, and Sohan and Daljit and Davinder all lived in a castle, but what about these other people? His finger strayed over the photo. What did all of these other people have to live in since they were not kings and could not live in a castle?

"They lived in a house," one of the children said, and tipped up her face to smile.

All in the same house? All together?

The little girl closed her eyes, pursed her lips, and hummed, while her feet swung back and forth just inches off the floor. Then her eyes sprang open and her hands flew out, as if she'd discovered something written on the inside of her eyelids. "They live in houses!" she shouted. "Houses!"

Mr. Manku nodded stiffly. "Of course." His dark eyes

steadied on the eyes of the ancient man. "And of course they live in God, my children, as you have been taught at home."

"Babaji?" one of the children said.

Mr. Manku nodded, "Eko Ankar, God is One."

True, the old man agreed, but Mr. Manku would forgive him if he added no comment of his own in front of these children, because this was a public school they were in, where encouraging thoughts of God, like advocating the practice of sodomy, was forbidden by the law.

At that moment a tiny face appeared at the nearest classroom door. "Grandfather?" It was little Kamaljit. He'd recognized the voice and tiptoed out to see.

Mr. Manku rose to his feet. "Yes, of course it is me. Yes, of course."

The child ran to him, threw himself into the open arms, and laughed.

"Just look, Mr. Bourne, just look at this grandson of mine. And tell me, have you ever seen such a beautiful face?"

The small boy giggled, then turned to grin at the old man. A tiny dark face, all eyes, and a mop of black hair.

Bourne fished around in his pockets. Those eyes would swallow him. So dark and huge. Only once, Mr. Manku, had he ever seen a face so beautiful. "And the light that shines in those eyes, Mr. Manku, I think he stole it from the girl Raimey, whose looks were so full of joy."

And look, he added. A whole bag of cookies, enough for us all.

When Mr. Manku rose to leave, brushing his hand down over his stomach and buttoning up his jacket, he cleared his throat several times as if he were not quite capable of making the break. More words were meant to be spoken yet, but what could they be? Joseph Bourne stood up, with a hand on the top of a child's head. "Tomorrow," he said, "we'll be learning all about families. Maybe you could come again then and help us."

"Yes, yes." This was what he'd been waiting for. He nodded, nodded, smiling. "Yes, yes, of course I'll be here. Now you little children behave yourselves until I am here again." Set free, he pumped the old man's hand, "Thank you, thank you," and hurried away with quick steps to push his way out the door.

He was singing, under his breath, when he encountered Gregory Wong, who was just about to hop onto his motorbike and go down to the library for a tutoring session. "Wonderful man," he stopped to tell him, but could only repeat, "Wonderful man."

Wong wasn't convinced, as he reported to Larry Bowman. True, Bourne had done a lot of good around here, as one of the ex-cons who still met regularly with him he ought to know—but that crazy old man was starting to poke his nose in where it wasn't wanted. Look what he'd done to Dirty Della. "She wants a little *respect* all of a sudden, the bitch. Thinks she's a high-class lady or something with her nose in the air."

What a shock. Greg was nearly in tears when he told it. Frustration and rage. With Dirty Della it had been anything you could dream up, no humiliation was too grotesque for her, for money she could turn herself into anything you wanted. Seven men at once, the only way to have it. He and his friends had got themselves all worked up the other night, ready for a party, all gassed up in the Kick-and-Kill, and down they went on their bikes. But her door was locked. Someone else had got there first. "Son of a bitch." They rode their bikes around the the house, banged on the windows, "Come on, Della, hurry it up, don't take for ever," and made as much noise as they could driving out the boardwalk and back. "Open up there, Della, speed that slowpoke up, dump him off and get ready for seven real men."

No answer. But she wasn't getting rid of them that easily, now they were all worked up. They sat on her step, chucked stones at a rusty car-body half buried in salal. *Clang, clang*, enough to wake the dead. Someone in one of the shacks hollered, "Shut up, you bozos!", so naturally it was more fun to test your aim out on his front door, the fartface, let him learn to keep his insults to himself.

But Della's door opened at last and Greg Wong couldn't believe his eyes, it was such a shock. It was that old man Bourne who came out. No wonder it took so long, such an old crock, he probably couldn't remember what to do, but, "Never mind him, now you can entertain some real men, Della, get out the hooch and let's get started!"

The door slammed and a bolt slapped into place. What the hell? "Open up, you. What's going on?"

"Not tonight," she yelled through the door. "Go on away, take off! Leave me alone!"

The stupid bitch. They'd break the door down, smash her windows, wake up everybody for miles around. Who the hell did she think she was, slamming the door in their faces? What gave her the right to get fussy? She'd taken their money often enough, it was more than she deserved, she ought to be paying *them* for the privilege, the filthy squaw.

She couldn't stand the racket for ever, eventually she had to open up. "Ah Della, what kind of game are you trying to play? Look, it's us. The dirt-bikers. Step out of the way and let us in."

But she stood in the doorway with one hand outstretched to grip the wooden frame. Her eyelids were half-closed over her dark eyes, her chin lifted like someone sniffing the air for the source of unpleasant odours; she looked at Greg Wong and then at the others on her step as if here were a painful decision she was making in her head, behind those eyes, something she just couldn't quite accept. She shook her head, sadly. "Ah boys, I'm sorry."

She half closed the door again. "Things around here are going to change. You guys better just go away, let a woman live in some peace and quiet. Show a little respect."

When Greg Wong leapt at her she stepped back swiftly and slammed the door in his face. Bitch! The bolt snicked into place, and no amount of rattling the doorknob could budge the thing. Break down this pig's door, boys, no filthy clootch was going to shut the door in their faces without being sorry. Smash down the walls of the pigsty, raise a racket loud enough to break the windows, bring the ceiling crashing down, don't let her get away with that kind of high-handed snootiness. Who did she think she was?

Nobody could raise a ruckus to match the dirt-bikers when they were insulted. They just didn't make ears strong enough to stand it for long—bike motors revving, broken boards banging against the verandah railing, curses foul enough to melt steel and scare rust in flakes off the old bodies of cars. "Who'd want to touch you, you two-bit hoor? Who wants your diseases? We wouldn't step in that door if you begged us to. Go take a bath in boiling water. Fill the tub up with lye!" Oh they made sure her ears were split, don't worry about that. They made her sorry she'd got so high and mighty with the dirt-bikers, he told Larry, no fat squaw was going to get snotty with them. And if she came crawling for their favours now, they'd only spit in her face, let her beg, she wasn't the only fish in the goddam sea.

"It's all the fault of that Bourne," he said. "Look what he's

done. Giving that slut ideas. And making a fool of herself—
public too, with her ridiculous strut. What does she think—
that she stepped off a freighter or something? Someone ought
to smash in her skull."

Such drastic measures weren't necessary after all, as it turned
out. Because Dirty Della, after a few days of this new touch-
me-not dignity, admitted that she was getting lonely all by
herself with just those kids of hers for company. She was
willing to compromise just a little.

What she meant by compromise, Angela Turner reported to
Larry, was only one gentleman caller at a time after this. And
only if they treated her like a real lady. She wanted to be taken
bowling. She wanted to go for joy rides in the mountains. She
wanted to park at the dump, watching the bears like everyone
else. She wanted a bouquet of flowers, or some chocolates. From
now on, anyone who wanted her favours would just have to
show a little respect. She'd told Angela this in the grocery store.

"I'm not just a pig," she smiled, and wanted to know why
there wasn't a boy handy, to pack her bag and carry it home
for her.

Obviously, Joseph Bourne was not going to be content with
renovating shacks and teaching children. He had something
else in mind. Larry dug out his stack of magazines from the
back room, to read through again, and study the pictures:
Bourne in a tuxedo, surrounded by society people holding
champagne glasses; Bourne piloting his own yellow plane with
purple lettering down the side; Bourne crawling out of the
door-hole of an igloo; Bourne at a desk, frowning over a piece
of paper. None of them helped him to understand what was
going on in this town. Did the old man have ambitions to be
some kind of wizard or shaman?

In Joseph Bourne, Larry thought he could perceive a powerful force at work—wonderful and terrifying all at once—
preparing to slip the world out from under everyone's feet any
minute. Ready to shake their foundations loose and whisk the
earth right away. Perhaps only those who had learned to float
with their dreams, like Bourne himself, had any hope of surviving. The others, like Larry, could brace themselves for a
fall. Force of nature, instrument of God, or only a common
mortal with accidental talents, Joseph Bourne was a man to
keep your eye on. Besides, there might even be something a

fellow could learn from watching him. Especially a man who'd always been obsessed with heroics. Was this ancient man a space-age equivalent of Sir Lancelot and the others? Instead of fighting dragons or slaying villains he challenged the limits of mortality.

Naturally, Larry was sceptical. After all, he'd read all those books, he knew about heroes, he was an expert on the nature of superheroic deeds. Being a hero had strict requirements. A code of honour. A grand enormous soul. It required courage and strength and patience and love and sacrifice. And outside of the pages of those books, where had he ever seen such a thing? Real people were usually just like himself, behind all their masks, small and foolish and scared. And selfish. There were no Alfred the Greats any more, no Socrateses, the idols of this modern world turned out to be all too human. Lord Jims and Lucky Jims were the best you got. There weren't even Don Quixotes any more, daring to look ridiculous to honour the code. If Joseph Bourne was beginning to act as if he belonged in an allegory, or an ancient romance, it was only natural that Larry Bowman should look for some gimmick, some flaw, some ulterior motive.

Every chance that came along he kept the old man talking in the library. Or stopped him on the sidewalk if it happened that he intended to go right past. They talked of books and poetry. They talked of travel. They talked of the old man's slowly growing poem about Port Royal. They talked of the beautiful girl off the Peruvian freighter who had changed the course of both their lives. And as they talked, Larry sought the secrets of his boundless energy, even while he watched for some sign of the expected flaws and twisted aspirations.

Though he preferred, of course, to believe. A hero, after all, was what he had hopes of becoming himself. He dreamed of rescuing people from flames, of leading refugees over the mountains, of masterminding a revolution of slaves, of raising the dead. If he died—for others of course—if he ever died, he would ascend to the sky in a blaze of gold light, be confused with a star. Why not go all the way? He would be someone whose very memory could transform lives for centuries to come.

Like Fat Annie walking the booms, women would go into mourning and call out his name so heartbreakingly that the

mountains would take it up and echo it back to them all
through their empty lives.

He did not, of course, confess any of this fantasy to Angela
Turner, though he did go so far as to admit—when she took
him in a borrowed boat out to the little island of Billy Goat
Jake—that the part he liked the best about Fat Annie's story
was the way she mourned for her men. "Imagine being so much
in love!"

"Love!" Angela searched the island for someone to share
her disbelief. "Listen to this man! Fat Annie in love? The old
hag just couldn't believe that anyone would desert her. Don't
go calling that love."

"She must have loved them. Her heart was broken." But
Angela's sceptical look was not about to soften. "Tell me,
then, if it wasn't love, what did she mean to her men? What
did she mean to this . . . Billy Goat fellow out here in his tiny
world? If it wasn't love what was it?"

"Fat Annie has always meant the same to everyone. Flesh.
Something you could get your hands on, flesh and earth and
good old solid matter."

The driftwood shack faced down the inlet, to the two sharp
treed slopes that seemed to meet where the inlet turned. Gulls
wheeled at the turning, cormorants rode on a floating log.
Larry walked down to the water's edge alone, then followed
the strip of tangled kelp and woodchips around to the other
side, where the town was visible, and the shacks of Squatters'
Flats. Small clusters of wooden boxes in all that green. A few
grey cabins at the water's edge, a few rows of roofs up the
slope—it was hard to believe there was enough there for anyone to care about. Or get excited over. Even the Mill—sole
reason for life here at all—was only a cement-grey stack re-
leasing a steady flow of thick whitening smoke that drifted up
the valley beyond the inlet's head.

Something, he recognized, was changing. Something un-
named was happening. He kicked at bones, trying to reassem-
ble them in his imagination. He saw goats roaming the island,
looking for something to eat among the grass that grew in
pockets of soil, nibbling at the few twisted trees which, he saw,
had been stripped of everything but their own trunks up as
high as a goat might be able to reach. They must have been
desperate. He imagined the bloodbath when Fat Annie took
her revenge.

"There's a poem in one of Bourne's books," he said, when he sensed Angela behind him. "One of his earlier books. About Fat Annie."

"Impossible. He couldn't have known about her before he came here."

He shrugged. Maybe. "She was someone who dogged his footsteps, in the poem, she wrote him letters. Obscene suggestions, mocking insults. Wherever he was in the world. Invitations to hell, he called them."

"Coincidence," she said, and took his hand.

"Well, now he thinks it's funny."

"What?"

"That he's operating right under her nose up there in that hotel."

"He told you that?"

"He told me it was only natural the two of them would end up in the same place here. The end of the world, he calls it, him and the old death-whore at the end of the world together, and only one of them—he says—with any hope of surviving."

She pulled his hand to her throat. "And us? What about us? What are our chances of surviving?"

He didn't pull away this time. No frightened reflex, no beads of sweat. He put both of his hands around hers and lifted her fingers to his lips. He'd come prepared for this. What else had he been able to think about since the day she'd made her move? His hands had kept on burning for days while he got used to what was happening. Now all he could think was how pretty she looked, with the drops of rain on her cheek, those beautiful dark eyes that always appeared slightly startled at first, until they softened with her laughter. There was little doubt in him now, only this warmth, this urgency, this sense of his own exhilarating fall through space.

Inside the driftwood shack he kissed her lips and felt her hot breath when she pushed closer to be kissed again. Honeysuckle on her shoulder. She whispered something with her lips so close to his that every nerve in his body responded to their movement, the soft movement of air. He kissed her ear, pressed his face into her hair, and felt the falling that had started in him long ago hit bottom.

A row of raindrops clung to the top of the doorway, collecting enough weight to tear themselves loose. One of them, directly in line with the sun that burned so pale behind the

whitened sky, suddenly flared up red, a sun itself, so bright he
flinched and had to look away.

The truth, Larry, the truth.

But not until he'd drawn her back into a darker corner of
the shack, and found a comfortable piece of floor. Not until
she'd curled up against him, her face by his throat, her hand
inside his shirt. There, though he knew he was risking everything, could ruin it all for ever, he told her all about the shame
of having been in love with a woman once who'd laughed in
his face. And told her about that other one, too, who'd strung
him along and then walked off and left him for a uniform.
Why were women such unknowable creatures? His head was
always full of the shapes of beautiful girls, his body was always
ready to make love, but the thought of getting close to a real-
life breathing woman scared him half to death. Until recently,
that is, and even now a part of him was ready to bolt, expecting any minute she would leap up and laugh at him.

"Do you hear me laughing?" she said. "I didn't get this bulge
in my belly without becoming the biggest joke in the universe.
Somewhere out in that world right now there's a lousy Peruvian sailor turning me into a joke to pass on to every man that
he meets. Don't forget to stop off at Port Annie, boys, for the
easiest you-know-what in the hemisphere."

So he didn't bother to tell her about the magazine ice-cube
images he studied every day, sometimes with his fingers between the pages under the counter while he stamped somebody's book with the other hand. Why push his luck? She
hadn't laughed so far, but even the most compassionate girls
must have their limits. Nor did he tell her about the romantic
novels he read, like a pre-adolescent boy, in which knights
killed dragons and rescued beautiful ladies, or the fat books
of old poems in which men knew how to be men and courage
was something that seemed to come easy. He even decided
not to remind her, yet, of the erotic images he couldn't help
finding in Joseph Bourne's poems, where others were finding
everything else. Time enough for those confessions later, when
she wasn't waking up every nerve in his body with hungry
kisses along his throat. She brought his face down to hers with
her hands, and ran her tongue quickly along his lips. "Who
cares about any of that, it doesn't matter, just forget it." She
pressed against him, forced his mouth open, ran her tongue
across his teeth.

No more dying like a schoolboy from fear or joy, the dying was dead, everything flamed to new life, rose up in him throbbing. Sweet as honeysuckle, warm as sun, she must have sensed it, known the sudden surge of life inside him. She moaned, softly, like a little girl, and nuzzled her face into his shoulder to find whatever his scent was, and encouraged his hands down to feel the hard swollen curve of her, the baby that was between them, and slipped her own hands inside his shirt to move against his skin and slide around until they met each other across his back.

People in town who'd seen the boat set out from the little dock by the cactus barge were sure they knew what was happening out there on the island, but the details were nobody's business. That was why it had to take place so far from prying eyes or accidental witnesses who would have been embarrassed anyway, or unbelieving. It was no concern of Rita Rentalla's, say, whether Larry Bowman, once awakened, remained the clumsy timid lover she suspected him of being, having to be coaxed and led by the nose all the way, taught everything as if he were born only yesterday, making mistakes and getting himself so worked up after all those years of waiting that he was only a disappointment to a woman, pleasing only himself. Just as it was no business of Linda Weins's keeping one eye on that white speck of boat from the coffee-shop window, whether Larry surprised himself by discovering he was already an incredibly skilful lover (as she imagined), ready to devour a girl with his hot mouth, his sharp teeth, his tongue, driving her crazy with all the manipulative talents of a man who'd lived for years with all the most sophisticated women of the world, instinctively knowing exactly what to do in order to make Angela Turner forget whoever it was that had planted that seed in her gut, poor thing. As George Beeton said to himself, standing in the open doorway of his service station, if he was able to actually watch what was going on he'd probably be disappointed, better to just imagine. After all, who said that what was going on had to be sex at all? Shame on everyone who jumped to that conclusion, there were other ways for people to get to know each other. For all anyone knew in town, George thought, those two could be the lovers of the century or they could be two lonely kids talking the ear off one another.

Whatever happened happened, the little white boat remained

beached on the island for several hours and people could spend
only so much of their time in guessing; life had other distrac-
tions. Jenny Chambers, for instance, didn't care one way or
the other what was happening on the island. As soon as she
was sure the mail had come in, nothing else mattered but getting down to the post office to see if her wedding-cake orna-
ment had arrived.

It hadn't. Only the telephone bill and a government pamphlet. Taxpayers' money to praise the party in power.

"Nobody loves you today," Ian McCarthy said, as he said
countless times every day.

Jenny turned to leave. She had no time for small talk with
that fuzzy otter-face. But she had to wait for the crippled
brother Crabbe to move his giant bulk out of the door before
she could get past. She was almost down the steps before she
realized he'd been walking on his own two feet, no crutches
anywhere in sight. This was worth a second look.

"What happened to you?" McCarthy said, peering at those
boots for some evidence of a trick device.

Jenny didn't need to hear the answer. "Joseph Bourne?"

The young man nodded and walked in a circle to show off
his perfect feet from every side. He walked backwards, he
kicked, he did everything that feet could do. He even did a
few short shuffling steps of a tap dance. His grin was so wide,
his face so red with pleasure, that he appeared to be taking
most of the credit himself. "Old Bourne," he said. "There ain't
nothing that man can't do."

"I don't believe you," McCarthy said. "What really happened?"

The cripple shrugged and reached for his handful of mail.
"Believe it or not," he said, and popped three dusty pocket
peanuts into his mouth. He didn't give a hoot for anyone else's
opinion; it was clear he knew what he knew.

"What are you feeding that old man up there anyway, Jen?"
McCarthy said. It was safer to hide behind a joke. "Must be
something in his porridge."

"Nobody's ever accused me of working miracles with my
cooking. I take no credit for this thing."

"Whatever it is, you ought to patent it, you'll make a fortune selling it through the mails."

Simple-minded people must be the easiest to cure, McCarthy
said as soon as the Squatter had gone. "They believe every-

thing they're told, no mind of their own. Bourne probably hid his crutches somewhere and this big lummox forgot he couldn't walk."

"Nice try," Jenny said.

Well there had to be a sensible explanation, McCarthy said. No doubt there were plenty of ways to explain it, nobody was going to treat him like a fool. "Everything in this world has its rational explanation."

"Don't count on it," Jenny said, and left. Naturally she didn't mean what she said. She counted on an ordered universe as much as anyone in town, but she wasn't quite so sure as Ian McCarthy was that all of it could be simply understood. There were still some mysteries left, thank goodness, and lots of room for new ways of looking at things.

III

AT TWO-THIRTY on the afternoon of November ninth, Angela Turner looked out the grocery-store window and saw Fat Annie Fartenburg crossing the square. Maybe it was an illusion, she couldn't be sure, this rain was coming down so heavy that you couldn't be certain any more if what you were seeing was there or not. A huge fat woman in long skirts, a thick-painted face, and great laced boots. But by the time Angela's mind had registered what she was seeing and she'd rushed to the door for a better look, the uncertain figure had disappeared. It must have been only a distortion in that streaming-down rain, this garish light from a white sky making a normal person look as fat as a pig.

Yet Mrs. Landyke saw her too. While she was hurrying home from the post office with a letter from her married daughter Irma bulging in her pocket, she caught a glimpse of the enormous figure passing across the bottom end of the street. It couldn't be anyone else. No one in this town had ever got so fat. And those clothes—straight out of a history book! If it hadn't been raining so hard Mrs. Landyke might have gone down for a closer look, but as it was, all she wanted to do was get home as fast as she could. The easiest thing was to believe that her ageing eyes were deceiving her, let it go at that.

But George Beeton also saw her, and there was nothing wrong with his eyes. Even flat on his back under someone's car he never missed a thing that passed in front of his service-station pumps. He bumped his head on the differential in his hurry to get out from under, but there was no question about it, this was definitely Fat Annie Fartenburg—exactly what he'd expected her to look like, exactly the picture he'd formed while listening to Christie's tales. A mess of white hair, an over-painted face, breasts like heavy watermelons, buttocks like two sacks of potatoes in that skirt made from acres of coarse red material—everything protected from the rain by a huge tent of transparent plastic that hung out around her like the display case of the cactus, only portable. A little shorter than he'd pictured, but it wasn't realistic to expect a legendary figure to live up to all your expectations. He nearly whistled, to call her back, but a sudden attack of shyness cut off the wind in his throat. If she turned, what would he say?

Instead, he followed her. At a discreet distance, of course. Who was she looking for? What kind of mischief was she up to? He couldn't help admiring the way she had plenty of life left for such an old woman, plenty of flesh. Look at the seductive way she managed to grind those sacks of potatoes against one another. No wonder those men used to call her their tub of love, and dream of tickling those rolls of fat.

She led him along the road past the Down Front houses, past the recreation centre, past the library. This rain had already soaked him through to the skin. The water on the sidewalk rose to his ankles. Streets already sprinkled with periwinkle shells and pieces of seaweed from the inlet were littered now with debris raked down out of the sky—needles and branches stripped off trees, moss off roofs, feathers from seagulls and cormorants and crows and the thousands of jays whose incessant movement seemed to keep the whole town alive and jittery twenty-four hours a day. She led him into the gravel pit and up to the little trailer that had been intended for a church. There she lowered her weight onto the step, which was sheltered by the trailer's projecting plywood roof, let out a long noisy sigh, and started to shrug her way out of her transparent raincoat.

"What are you staring at, Beeton? Put your eyes back in your head, haven't you seen a beautiful woman before?"

The jolt of recognition that hit George Beeton nearly knocked him off his feet. She was talking to him with the voice of Gregory Wong. How was such a thing possible?

It was possible, of course, because she *was* Greg Wong. He saw that soon enough. Behind all that thick greasy make-up there was Wong's round face looking at him, ready to laugh at this fool who really believed he was following Fat Annie Fartenburg down the street. And behind him, in the doorway of the trailer, there was Jacob Weins in his Dieter Fartenburg costume, a logger's outfit complete with hacked-off jeans and wide elastic braces.

"What the hell's going on?" George said. "Why's this ass parading around like an old hoor?"

The mayor invited him inside, into a mess of boards and sawdust and sawhorses and tools dropped just wherever they happened to have been used. "I'm trying to make something useful out of this thing, and practically single-handed too. Turning it into a cultural centre for the town."

By cultural centre, he explained, he meant a tourist-information bureau. Also a headquarters for his campaign to prepare the townspeople for the inevitable exciting future, as well as a publications depot for the pamphlets and news releases and photographs that would be sent out to every newspaper in the world. It was stupid to think of this church sitting here empty, no use to anyone, when a little bit of hard work could convert it into something valuable. He showed George the posters and banners he would be putting up on the walls, over the door, in a glass case out by the road.

"Something to give this town a shot in the arm," he said. "Wake those lazy drag-backs up a little, get them excited about the future."

As for Gregory Wong, he was a walking advertisement. Employed by the city now to work up a little interest in the Fat Annie Festival coming up at the end of the week. And don't forget, Jenny Chalmers' wedding wouldn't be the only thing happening in the Kick-and-Kill that night, there was also the yearly round of noisy entertainment aimed at shaking the old girl loose from her nest in the second storey.

"This year I'm sure the miracle is going to happen at last, and about time too. We've waited long enough. It's high time that old hag made herself useful for a change instead of hiding up in her room while people guess when she'll decide to come down. I've done her deciding for her, this is the year."

Gregory Wong bounced his breasts in his hands, gave his

colossal hips a suggestive shake, and pouted his painted lips at George. "It's so thrilling to be followed by such a handsome stud, someone who knows where a piston goes, a grease monkey with the magic touch when it comes to starting a girl's engine."

George might have thrown the electric drill if the mayor hadn't laid a cautioning hand on his arm. "You see what a hit she's going to be?" Weins said. "In costume for the whole week, even when she's out at the Mill."

Only a stopgap measure, though; the mayor had bigger plans. He couldn't tell George this yet, or even breathe a word of it to Wong, but he hadn't pried that plywood off the windows and hacksawed through the lock and put himself through all this work to produce nothing more important than a cultural centre. Just as he'd decided that this was the year Fat Annie would descend, no question about it, he'd also decided that once she was down she wasn't going back up. He himself intended to see to that. Where she would live out the rest of her life was right here in this trailer he was fixing up for her, a comfortable home, where she'd be always available to curious visitors when they came in to town—tourist attraction, living history, and the spirit of Port Annie all rolled into one. He had a vision of her enormous figure in the doorway, dressed in something suitably old-fashioned, like that skirt and blouse of Wong's, telling off-colour tales of the good old days while grateful visitors shook the mayor's hand and congratulated him on his astute public-mindedness in keeping the spirit of the town alive, quite literally, to be enjoyed by one and all. He wasn't such a fool as to believe she would be still in her prime after so many years alone in her room, but as long as she wasn't totally senile she could still be put to good use.

Not long after George's arrival, Jenny Chambers yoo-hooed at the trailer door, she needed a rest in her daily weight-losing walk and this looked like a good enough place. Three of Slim's kids, playing hooky from school, poked their noses in just long enough to sneer at this proof of adult insanity, then went out to continue their assault on the boat in the tree. Throwing rocks hadn't budged it, and so far no one had been able to climb the trunk high enough to reach it, but today they'd brought somebody's broken ladder. If they ever got up as far as that boat, they had plans for bringing it down on top of somebody's head. Otherwise, what was the point? You could always hope, of course, as Weins did, that they'd climb inside it and crash to their deaths. Or better still, go sailing off into space and never be heard from again. Wynken, Blynken, and Nod.

Jenny gave Gregory Wong the once-over, then slid a look at Weins. Chewing gum as always. "You two planning to set up housekeeping together here?"

Weins hadn't noticed before how much she'd improved her appearance now that she'd become a bride. Pretty enough to turn a few heads. A trim new figure, a dancer's smart walk. She was still too mouthy for his taste, but he couldn't deny she was easy on the eyes.

"His newest toy," George Beeton said. "Let's hope it doesn't go the way of his friend in the barge." He tilted his head in the direction of the Giant Cactus, which could be seen from the doorway of the little trailer-church. The poor thing had been subjected to such a series of shocks—uprooted from its native soil, transported over land and sea, rained on and saturated to the point of nearly exploding, burned by heat lamps, dried out by electric heaters, and stared at contemptuously by one family of tourists from its own home state—that it had shrivelled and dropped in its enforced afterlife and slumped against its glass wall like a boneless drunk. Not another tourist had come in to see it. A good thing maybe, it looked so defeated and ugly.

But never mind, never mind, Weins insisted, in case they thought he was brooding over that conspicuous failure. How could he be, with this new project already under way, the best one of all? "I've been far too busy to give that cactus a passing thought."

He'd had to pile all the pews up at one end of the room. A good bonfire was what they looked ready for, but he supposed he'd better haul them away to store in his basement. Just in case. Lucky this was meant to be an all-purpose church, not one of those fancy cathedrals full of statues and crosses and pipe organs. As it was, he'd nearly got a hernia trying to crowbar the pulpit away from the floor. Other than that, there was no evidence that it had ever been intended for anything but exactly what he was using it for, except for all the gold-leaf messages printed on every wall. Churchy people were the worst offenders when it came to slapping up quotations everywhere you looked. "Look at this one," he said. "I'm using up half my supply of posters just to cover up all their warnings."

For he that loveth not his brother
abideth in death.
                              I John 3:14

He sorted through his posters until he found one large enough
for this particularly offensive quote. Fat Annie's face, larger
than life, grinned out at them over a huge green-lettered
command.

Grab your chance
Don't think too small
The future's coming
With fortunes for all.

"That's better," Weins said, and stood back to make sure he'd
stapled it level. He had. This place was beginning to take on
new life, he could hardly wait to get it finished. An ordinary
office with desks and a counter would be good enough for
now, in this bigger room anyway, but he hoped to decorate it
with things dragged up off the beach, to give it a local flavour.
Driftwood and dried starfish, fishnet draped across the end
wall, hanging with cork floats and chunks of bark. Maybe even
bring that hull down out of the tree and drag it inside, fill it
with dirt and plastic flowers.

"Do you think this is right?" George wondered. "Just taking
over a church like this?"

"A church? A church? And when was the last time anybody
wanted into this church? Letting a piece of real estate sit
around unexploited like this is a mortal sin as far as I'm concerned. I'm delivering it from the evil of stagnation; I'm turning it into something useful. A real salvation, and no kidding
either. God helps them who help themselves and that's exactly
what I'm doing, helping myself."

"Helping yourself is right," Jenny said. "This is all part of
your plan to ram that fancy playpen of a resort down our
throats. And all that comes along with it."

She may be something to look at now, but she was just as
mouthy as ever. Weins took a deep breath, no use losing his
temper over this. She just needed to be convinced with logic.

"You might as well try to hold back the clock. Port Annie
is on the march, full steam ahead, on soaring wings! No more
using that lousy catalogue to do your shopping, like somebody
out in the sticks. No more taking that pain-in-the-butt down-

island trip, you'll be able to buy everything you need right
here. You'll never have to go anywhere else for the rest of
your life!"

"Some of us like this place the way it is," George said. "Why
d'you want to change it?"

Weins might have let loose with some of the rage that he
felt whenever he heard that kind of talk if Mr. Manku hadn't
stepped in through the door at precisely that moment. The big
Indian always looked so controlled and dignified that you felt
like an idiot demonstrating any kind of excitement at all in
front of him. "Some people are blind," was all he could think
of to say. "And some people are just plain stupid."

Mr. Manku permitted himself the luxury of a curious glance
around the room, but obviously he had something else on his
mind. He was on his way home from a visit with his friend
Mr. Magnani at the recreation centre, he said, and would anyone like to guess who else was there?

Weins shrugged. Who cared? Magnani was a write-off, an
emotional wrong-headed Italian. Someone he tried to ignore.
And who invited Manku to poke his nose in here where he
wasn't needed?

The surprise, Mr. Manku said, was Mrs. Magnani herself.

"Out of bed?" Jenny said.

Weins lowered his stapler. Rosa Magnani hadn't set foot
outside her house in years, not even outside her bedroom. The
only way that woman would ever come out of her house was
inside a coffin, with Papa Magnani wailing and carrying on in
a typical old-country way behind her. Everybody knew that

"Out of bed," Mr. Manku said. His thick lips stretched out
thin in a smile. "Out of bed, and on her feet."

"What is he trying to do, kill her?" Weins said. From what
he'd heard she'd do anything her husband said, including dragging herself out of bed and propping herself up at the rec
centre if it pleased him. Some people had no minds of their
own. "I hope you told him to get her home fast, and no stalling either. Did you call the doctor? He ought to know what
that Eyetalian is up to."

Mr. Manku shook his head, still smiling. "She was well
enough. She doesn't need Dr. Harmon or anyone else. She is
just fine, thank you."

Oh how Mayor Weins hated smugness. Above all he hated
to see smugness in someone like Mr. Manku, whose face as

far as he was concerned had no business expressing anything
but gratitude. How many opportunities would he have had to
look smug in India? "What do you mean? Don't be stupid.
You better get back there and talk him out of this nonsense."

"Just wait a minute, Weins," Jenny said. "Hold your horses.
Did she tell you anything else, Mr. Manku? Did she tell you
what had happened?"

"Yes. Yes, of course."

"And she told you . . .?"

"Joseph Bourne, of course."

Weins lowered his stapler. Rost Magnani hadn't set foot
name. These people were crazy. "Go tell that woman to get
back in her bed where she belongs. If I hear any more of this
kind of talk I'll be sick to my stomach, and no kidding either.
There must be some kind of law he's breaking, people need
to be protected from men like him. Somebody ought to sick
the police on him, fooling around with people's lives."

"Don't have a heart attack over it," Jenny said. "Look at
the colour of your face."

"Mrs. Magnani is in perfect health," Mr. Manku said.
"There is no need to worry about her now."

"How did it happen? How did it happen? What's going on
in this town?"

"You'd better sit," Jenny said. "You're shaking, you'd better
calm down."

"Whaddya mean calm down! I want to know what's going
on. I want to know what he thinks he's doing. I want the police
to look into this."

"There's no law yet against helping your neighbour," Jenny
said. "Even if some people think it's a hanging offence."

Weins took back everything he'd thought earlier about her
looks. There was nothing pretty about a women whose tongue
was dripping with sarcasm. "Encourage this kind of thing and
the next thing you know he'll be setting up a circus tent, right
here in this gravel pit! Do you want to see someone make a
mockery of this sacred place?"

Jenny laughed. He couldn't guess what she was thinking.
These people all come from another planet. "Mr. Manku, I
think somebody better call a doctor in here. If Weins doesn't
get himself calmed down he's going to explode all over his
Fartenburg costume."

"I'm calm, dammit," he said. "I'm calm."

And he was, suddenly. Why should he get himself upset?

How could anything that Joseph Bourne might do affect the only thing that mattered, the future of this town? Let him pull his little tricks, act the mighty healer if he wanted, none of it came to much in the face of all that was yet to happen.

"Instead of getting all upset with so little to go on," George Beeton said, "I'm heading across to get it from the horse's mouth."

"Good idea, George. Please do," Weins said, putting the pieces of his stapler back together. He couldn't stand around and chew the fat all day. There was work to do around here, anybody who didn't want a job had better clear out fast. Greg was heading down to the Kick-and-Kill, just to try out his costume on the drinkers, and he himself wanted to start building a display rack for tourist brochures just as soon as he'd covered up this one last stupid quotation on the wall.

> For whatsoever is born of God
> overcometh the world.
>   I John 5:4

A relief to see it disappear behind another Fat Annie face, and a more appropriate message.

> When opportunity knocks on your door
> will you answer the call
> or hide your head in the sands of lethargy?

Outside, Mr. Manku peered up into the giant fir, where the fishboat floated in the limbs. "And what have you children found up there?"

One of the Chamber-Potts youngsters was still on the ground, at the foot of the ladder, but the others were nothing but feet, dangling down out of the thick boughs. A voice answered: "This goddam thing is full. It won't move. It's heavy as hell, full of water."

"Watch your language," Jenny said. "Naturally it's full, it's all this rain. A wonder it hasn't crashed to the ground."

"Sea water," the disembodied voice continued. "And rocks covered with barnacles. Crabs crawling around. Sea cucumbers. Oysters."

"I don't believe it," Jenny told the mayor, who'd come to the door. "It isn't possible, is it?"

"And fish! A school of tiny fish!"

"You kids get down out of there," Weins yelled.

"And an octopus!"

"That wave must've picked it up off the bottom of the sea," George Beeton said. "It must've been sunk for a while."

"And a dead whale! And a sunken ship!"

Weins shrugged. "You kids come on down from there—you'll fall and break your necks." He turned to the others. "Which mightn't be such a bad idea." Even Jenny smiled at that. He bet she'd wished the same thing a thousand times.

One pair of feet found the ladder and started down. Then the other pair. The smaller of the two boys held a six-inch crab in one hand. "Didn't believe us, huh? Look at this." The legs scratched at the air, the pinchers opened and closed. "There's a half-dozen of these things up there, crawling around."

Jenny stepped back and wrinkled her nose at the crab, ugly creature, one of the reasons she seldom went near the water. But suddenly the thing arched out through the air and landed on her shoulder. It caught for a moment in her threshing hands, then dropped to the ground by her feet, where it hurried sideways off across the gravel. "Albert—you miserable creep! Cripes, those monsters ought to be locked up and horsewhipped, a bunch of savages. Just wait till I get you home."

Weins was relieved to see them leave, he had no time for visiting. He was only concerned with how much work he'd cut out for himself in this campaign, nearly all of it to be done alone. Was he the only person in town who cared? Sometimes he didn't think they deserved him. It would serve them right if they elected someone like Beeton in the next election and then sat around stagnating forever while the rest of the world passed them by.

You'd think he could have counted at least on Jeremy Fell for some help in this all-important task. This was exactly what that storekeeper had come into town for in the first place, and now he was completely useless, no help at all. He hadn't even stuck his nose inside the trailer since Weins had opened it up. All he could talk about was how much he despised Bourne, all he was interested in was hanging his corpse around that old man's neck as fast as he could. Perverted. News of the cripple's corrected foot had nearly driven him crazy—he refused to take his quinidine tablets, he refused to eat, he wouldn't talk to his doctor. Wheezing, panting, almost too weak to lift a finger, all he'd managed to do was frighten his wife so badly that she'd packed up and gone back to Victoria.

Weins had no patience with such selfishness, especially at an important time like this. The sight of that pale face disgusted him, reminded him of a parasite plant which has no need for green leaves or any other colour, just sucks its life from others. He'd spent five years of his life sucking information out of people in this town to help that development company out, and now he wasn't doing a thing with what he knew, only sitting on it and waiting for the end. The only time he ever stepped outside was to go down and gaze at those yellow bulldozers parked above the Flats. Fell was in love with them, not a bit of help to Jacob Weins in his fight to stop those backward people from keeping Port Annie in the Dark Ages.

Well he knew a few things about these people himself, and he hadn't had to snoop around like a spy taking notes for five years, either. Even after a day of working like a Trojan in that cultural centre (Mabel holding down the magazine shop for him) he still had the energy and enthusiasm left to get out into the community and sell what he had to sell. With Gregory Wong in his Fat Annie costume he visited house after house, a box of posters and photos and pamphlets under his arm. *Good day to you, ma'am, could I step in a minute? I have this certain matter I want to talk about, and no beating around the bush either, this is important, the most important thing that ever happened to this town. A poster to staple to your door and, look, it has a big picture of Fat Annie on it, symbol of this town, modelled of course on this gorgeous example of womanhood who is going everywhere with me on my arm.*

The gorgeous example of womanhood was content to primp and titter, rolling her hips, there was nothing in her contract that said she was expected to talk. If Weins wanted her to dance, she would, or even show off her legs, but as for trying to talk somebody into something they didn't want, forget it. She knew where to draw the line. After all, she did have a little pride.

But this was no time for pride as far as Mayor Weins was concerned. He had a job to do, and pride was a luxury he couldn't afford. Too much was at stake here. Everything, in fact, was at stake. It was time to pull out the plug, go whole hog, turn these people around and get this matter settled once and for all. If he actually knew what he thought he knew about people, then changing their minds shouldn't be all that hard. Giant department stores were what he pictured

for Eva McCarthy, if that resort came in and the town
started to grow, shopping malls all over the place, and every
one of them full of the latest designs in furniture, carpets,
hardware, all a person needed to keep her house the nicest
on the block, the envy of the whole neighbourhood. How
could she turn down a promise like that? She couldn't, any
more than Mrs. Barnstone could resist his vision of honest-
to-goodness culture flooding into town, Hollywood screen-
writers and people who wrote television commercials moving
in, all eager to join the Creative Writing Club. A pushover,
a snap, like telling his own wife about all the doctors who
would be moving here just the minute they caught a sniff of
that Hollywood money down at the resort, and finding herself
overnight with a whole new exciting array of medicines and
pills, every colour under the sun, bottles and bottles in her
cupboard, a different medicine for every inch of her body. It
was easy. Everyone had dreams, just like himself. All he had
to do was promise to make their dreams come true and his
own would just naturally follow. And about time, too, he was
sick and tired of watching those Mill managers drive their
fancy big cars while he still drove a nine-year-old Ford; he
was sick and tired of having to watch the pennies while everyone else spent money like water.

The women weren't the only ones who needed a little of
Weins's help in order to see the light; he made sure he
cornered as many men as he could too, some of them as they
crossed the square on their way home from the Mill. Greg
Wong was a big help, an attention-getter, willing to play his
role to the hilt and no hanging back, either. No one could
have guessed he'd turn out to be such a natural clown, with
his eye-balling and his hip-rolling and his mock flirtations,
not afraid to make gestures and suggestions so crude that no
one could help but laugh.

"Better watch out, Weins," said Ian McCarthy. "This guy's
so good he'll be going off to work in a nightclub somewhere
one of these days."

In front of Ian McCarthy's nose he dangled the opportunity to get into real estate, a killing to be made for anyone
with a sense of adventure, not too scared to invest a little
money in land, in the lumber business, a whole new world
opening up. He himself had already invested his whole life's
savings, every penny, that's how much faith he had in the

future. And every cent of Mabel's inheritance, too, though she didn't know it yet, so hold your tongue about it. To Slim Potts he put forward the idea of turning that row of machines into a museum, they were in such perfect running order and all polished up, people would be happy to pay admission. And who knows, the provincial government would probably give some financial aid to a scheme like that. For George Beeton, that doubting Thomas, he called up a vision of cars coming in over that road, every one of them thirsty for gas, half of them needing repairs, a few of them wanting complete over-hauls. "Just think of those great big gas-guzzlers, all the way from California some of them, sputtering down that final mountain on their last ounce of gas, desperate for a pump. Can't you imagine getting your fingers into those expensive parts, a chance to tear a *high-class* vehicle apart for a change instead of these ordinary cars that most people drive in this town?"

In the Kick-and-Kill he flashed photographs of movie stars around. Handsome or beautiful, nearly naked, with sun-golden bodies and perfect teeth. All those Hollywood people were dying to spend their holidays in a place like Port Annie, and no kidding either. Build that resort and the streets would be crawling with them. Old-time stars like Bette Davis, just you watch. All those luscious successors to Marilyn Monroe. Child stars. Teenage rock-idols. He slid a coloured photo of Robert Redford under Rita Rentalla's nose. Did she think he'd be able to resist, once he heard of this place? And once they arrived there was no doubt some of them would want to shoot a movie here, maybe even use some of the local people for extras, or minor roles. The stars of tomorrow could be discovered right here in Port Annie. Why not? They had to come from some-where, didn't they, why not from here?

Oh, Jacob Weins was pleased with himself, he really knew his people, no doubt about it he was better than any psychiatrist at knowing exactly how to hit them where they lived. Wasn't it true that everyone at his core was greedy? Nothing to be ashamed of, he even believed that greed was a healthy thing. The Creator of this world made people greedy so they could get ahead, he told himself, and gave Jacob Weins all this extra energy so that he could go around setting free this greed that everybody else was trying to keep hidden so unnaturally. As for himself, he was fed up with being just a nobody, hiding his light under a bushel. All this talent, and mayor as well, but in this place he was still a Mr. Nobody, not even as important as the assistant to the Assistant Manager at the Mill.

He wasn't only tired of seeing the Mill workers driving their expensive cars, he was also tired of watching the management people go off to Hawaii every Christmas. He was fed up with eating his heart out with desire for one of those Down Front houses he could never afford, and would never be given the opportunity to buy, even if he could afford it. And how did it feel to pick up a down-island newspaper and see all the attention those other mayors were always getting? Invited to ride in parades. Asked to make speeches in front of businessmen who understood how forward-looking people thought. Called on to lead the way in fund-raising marches. Required to settle important controversies. Urged to attend colourful banquets and balls. Persuaded to run for the legislature in Victoria, or even for Parliament in Ottawa. Expected to dance with debutantes and society matrons. Begged by others to dream up breathtaking schemes for drawing attention to their towns and increasing the influx of tourists. Pressed to appear on television shows and news reports seen all across the province, even across the country. It was depressing to think how all his talent had been going to waste up here in this town where nobody cared, nobody noticed, and the rest of the world was so far away. All he wanted was to be a little appreciated, a little celebrated, not too much to ask. No wonder he didn't mind wearing himself to a frazzle canvassing the town in order to get his important message across.

But was it getting across? Only time would tell. People's minds were funny things and could change one way as quickly as another, and then change back again. All he could do was keep up the campaign, never relax his efforts for a minute, and count on good sense to win out.

If he thought, for instance, that Jenny Chambers was going to be seduced by his enthusiastic efforts, he had another think coming; she didn't even answer the doorbell when he rang. Jenny was in far too good a mood to bother with anything that didn't interest her much. The happiest person in town, maybe the world for all she knew. She hummed to herself (the latest love song from the radio) as she flipped through nearly untouched recipe books looking for something exotic to whip up for supper. She sang right out loud as she vacuumed the house, tidying up, even dusting, making some of the rooms look neater than they'd been in years. She paused long enough to execute a few steps of a provocative dance she thought she'd almost forgotten. And flipped one more time through her well-worn scrapbook beside the bed. Sally Rand and all the other girls looked out at her. What did she care about Jenny Lee's Hall of Fame now? What did she care about this newest clipping, a stripper who prayed for her customers and claimed she saw haloes above the men's heads when they'd been saved? All of them were history, part of the past, Flaming Jenny was alive again without them, let them rest in the scrapbook where they belonged.

Was it because she was about to become a bride that Jenny was so happy, her wedding less than a week away now and everything almost ready? Maybe she was dreaming of the hour when she would follow all those bridesmaids into the Kick-and-Kill to say her vows, floating in her layers of expensive white material. Not on your life. Far from it. She had quite another reason for all this singing and cheer, as Joseph Bourne was to discover almost as soon as he stepped in the door.

Steaks were ready to go under the broiler. Mushrooms simmered on the stove. An angel-food cake, buried under a mountain of sticky icing, sat on the counter waiting for the knife. Even a bottle of Slim's homemade blackberry wine stood ready in the middle of the table, which Jenny was setting with her best silverware.

"High heels and jewellery," Bourne said. "This must be some kind of occasion that nobody told me about. Should I have brought some flowers?"

She took a deep breath. "The wedding is off," she said. "I've cancelled it."

Here was her reason for singing, for outdoing herself with a beautiful meal, for using the best silver. Here was her reason for being the happiest person in town. The bride was no longer a bride. No, she didn't mean postpone, she said, cancelled was what it was. Cancelled. Forgotten. Erased. Nine bridesmaids, two flower girls, a best man, and several ushers were out of a job. Four thousand yards of crepe-paper streamers for decorating the Kick-and-Kill would have to be given away. Tons of food—representing hundreds of hours of work by dozens of women—would have to stay in basement freezers all over town until someone else decided to get hitched. Either that, or be gobbled up at the Festival by those hungry people cheated out of a wedding. That beautiful wedding dress, acres of net, a Paris style, would have to go into mothballs, never used. She'd never been so happy in all her life!

"And Slim?"

"I haven't told him yet but he won't care. I didn't say I was going to cancel the marriage, did I, just the wedding." The only difference any of this wedding business had made to Slim was the acquisition of a new suit he'd never wear. The tie and shirt, still unwrapped, could be returned to the store. And underwear—who didn't always need new underwear, even without a wedding? The long black socks, on the other hand, could probably be given away as Christmas presents, to people with the right size feet.

To tell the truth, now that she'd let it out, she didn't feel quite so terrific as before. Not quite so wonderfully happy. A bit of the edge had been taken off, it wasn't the same once a second person got ahold of your news. Especially since she would have to try to explain. Joseph Bourne was waiting. He knew that such a drastic decision had to have a pretty good explanation. He might even be wondering if she'd thought yet about the people she was letting down.

"I was worn out," she said. "Just plain exhausted from the effort of entertaining all those women every day, breaking my neck for the wedding. What was the point? All this popularity was just as much of a pain as the loneliness was. And nothing else has changed."

"You cancelled a wedding because you're tired?"

"Because I'm ashamed of myself. I never wanted a wedding, I . . . I only wanted the fuss."

Now her mood was really spoiled. She even felt like crying. How could she go so fast from the top to the bottom, from the peak of happiness to feeling rotten?

"It was dishonest, Bourne. I couldn't go on with such a farce." Dammit, she hated women who turned on the taps; it made them look as if they were after sympathy.

And he was to blame, if he really wanted to know. If he hadn't moved into her house she might never have questioned what she was doing. But there he was, every day, a constant reminder of how good he was, how selfless, how dedicated to making other people happy. A model of generosity. And there she was, taking advantage of all those women to make herself more popular, scared to death that without the wedding she'd be an outsider again, friendless, a lonely has-been getting fat and not having any purpose in her life. Cripes, how could she help noticing what a gulf of difference there was between them? He ate, he laughed, he used the toilet just like anybody else, and yet he was still capable of working marvels everywhere he went—so what was the matter with her? She was a cheat, a hypocrite, a phony, and he was—what?—a paragon, a walking daily rebuke. So it was all his fault, nobody else's, if everybody was going to be disappointed about being done out of a wedding!

"But leaving it so late," he said. "What would be the harm now if . . ."

"If I went on pretending until Saturday? Then what?"

He smiled. Of course he hadn't expected her to do anything of the kind. Already she was beginning to get some of the good mood back; it hadn't disappeared completely after all. Not even when he brought up the spectre of her angry bridesmaids' faces was she tempted to reverse her decision.

"Just don't imagine that they're going to take this sitting down," he said.

And Eva had already given her a shower. No matter that it was only a typical Eva shower, where she asked everybody else to bring the sandwiches and cakes, which she passed around only once and then put in the freezer for herself and Ian to nibble on for the rest of the month. "But what am I going to do with the presents?" All those pillowslips and bowls and Tupperware that had been given to her in a cardboard box painted up to look like the Mill. "If I have to give them back, what am I going to do about that macramé plant-hanger that one of the brats tried to stuff down the toilet?"

"Wring it out and wrap it up and give it back. When you explain what happened they'll probably insist you keep it."

Now she really was feeling much better, nearly as happy as she'd been when he came in. She offered him the plate of hors d'oeuvres—smoked oysters and cubes of cheese and chunks of George Beeton's smoked salmon. "Only one each for now, just a taste, then we wait for Slim and the kids." She wasn't even going to put the steak in the oven until he was home and washed up and ready; for a change she wanted to cook his meat just the way he liked it, give it all of her attention.

"Come and sit down," she said. "Don't go into your room

and shut your door on me like you usually do. Come into the living room." Usually such a mess with all the bridesmaids' work left lying exactly where they left it, on top of the normal mess of eight rambunctious kids, today the living room was neat as a pin, everything in its place. "Oh, I know there'll be hell to pay when they find out. I don't know how I'll be when they decide to get even with me, but I won't be bullied. My mind's made up."

"Maybe one day you'll make it up to them. Maybe one day you'll—who knows—even dance for them."

She laughed. "The hell I will." Just imagine their faces if she ever tried such a thing. Heart attacks and apoplexy! Eyes bulging and throats choking! Mrs. Barnstone would drop dead on the spot. *Honestly, I could spit.*

But he was serious. "I think you will. Sometimes the only way we grow is by pushing against the limits that try to hold us back. I think some day you'll dance for them, you'll make it a gift, the thing you know how to do."

Who knows—maybe she would. Cripes, anything was possible. In this mood she was already forgiving herself for letting people down, forgiving those bridesmaids ahead of time for the anger they were bound to feel, she was already looking forward to a time when the air would have been cleared, all of this forgotten. Who knows—maybe then she'd be ready to dance again for somebody.

"That oyster was delicious," she said. "I think we ought to sneak a second one while we're waiting. Slim'll never know."

Just as Jenny expected, bridesmaids all over town went to pieces when they heard the news. What kind of game was that lame-brain traitor trying to play? How could she do such a thing? She could certainly expect a cool reception for a while; this wouldn't be quickly forgotten. Eva, of course, had one of her hissy-fits when she heard the news. And Mrs. Landyke wanted to know who was going to pay for this dress and the shoes that she would never wear. Did she think a widow had nothing better to do with her money than throw it away? It wouldn't have hurt the woman to go through with it; after all, what real difference would it have made? Especially since it looked as if she intended to go right on living with Slim just the same as before. Some tempers refused to cool down until husbands had promised weekends in Vancouver, with exotic ethnic dinners at only the best, and a night of dancing and fun at the top of the highest hotel.

Only Mrs. Barnstone remained unruffled. Despite the fact that she'd been included as the ninth bridesmaid just at the last minute (after a considerable amount of hinting) and had to break her neck sewing the dress in record time, she didn't really care. Something more important had come up. Inspiration had struck like a bolt of lightning from the blue, just as she'd always suspected it would some day. When Jen called to break the news of the cancelled wedding she snapped: "No more talk. I'm hard at work. I'm going to take my phone right off the hook."

A marvellous idea for a poem had struck her, just what she'd always wanted, a grand epic in the tradition of Homer and Milton, with a touch of Robert Service thrown in, based entirely on the things that had been going on in this town. This was the opportunity she'd been waiting for, her big chance, maybe the gateway to fame and fortune, and all in heroic couplets too. Her pen was running away with her; she'd never been so inspired before in her life. She was even hoping to break all records and have it ready for Saturday night when she might be persuaded to read some of it out at the Festival.

Her arm soon ached. Her hand felt as if it would drop off at any minute. But nothing could hold her back from her destiny now, she was a woman possessed. Only her husband was allowed to interrupt, and then just to bring her a tray of food to keep up her strength, and to report the latest news from town. What ludicrous schemes had Weins dreamed up for today? Had Jenny Chambers stepped out of her house to face the music yet? Would Jeremy Fell choose this day to drop dead at last and hang his corpse around Joseph Bourne's neck? What insulting letters had been published in the *Port Annie Crier*? And most important of all, had that real-estate developer shown his handsome face again—a certain sign that the battle was finally under way?

Because there was no doubt in Mrs. Barnstone's mind, or in her poem, that this was war. Real war. And that more than the few acres of Squatters' Flats were at stake. This was even, she decided, a matter of life and death. Whether this last bit of insight was something she'd dreamed up herself, or something conveyed to her by her muse in the lightning bolt, even she didn't know for sure. Nor was she about to question it. A poet, she knew, had to respect the mysteries. Her job was just to record.

And she recorded everything in sight. The rain. The jays. The floating hull. Fat Annie's monstrous double hauling her bulk from place to place, wherever a crowd could be found. Canada's Largest Natural-Growing Cactus, dead as a dodo in its upright coffin of glass. The little trailer that no one had ever used for a church gradually changing into a cultural centre, as Weins liked to call it, with a spectacular banner draped from the pole on the roof (formerly a poor attempt at a spire) across the gravel pit to a tree. PORT ANNIE, WHERE THE FUTURE WILL GET ITS START. Posters everywhere. Fat Annie's face grinning off every pole, off every blank wall, off every second tree. A huge model of the promised resort, sent up from the south and displayed under a bubble of glass just inside the hotel lobby door. Those three yellow bulldozers parked at the top of the road to the Flats, decorated with obscenities in various colors of paint, all smeared by the incessant rain before they had time to dry.

Mrs. Barnstone, of course, did not record the actual words that were painted on the bulldozers. She wanted her poem to have the widest possible appeal, appropriate for memorizing out of classroom textbooks and reciting at Christmas concerts. "Rude words" was what she called them. "Scatological unpleasantries" was the furthest she would go (to rhyme with "unbelievable peasantry" in the previous line, a reference to the Squatters and their unsportsmanlike behaviour in this time of civic stress). Though she hadn't actually seen anyone paint those crude embarrassing messages on the yellow cats, she was sure that the language was the kind that only Squatters would know how to use, people who were used to living without any standards of decency. Besides, one of the words was misspelled.

Not a single action was overlooked. Whether it was witnessed by herself or passed on by her husband, everything was absorbed by her teeming mind and reordered into iambic pentameters. Papa Magnani slamming the door of the recreation centre in Mayor Weins's face. Jeremy Fell skulking at his window, leaning weakly against the wall to watch Bourne, wheezing and holding his heart but still alive. George Beeton ripping the posters off his service-station walls and making a bonfire of them in the middle of the street. Charlie Reynolds moving all his newspaper business inside the Kick-and-Kill, where he caught up to Belchy McFadden in the beer-drinking race and even passed him, chuckling as he read the latest letters from the stirred-up populace, deciding which to include in the *Crier* and which to throw away. Smart enough to know a good thing when it hit him in the face, even in his boozy state, he'd turned his weekly paper into a daily for the occasion, and filled its pages with nothing but letters, a chance for people to get their feelings off their chests and make their positions clear. Some of the letters were perfect material for the epic, though very few could be easily rearranged into the rigid structure of heroic verse. A number could be found, however, that supported Mrs. Barnstone's thesis—promises of sabotage, threats of arson, warnings of divine wrath, hints of tar and feathers, demands for a reversal in policy, boasts of hidden weapons kept in reserve, talk of impeachment, threats of strike, and declarations of loyalty.

One writer, signing himself "Disgusted", insisted that the mayor had gone mad and ought to be thrown behind bars. But another, "Born in Belfast", declared himself to be behind the mayor every inch of the way and would gladly kick the teeth out of any bastard that refused to see the light. The accompanying cartoon, he said, would make his position clear. But the only cartoon that Reynolds printed that day was by someone who signed himself "Don". An enormous thing, it showed a tiny round elf of a mayor and an obscene sexy cow of a Fat Annie dragging the handful of Port Annie houses on a skiff through the knee-high rain towards a place labelled "The Future", a wide expanse of skyscrapers full of miniature people shooting one another and men jumping out of windows and crowds stomping right over top of fallen children, and naked men chasing naked women who were eating their babies as they ran. The whole city was surrounded by a wall of wrecked cars, and entered by a gate flanked by skeletons and bodiless skulls.

Mrs. Barnstone, though warmed by the support the cartoonist's vision gave to the premise of her magnum opus, was so repelled by the details of the picture that she couldn't bring herself to mention it in the poem. And besides, who was responsible for the thing? No one in this town. It was probably mailed in by some nosy outsider keeping an eye on the local bickering from a safe down-island easy chair.

The overt violence that Mrs. Barnstone looked for did not occur until the very day of the Fat Annie Festival, when she'd hoped to be drawing her epic to a close, with a few hours for going back to polish some of those rough spots she'd hurried over. Never mind, she would write until she dropped, if necessary; when she heard about this latest development there was no doubt in her mind that it had to be included. Just as she would have predicted, if she'd thought about it, the first incident of out-and-out warfare did not take place in town— not at the trailer or the recreation centre or even at the Kick-and-Kill, where body-bashing was a way of life—but down the inlet in that collection of Squatters' shacks.

Larry Bowman saw it. So did Joseph Bourne. The two of them had been talking in the library—about "poetry and the artist's role", of all things, nothing to do with the celebration or with the divided town at all. This was a conversation that would have bored Mrs. Barnstone to tears, though she might have smiled a little if she'd heard Larry ask the old man why he wasn't spending all his time writing poetry, was he letting Mrs. Barnstone's rumoured masterpiece scare him into retire-ment? She would definitely not have smiled at the long-winded answer, however; she'd have had a prolonged fit of yawning. Caught in the exciting grip of wild inspiration, line after line flashing into her consciousness faster than she could write them down, what would she care that Bourne was taking his time, looking over every line from a dozen different angles before recording it, and even questioning the value of his work while he was at it? The old metaphors for eternity didn't work any more, he said, peeling an orange. We know too much for that. Keats and Byron, if they were around today, would have to take another look at their urns and oceans. Works of art could be burned or smashed, oceans could be killed off by men, even that famous steadfast star could have burned itself out years ago. "If symbols don't work—and what else can a poet use?— then eternity can only be expressed by implication, by the way we live our lives."

Pretty fancy talk, and not at all to Mrs. Barnstone's taste. She might have been more interested if she'd been able to read Larry Bowman's mind, which tried to keep itself anchored to all this talk of poetry and life—after all, it was something he cared about and how many opportunities did he have for this kind of thing?—but couldn't keep from slipping off to dwell on other things. Angela Turner for instance. Angela Turner's eyes. Angela Turner's laugh. Angela Turner's expected baby.

Angela Turner's hands. When he'd been spending all those months fantasizing a sex life for himself he'd never dreamed that he would end up falling in love.

Mrs. Barnstone might have been interested in a peek at some of these thoughts, but she wouldn't have used them in her poem—too suggestive, and definitely off the topic. What interested her most, to feed the greedy maw of her hungry work of art, was what happened when Bourne took Larry down to the Flats, to show him some of the books he had stored away in the upper floor of The Paper House. Just as soon as they'd stepped inside the door a siren started wailing somewhere, and bodies all around leapt into frantic action. Hill Gin, who'd stepped forward as if she intended to greet them, suddenly threw herself down on the linoleum, where she started tying one of her wrists with a piece of rope to the leg of the cast-iron stove. One of the pony-tailed youths jumped into a closet and slammed the door. Another, his twin, stood on a chair and pulled himself up through a hole in the ceiling. Just as his feet disappeared, a running shoe without laces fell off and dropped to the floor. Larry stepped back to the wall, anxiously pulling Bourne with him. What kind of madness had they walked in on?

Whatever it was, it wasn't over yet. Louise Ganton, who'd been flapping around the room like a frantic chicken, finally jumped inside her plastic bag of newspapers and old rags and rolled across the floor to wedge herself between the sink and a heavy table. Only her hands reappeared, to clamp themselves around the gooseneck pipe. "If they want to take me, they'll have to pull out twenty feet of plumbing while they're at it."

"What's going on here?" Larry said. These people looked silly enough to be laughed at, but his heart, unsure, was beating far too fast.

One of Hill Gin's yipping dogs streaked in through the open door, tried to stop, and skidded right across the linoleum to slam up against her hip. "Git out of here you, git!" she shouted, and gave him a clout on the nose that provoked a yelp but did nothing to chase him away. He limped around the room, whimpering, and finally curled up on the floor behind the stove.

Outside, running feet sloshed past in the mud. Someone called: "Where's Tim?"

"It's a practice run," Gin explained, her tone daring them to laugh.

"For their eviction when it comes," Bourne added. "They refuse to leave, no questions about it. And they also refuse to fight. They'll have to be dragged away one at a time, dead weights, and then they'll come back the next day and have to be dragged again."

"And if the shacks are burned?"

"They'll have to be dragged off the land. And then they'll have to be dragged off the construction site. And then they'll have to be dragged out of the fancy resort. But they don't expect it to come to that; they're not a bunch of bull-headed clowns, they've got their plans. They expect the builders to give up and leave them alone, maybe build their hotel a few hundred yards down the beach. Or pay to have these shacks moved down a ways."

Hill Gin raised her head. "Personally I'd rather fight the buggers, but you got to work together. That siren means them Crabbes are sneaking up to surprise us any minute now, to try and drag us away like they was cops. Our job is to hang on tight. Nobody's ever got me away from this stove yet! And nobody's ever managed to drag the stove out through the front door either! We're getting better at this stuff every time we do it."

Larry looked at Bourne and lowered his voice. "And you encourage them in this game? A lost cause like this?"

The old man's hands were busy ransacking his pockets. "I don't encourage them, I don't discourage them. This is just what happens when you anchor your life to a place or wrap your roots around *things*." He halted the search and raised his voice for the benefit of Hill Gin, an edge of teasing in it now. "I've told them to try sinking their roots into something a little more solid and lasting than a piece of earth, but nobody listens to me down here any better than they do in the town."

Hill Gin grunted. "Babble, babble."

"Solid and lasting like what?" Larry said.

"Like what?" One hand emerged with an apple, which he held up by the stem and examined. "Like those good old invisible things that can't be stolen or disappear." He polished the apple on the front of a sweater. "What our grandparents used to call the things of soul." And bit.

"Babble, babble," Hill Gin said. "People still have to live somewhere. That old fool would have us floating off into space like ghosts."

Bourne accepted the rebuke with a nod. "So you see, Larry

Bowman, there's nothing left for me to do but . . . what?"—
his hands turned up in a gesture of mock helplessness—"but
love them, I guess."

The old woman, recoiling, cracked her skull on the floor.
"Crap."

Bourne laughed—and sank his teeth once more into the
apple.

Larry looked at Hill Gin rubbing her head with the hand
that wasn't anchored to the stove. How did you bring yourself
to care for a hag like that? Lowering his voice again: "Is it
even possible?"

The old man suddenly became very serious. "Is it ever any
easier?" He turned away, as if to keep his words from reaching
Hill Gin's ears. "Isn't love of any kind an attempt to see what
God must see—with *His* perfect vision? Which means," he
added, with a nod that directed Larry's attention back to the
woman on the floor—old, foolish, cranky—"that you have to
be prepared to see *through* quite a bit!"

A good thing Mrs. Barnstone heard none of this. This kind
of talk not only wouldn't get into her epic poem, it might have
put her off her food. Some things were all right perhaps to
read, in certain books, where you could skip right over them
and decide they didn't matter, forget them fast or throw the
book away. But they certainly weren't the kind of thing that
normal people said out loud. What *she* was after was the action, the exciting part, which luckily happened right away before this conversation had an opportunity to go any further.

The sound that everyone heard, as soon as the siren died,
was the sound of a Caterpillar engine moving down the gravel
slope from the pavement. Hill Gin screamed, tugged against
her rope, pulling the metal chimney apart. It clattered onto
the top of the stove, sprinkling hot soot on her head and releas-
ing a weak stream of smoke into the room. "Those bastards!
Nobody thought they'd think of doing a thing like that."

"Shut up, Gin," Louise Ganton said from inside her plastic
bag. "Don't move. It's a trick to fool us into letting go. You
know those brothers when they get started."

"This is something new," Bourne said. "It should be interesting to see how they handle it."

"If we don't choke to death in this smoke."

"They can't smoke us out either," Hill Gin barked. "You
two just stay where you are."

Larry put his hand over his mouth, leaned closer to the

broken window, and listened to the bulldozer getting closer. When it was near enough to rattle windows he expected to hear it stop, he expected to see one of the Crabbes come in through the door. Instead, he heard the chilling sound of boards splintering.

"Damn them!" screamed the old woman on the floor. "That sounds like my house they're bustin'!"

"Shut up, Gin!" Louise Ganton hissed. "It's a trick. They're pushing down one of the empty shacks to see if we'll let go and be lured outside."

By the time Preserved Crabbe finally burst in, everyone was coughing. Only the open door and broken windows made it possible to breathe at all. "What's the matter with you guys?" Crabbe shouted. "You're lying around here like a bunch of dummies while they're out there pushing down Hill Gin's house!"

"Shut up," said Louise Ganton under the sink. "We know your tricks when we hear them. We're not budging." Her hands strengthened their grip on the gooseneck pipe.

"Then stay and suffocate in the smoke. That's Jeremy Fell on the Cat, and there goes Hill Gin's roof!"

A crash. More splintering boards. Breaking glass. The bulldozer motor roared, changed gears. Tortured nails squealed. Something clattered and rolled. This was no trick, it was real.

And it *was* Jeremy Fell. Larry was right behind Preserved Crabbe going out the door. The pale storekeeper worked those levers like someone who'd been trained to do it, his face pulled into an expression of grim determination. With that decorated bulldozer he pushed Hill Gin's fallen walls towards the centre of the heap, backed up, came forward again pushing posts and chunks of rotten floor.

In shacks all over the Flats, faces appeared at windows, people appeared in doorways. Voices screamed, or roared in protest. From everywhere, almost at once, people came running, descending on Jeremy Fell. Someone wielded an axe, another carried a crowbar. Someone else bent to pick up a handful of stones. Rushing towards that bulldozer, they were joined by the pony-tailed youth from the closet, the pony-tailed youth from the ceiling, and Louise Ganton with her legs pushed through the bottom of her plastic bag. Hill Gin was still behind in the smoke, coughing and cursing the stove as she tried to fight herself free.

Fell, ignoring the uproar, kept the machine moving ahead through the heap of rubble, pushing board and furniture and some of Hill Gin's barking dogs ahead of it. Preserved Crabbe wrenched a board off Hill Gin's demolished house and set off through the rubble. "Bash his goddam brains in," someone shouted. The pack of dogs stopped their barking at the bulldozer and leapt on Crabbe, bringing him crashing to his knees. For a moment they swarmed over him, as if they'd found something to eat, but he came up roaring out of their midst, driving them back, kicking at them, swinging at them, growling at them until they retreated, yelping, to hide in the dark spaces under The Paper House.

But Fell ignored Preserved and the flailing board. He ignored too, the rocks that bounced off the metal framework around him. He kept that bulldozer moving across the grass— adding a thrown-out chair, a few fence pickets, and a shovel to the heap of assorted junk in front of its blade, then pushed the rotted clothes-line pole to the ground and dragged the rusty wire with its decoration of clothes-pegs and plastic bags and rain-drenched rags behind it in the direction of the stand of alder trees.

"The man's gone crazy!" someone shouted. Several rushed to help Crabbe, but the pack of yelping dogs swarmed out from under the house again, eager to be part of all this excitement, and sent people sprawling in the rubble. Others preferred to shout encouragement from the road. "Jump up on the back and bust the bugger's skull wide open!" "Grab the key!" "Watch out for those goddam tracks, he'll run right over you!" Some were for putting the creep right out of his misery fast— "Where's Hill Gin's gun? Everyone knows he wants to die; give him his wish and maybe he'll thank us for it."

"These people give new meaning to passive resistance," Larry said. "All that practising really came in handy."

The bulldozer abandoned its gathered load against the alders and backed away to turn and head once more for the collapsed house. There was no indication on Fell's face that he was even aware of the people around him, shouting and throwing things and clanging boards against the side of his machine.

"Somebody's got to stop him," Larry said, and sensed with weakening knees that it was going to have to be himself. He turned to Bourne beside him but the old man wasn't there. Out in that milling crowd? No—he was moving out alone ahead of the pack. And shouting—commanding—in his richest radio-announcer voice. "Fell! Jeremy Fell!" Though there was not much chance of being heard by someone sitting in the midst of that engine's noise.

Yet Fell's head jerked up suddenly. His mouth moved—some kind of sound was torn from his lips. The blade lifted a little, abandoning a heap of bricks and furniture legs and cooking pots; the machine turned with quick jerky movements and started in the direction of the old man. Fell stood up and leaned forward, holding on to the metal roof-props as if he were impatient with the bulldozer's progress and intended to leap ahead. He screamed something, his face red and his throat swollen, but his words were lost in the rattling exhaust.

"What the hell is this?" Larry leapt down off the porch. "What's he think he's going to do?"

But someone's fist clamped around his arm and held him. One of the Crabbe giants. "Leave him alone. It's okay."

Bourne stopped directly in the path of the bulldozer while others moved away, leaving him standing there alone. Larry spat out a piece of thumbnail. The old fool. Did he think there was something noble about placing himself in the path of a madman?

"Get out of the way, old man!" someone shouted.

"Christ! Why are we just standing here?"

Even Preserved Crabbe was just standing, not doing a thing about what was happening. Against the side of The Paper House he stood, with his mouth dropped open and the board in his hand resting against his foot. Like everyone else he'd become a spectator.

If Bourne thought he was being heroic, Larry thought, he ought to know that what he looked like now was just a stubborn old man—his white hair drenched with rain, his black plastic makeshift cape snapping and fluttering behind him, his gumboots ankle-deep in mud. Without lowering his gaze from the advancing Fell he fished with a hand in one pocket after the other of those layers of sweaters until he came up with a half-eaten sandwich, which he unwrapped from the waxed paper and bit into. Larry groaned. Eating—even now he was eating. The man was never without something to stuff in his mouth—when in fact he could probably have done without food at all if he'd wanted to. This was likely some kind of act he'd cultivated in order to hold onto at least that much of humanity in common with everyone else—in order to keep from slipping off into some perfect ideal or disappearing altogether into spirit.

"He's going to let that prick run over him," someone said.

"And us?" one of the pony-tails said. "We're just watching."

"Do you feel like a fight with that blade and who knows how many tons of steel?"

When that blade touches him, Larry thought, *I will . . . what?* He couldn't imagine what. Leap up onto the bulldozer and beat that breathing corpse with his fists? Somehow the notion seemed ridiculous here, to say the least—compared to the old man's behaviour. He couldn't imagine himself doing anything at all, except maybe rushing out to drag Bourne out of the way.

But it wasn't necessary. The bulldozer stopped a foot or so in front of Bourne. Fell, still standing up and leaning ahead of his controls, continued to glare in rage at the man in his path. His mouth moved; he was evidently saying something with restraint this time, the sounds were torn away and buried in the idling motor exhaust. If the look on that face means anything, Larry thought, and if I continue to stand here doing nothing, then a murder will be committed right in front of us all.

What might have become murder became a terrible silence instead. The motor died. Jeremy Fell lowered his face to his hands. No one moved or spoke.

Then a Hill Gin war cry shattered the quiet. Free of her stove leg, she was out on the porch with her shotgun up to her shoulder. Two hammers snicked. One eye squinted, the other shut. A finger pulled one trigger. She turned her face away from the bitter smell and spat.

Jeremy Fell raised his head. He wasn't hit, but a sturdy hemlock beside him shed bits of its limbs like pale green feathers that floated in the air around him.

"That's one barrel, Fell, there's another one to come!"

Jeremy Fell didn't argue. He stayed where he was and contemplated the raised gun. It appeared to make no difference to him at all.

"Careful Gin," someone said.

"It mightn't even kill him," Gin said, with contempt. "He wouldn't be the first to collect some buckshot in his hide and live to tell about it."

"On the other hand you could put an end to the Flats," said Joseph Bourne. "If you hurt that man, how long do you think they'll let anyone stay on here?"

"Horseshit, Bourne! We're finished anyway. We haven't a hope of winning, so we might as well go down with a decent fight."

"Hill Gin thinks the end of the world is coming any day," someone said. "What's she got to lose?"

"Nothing."

Louise Ganton in her plastic bag began to cry. Once she got started she could shed more tears and work up a louder wail than anyone else in the Flats. Nothing could stop her now.

Except that second shot. When it happened she screamed. Too late to sob about it now, curiosity dried those tears up fast. Like everyone else, she looked at Jeremy Fell to see if he'd slumped over dead.

He hadn't slumped, but Hill Gin had. Jeremy Fell was off and running. Hill Gin's ancient gun had exploded in her face. Down on the ground she covered her eyes with bloody hands and groaned. The shotgun was up on the roof of the porch. The terrible smell in the air was like nothing that anyone had ever experienced before. Her pack of dogs swarmed out from under the porch to smother her with tongues and whimpers and insistent noses.

It took Larry Bowman and Joseph Bourne and one of the nameless pony-tailed youths to kick the dogs out of their way and haul Gin inside The Paper House, away from the rain, where they could stretch her out, force her hands down off her face, and confront the bloody mess beside her eye. "Nothing to worry about," Larry said, trying to sound reassuring. It was a lie. He was afraid to wipe away the blood and see just how bad the mess really was.

The old woman glared up at him from the unharmed eye. "Nothing to worry about? That son of a bitch got away, didn't he?"

Bourne told everyone to get out of the house, leave him alone for a while with Gin. Even Larry. "Go on—help settle those people down—leave us alone." Even before he'd closed the door on them he was turning to the woman laid out on the floor. "Go ahead and pretend you're mad you missed him if you want, old lady, but you know you're not really sorry."

"My foot she isn't sorry," said Mrs. Barnstone when she'd

heard the tale. "That woman won't be happy until somebody's dead." When her husband told her about the skirmish down at the Flats (after hearing it in detail from George Beeton, who'd picked it up from Angela Turner, "who's heard it straight from her lover-boy's lips, less than a half-hour ago") she hastily wrote it up as Canto Sixty-five in her poem but refused to believe the story was over yet. "You can't tell me the police will allow this to go unanswered."

Her husband didn't try to tell her anything of the sort. He simply waited until he could report that she'd been right. Jeremy Fell hadn't filed a complaint, quite understandably since it was in stepping outside the law that he'd started this mess in the first place. But Jacob Weins dropped everything when he heard of it and burst into the police station already in high gear. Crimes were being committed all around them, he accused, and what were they doing about it? You'd think it was the Wild West, or a place that didn't have laws, guns going off and people's lives being threatened, now get on down to the Flats and get rid of those people fast.

And just to make sure that they did their job—no more of this pretending just to humour him—he decided to go along too. He even gathered a crowd, in case those badly trained cops needed a hand in throwing those Squatters out of the Flats. Gregory Wong of course, his shadow. And some of the biking friends. Belchy McFadden and Charlie Reynolds, collected from the Kick-and-Kill, where they were getting a head start on the Festival celebrations. Ian McCarthy. And several Mill workers, ready to head out for the afternoon shift but more interested in finding out where this posse was going first. No amount of patient persuading from Constable Nevers could convince any of them that their help wasn't needed. "Just get this show on the road," Weins said. "A man was nearly killed."

"But it was a wasted trip, my dear, and I don't know how you're going to render this into poetry at all. Their siren went off before the party had even entered the Flats. By the time they arrived, nobody answered a door, nobody looked out a window, you'd think the place was deserted. Maybe they're already gone, somebody said. But naturally Weins wasn't so easily satisfied, he demanded the police bust in, which they were happy to do."

"Yes, I can see it now," Mrs. Barnstone said, already writ-

ing. "The mayor must have nearly gone crazy. People tied to
stoves. People hiding in closets. People anchored to plumbing.
People hanging onto rafters. People wrapped around posts.
People inside trunks and under tubs. I know, I know, I know."
She waved her husband away, she didn't even need to hear the
rest.

"Mayor Weins ranted and raved at the police and they refused to do anything else but ask a lot of questions. He ranted
some more and they told him to go on home where he belonged, they'd do their job their own way without his butting
in. He ranted at his followers, tried to get them worked up,
but they only laughed and went from shack to shack throwing
open doors to see what people were hanging onto. Ice boxes.
Car bodies. Beds. Weins, no doubt, came back to town breathing fire and promising vengeance."

So the battle hadn't really developed into all that much,
certainly not the all-out war that Mrs. Barnstone had counted
on. Maybe the people of Port Annie didn't have the energy
for the kind of fight she wanted. Maybe because they lived in
real life and not in a poem they were too uncertain about the
issues to see things in terms of black and white. If Port Annie
was caught in a life-and-death struggle, as she believed it was,
then how could you tell which side was which? If the real
war that was going on here wasn't between the town and
the Flats, if it wasn't between Weins and the people who ob-
jected to change, then where in the world was it happening?
Why couldn't she see it? She had the uncomfortable feeling
that, though her masterpiece was recording all the action she
could find, the real story was going on behind it somewhere,
perhaps invisibly, or just out of range of her vision. Nothing
to do but keep on going and wait to see if it surfaced.

Already she had something new that needed to be crowded
into her poem: everyone rushing down to the Kick-and-Kill
in time for the Fat Annie Festival. Even while she was getting
dressed herself (in her bridesmaid dress, of course, no use
letting all that hard last-minute work go to waste) she watched
from her window and recorded all that she saw. The Magnanis,
both of them dressed up as if they were about to be introduced
to royalty. Two carloads of Mankus, packed tight. George
Beeton in a suit—unbelievable! Rita Rentalla dressed fit to
kill. Damon West—sprung as if by magic from wherever he
lived—in his white Porsche. People ran to their cars, drove

down and parked, then ran again for the hotel—suits would be spotted, dresses would be splashed. What was the matter with those clods of men that they didn't drive up to the door and let the women off, like city people? No sign of Jenny Chambers, of course, or Slim. That turncoat ex-stripper was probably watching it all from her own window, knowing there were nearly a dozen women down there who would be glad to skin her alive. She wouldn't go near that place for a million dollars.

And a wise decision, too, because Eva McCarthy was ready to scratch out her eyes. One of the first to arrive, Eva sat where she could keep an eye on the door in case that traitor had the gall to show her face in public. Just see what happened if she did. In the meantime this was an ideal spot to see who was coming in, have a good look at what they were wearing— mostly dresses she'd seen before, and seven other bridesmaids' dresses just like her own. The place filled up fast, the smell of bodies and perfume was soon strong enough even to block out the stink of beer.

Her rash was driving her crazy again, worse than ever, she didn't know what she would do about it. But never mind that, sit down here, Mabel, she was thinking of having the living-room wall taken out now, extend the room right through the dining room and add a new dining room out the back of the house with steps down into it, shag carpet, with its own sand-stone fireplace and a sliding glass door out onto a sundeck. "Just like this picture, I think I've brought it in my purse to show you, yes, here it is, out of a magazine, now isn't that something?"

Drinking. Hollering. Everybody trying to be louder than the next fellow. Christie didn't like it when the place was this full, eh, it wasn't like the Kick-and-Kill at all. But since it only happened once a year he might as well stick it out. With one arm around Rita's waist he leaned on the table and tried to tell George all about the mess at the Mill today, drains over-flowed and water all over the place, eh, people everywhere you looked trying to suck it up with their dinky pumps. What a mess! But the noise got so loud he soon gave up on any kind of serious conversation. Nothing to do but drink.

"Who're those guys over there with Bourne?" George said.

"Nobody." Rita had already been over to check them out, the only out-of-towners in the place so far, except for West.

"I don't know who those two guys against the wall are supposed to be, but the handsome fellow with the moustache, he's
a book editor, from Back East. The one that's tapping his teeth
with a pencil."

"Back East!" Christie waggled his shoulders and head, and
pulled a la-di-da face to show that he wasn't impressed. Back
East, of course, meant people who worked in television and
believed that the country ended just outside their own city
limits. "I hope he's not finding it too much of an effort, eh,
slumming like this."

"They've found the old man's hiding place, I guess. Lord,
who knows what they'll do with him now."

Greg Wong sashayed from table to table, swinging his padded behind in those old-fashioned skirts, sitting on men's knees
and puckering his overpainted lips up to be kissed, "Get off me
you fruit," while he batted his eyelashes and threw his legs up
in the air to show off his garters and hairy thighs. When he
reached Bourne's table he gave the old man a big smack on
the top of his head while he swung his rear end to perch on
the book editor's lap. One arm around that Back East neck,
"Welcome to Port Annie darling," and he threw his mouth
open for a wide soundless laugh in the direction of the hooting
crowd. The editor, despite his embarrassment, was willing to
laugh—lucky for him. His reward was a big greasy kiss on
the end of his nose.

Even this went into Mrs. Barnstone's poem. Book editors
deserve immortality too. She sat at a corner table, behind most
of the crowd, scribbling madly on her huge sheets of newsprint, caught up to the present time now in her epic and trying
to record everything that was happening before her eyes. Including the entertainment taking place up on the makeshift
stage.

Speeches. Homemade poems. Songs. Imagine the courage it
must have taken for Gloria Anderson to sing the forty-six
verses of some incomprehensible Scottish ballad that no one
listened to, and with *her* voice too. Nothing to the courage it
must have taken Mabel Weins (gulping Valium pills while
they persuaded her up onto that frightening stage) to warble
through a short lyric written especially for her, and for the
occasion, by her husband: a hymn of praise to the town, of
course; he had hopes that if she sang it well enough someone
would suggest it be adopted as a municipal anthem. No one

suggested such a thing right away (too spellbound by the look on Mabel's face perhaps), but no doubt someone would bring it up soon. Comedy sketches followed, including one in which fourteen Fat Annies materialized from somewhere to engage in a free-for-all that saw bodies thumping and snorting around on the stage, and more than one display of the martial arts that left padded bosoms gasping for breath on the floor. Two of George Beeton's children sat down side by side at the piano to play a duet—something classical and boring—but soon turned the performance into a race to see which of them could get to the end first; the girl won, and had time to gulp down somebody's glass of beer before her sweating brother hammered out his final chords. Several accordion solos followed— the town still hadn't recovered from the arrival of an accordion teacher last year, but thank goodness her husband had found a job somewhere else, and children could be counted on to lose interest pretty soon in the two pieces that everyone had learned. Tap dancers, barbershop quartets, stand-up comics, everyone got in on the act, there was no end to the talent. Who would have guessed that Mrs. Landyke could almost stand on her head?

Mr. Manku saw that it had been a mistake to bring the whole family to this. Already the women, upset by so much shouting, had taken the children out to wait in the cars. Only he and his sons and his nephew Daljit were left, feeling very foreign in this boisterous crowd. Raminder had drunk up all of the beer they had ordered for courtesy's sake, and already he was red-eyed, with his face down on the table, looking witless and ill. Then why not go home? Why not take his family out of here and go back to the house where Joginder was engaged in his three-day reading aloud of Guru Granth Sahib? At least there it would be quiet, with only the sound of the boy's voice droning on in his room of worship, not the ear-splitting racket of this rowdy company. But it was most necessary that he be seen here at this event. Local rituals had their importance. "Drink up, old man," someone said, and slapped him on the back. "Try to have some fun."

Larry Bowman wasn't paying very much attention to what was going on around him. All he wanted to think about was tomorrow morning, when he and Angela would be getting out of this town for a few days—a weekend together on the mainland, his first time out of here in more than three years, not counting that quick trip out for his ridiculous clothes. George Beeton had even let him borrow that old beat-up Chev he kept parked behind the garage for customers who needed transportation while he worked on their cars. Of course it had no brakes —something that could be a problem in the mountains—but it was in good shape otherwise, a chance to be alone together in some place other than this town where eyes watched everything you did. Privacy. A luxurious city hotel. Movies and cabarets and plays they could go to, holding hands, having a good time but torturing themselves with the need to be alone again. Bright lights at night, the voices of strangers, people who didn't know all your business. A chance to act the way other people in love had always acted, without nosy neighbours watching your every move. It could even turn into a honeymoon. Who knows—they might even decide not to come back.

Now Damon West was up on the platform making a speech. A hymn of praise to the future was what he delivered, a psalm to the glories of progress, a song of faith in the indomitable spirit that kept man evolving through time—enterprise, energy, and exploitation. "*Seize* the chance, my friends, leap on the chance to go forward with the rest of the world into tomorrow, jump when opportunity knocks—the world was put here to be used, ladies and gentlemen, go out there and *take* it! The spirit we are here to celebrate tonight is the spirit that has made the world what it is, the spirit of the frontier, the spirit that made people like Fat Annie Fartenburg and her husband roll up their sleeves, put their shoulders to the wheel, spit on their hands, and yell *Go!* Progress! Moving with the times! Recognizing that the world is all we've got and we've got to take advantage of it."

"Oh hush up," someone shouted. "Get down off there and let someone else have the floor."

"Let Mrs. Barnstone read her poem."

"Yes. Let her read that thing she's been writing on."

Mrs. Barnstone screamed, though didn't stop the movement of her pen across the paper. "It isn't finished, it isn't finished, it's happening faster than I can get it down!"

Nevertheless she was picked up, chair and all, still writing on those sheets of newsprint, and led across the floor to the stage, where someone else grabbed her arms and hoisted her up, turned her to face the crowd from behind a hastily cleared table. She stared down Damon West, who could have been talked into continuing his speech, then cleared her throat. Ahem, ahem, she cleared it again, the pen in her right hand still writing, and waited until the crowd had grown quiet enough. The first few lines she read apologetically, nervously, as if she were ready to take them back, eat them even, if people didn't like what she'd written.

> Of life and death, oh Muse, these lines will sing;
> Ambition, love, the soul, and other things.
> Of streets still strewn with seaweed, all a mess;
> Port Annie people living under stress.
> Say first, what sent that sexy stud our way
> The handsome devil, has he come to stay?
> When that mysterious fellow first drove in
> And set a hundred female hearts a-spin,
> Who could have guessed that what he'd come here for
> Was nothing more or less than start a war?

Already, she was rewarded with a round of applause. Even Damon West granted her a smile, to show what a good sport he was. Encouraged, she cleared her throat again, ahem ahem, and pulled her chair up closer to her sheaf of papers to read in an even louder voice, the writing hand compelled to look after itself now that all her attention was on the words she was reading. Everyone in town was in the poem, just as promised. Rita Rentalla, painting her nails. Linda Weins sighing for you-know-who. Christie telling another of his unbelievable tales. Cheers went up whenever the name of someone present in the Kick-and-Kill was mentioned, slowing her down considerably, of course, and causing that right hand to go frantic; but it meant that between the cheers everyone leaned forward straining to hear every word, mouths open and ready to scream with laughter or shout with glee. And yes, no one was disappointed, Mrs. Barnstone threw everyone in, there wasn't a person left out, there wasn't a personal mannerism or a personality fault or even a peculiar way of walking that escaped her notice, everything found its way into her poem—even Eva McCarthy's famous imitation coffee and Larry's former attachment to liquor ads in the magazines. Names, names, lines were chock-full of names, Mayor Weins and his precious cactus, Greg Wong in his ridiculous dress. Everyone's biggest

weakness and obsession got mentioned somewhere in the pro-
logue: Eva's one-and-only love, her house; Slim Potts's row of
unused machines; Jen's catalogue clothes; Mabel Weins's endless supply of aches and pains, with an equal supply of pills
to go with them; Charlie Reynolds' weakness for the bottle;
Preserved Crabbe's wandering penguin; even Mrs. Landyke's
precious plot in the tiny overgrown cemetery. Never mind if
a few feelings got ruffled in the process, even the people being
made fun of had to laugh it off or look like hopeless sour-
pusses with no sense of humour. After all, Mrs. Barnstone was
only poking gentle fun at them, hardly a scratch on what
might have been done by someone with a sharper tongue. Look
at the way Mayor Weins guffawed when the poem spent a line
or two on his affection for the camera—he didn't mind, in fact
he dragged Charlie Reynolds out of the corner and demanded
to have his picture taken immediately with his arm around
Greg Wong, giving that greasy face a great big kiss. And did
Greg Wong take offence when she chided his affection for a
certain two-wheeled machine he was never parted from, more
important to him than anything else in the world? Certainly
not, he laughed the loudest of anyone in the room, and laughed
even louder when George Beeton got up on the stage and surprised everyone by improving on the couplet.

> Unzip his fly and see what waits inside—
> That thing is just a motor-bike to ride.

A little too strong for Mrs. Barnstone, who frowned her disapproval—there was not a speck of smut in all that stack of
pages—but Gregory Wong himself thought it was so funny
that he hauled up his skirt to show them it wasn't true.

It became clear, as soon as the story itself got started, that
in Mrs. Barnstone's poem (if not in fact) absolutely everyone
got into the battle of life and death. Casual comments became
blows. Disagreements became skirmishes, active campaigning
became all-out war. And not only individuals got mentioned.
Every club in town, every group, had some role to play. The
Creative Writing Club was mentioned, naturally. And the
Anti-Vivisectionists (Mrs. Barnstone being a still-outspoken
past-past president in defence of helpless animals, poor things).
The Committee for an Independent Canada had no trouble
justifying its entry into the fray, nor did those admirable stal-

warts, the Committee for Stopping the Oil Tankers Now. Old Ban-the-Bombers, long inactive, marched again into battle, with the Home and School Association right behind. People who belonged to the United Protesters Against Public Indecency, having survived a dull summer of no activity (all that rain—who was crazy enough to go in swimming, nude or any other way?), were happy to find a newer cause to support. The Breast-Feeders' Association did not have any trouble choosing a side in the dispute, just as soon as they saw which side the Anti-Breast-Feeders' Association was supporting. Nor did the Good Christians for Bringing Back the Strap, the Good Christians for Bringing Back the Noose, the Society for the Protection of Tent Caterpillars, and the three members of the Ecology Club. Natives in Favour of Total Revenge, Western Separatists, North Island Separatists, Port Annie Separatists, Champions of the Pacific Salmon, Save Our Old Buildings Society, Friends of Culture, Friends of Amateur Sports ("Culture Is For Pansies" their motto), Hockey Mothers' Association for More Exciting Sports, Save Our Children from Pornography and Perversion Alliance, Non-Smokers for Clean Air (a bunch of whining goody-goodies, according to Rita Rentalla), Civil Rights for Smokers (of which Rita was Founder and current President), and that world-famous organization to which all the Down Front Wives belonged, without exception, Bridge Players International. Not even the Port Annie branch of the Temperance Movement was left out (kept alive by Mrs. Barnstone herself, its only surviving member). No one had realized that so many clubs existed in Port Annie, but neither could anyone deny that they all deserved their place in this epic poem.

The story according to Mrs. Barnstone stumbled ahead from laugh to laugh, through guffaws and cheers, past hollered-back comments and outbursts of friendly backslapping, finding its way past sudden interruptions by people who felt they could improve a line by rewriting it for her and people who felt they could improve a line by acting it out for her. Only Jacob Weins in all that crowd had ceased to listen to the poem. He was brooding. Once again that old beached whale upstairs hadn't budged, wasn't showing any signs of coming down; once again he felt like an empty-handed fool. Look at all these people kicking up such a ruckus on her behalf, and what did she do in return? Nothing. Such contempt was just not acceptable in any town that was run by Jacob Weins. Who did she think she was?

And he really had counted on it happening this year, too. Just what he was looking for to give this town a shot in the arm. At a time when so many of his schemes had come to an unfortunate end, he needed to have that old woman come down, set herself up in his trailer-church, and become the visible spirit of the town. Maybe then, maybe at long last, all those elusive tourists would have a reason to come through the mountains to spend their money here.

"Come on," he said to Damon West, "let's go up and bring her down."

Through the crowded room they made their way, heading for the door to the lobby. Not even Vincent's "Oh no you don't!" could stop him now. He led a parade up the carpeted staircase, West behind and Vincent trying to stop them both. Up the staircase and down the hall, he knew exactly where to go. "You can't go in there!" Vincent yelled, but Weins had got inside the room before either of the others had caught up. "Where's the goddam light switch?" The air smelled of rotting vegetation.

"There is no light."

"Where the hell is she?"

He stumbled across the dark room to the window, and pulled the drapes open. Electric light from the square crept in, as if afraid of this unaccustomed place, slid out across the carpet and a bed dusty with age, and moved up the dry papery walls, hung with trailing strings of dust and cobwebs like mossy lichen, and along a row of glass fish-tanks, all the way to the far side of the room, where a rocking chair gently moved, perhaps from the stirred-up air of their entry.

"Annie," Vincent said gently, pushing past.

What Jacob Weins thought for a minute he was looking at was a dry white shrivelled-up parsnip. "My God," he said, "what's that supposed to be?" What kind of a joke was this? A shrivelled parsnip head and tiny legs that didn't reach the floor.

Vincent put his hand on the chair to stop its movement. "This here is Annie."

West leaned in for a closer look. "My Christ, is it still alive?" Those eyes, so used to smouldering promises and indecent questions, were full of annoyance now. He looked around the room as if anxious to get his hands on the person who'd pulled this joke.

"She's alive," Vincent said. "She's just old."

There were no real features left in her face, just creases and wrinkles. There was no hair left on her head, just a few nearly invisible floating threads. A dry shrivelled-up vegetable root— how could anyone tell she was still alive? But Weins was already busy recovering from this blow. So long as she was breathing, so long as she was really Fat Annie Fartenburg, what difference did it make that she wasn't the giant that he'd expected? Somewhere inside that decomposing head there was probably still enough human sense left to appreciate the plans he had for her. A little make-up, an old-fashioned dress, perhaps a wig and a bonnet, she could still prove to be more than useful. He had a lifetime behind him of making readjustments, plenty of practice, he was a master at changing his goals before they had a chance of disappointing him.

"Okay, okay," Vincent said. "So now you've seen her. Everybody out. Let's leave the poor old thing alone." He held the door open—like a cranky nurse, or an overprotective parent. "Who knows how much damage you've already done?"

Weins turned his back, "Don't rush me," and peered into one of the glass tanks. The insides of the walls were caked with black muck, and a string of tiny discoloured bones lay across the green shrivelled slime of the bottom. "Some nursemaid *you* are, leaving a thing like this in an old woman's room."

"She won't let me touch them. Come on, leave her alone."

"Them?" Weins felt the sweat break out on his forehead. His hands were damp. There were skeletons on the bottom of every tank. Six of them. "Is she crazy too?"

And if she were a gibbering idiot, what good would she do his plans then?

But Vincent was tugging at his arm. "Look—if you don't get out of here I'll have you thrown out. You're bloody well trespassing, Weins—get out of this room."

Weins shrugged off the hand. "Get out of the way." He felt as if he would drown in the gallons of sweat that had boiled up out of his head, tightened his hair into damp curls, and poured down over the burning skin of his face. "Get out of the way, Vincent, we came up here to take her downstairs."

West took a cigarette out of a silver case and lighted it. "Forget it. What'll you do with a thing like that? Use her for a bean bag?" He slipped his lighter back into a pocket and walked to the door. "Lock her up and forget the whole thing."

"Nobody's touching her," Vincent said.

"That's what you think," the mayor said, and elbowed Vincent aside. From behind he scooped the rocking chair up off the floor by its arms and walked forward to the door with that tiny body directly in front of his face.

"Don't you drop her, don't you hurt that woman!"

Vincent, frantic, didn't dare try to wrench the chair out of his hands, for fear of doing the old lady some damage, so all he could do was follow the mayor down the staircase—West cursing under his breath behind him. Weins took each step with care, peering through the bars behind the wrinkled head and chuckling to himself. What a coup! What a day in the history of this town! Fat Annie Fartenburg down from her room at last, and thanks to him. "What took you so long? Didn't you know how we needed you here?" But none of the creases opened to answer him. The head lolled a little to one side, then righted itself. Weins was so excited at the thought of his own triumphant entry through the door of the Kick-and-Kill, his marvellous realized dream between his hands, that he held his breath to keep himself from laughing.

And then he tripped. One foot slipped off the edge of a step, a corner of loosened carpet. Vincent yelped, reached out. Too late.

Jacob Weins staggered forward, out of control, down two more steps, holding the rocking chair aloft. It looked for a moment as if Fat Annie Fartenburg might ride this out unharmed, but he twisted his ankle, fell to the side, let go of the prize. The chair flew ahead through the air as if, for a moment, it intended to take off through the first open window it could find and ascend to the rainy sky. But somewhere near the lobby chandelier it changed its direction and hurtled floorward, landed on its rockers, and somersaulted backwards, propelling the tiny figure out across the floor.

Larry Bowman was the first to see her rocket through the door of the Kick-and-Kill, but he had no idea for a minute what he was looking at. A bundle of rags? A gnarled root? A wind-up toy spinning towards his leg? When she came to a stop against his ankles he sat and stared for a moment, trying to clear his head.

People closest to the door fell silent. Even Mrs. Barnstone's shrill excited voice trailed off. Farther back in the crowd individual voices still rose in unselfconscious argument. They had no way of knowing that something was going on at the door. "Then we damn well *ought* to strike, those bastards have pushed us all we can take!" . . . "Maybe you can afford to pay a maid but me, I have to do all the housework shit myself." Eva McCarthy gasped and stood up when she saw the body, but it was Belchy McFadden who elbowed his way past others to be the first for a closer look.

"It's Annie," he said. "They've killed her."

Weins got up off the step and limped closer to peer at the tiny figure on the floor. He blinked, confused. What was this? What had happened? Maybe the fall had done some damage to his skull, he felt a terrible pressure in his head.

"You killed her, you bastard." McFadden's tight-lipped mouth sprayed spit all over Weins. "Look at her now, she's dead."

Weins looked, but he couldn't believe it. What was this? What had he done? He looked at those faces, looked down at the lifeless root, and felt a terrible cold doubt fill up his body. Something new, he couldn't remember ever feeling this before. Cold doubt. Where was the old ability to bounce back almost before it was necessary? Why wasn't he raging at the way he'd been cheated again? He had no more intention of accepting responsibility for this unlucky break than he had of accepting responsibility for the never-ending rain or the giant wave that had washed over the town. "How do you know she wasn't already dead?" he said—to Belchy, to the others—"How does anybody know that she wasn't already dead?"

There was no conviction in his voice, however, and everyone in that room, including Mrs. Barnstone, who was madly recording even this, could see that though the mayor refused to take responsibility for anything that had happened up to now, he was clearly preparing himself to accept the blame for everything that happened next. The future, whatever it may include, was already all his fault.

IV

WITHIN MINUTES OF THE DEATH of Fat Annie Fartenburg, everyone saw Damon West drive out of town in his expensive car. And not alone either; everyone saw Linda Weins go running after him in the rain, screaming, absolutely shameless, until he stopped and backed up his car and flung open his passenger door. Everyone saw her climb in without so much as a backward glance at her mother watching from the door of the Kick-and-Kill. "Not an ounce of sense but, oh well, some people have to learn their lessons the hard way." Everyone saw the way she flung her arms around the handsome devil's neck, like a person drowning, and held on tight while the car pulled away again and started moving along the road that led to the mountains.

Such a collection of competent ever-watchful eyes, they never missed a thing, but where were they looking when the resurrected man made his quiet escape? Why did no one even catch a glimpse of the restorer leaving town? It hardly seemed possible that such a thing could go unnoticed by a gathering that included such alert observers as Eva McCarthy, Mabel Weins, George Beeton, and Mrs. Barnstone (who'd stopped reading her poem aloud but hadn't stopped writing it yet, a little panicky that she might be writing it forever, recording everything that ever happened in this world). Did he wait, perhaps, until everyone was asleep—some at home where they belonged and others in the Kick-and-Kill exactly where they dropped—too worn-out to notice an old man sneaking off in the dark with a moustached Back East editor?

Of course he may have simply disappeared in a soft explosion of smoke. Some would believe such a thing. But as Jenny Chambers reported the following day, wherever he'd gone—Toronto, Jamaica, wherever—he must have intended to go on much as before. While she'd tossed in her bed, asleep, he'd come in and cleaned out his room: manuscript, clothes, all that he owned had gone. Naturally you didn't expect that when he left he'd leave like anyone else, in daylight, standing with his beat-up suitcase in front of the hotel until the minibus came in to take him away. But neither had he gone out of his way to make you think he could snap his fingers and disappear, or turn himself into a breeze to blow out of town. He was a human being too, Jenny said, for all the marvels he performed, though quite a bit more talented than most, and much more impatient with human evolution.

V

A SPLITTING HEAD, dizzy spells, eyes that couldn't stand the light. When was George Beeton going to cut down on his drinking as he was always promising himself? Holy toledo, he had to sit still, scared to move, nothing was worth this price he had to pay the morning after. If the earth was trembling beneath his feet, well what of that?—it was only another sign that he'd overdone the celebrating once again, and hadn't had more than an hour or so of sleep.

Something else besides that trembling was different, too, but he was in no condition to determine what it was. It was Larry Bowman who saw what had happened: the rain had stopped, the sun had burned through the high white cloud, the world had changed its colour once again. Something was about to happen. While he was trying to get the twisted trunk-lid of the old Chev closed down over his suitcase, Larry looked up and saw a piece of the mountain's face begin to slip, trees and all, as if an invisible knife had sliced it away. It was so unexpected, so incongruous, that he laughed. This was impossible. All over town jays exploded up into the air and flew off in the direction of the inlet, where gulls, already screeching, led them away. The air vibrated: a low rumble, a threatening growl. He got into the car, quickly—he'd witnessed slides before now, the world was about to fall in. Only a few minutes left to get Angela away from her apartment where she was packing her suitcase. Even as he drove the old car towards the square, the sliced-off piece of mountain collapsed on itself and disinte-grated, trees disappearing in mud while others leapt up spin-ning in the air. Below it the hillside seemed to buckle, heave, roll in waves, its birches whipping from one side to the other. People burst out of houses, searching the sky for the cause of this racket. By the time he'd run the Chev into a cluster of shrubs to stop, the siren had already started to wail.

Mr. Manku had never seen anything like it. How fast was this going to be? From his kitchen window he saw an enormous raw gouge open up in the mountain's face. Then whole ridges, whole valleys, fell in, started moving, rolled forward in waves gathering everything, heaving up stones, tossing trees, churning up mud, descending. "Kamiljit! Harbans!" He hurried through the house, banging his hands on the walls, kicking the furni-ture, making as much noise as he could, "Harbans! Kamiljit! Raminder!" And opened the door to the basement suite, "Leave. Quickly." People came out of every room: What was the matter, had he gone crazy, why was the house shaking like this? "Coats, coats, everyone into the cars. Quickly." Joginder had to be interrupted in his reading of Guru Granth Sahib, "Quick, no time to put him to bed, just come," but the boy only looked confused until Mr. Manku seized the book himself, put it down on the manjie sahib, then pulled at his son's shoulder, "Into the car." He found his wife hiding under the table, her hands over her head. "Hurry, hurry!" He dragged her, coaxed her, pushed her out through the house. "The mountain is falling." Out on the street his sons had the two cars already started, the doors open. But the children seemed unable to understand what was happening; they ran from one end of the yard to the other, whimpering, biting their hands. "Kamiljit!" Mr. Manku shouted. "Into the car. Quickly!" But as soon as he seemed to have everyone gathered at last, crammed into the cars, Joginder erupted from a back seat full of children, "Wait! Wait!", and struggled free to run for the house. Guru Granth Sahib, he said, he couldn't leave it behind.

"Slim!" Jenny clawed at the thickening mud, down on her knees. A shovel! Where was the shovel? But not even a shovel would have helped now, the tractor itself was buried. Down on her knees she dug with both hands in the muck as fast as she could. Her nails were broken, her fingers bled, but he was deeper below her every second, a whole tractor between them. And that wheel. The wall of gravel and muck had filled up the yard, was pushing the machinery against the house. She could hear the boards creak. All along the street people were getting into their cars, driving off down the hill. If she stayed she'd be under there with him. And the kids? Where were the kids? Some of the other houses along the back row had begun to move forward off their foundations, groaning. A carport collapsed under the pressure of the moving mud. A pile of boards, soon buried. She'd have to save the kids, too late now for Slim. "Regina! Liz! Regina!" Falling, running, half-swimming through mud, she fought her way clear and started to run down the hill. "Regina! Albert! Liz!"

"Son-of-a-bitch!" Greg Wong leapt onto his bike, still dressed in those skirts he'd slept in. His side ached, his lungs burned like a chest full of fire, yet he was faster than some of those cars. He took short cuts—across yards, through carports —to angle his way down to the only road out of town, to get out of this place before it could bury him. Skirt fluttering up around his hips. And—"Son-of-a-bitch!"—a car going too fast grazed his leg, tossed him into the ditch, then rocketed down-hill even faster, while the bike, on its side, crawled in an arc across the gravel.

In the square, hurrying towards Angela's apartment through the rush of fleeing people, Larry Bowman felt himself bumped and shoved, pushed aside by people rushing the opposite way. Once he spun right around and nearly fell. The faces that rushed by were more intense than frightened: this had to be done fast, there was no time to be scared until later. "Everything! Everything!" someone cried. And another, "Never mind that, keep on moving." A child stood alone for a moment, knee-high in that rushing confusion of legs, screaming. A hand reached out of the crowd and yanked it along. "Not even my coat, I've forgotten my coat." A groan passed through the crowd, someone fell to his knees in the mud, "My glasses, my glasses!", and fought his way upright again, to be carried ahead by the crowd.

The muddy water, thickening, pulled at Larry's ankles, everything rushed downhill towards the inlet: sticks and clots of grass hurried past, spinning. But Jeremy Fell in the centre of all this commotion seemed to be transfixed, watching the world fall in on himself. "Start running, you fool!" Larry yelled, searching the crowd streaming out of Angela's apartment. "Come on, this is no time to be sightseeing." But Fell remained rooted to the spot, watching houses above him collapse and go under, splintering, mud rolling over everything, trees shaking loose as if some giant hand had hold of their roots, "Go away, Bowman, leave me alone." And here was Angela, coming this way up the slope from her apartment. "What took you so long?"

"My God, let's get out of here." She leaned her weight into him. "Oh don't make me run, I can't run, oh God Larry, it hurts."

But he told her to run anyway, get going, move her legs as fast as she could to his car, while he grabbed Jeremy Fell by the shoulder, "Come on, you can't hang around here." Almost no one was left now, cars were bumper to bumper funnelling out the town's only road to safety, horns honking, "Hurry up, hurry up," past Constable Nevers waving them on, while children's faces pressed against windows watching the mountain fall in.

Fell resisted, yanked himself free, "Get away, Bowman, take your hands off me." Idiot, he could stay then, Larry Bowman didn't have time to hang around arguing. But just as he turned to run, to catch up with Angela, Fell started to sway, collapsed into the mud. Larry felt stupid and thick-headed, confused. How could you leave a man lying like that? Maybe he was dying. Or already dead. His face was blue. There was no one else left to make the decision, the place was deserted, a river of mud, while boulders and logs were already moving down from behind the hotel. Angela screamed at him from the car, "Hurry up, hurry!" He dragged up the body by the armpits and ran, the earth vibrating beneath him. It was like running down the back of a bucking bronco. Half carrying, half dragging a wet slippery corpse that dripped mud down the front of his pants.

"Let's hope this crate'll move in the muck." The corpse could ride in the back. And inside Angela had already got the engine started. "Get in, get in." Houses a hundred yards away were moving, he could hear windows explode. "Come on, baby, move," and it did, it whined out into the space where the road ought to be, while Angela—up on her knees and reaching into the back seat—searched for some sign of a pulse, first at the wrist, then at the throat. "Damn," she said. "I think the poor fellow's finally got what he wanted."

But Larry could waste no attention on corpses, the cross-pull of the current made steering almost impossible, the wheel shuddered and tried to pull free from his hands. Still, he put his foot to the floor, tried to push through. "Come on, come on." Like trying to ford a river. No, a falls, a muddy falls. The front end swung to the left, headed for the buried sidewalk. Something crashed, the car shuddered. A small tree fell across the road, blocked it for a moment, then dragged its shallow roots behind it into someone's yard, up against someone's window. "Keep on going, Larry, don't let her stop now, we're almost there." With his leg stiff from pushing on that accelerator, he aimed for the bottleneck of cars and people milling around at the junction, far enough out of town to be safe, people standing all over the road and up on the tops of the two bulldozers, looking back to watch this thing happen.

"We made it!" he yelled out, breaking free of the mud, laughing now, what a fool, and put his foot on the brake pedal to slow down. "No brakes, my God I forgot!" They were free-running, out of control. He geared down, while Angela put her hands over her face. Geared down again. The car backfired. People standing on the road began to move, stepped back, ran for the ditch, and he drove with one hand on the horn all the way down to the end of the two rows of cars holding his breath, then swerved and ran the Chev into the ditch where it bumped, jumped up, settled, and died.

Silence. His legs trembled. "What a hero!" she said, laughing, and turned for another look at the corpse in the back.

But the dead man was already pushing the door open to escape. He fell out onto his knees on the pavement in his hurry, but scrambled upright and, glancing back just long enough to give Larry a malicious look, hurried away.

A burst of smothered laughter from Angela. "I don't think he's very grateful." She put her forehead down against his shoulder.

When Larry felt life return to his watery legs and climbed out of the car, everything seemed to be over; there was a great long scar where the town had been, humps of stones settling into place, a dark lumpy slope down into the sea. The town had been scraped off the face of the mountain, leaving little behind but a strange dangerous smell. A few splintered boards broke the surface of the mud and gravel. The gable end of someone's roof. An automobile tire. A triangular slab of concrete like the prow of some subterranean ship emerging from the underworld. Here and there in the mess upended trees had their crowns buried in earth, their roots clawing upward for sky, as if they'd decided to take their life from another source. The air hummed with a low echo of the roar, sent back from the mountain across the inlet.

People leaned on cars, some paced aimlessly on the narrow pavement, others stood in groups. Excited voices broke like sound-splinters above the general babble. Children cried. The police were kept busy trying to calm people down, get families back together, "Cut it out now, you're alive and that's something," and talked on their radios to police on the other side of the Island who were already on their way, folks, and bringing an ambulance as well as the volunteer fire department to do what they could.

"What's there to do?"

Some looked back down to where the town had been, as if they still hoped for something more to happen—for a hole to open up and swallow the rubble perhaps, or for rooftops and houses to rise up undamaged, and for time to reverse itself. Some men had already gone back to prowl in the debris. Looking for what?

"Everything!" A shrill woman's voice. "We've lost everything!"

"Hush."

Someone else. "Mrs. Landyke's been hurt."

But Mrs. Landyke, leaning against someone's car, tried to keep something hidden. Her hand. "It's nothing." But, "Let me look at that," someone said, and, "Oh my goodness, Mrs. Landyke, oh my good gracious."

"The ambulance will get here pretty soon. Where's Doctor Harmon?"

"Never mind the ambulance, get her into a car. Get her across to the hospital as fast as you can. Somebody help."

Greg Wong, too, was waiting for help. His leg was torn open, fellas, a goddam runaway car, he thought he was a goner there for a while.

"Someone better hold Ian McCarthy down, he's going nuts. The best thing they could do is get him out of here."

"Why?"

"Poor Eva."

"The Andersons didn't even stop, they kept right on going. Gloria put her head out the window long enough to promise a postcard from California and to hell with this place."

Mrs. Barnstone wasn't far behind. She couldn't get out of here fast enough. Some time during the panic of falling houses and sliding earth she'd begun to get a glimpse of what her epic poem had entirely missed, and the faster she put it all behind her the better. "Just keep on going," she told her husband, and braced herself for the mountain roads ahead—miles and miles of climbs and dips and hairpin turns through hills of blackened stumps and fireweed stalks gone white with seed. "Just keep on going."

Jenny Chambers, standing in mud beside one of the yellow bulldozers, shivering in her muddy clothes, chewed gum faster than ever before. All her kids stayed close, silent; no one had ever seen such a thing. Maybe they were scared for the first time in their lives.

"Slim," Larry said. "Where's Slim?"

Jenny looked at him a moment, as if she had to force herself to pay attention. Her lips tightened, she shook her head, "Under one of his stinking machines." Angry, as if she could easily start slashing at trees, hammering on cars. "Under one of his goddam stinking machines! The tractor rolled ahead, I saw it happen. I *tried* to get him, I tried to dig him out but I was too late."

"Let's get out of here." A bitter masculine voice.

Others began to think the same thing. Why torture yourself? You had to leave some time. Good riddance to this dump, it's a wonder we weren't all killed. What if it had happened in the night? Never want to see this arse of an inlet again. Cousins in Port Hardy had extra beds. Port Alice people would help, they know about slides. No hope of digging that mess out. No way a person could help. It would be a relief to turn your back on this town and start a new life.

Doors slammed. Motors started. No one said goodbye to anyone else; faces were harsh and tight, lips set, as if the spray of gravel and contempt were meant not only for the disappeared town but for the other people as well—good riddance to the lot of you—and more than one family hurrying away said that if they ever saw anyone from Port Annie again it would be far too soon.

Mayor Weins was amongst the first to escape, still dressed in his Fartenburg costume. Mabel's nerves, he explained, she was going all to pieces under this strain—all her pills had been buried—and he wanted to get her across to a decent doctor as fast as he could, no fooling around with Harmon. Though he had to admit, to Jeremy Fell, that he would go crazy until he found out whether this slide would make any difference to that real-estate company. He could just imagine all his savings and his wife's savings and his wife's father's savings washed into the inlet with the town until he heard from Mr. West himself that the resort hotel would still be going ahead. The first thing he would do when he hit the other side, he said, was telephone south.

Then he would hurry back just as fast as he could, don't worry, because there'd be photographers and newsmen flocking into this place any minute like vultures, he said, all disappointed if there wasn't a mayor around willing to be coaxed into having his photograph taken in front of that slide.

Jeremy Fell only shrugged, no skin off his nose, Your Worship, as far as he was concerned he ought to be dead in that rubble, buried and done with, a thing of the past.

Jenny looked around for someone who wasn't deserting. Another car roared away up the hill. What was the rush? It was true that they had to leave, but what was the big fat hurry? Shouldn't someone be trying to do something? Shouldn't people be starting to dig? You couldn't just up and take off and leave all the clean-up for somebody else.

And besides, where was she going to go?

The children stayed close, sniffling, all looking as if they'd just seen the world come to an end. Even snooty Regina looked scared. They only made her feel more like crying than she already did, ready to break down and start howling like a baby right here in this mud. But that big stupid lump in her throat would just have to give up, she wouldn't let loose and bawl, not in front of Slim's kids.

But those who weren't roaring away in their cars, or going back to poke around in the debris, were moving downhill towards the Flats. Strangely quiet, talking in whispers. Hill Gin had a crowd of those Manku children in tow, leading them down the gravel. Mr. Manku, with one hand on his enormous belly, stayed behind a moment, great furrows in his forehead, searching this way and that with his heavy brown eyes.

"Aha!" And Papa Magnani rushed up to him, pumped his hand. The two men for a moment held hands and congratulated themselves on finding each other. "But where is our friend Mr. Bourne?" Mr. Manku said.

Jen butted in—who cared about manners at a time like this? "He left in the night. He's gone. Probably back to that woman in Jamaica."

Mr. Manku turned slowly, his two hands pressed palm to palm. Such gravity. "But so suddenly!"

"Maybe he'll be back," Mr. Magnani said. "Maybe he'll come back to say goodbye at least."

"Maybe," Jenny said. Don't bet on it, she thought.

"Yes, yes," and Mr. Manku frowned downhill in the direction of his retreating family. "But where is your . . . where is Mr. Slim Potts?"

Oh, those stinking traitors of emotions! That lump that swelled in her throat, those tears that burned in her eyes! Suddenly it didn't matter if those kids were watching her with their mouths open, it didn't matter if Papa Magnani was in danger of wringing his own hands right off at the wrists. She gave in, she let fly, got it all out, put on a good show for those cold fishes of babes standing around watching and wondering at the bad taste of this public display. And once she'd started making a fool of herself, breaking down like this, she might as well do a good job of it, these trees had never heard such sobbing,

Mr. Manku's jacket had never soaked up so many tears, those rotten brats of kids had never witnessed such a violent demonstration of her emotions. Cripes, she was acting like one of those Europeans in a movie, Slim, and even felt like throwing herself on the ground, pounding those trees, kicking at the cars, she was so mad and frustrated and sorry and upset. A turmoil of womanly sorrow. If she thought it would make her feel any better she'd have gone screaming back into the rubble, digging in the mud, rooting around like an old pig trying to find him down there. That would open up a few of their eyes! But she'd seen the whole thing happen, Slim, she'd watched that stinking tractor roll ahead, she knew there wasn't any hope. For the rest of her life she'd find herself looking out that window in her mind, feeling the vibrations of a world with its death dance, and see that tractor roll over him. Too bad if Mr. Manku was embarrassed, too bad if Papa Magnani had started to cry himself, too bad if those Down Front wives were offended by her lack of control, it was time they found out she was a passionate woman, not a cold fish like some other people she could mention!

Larry saw right away that the Flats had become a camp for refugees. People and seagulls everywhere, what a racket! All of the shacks were wide open, people huddled inside. Hill Gin seemed to have taken on the job of meeting people and hauling them off to whichever of those buildings she'd decided was the best one for them to recover in. Hardly a trace of yesterday's accident on her face. "Come on, Mr. Librarian," she said, grabbing hold of Larry's arm, "let's get you inside and put some coffee into you."

Larry shrugged himself loose. "I'll have a look around first, see how people made out." He wondered if she was disappointed that her end of the world had turned out to be only this.

Angela, however, was happy enough to be dragged away. "Go ahead if you want, I'm feeling the weight of this belly." She laughed. "Big hero, the man who rescued a corpse!" And shaking her head, still laughing, she leaned into the old woman's shoulder.

Wandering through this shacktown chaos, he saw that some had decided it was never too soon to start laying blame. A democratic crowd, they spread the guilt around equally, no one was getting left out.

The Mill owners knew it was going to happen, those lousy money-grabbers. They were just looking for an excuse to close the Mill anyway, this was what they hoped would come along and solve all their problems for them.

That damn government knew it was bound to happen sooner or later. They sent their inspectors up to look things over after the other slides, they could've done something to stop it then, but what did they care about Port Annie? They knew the town had supported the Opposition.

Those logging companies were the ones who'd started it. They should've refused to cut the timber off that hill, the dumbest thing anyone had ever heard of, not a brain in their heads. Some people would do anything for money, no matter how stupid.

Not as stupid as the guy that planned the town. They could've built it somewhere else without any trouble but no, in his city office he liked the idea of streets that climbed a hill like an amphitheatre. That way everyone would get a view.

A view of mud and fish.

Of course everyone agreed the actual culprits were the real-estate people, no question about that. They'd wrecked everything else they could get their mitts on up and down this coast, they could easily have engineered this thing too. There wasn't a one of them with a conscience. Now there was nothing to stand between them and their big fancy resort. Money falling into their greedy hands.

And content that everyone concerned would soon be sorry, they turned to other things. Jobs. Houses. Insurance (they had none, no company had ever been found to take such a risk as that). The stinking rain that didn't stop until it was too late. This stinking noise of birds. Preserved Crabbe's woman. Jeremy Fell, that walking corpse.

"And poor Ian. Couldn't pull her out of her house, she just wouldn't come."

"Not even when it started to slide, he told me, and the walls started to buckle. She wouldn't be budged, such a tiny person but she found the strength to hold on, he just had to leave her or get killed himself."

"How will he be able to live with it?"

Rita Rentalla called Larry over to the step of a nearby house, where she smoked a cigarette. Her head was still spinning, she said, she felt weak. She should have gone in the ambulance with Wong, she told him, she should have gone along just to keep him company. But Lord, one look at his leg and she'd nearly fainted, she couldn't stand blood, they had to hold her head down by her knees to bring her around.

Even now, while she allowed ribbons of white smoke to shred away from her lips, her eyes just automatically travelled down the length of a man. "They'll all go," she said, pressing her lips together and sliding a look full of blame off in the direction of the others. "You too, everybody'll go, there's nothing for anyone to stay for now. The place is finished. Guess who is the only one who'll never get out. Guess who'll be right here forever."

The lips pressed even tighter, the accusing eyes swept across all they could see. "Come back in a few years and see. Rita Rentalla working in that big tourist resort, I'll bet, waiting on their stupid tables or something, and being dragged over to tell these newcomers from California, please miss, all about the history of the town that used to be here. Just wait, I can see it now, boring the guests with tales about Christie and Fat Annie and Joseph Bourne."

"And me."

"And you?" She looked at him coldly and raised an eyebrow. "What did you do?" Again those eyes travelled down his length, appraising something.

"Well . . ."

"You escaped. We all escaped, Bowman, nearly all of us. That doesn't mean anything except that we're still alive."

"Are you scared?"

"You bet I'm scared. I've never lived anywhere else. I was born in this town."

Strange, but he wasn't scared. The town had gone, but he didn't feel that he'd lost a thing that mattered. No one had. The community still existed. Some would find another isolated town, there were others like Port Annie. Some would go out to join the city crowds. Either way, they'd been freed from something—don't ask him what—they'd been given a chance to find out what they were capable of being, a chance they would never have had as long as they'd stayed rooted to that mountain.

The inlet seemed calm. It lay there brilliant in the unaccustomed sunlight, already settled again after swallowing that mountainside whole, houses and all. No doubt it had suffered convulsions at first, swelling up and throwing itself at the shore in a fury of waves, but all of that was over, the town and the mountain had been gulped down and accepted. Out there, pieces of wreckage had surfaced—boards and garbage cans and pieces of wall, some shapeless lumps that could have been anything from clothes to mattresses—all drifting seaward. And along with everything else, something that must have been the hull of that derelict fishboat floated past, released from its tree. It rode low in the water, weighed down by its crust of barnacles and its freight of—what were those kids supposed to have found inside?—a whole aquarium of uprooted sea-plants and crabs and shellfish. A colourful living stew.

At the high-tide mark, two pilings stood up like rotted teeth, charred to the water line. This was where Joseph Bourne's shack had been, now a black patch of ashes, a heap of burnt rubble, shiny with rain in the pale drowned grass along the sea-edge. The papery sea-pink flowers bobbed and dipped on the end of their too-long stems. Nothing else remained.

And where was Joseph Bourne? On his way to Toronto with that editor, he supposed. Or heading to Jamaica where his brown-skinned wife may still be waiting for him in her shack above Port Royal's sunken bells. Or was he already hatching some new secret plan for disappearing off the face of the earth again? Larry saw that seabird walking the streets once more, driving everyone crazy with her incredible walk, her perfect feet, her beautiful eyes that could make the whole world lurch for him and change the colour of his life. Look at all she had started, along with that crazy wave! The rain had finally washed all trace of the wave back to sea—seaweed, shells, and even that fishboat hull—but not even rain could wash the girl away. All of them would be carrying a little of her around for the rest of their lives whether they liked it or not.

Dirty Della, hurrying by with an armload of blankets, broke the rhythm of her steps just long enough to give him the once-over. She looked for a moment as if she regretted those blankets, this mission she was on, and could have dropped everything if only Rita Rentalla hadn't been sitting beside him. But she remembered in time that she was part of an army and hurried away—to rescue, to comfort, to bind up the wounded. Florence Nightingale dragging her skirt through the mud.

The rest of The Flats population seemed to have leapt into life as well. Those nameless pony-tails from California distrib-uted dry clothes wherever they were needed. "Here, let's get them threads off you, man, you're mud clear up to your ass.

These rags'll get you warm at least." And red-eyed Louise ran past with a full coffee pot, ran back with it empty—biting her lip and frowning with the responsibility of the moment. The floating bunkhouse of the brothers Crabbe appeared to be a supply depot for something else—three of the brothers distributed fruit jars of liquid clear as water. It smelled and tasted like turpentine, but did no immediate damage to the spirea bush where Larry threw it after an experimental sip.

"What a waste," Rita said, holding her own jar close. "At least it warms you up."

Preserved Crabbe, unlike his brothers, was making no effort to act the host. With panicked eyes ready to pop out of his big red face, he lumbered past, nearly past, then grabbed Larry's arm so roughly that he almost pulled him off the step. "What do you want, Crabbe? You're breaking my arm."

"You seen my Marguerite?"

Rita groaned. "Not again!"

Larry shook his head. No, he hadn't seen her. But he hoped this didn't mean another long-distance chase of epic proportions. He didn't stay around to talk with the frantic giant, though, he'd caught sight of Jeremy Fell walking down along the beach. "Excuse me," he said, and set out to head the storekeeper off. There was some unfinished business he wanted to straighten out.

But Fell didn't even turn when he heard Larry approach. He kept his eyes on something out on the inlet.

"Looking for what?" Larry said.

"Nothing." The mud on his clothes had nearly dried. His face was streaked from attempts to wipe the dirt away with his hand.

"Well, I hope you'd rather be here than down at the bottom of that."

Fell's eyes blinked, shifted in their deep sockets to look at Larry. He almost smiled. Tilted his head and looked away. "I don't seem to be given much choice in the matter." If gratitude was what Larry expected to hear in that voice he was disappointed. Bitterness was what he heard. *Brave man, he rescues corpses.*

A new throbbing in the air. A helicopter approached from behind them, curved out over the inlet, and angled in across the slide. Cameramen. The newsmen were beginning to arrive. Soon the whole world would know about the death of Port

Annie. "Cynthia," Jeremy Fell said, suddenly agitated. "Cynthia will hear about this. She'll want to know . . . but the telephone lines will be down."

"The cops could get a message out for you."

Fell looked at Larry again. "Will you?" He shuddered, as if to demonstrate that he hadn't the strength himself.

"I'll ask. Where'll they find her?"

"Victoria. The Museum of Evil."

Still looking for that tiny scrap of gratitude, Larry couldn't resist: "*She* at least will be happy to hear that you weren't left behind in the slide."

Jeremy Fell let his eyes rest a moment on Larry's face, then shift to the inlet again. "I hate that man," he said. "He's playing some terrible joke on me, I know it. I wanted to see him fail."

To see him fail at what? With Bourne, the marvellous seemed to be perfectly natural, something he couldn't help. Caring was as normal to him as breathing, reviving and restoring were as natural as eating food, he simply recognized no alternative to life. Only Jeremy Fell could see it as some kind of threat.

Or maybe there was something in us all. Did our cave-dwelling grandparents fight this hard to resist standing upright, Larry wondered. Or hate the man who did it first and showed them how it was done? Did they panic when hair began to thin out on their shoulders; did they fight the beginnings of speech? Or was it possible that crouched in their dark caves they would be disappointed to see how we still object to whatever would take us higher?

Too many questions on a day that had started so badly. He would get a headache. It was a good thing Angela Turner decided she'd had enough of resting under Hill Gin's witchy eyes and came outside to find him. She made everything else fly right out of his skull; she was getting prettier every day, and cheeky as well—she knew exactly what she was doing when she slipped her hand inside his hand and tickled his palm.

"Too bad I left every stitch of clothes in that apartment," she said. "I'll have to buy everything new or spend the rest of my life naked. The mud will never come out of this thing I've got on, I'll have to burn it."

He was all for starting a bonfire now, right here on the beach, but she told him to wait. In the shape she was in, nobody but an idiot (like him) would thank her for stripping in public. She'd be hauled away and buried, an unsightly blot on the landscape, an eyesore and a public nuisance.

At any rate, she wouldn't allow this kind of talk for long. Already he could see the look coming over her face that said she wanted to move on to more serious things. Being in love wasn't everything in life, she was a girl with important plans. Any minute now she'd want to know if the College would replace her business-administration course lost in that slide, if he was still going to be her tutor on top of everything else, if he was ready yet to consider where she ought to look for her first administrative post, some place where he could get himself a labouring job if nothing came up in the way of library work or tutoring. Of course if nothing at all could be found for him (she was bound to suggest) he could always stay at home and change that Peruvian baby's diapers. And naturally —because he loved her—he'd understand just how important her career would be to her and he wouldn't mind taking a back seat for a little while, just to help her get started. That wouldn't stop them from turning into a perfect couple, perfect partners, doing all those things that he knew a perfect pair of lovers were supposed to do.

By early afternoon most of the wounded had been taken away. Families with relatives in the North Island region had gone, promising to sit by a radio waiting to see who was going to pay for this mess, what kind of aid they would get from the government, what plans the Mill had for their future. And those who remained were soon worn out from answering the same questions for every newspaperman and television man and radio man who came through with a microphone and a camera. What did it feel like to be homeless, they wanted to know. And pushed their cameras into Ian McCarthy's face, swollen and red from weeping. Even when he turned away, blowing his nose, the cameras continued to purr. Did he feel the government was responsible for his wife's death? Did he feel like suing anyone? Or was he willing to call it just an act of God? How much did they feel they'd lost here? Could anyone give an estimate in dollars? Where would they go now? Microphones shoved into Jenny's face did not go away just because she swatted at them and gave them a look that should have melted their cables. Didn't she think that someone down in Victoria should have foreseen this and tried to stop it? If there were an election tomorrow would she change her vote? Would she be willing to ride in the helicopter and give their viewers a blow-by-blow report while the cameras played over the hideous devastation of that mountainside? Wasn't this proof once again that the federal government was spending too much of its attention on Quebec and not enough on the Coast?

By late afternoon, however, when everyone had been interviewed to death and the light had begun to fade over the inlet, the men brought tables into The Paper House, the only building in the Flats big enough for all this crowd. Women carried in food they'd cooked in the various shacks along the waterfront. Fish soup was what they called it, but what each person was given looked more like a bouquet of flowers—a bowl of steamed-open shells: dark blue mussels and creamy clams and pure white oysters and other colourful shells that no one had thought of eating before. "Lord, we're all of us ruined so we may as well eat!" said Rita Rentalla, throwing her hands up in air.

But before anyone had time for more than a taste of the delicious soup, Mayor Weins arrived on the scene, flushed and excited from his hurried trip across the Island and back.

Unpractised at fading into the woodwork, he naturally assumed that everyone in the house wanted to be brought up to date. A gathered crowd was an occasion to make a speech. Mabel had been turned over to a doctor, he reported, no need to worry about her now, she was in good hands. But he hadn't been able to catch up to Linda and Damon West, his future son-in-law. What he had done, ladies and gentlemen, was put in a few phone calls to the south. Incredible, but those people had already heard about the slide, don't ask him how news travelled so fast, and every one of them sent their sincerest sympathy and best wishes for the future. Their concern was genuine and touching. It didn't hurt to remember that out there people really cared.

A television cameraman was struggling with his machine, trying to get a good angle without causing a disturbance, so Weins—always eager to help the media wherever he could—turned so that the light would fall more completely on his face. Dreams had fallen apart right and left today, shattered in every direction, he said in his most sombre tone for the benefit of those big-city viewers in Vancouver, in case they thought this was only an entertaining diversion put on for their benefit. "But this is no reason to sit down and quit. Life is still meant to be lived." He turned to look directly into the eyes of those viewers in Kelowna and Saskatoon and Ottawa and Halifax, in case they thought he didn't mean every word he was saying. Jacob Weins had never been so serious. "Let me tell you the world hasn't ended here," he said. "Far from it. Homes, automobiles, jobs, stores, even some lives have been wiped out, but that doesn't mean the end, no kidding. We'll find the strength to pick up and carry on."

He hauled a handkerchief out of his pocket and mopped his sweaty brow, giving the people in Moose Jaw and Toronto time to register their admiration for this plucky mayor, so quick to spring back to life from the ashes of disaster. Then he added, "It could even be the beginning."

"The hell with beginning, Weins," someone shouted. "I'm getting out of this dump as soon as my belly's full."

The cameraman swung around to take in all the laughter— people rolling their eyes, and muttering under their breaths, and elbowing one another. In order to remain part of the picture, Weins had to take several steps down the table and push in between two pairs of broad shoulders; his big ears burned a violent red. For those with the courage to stay, he told them, there would be the joy of seeing that luxury hotel rising right here on this spot they were sitting on now. The Cathay Towers Resort, swamped with thousands of glamorous tourists from the south, all with more money than they knew what to do with. And what did he care if some people were snickering, no doubt a new boom town would grow up, perhaps in the mountains where it was safer, a modern town with the latest in shopping malls, the most carefully designed subdivisions, the most tasteful rows of fast-food outlets and car-dealers and tourist attractions. Laugh all you want, but Port Annie the Second, whatever they called it, would have blacktopped parking lots, and towers of glass scraping the clouds, and even stoplights, just wait and see!

"And a tollgate owned by Weins before you can get in."

"With a statue of Fat Annie on the top."

Scattered laughter, but he didn't hear. Once again he sought the eyes of his viewers out in the world, those people who would understand and appreciate a man like him, people who would have no trouble seeing that his was the voice of progress and sanity. And that hideous scar where our town used to be?

Don't worry, he answered, it wouldn't go unmarked. "Famous is what it'll become, one of the wonders of the world, awe-inspiring, its picture in every magazine you can name, every paper. In California and Japan and Europe, all over the world people will leave home in order to travel to this incredible spot." He thought of the Minister of Tourism down in Victoria applauding him, and turned on his biggest smile, to show that he'd paid attention to that pamphlet of suggestions the govern-ment had sent him once. "No, no my friends, it won't go un-marked. Even if everyone else moves away you can be sure that I'll stay here and see that a proper memorial is erected, a huge cairn in the centre of that scar, with floodlights beaming down on it at night, and a proper inscription for all those tourists to read and take pictures of."

But poor Weins was unable to continue, not even with three television cameras whirring in his face and two newspapermen jotting his words down on notepads. He was so chocked up at the way so many of his dreams had come true all at once that he was unable to spit out another word. All he could do was wave a hand at them, cover his face with his handkerchief, and sit down before his heaping bowl of food while he struggled to regain control. What a crazy way for his dreams to come true! He couldn't stop shaking his head. Wasn't it funny the way the world picked to make all your ambitions start to take shape? Not what you'd expected at all.

No one felt much like eating after he'd finally shut up. How could they with their stomachs all in knots, the whole world watching? It was a great feast, no one could deny it, heaps of delicious food. And no one could get over the way those Squatters women knew how to cook just like ordinary people —delicious food, even the Mankus seemed to approve. But in the circumstances, no one wanted to eat very much, only enough to be polite. That mayor with his raving had taken their appetites away.

Afterwards, no one would remember what he'd eaten any-way. The only thing that mattered was Jenny Chambers' dance. Everything else was pushed aside, forgotten. It came as such a shock—who would ever think she'd do a thing like that when she was so recently a widow with eight kids to look after, old Slim still lying underneath the mud, dead as a mackerel? And even once you'd got used to the idea and figured it was as good as any other way for someone to work off her sorrow, there was still the surprise of discovering the woman still had the talent. She was good. As George Beeton whispered to Rita under his breath, if he'd known there was a body in town that could move the way Jenny's did, he'd've dumped his Gerda in the inlet years ago and given old Slim a few things to worry about. People could just barely remember the last time she'd danced, at the Kick-and-Kill, a stranger in town. Flaming Jenny, a memory of high-kicking legs and plenty of skin. She was a knockout in those days, they knew that, but somehow they'd got used to seeing her as just an ordinary woman around town. And two years of being on the picket line had done nothing to keep the old image of a high-stepping dancer alive. Certainly no one had ever suspected that she'd kept up her skills. They assumed, quite naturally, that a retired stripper just let herself go all to pot.

But when Jenny stood up to dance it was clear that she hadn't forgotten a thing.

"This place is too full of that slide, someone's got to drive that rotten stink of it right out of here!"

"You show 'em Jen!"

She laughed. "I've made a public ass of myself once already today, a second time won't hurt a bit."

"Dance that bloody slide right off our backs!"

"For Joseph Bourne."

"For Slim."

Not until they'd turned down the lights. Cripes, did they think she was still a young girl? Everything out but a couple of candles. And turn off those cameras right now. This wasn't for the whole world to see. Ray Crabbe strummed his guitar and a pony-tail ran for his flute. "Start out slow and sad, I've got a lot to get rid of before I get myself worked up"—and people moved back to give her some room, shoulder to shoulder at the tables, standing or crouching around the walls. All she had to work with was the staircase and a piece of the floor. And someone else's dress she'd put on when they'd stripped off her muddy clothes. She stepped between bodies to pull curtains down off their rods, dusty panels of flimsy lace, and snatched off the scarf from Rita Rentalla's throat; who else in town would be dressed like a fashion plate when the end of the world arrived?

She climbed to the top of the stairs and waited for silence with her back turned to the crowd. Then gave the guitarist a nod. This was going to be hard, she'd never even heard this haunting song before, it was certainly nothing she'd ever stripped to, that was for sure. But she took a deep breath and snapped her body into position for starting: one hip cocked to the side, one hand on her waist, the other hand reaching for sky. The dust in those bloody curtains was threatening to make her sneeze.

But she began anyway, she could sneeze later. She started her descent before she had time to change her mind, letting the music work into her bones. A slow piece, but with plenty of cheeky life to it. Unexpected chords, sudden changes, a teasing melody, steady but capable of bursting into almost anything. Like tiny flames, licking at the air. This was a staircase descent that no one in the world could match—she was the champion and knew it, always had been. When it came to descending a staircase she could make all the rest of those babes look like clumsy gorillas. Sexy, seductive, voluptuous; she knew how she looked. Like nothing ever seen by George Beeton or Larry Bowman or Bald-headed Pete except in movies or dreams. The descent of angels, the descent of grace, had never been gentler, or more exciting. Her body was music itself, fluid as eelgrass under the sea. Nothing like it had ever been seen by the people of this town, she could tell by the looks on their faces.

And she was right. Larry Bowman found himself gradually standing up, as if he'd been pulled from above. She'd inherited the seabird's grace. You didn't hear the music with your ears, you heard it with your eyes, it flowed in the lines of her body. And look at those hands, so white, like gentle birds cutting arcs in the air, caressing the banisters, making love to one another. Dragging those streaming curtains behind them like moving water. And she was barefoot, too, no one had noticed before—suddenly those two small feet were every bit as important as those hands. Birds, that tested air, that flew up and swept through clouds and glided down, that one after the other teased its mate with slow caresses and arced away before coming back to tease again. The hands swept down to touch, to slide back pulling their frothy streamers of lace, which tore loose and kept on rising to the ceiling, pale fountains that fell like wave after wave of water around her, frothing, bubbles breaking on the sand.

Oh Jenny! Someone was crying. Oh Jenny! So go ahead and cry, she was crying herself, but wouldn't be crying for long.

Her fires had been rekindled. Life blazed up in her heart. Several people were tapping time with their fingers against the tables. She wished she could do a strip, do it up right, but these weren't the clothes for it, this wasn't the place. Not with Slim and everything. Oh Jenny! No clothes to take off, but cripes she had plenty to shed in this dance. Slim Potts had to be shed before anything else, she would cry for him later when she found out what it was like trying to bring up those kids on her own. She dropped him gently on the step with Rita Rentalla's scarf so she could go back and find him when it was time to have a good cry. Down a few steps and she shed all of those closets full of clothes that she couldn't get enough of—who needed them?—fancy rags to hang on her body, decorations, trying to bury herself in a cocoon of stylish possessions. The music quickened. Someone was beating a pot, others were softly clapping. More steps and she shed all those long years of loneliness in town, desperately wanting friends—a great weight, she nearly sighed right out loud when it fell—and shed the humiliation of her desperate wedding announcement just to get all those babes running to her, making her popular. Around her feet everything fell, like the lace, and trailed behind her, left on a step without even a backward glance, good riddance. The worst burden of all had to wait to the end, nearly the bottom step, while she worked up the courage to shed it. The music had gradually picked up tempo and now it was nearly wild, she was wrestling with something, trying to get something off, no one had seen a body move so fast and stay so graceful at the same time. It was fear of those eight rotten brats who hated her guts, that she would have to bring up all on her own without a notion of where to start, whom she would love if it killed her, dammit. That one remaining curtain flew like a great tongue of flame above her, whipped itself over her shoulder, twisted around her body, under her arms, then slipped free and flew mockingly out to snap, like a whip, and come back.

Everyone watched while the pale thing wound itself right up her leg, then up her arm, threatening to strangle her. Whatever it was she was struggling with, there were people straining forward to help, there were people who could hardly stand it, Jenny, just sitting here while you were in such terror. Mr. Manku. Jeremy Fell. All those others who were much more than simply survivors too, like herself. All of them keeping the rhythm. Larry Bowman's chest was so tight from the tension that he was ready to shout out for the music to stop, get it over with, this was a torture for everyone here. Angela's grip on his hand was so hard that his fingers felt crushed.

Yet everyone strained, he could feel that they tensed. And he knew that none of them was sure what Jenny was wrestling with. What was it then that they saw? What were they watching? Was she shedding something for them as well? Their own contributions to the music's beat, the body movements, the frenzy of her need to free herself from that thing, all of it united them somehow. This old earth could throw you off its back like a bronco any time it wanted, but it couldn't break that link which ran from soul to soul.

Ah Jenny, Flaming Jenny, was afire again. Even the face of Jacob Weins was turned up to her now. Like a child excluded from some game, he seemed to suspect that something wonderful was happening here, but had no clear idea what it might be.

Larry looked from his face to the others, around the room in this flickering dark, to see what sense there might be in the survival of this untidy crew. Love and perfect vision were the same, old Bourne had said. He remembered now. But was he capable of seeing clearly what anyone else in this room might be? Except human, like himself. Neighbours somehow linked. People who acknowledged, as he did, a hunger in themselves for things they didn't understand, or couldn't put their finger on—like forgotten dreams of childhood or some flash of insight into broader life. In Jenny's dance they all saw something different, something the same. Together they laboured hard towards the pleasure and relief of seeing this woman shed that final piece of lace.

But would she ever shed it? Larry saw her hesitate a moment, as if she'd danced beyond her limits and had to stop. But she recovered fast and didn't seem to notice when he stepped ahead to offer her a hand. Instead she danced unseeing, as if she were charged with dancing life back into things, or into *them*, as if she were filled like everyone else with the steady hurried throbbing of the guitar chords and the beating hands and the various makeshift instruments around the room. And Larry, too, began to tap one foot on the floor while he swayed to Jenny's motions, with Angela now beside him, holding his hand and moving too.

Others stood up to join them. Not a dancer in the lot, but still they danced, they leaned on one another and tried to imitate a dancer's grace, or simply clapped their hands and let their feet create some patterns of their own. Rita Rentalla got up, of course, with George beside her, both a little drunk from the homemade hooch. Mr. Manku moved with the slow and splendid formality of an elephant seal, his head held high and his eyelids closed, while Papa Magnani with his Rosa bobbed and kicked and hopped in circles around him. Others stumbled, laughed, and mocked themselves with exaggerated imitations of their own ungainly efforts. Soon everyone who wasn't up was thinking of it. "What a pack of crazies!" Christie shouted, and leapt to join them.

So no one even noticed when Jenny stopped abruptly and leaned against the wall to watch. No one saw the way she ducked to hide her smile and used that piece of cloth to dry her throat. Cripes, she was nearly out of breath. Afire again or not, Flaming Jenny wasn't going to shed that final piece of lace at all tonight. Forget it. She was pooped. It would have to be dropped some other time and probably some other way. Let these others carry on if they wanted to, like a clumsy chorus line of salvaged bones, but she wasn't going to break her neck to complete the dance. She'd rather it hung in the air un-finished. After all, as some of them knew, the things that aren't seen never end.